Drawing Lessons

Patricia Sands

LAKE UNION
PUBLISHING

Text copyright © 2017 Patricia Sands
All rights reserved.

No part of this book may be reproduced, or stored in a retrieval system, or transmitted in any form or by any means, electronic, mechanical, photocopying, recording, or otherwise, without express written permission of the publisher.

Published by Lake Union Publishing, Seattle

www.apub.com

Amazon, the Amazon logo, and Lake Union Publishing are trademarks of Amazon.com, Inc., or its affiliates.

ISBN-13: 9781542045872
ISBN-10: 1542045878

Cover design by Ginger Design

Printed in the United States of America

Be ready, heart, for parting, new endeavor,
Be ready bravely and without remorse
To find new light that old ties cannot give.
In all beginnings dwells a magic force
For guarding us and helping us to live.

Serenely let us move to distant places
And let no sentiments of home detain us.
The Cosmic Spirit seeks not to restrain us
But lifts us stage by stage to wider spaces.

—*"Stages" by Hermann Hesse*

PROLOGUE

The first time her life came to a screeching halt was twenty years earlier when the predawn phone call came from Greece where her parents, Sophia and Nikos, were vacationing. Everything changed with that tragic car accident. Arianna's father was dead. Her mother had minor physical injuries but was emotionally scarred forever.

In her typically close-knit Greek family, daily interaction was the norm between the generations. Nikos Papadopoulos had been the head of the household in every way with his loud and loving Zorba-the-Greek personality. His absence left a void that slowly filled with memories. His spirit remained ever present.

Arianna's husband, Ben Miller, took over full responsibility for Papa's on the Danforth, the popular Greek bistro he had run with his father-in-law. Arianna left her career as an art historian at the Art Gallery of Ontario to help patch their world back together.

They worked in tandem to maintain the spirit and reputation of the restaurant. Ben moved between the kitchen and the customers with his creative cuisine and his contagious high spirits. Arianna worked behind the scenes, keeping the staff organized and the menus updated, as well as handling accounts.

As time went by, they gently guided heartbroken Sophia into her changed life.

Helping Sophia adjust to her role as a widow had been a challenge. Arianna was thankful her son, Tadeus, was a responsible teenager with a strong sense of self. He easily stepped into the role of helping his dad. The same could not be said for his sister, Faith, two years older, who had fallen apart at the sudden loss of her beloved *pappouli*.

As it does, life slowly moved forward. Roles shifted. Where Sophia had been the dominant matriarch of the family, she now acquiesced to the decisions Arianna and Ben made about the business. The family weathered the storm and began again to live a life that was full and no more complicated than most.

Then, twenty years after that heartbreaking call from Greece, Arianna's life came screeching to a halt once again.

Her children were adults with busy lives of their own. Sophia was settled and content in a seniors' residence.

Now Arianna Papadopoulos-Miller had choices to make that were hers alone. A new life to lead—or not. It was up to her.

CHAPTER ONE

They sat together in the office of their longtime family doctor. Ben reached over to take Arianna's hand.

Gripping a tissue, unaware her nails were digging into her palm, Arianna let Ben gently unclench her fingers. He nestled her hand in his. In spite of his over-the-top personality, he was always a calming influence, and she loved him all the more for it.

A battery of test results—including blood work, neuropsychological assessments, and neuroimaging—had been assembled over the preceding weeks. In this office, finally, they hoped to find the answer to the puzzling and troubling changes Arianna and others had observed in Ben.

Ben stared straight ahead at the doctor, who was as much their friend as their physician. Dr. Russell Spencer had delivered their children. Their families often vacationed together. The men played poker with a group of close friends once a month. Arianna and their doctor's wife, Karyn Spencer, danced their hearts out once a week in the same Zumba class.

They had already greeted each other warmly and exchanged the usual friendly small talk. But something hung in the air, an anxiety absent from every previous appointment.

The doctor busied himself shuffling papers on his desk and opening documents on his laptop. Then he quietly cleared his throat and slowly looked up, directly at his friends.

"I'm so sorry, Ben . . . and Arianna . . ." He paused, his eyes dropping down before meeting their questioning gazes once again. "There's no easy way to tell you this. I'm heartsick to deliver this news." His voice clearly reflected the pain his words were causing him.

"The diagnosis is frontotemporal dementia, FTD, also known as frontal lobe dementia or Pick's disease. There's no way to make this sound better. It's not good. It certainly explains your ongoing stumbles and memory loss."

Dr. Spencer's eyes searched those of his friends for a moment. He wished he could offer his friend and patient some words of hope or consolation, but he knew there were none.

"Frontotemporal dementia consists of several disorders that affect the frontal and temporal lobes of the brain. Personality, emotions, behavior, and speech are controlled in these areas of the brain. Currently, there is no cure for FTD, but there are treatments that help alleviate symptoms. We'll do more tests to chart how far along it is." A deep sigh slipped out.

A rogue tear rolled silently down Ben's cheek. Arianna gasped and sobbed loudly in the chair beside him before she buried her face in a cluster of tissues.

Their hands fused together.

Arianna would remember forever that this moment was accompanied by the sound of an enormous door slamming shut in her head. There were no thoughts now . . . just black emptiness swallowing her as she fought to breathe.

Dr. Spencer came around his desk. His face was flushed with worry as he leaned down to hug Arianna. Now her arms hung limply at her sides.

Ben stood to embrace his friend. They clung to each other as only close friends could. The doctor mantle slipped off.

The room was filled with sorrow.

Collecting himself, Dr. Spencer pulled up a chair next to them. "Goddamnit! I'm so sorry. I thought it would be better for me to tell you than have the specialist do it. We've been through so much together. But there's nothing that makes this easier . . ."

Ben nodded and put a hand on his friend's shoulder. "Thanks, man. I'm sorry you had to do it . . . but I'm grateful you did."

Arianna mumbled and nodded in agreement. Her shoulders were racked with sobs, and she accepted a box of tissues Russ handed her. Ben pulled his wife into his arms. "Come, come. We will deal with this. We have to."

Arianna tried to speak, but she couldn't find any words. Her sobbing was muffled in Ben's shoulder as he held her tightly, stroking her back. Russ and Ben shared a look that conveyed the depths of their friendship and their despair.

"I'll go get some water," Russ offered, his voice strained as he left the office.

When they were alone, Ben pulled away slightly. Tracing his finger lightly down Arianna's cheek, he lifted her chin so their eyes could meet. "Sweetheart, we have to accept this. We'll cry when we get home . . . and many times after, I'm certain. But let's pull ourselves together now and listen to Russ."

Arianna nodded. Her breath came in gasps, catching in her throat. Her thoughts swirled, impossible to calm. She'd never felt so out of control.

After discreetly taking his time, Russ returned with his doctor persona back in place and a pitcher of ice water and glasses. He poured a drink for each of them.

Then, barely composed, the three friends sat and began talking through the prognosis. The reality was grim. Arianna felt completely outside of her body as she listened to the words the doctor was obliged to share.

"Most people with a frontotemporal dementia disorder live an average of six to eight years after the first symptoms appear. In some cases, people live as few as two years. It can't be predicted."

Dr. Spencer had collected an assortment of literature for them. He had also compiled a list of medical websites that offered additional information.

"There's a support group at the hospital that I believe may be helpful for you. They meet every Monday evening, and I've heard positive feedback about it. You might give that a thought . . . when you are ready . . ."

After a short while, they all agreed they were flailing for words. It was impossible to digest the facts and think clearly.

Arianna asked, "Russ, would you and Karyn come over to our place tonight and help us break the news to the kids? I'm pretty sure they will be available—we'll arrange for Faith to join us on Skype. She's still up north."

Ben patted her hand. "Good idea. They'll have a lot of questions we won't be able to answer on our own."

Russ said, "Of course. Just give us a time, and we'll be there. In fact, why don't we bring over dinner? Just go home and hold each other."

"I'll check our supply of Scotch," Ben mumbled. "I have a feeling we may need a few stiff ones."

Russ nodded. "No question."

Walking slowly, hand in hand, Arianna and Ben left the medical building. Shock could not begin to describe their state. They had been blindsided.

Arianna's legs felt like rubber. Each step she took was faltering and irregular. Ben held on to her tightly, as much for his own steadiness as hers.

This was not what they had anticipated. They had expected a problem, not a death sentence. They'd known there had to be a reason for some of Ben's increasing forgetfulness, stumbling, and unpredictable personality shifts. More recently he had struggled to find words, which resulted in frustration and sometimes a loss of temper. Never before had that been part of his warm personality.

They'd known something was wrong. But not this.

To receive such a final, definitive statement of how Ben's life would soon drastically change was difficult to process.

"Let's look at the positives here," Ben said, attempting to control his emotions as they sat in the car. "I've had an amazing life. It ends for all of us at some point, and many people are not as fortunate as I've been. Let's keep remembering that."

Arianna wept again.

And that is how Ben Miller accepted the end of his life.

Until he no longer could.

That night, Arianna and Ben lay awake, tossing and turning. Breaking the news to Faith, Tadeus, and his wife, Christine, had been sorrowful and difficult. They would wait a day or two and consider how to tell Sophia.

In the following weeks, there was a flurry of meetings with their lawyer and accountant. Demetrios, the young man who had worked as Ben's assistant manager in the restaurant for the past two years, put together a group of associates to purchase the business. The purchasers asked if they could keep the name, out of respect. It was a bittersweet gesture that brought Ben some satisfaction in the midst of such turmoil.

The next month, Ben sweetly handed a rose to Arianna and suggested they spend the weekend at the Whispering Pines Inn, a rustic lodge with a popular spa an hour away from Toronto. They had celebrated many special times in the calm splendor of its setting. With their son's help, Ben had arranged a limo with a chilled split of champagne and assorted hors d'oeuvres. Ben had thought long and hard about this weekend.

"Oh, Ben. Look how glorious this lane is today," Arianna said as the car brought them down the long driveway, which was carpeted in red, orange, and gold. "I'm surprised there are still so many leaves on the trees. It feels like we're entering a magical land."

Later, they ambled along woodland paths, leaves crunching and crackling underfoot as the earthy, musky smells of autumn filled the air. Ben stopped at one point, inhaled deeply, and waved his hand at the surrounding forest. "I want to savor all of this. I think I will miss this season the most."

Arianna swallowed hard and felt every muscle in her throat tighten. She silently slipped her arm through Ben's and nudged him forward. She knew if she said anything at that moment, her heart would break into a million pieces.

Today there was no mistaking the chill in the air. Thanksgiving had always been their favorite family holiday, and they loved the time leading up to it: the changing leaves of early October, pumpkins and gourds decorating front porches and mantels, the smell of wood-burning fires in the air.

They chuckled as they strolled and exchanged memories.

Ever since they'd gotten married, the kitchen was Ben's domain at Thanksgiving, off-limits to everyone except Arianna. Ben would open a bottle of wine and pour them each a glass. Arianna always prepared the stuffing and tackled getting the bird ready for the roasting pan while Ben made scrumptious appetizers and flavorful veggies. His mashed potatoes drew raves, and he held tightly to the secret of his rich gravy.

Sophia always brought her homemade *kolokythopita*, the Greek pumpkin pie with phyllo dough. In the early years, Nikos kept the ouzo supply topped off. He could be counted on to entertain with reminiscences of their early life in Greece, ending with a toast of thanks for the family he adored.

"Family, friends, and food: the perfect combination," Ben always said.

"And no shopping for presents!" Arianna would add.

That exchange had passed between them so often at Thanksgiving that Tad and Faith expected it and teased them every time. It was one of the many endearing habits they had established over the years. One Christmas, Faith had even presented them both with needlework pillows on which she had stitched their exchange.

"The gifts we give each other at Thanksgiving are priceless," Ben reminded Arianna now. "The best kind—love, laughter, and lots of delicious things to eat."

He slipped his arm around her shoulder and drew her close. They stopped in the middle of the path and faced each other. Ben kissed her forehead, then the tip of her nose, before their lips briefly met in a quick, caring kiss, in some ways more meaningful than one filled with passion.

They stayed in a long embrace before they continued to walk and reminisce, hand in hand.

Absorbed in the pleasure of those memories, they explored the property for almost an hour. Arianna noticed Ben's gait was growing more erratic, and she held gently to his arm. When they reluctantly admitted they were beginning to feel cold, they returned to their suite, where Ben had planned everything perfectly.

A couple's massage was next on the agenda. Massage tables were set up in the suite's spacious living room. Soft music played, and the masseuse asked if they would like a scented candle.

"Absolutely!" Ben enthused. "The more atmosphere, the better!"

Dinner was served in their room by the gas fireplace. But as delicious as the meal was, much of it remained on their plates.

That night they lay sharing tender thoughts as their lips and fingers retraced memories. Intimacy had become increasingly difficult for Ben in recent months. Tonight, Arianna made certain Ben knew how deeply she loved him. How his touch had pleased her throughout their life together. How he filled her with laughter, happiness, and respect during a wonderful partnership as a lover, husband, and father. How she had no regrets.

As much as they tried, reality could not be ignored.

They had promised each other this weekend would be a celebration of all that they'd been and still were. They had sworn there would be no tears.

But wave upon wave of torrential sadness engulfed them—a tsunami of disbelief, frustration, and sorrow.

Once again they wept themselves to sleep wrapped in each other's arms.

CHAPTER TWO

Ben appeared to respond well to some of the prescribed medications over the winter. In spite of that, his need to have Arianna close by at all times was increasing noticeably.

This spring day was a turning point.

Ben left to drive to the nearby mall to meet friends at the Irish pub at noon for a corned beef on rye and a beer or two. The guys had been meeting on the last Thursday of the month for years. The mall was a five-minute drive straight down the street from their apartment.

Arianna knew how much it meant to Ben when he went somewhere on his own. She also knew that she'd worry until he returned. The doctor had said it was important for him to have this kind of independence as long as he could handle it—and so far he had.

When he hadn't returned home by three p.m., Arianna called his cell phone. The call went straight to voice mail. Ben had been finding his phone confusing recently. Arianna called him on it every day, even when they were in the apartment together, just to keep him connected to it. Lately, though, the ringing had upset him.

She then called his good friend George Castellanos to see if he was still with Ben.

"Gosh, Arianna, I watched Ben leave the parking lot around two o'clock. We all got into a serious game of darts and stayed longer than usual. He seemed to have a good time . . . you know, as much as he can these days. We all noticed he was a bit quieter, and the scoring was confusing him, so we just let that go. I mean, who cares, really? We're just glad that he still comes each month. I guess you called his cell?"

Arianna told him the call had gone unanswered. "That's happening a lot now."

"I think we better call the police," George replied, sounding concerned. "Is anyone with you?"

When Arianna said she was alone, George and his wife, Marlene, came straight over. Arianna called 911, and two police officers were at the door within five minutes.

They asked a number of questions about Ben of Arianna, George, and Marlene and took the addresses of Sophia and Tad. Arianna began to feel as if they were all under suspicion for some sort of crime. The police also e-mailed a photo of Ben, along with a description of him and his vehicle, into the police system.

Next, the officers searched every nook and cranny of the apartment and their restaurant, where they also interviewed the staff.

Finally, one officer left to search the area around the Irish pub. The other officer remained at the apartment with Arianna, George, and Marlene.

As the hours passed, Arianna's nerves frayed. Tad rushed over after work. They had agreed there was no need to let Faith in on what was happening until they knew more.

George and Marlene also insisted on staying. Marlene retrieved a casserole from her freezer, and Tad went downstairs to the restaurant to get a Greek salad to go with it. They forced themselves to eat and talk and tried to be optimistic.

The officer was receiving updates regularly and told them no accidents had been reported in the city or on any of the local highways. He suggested Arianna try to get some sleep, but he understood when she told him that would be impossible.

Finally, the officer received a call at two a.m. Lifting a hand to calm Arianna's frantic reaction, he said, "Mrs. Miller, your husband has been found. He is fine . . . he had driven east from Toronto to just outside Cornwall. One of our officers recognized his car from the province-wide alert. Your husband had pulled off onto a small side road. Ran out of gas and had probably been sitting there for some time."

"Jesus!" Tad blurted. "That's about a four-hour drive away!"

The policeman's face blurred in and out of focus through Arianna's tears, and his words became indecipherable to her. Tad quickly put his arms around his mother as she sobbed with a mix of relief and dismay.

"The officer has taken your husband to Cornwall Community Hospital to be checked out. They will keep him there until someone can collect him. The officer reported that Mr. Miller was calm and did not show any sign of distress."

George and Tad insisted they would leave immediately. "I'm going too," Arianna said. "I want to be with Ben."

The police officer advised otherwise. "You won't be doing Mr. Miller any service by jumping in your car right away. The hospital will take good care of him. They will give him something to eat and a bed to sleep in. I imagine he's exhausted. Now, please get some rest before you drive to Cornwall."

As much as Arianna wanted to leave immediately, Tad convinced her that a few hours of sleep would help them all.

As usual, Tad's quiet common sense had been wise. They all felt better when they awoke in the morning.

Russell Spencer called. They had been keeping in touch with him the day before and had texted him at two a.m. He wanted to make certain his help was not needed.

"I'm on hospital duty today but have left instructions you are to be put through to me," he told Arianna. "A word of caution when you see Ben: be calm. Do not act as though anything is wrong. That will be important for both of you."

"Oh, thanks, Russ! I would have rushed right over to him. I'm sure of that! I will pass that on to Tad and George."

When Tad, George, and Arianna walked into the hospital in Cornwall that afternoon, Ben was sitting calmly in a lounge watching television. He showed no awareness that anything was amiss.

Arianna's emotions were in turmoil. She was relieved he was safe, sad that his judgment was so impaired, helpless that she could not fix this, and frightened about what might happen next. The unknown was terrifying. Her heart was breaking apart, piece by piece.

Back at home in Toronto, a police officer called to make an appointment with Arianna the next day. While Ben watched television, the officer explained to Arianna that her husband would have to give up driving. She understood completely but was worried about how Ben would respond to that. As it happened, the first time they went out in the car, Arianna simply suggested she would drive. Ben did not protest, and he never mentioned driving anywhere again.

Later that afternoon, Arianna and her friend Gloria sat shoulder to shoulder on Gloria's sofa, their feet sharing a large leather ottoman. They had sat like this since they were teenagers sharing confidences, and somehow they had never stopped.

"I'm tired of crying," Arianna mumbled, smearing her mascara as she wiped tears away. "And I'm so glad you insisted I come over here. George and Marlene were happy to spend some time with Ben. They brought him Marlene's famous chicken pot pie . . . you know, it's about the only thing he will eat these days."

Gloria nodded wordlessly, crumpling another tissue in her hand. She had also been crying as Arianna related the details of the previous two days. Gloria and Arianna had been best friends since high school, when Gloria had originally been Ben's girlfriend. They knew each other well.

"And the worst part was—after all my worrying, picturing Ben dead somewhere—when we walked into the hospital to get him, he simply looked at us and said, 'Hi' . . . like nothing had happened. That's when reality hit me smack in the face, and I had to stop pretending things were sort of okay. They just aren't."

"I feel so helpless," Gloria said, her voice barely more than a whisper. "I don't seem to do much more than cry with you these days."

"You have no idea how much you help me just by doing that," Arianna assured her friend. "Who else could I do this with? I'm so lucky to have you."

By the following September, Ben's condition had deteriorated to the point that he could not be left alone. He lost all perspective and often attempted to leave the apartment with no idea why. His personal hygiene had been abandoned, and he was struggling with incontinence.

There were unexpected periods when a conversation seemed almost normal. Then, suddenly, a look of panic would come over Ben's face. His jaw would tighten and his eyes widen. It felt to Arianna like a silent cry for help just before it was replaced by a blank stare, and he would reach for her hand.

Arianna felt trapped in a nightmare. The pain in her heart was oppressive as she watched her life partner slip away from her. Some days she worried about her own grip on reality.

Their sprawling apartment above the restaurant was now fitted with railings and safety bars in the bathrooms and hallway. New locks were installed on the doors. Regular caregivers provided some relief from the physical and emotional demands on Arianna.

Ben was not happy when these strangers were in his space. His calm demeanor changed as he suggested harshly that these uninvited guests get out of his home. Arianna wondered at times if it was even worth it.

Dr. Spencer insisted, taking her aside after an appointment with Ben, "Arianna, as your physician, and even more so as your friend, I assure you that this assistance is necessary. It's as much for you as for Ben. If he is upset when you leave him for a few hours, so be it. He will be fine when you get home and won't remember, anyway."

When she explained how embarrassed she felt for Ben, and for herself, at his uncustomary rudeness, the doctor reminded her that these caregivers understood and were used to this behavior. "It goes with the territory, and I'm sure you've noticed how well they cope. They feel your pain."

Ben's friends did their best to spend time with him, but he could no longer go out to the pub or a coffee shop. For the most part, he would simply stare at the television. Still, they persisted and tried to entertain him with their running sports commentaries. Ben's responses were dull and muted, if any.

Everyone was suffering as they watched Ben slip away from them.

Arianna tried to spend as much time with Ben as she could, but often the restaurant required her presence. Once the business was sold, there were still frequent meetings of one kind or another. And other times she knew she was purposely avoiding being with her husband. Which caused her all kinds of guilt and sadness.

Because when she was being honest with herself, as much as her love for Ben did not fade, she often dreaded the time alone with him. It was torture for her to see his loss of control over his words and emotions, as well as his body. Even simple conversations were becoming difficult.

It was also a test to constantly have caregivers in the house, as much as they tried to melt into the background when not needed. Most were kind and helpful and respected Arianna's privacy. Nevertheless, there was always an unavoidable extra presence.

In mid-September, Ben's elderly parents, both in frail health, flew in from their retirement community on Vancouver Island. They had never been particularly close in the fifteen years since they had moved west. The weeklong visit was awkward and emotional, and it was a relief they only came once. Arianna dutifully called every week after that and filled the conversation with news about Tad and Faith and the great-grandchildren.

Faith Skyped nightly with her mother. Ben enjoyed talking to his daughter this way at first, but as his illness progressed, he became frustrated that she was in "that box."

In early October, Faith took a leave from her teaching position in Nunavut and returned home to Toronto.

Arianna was deeply touched by her daughter's sensitive and tender manner with Ben, even in his worst moments. Those moments were becoming more frequent. With Faith at home, they were able to dispense with the night nurse for a while as, most nights, Ben could be sedated to sleep through until morning. If he did wake up, there was help for Arianna.

"Mom," Faith said one evening, after they had settled Ben for the night, "I know it doesn't make things better, but at least Dad doesn't realize what's happening. He is slipping into his own world. Somehow that's comforting to me."

Arianna ran her fingers through her long hair before she twisted it into a tight knot, her tension showing as she gripped it behind her head.

"I hear you, but it hurts my heart to the core to see it happening. My Ben—your dad—is vanishing in front of our eyes. Nothing about that is comforting to me." Tears fell easily.

Faith passed an ever-present box of tissues across the table to her.

⚜

For the first time ever, Thanksgiving was quietly acknowledged with a simple family dinner to which Ben contributed nothing but sadness. Ben's unawareness of the holiday made it that much more difficult. He became restless at the table, and Arianna helped him off to bed, as their grandchildren, Nicholas and Isabella, sat teary-eyed while they finished dinner. An atmosphere of gloom settled around the table, even though Faith attempted to cheer things up with dessert and offers of a movie.

Tad was still trying to accept his father's condition. His wife, Christine, leaned over and put her hand on his shoulder as the adults spoke over coffee. The children were happily settled with their movie choice. "There are times I look at Dad, when he's sitting quietly or snoozing, and I feel he might still be there. We might be able to have a conversation. But after today, I can see that's never going to happen. Dad, as we knew him, is gone."

Everyone nodded silently.

Tad reached across the table and tenderly took his mother's hand. "Mom, you're being so strong and handling this in the best way possible. I know your heart is broken to see Dad this way."

Arianna gulped back tears. "My heart's broken for all of us and especially Dad. He had so much more life to live. No one is ever prepared for something like this. I know we aren't alone, and the support group at the hospital has been incredibly helpful."

Faith agreed and said to her brother, "I went to the group meeting last week with Mom. Maybe you and Christine should come with us the next time. It was so beneficial to talk with others going through the same crisis in their family. I came away with more strength to deal with it."

CHAPTER THREE

Christmas was a disaster.

Arianna and Ben had always hosted, and every year, the house was filled with ever more joy as their children were born and grew up, and then grandchildren became part of the celebration. Traditions, large and small, began early in December, and the apartment was decorated with treasures collected through the decades.

Year after year, Ben lovingly teased Arianna. "You are truly Mrs. Claus, if there ever was one."

"And proud of it," she would reply, returning his warm smile. She felt grateful he had always been so supportive of her holiday indulgences.

Tad and Christine's children, Nicholas and Isabella, were the apples of their grandparents' eyes. Now ages eight and ten, they clearly noticed Ben's odd behavior. Their *pappouli's* inability to remember their names confused them, even though they understood he was not well.

Faith convinced Arianna they should go ahead with their Christmas traditions. Arianna had let Faith gently persuade her to unpack the boxes of house decorations. They had gone to the nursery to purchase cedar and pine boughs for the fireplace mantel and doorways. The scent of the fresh cuttings filled the apartment with the Christmas spirit.

Arianna loved watching the grandchildren help Faith set up the collection of Santas, exclaiming and giggling as they examined each one. Tenderly, they unwrapped the buildings and figures of the beloved Christmas village that had grown with each year and placed them on the mantel.

As decorations were brought out, the happy memories that accompanied them made Arianna feel distraught. "I don't know how much more of this I can take. Sometimes when I look around at all these reminders of our happy Christmases, I feel overwhelming sadness. I can't imagine ever loving this time of year again."

Yet each time Arianna began to object, Faith would put her arms around her mother and try to be encouraging. "As much as I hate to say this, it might be Dad's last Christmas. Let's do all the things that he loved."

"I'm not sure it will mean anything to him. But, okay. I feel guilty for having these moments of self-pity, but I can't stop them."

"Oh, Mom." Faith's voice cracked with emotion. "I'm so sorry this has happened to Dad, you . . . all of us . . ."

They put off buying the tree until Christmas Eve. It had taken Faith that long to break down Arianna's completely out-of-character resolve not to have one. "We must! For the little ones, if for no one else."

Faith prepared a platter of raw vegetables with a bowl of tzatziki sauce and opened a bottle of chardonnay. Arianna poured Ben a glass of iced tea, his favorite, but Ben refused every effort they made to cajole him into eating or drinking anything.

A soundtrack of their favorite carols played softly in the background.

They began trimming the tree with ornaments collected through the couple's thirty-seven-year marriage. From time to time, they gently encouraged Ben to take a treasure out of the box and hand it to one of them to place on the tree. They would remind him of the memory attached to it, and occasionally he would nod or smile weakly. His interest flagged quickly.

"This feels like an exercise in futility," Arianna mumbled under her breath to her daughter. She suggested they stop more than once, but Faith was determined.

"Maybe one of these ornaments will jog a memory for him . . . I keep hoping. He loved going through them every year. I remember when we were kids we used to get bored because he insisted on telling us about every single one. Each one had a story, or he would make one up." Her eyes filled with tears.

"Now," she continued, sniffing loudly, "I would give anything for him to say something meaningful."

Arianna said nothing at first. In time, it was more than she could take. She placed the ornament she was holding back in the tissue-lined box.

"Sweetheart, I'm done for now." Her wine sat untouched.

"I'm sorry, Mom. I didn't stop to think how this would affect you."

Arianna took her daughter in her arms. They rocked back and forth in silence. "It's okay. I understand. Let's turn out the lights and go for a walk while the nurse takes over. We can finish decorating when we come back."

On Christmas morning, before anyone could stop him, Ben suddenly pulled the tree over and tried to drag it out the apartment door. Ornaments crashed to the floor, sending bits of glass flying across the hardwood. Her voice caught somewhere between her heart and her mouth, Arianna watched memories of their life together smash into pieces as she scrambled to grab at branches and end the chaos Ben was creating.

The noise was calamitous. A lamp was knocked over, and water from the tree stand added to the mess. ·

The caregiver attempted to calm Ben after he yelled and pushed Arianna down and Faith away when they tried to stop him. He glared at them both as the nurse led him to the bedroom. It was the look of a man Arianna did not know. It was not her Ben.

As she sat where she landed on the floor, Arianna was too stunned to cry. Her face drained to the palest of pale, and she trembled as Faith took her hand and helped her to her feet.

Finally finding her voice, she murmured, "I can't believe he did that. I knew it might happen one day, but never really accepted it. I—I—" Her face reflected despair and anguish as her words caught.

"Mom, Mom . . ." Faith whispered, holding her mother. "I'm so sorry. That wasn't Dad. It was the disease that has stolen him from us. We have to let him go."

With her arm around her mother's shoulder, Faith guided her to the kitchen. "Sit here, Mom, and I'll make us some tea."

Arianna felt numb, her thoughts jumbled. Her voice was just above a whisper. "I've hit a wall, Faith. I don't know what to do."

Arianna's heart was wrenched even more as she felt Faith's despair. She appreciated the comfort her daughter was offering. It wasn't supposed to be like this. She knew Faith wanted to make it better, and she also knew that at this point nothing would. Her heart ached for her entire family.

"Don't do anything, Mom. Just sip your tea, close your eyes, and try to feel calm. You know how we've been meditating. Try to do that now while I clean up."

Silent tears slipped over Arianna's cheeks. "There's something so terribly sad about seeing a fallen Christmas tree and broken ornaments, even if it was an accident. But this is so much worse. I feel awful that you're cleaning it up. I should be doing it."

"There, there, Mom." Faith's voice was soothing. For the first time, Arianna became fully aware of the reversal that was taking place. Her child was assuming a parental role. As much as it was appreciated, it was also disconcerting.

Faith gathered up all the food, including the traditional holiday treats that had been collecting on the table over the previous week. She knew it would be unthinkable to leave behind the sweet *melomakarona* and powdered sugar–covered *kourambiethes*. No Greek Christmas was complete without those delicacies.

When Arianna protested, Faith decreed they would eat themselves back into the Christmas spirit. Then she bundled her mother into the car to go to Tad's house. They stopped to pick up Sophia on the way, after Faith called to explain they had been delayed. She felt it best to wait to share the details.

Faith followed her grandmother to the car, carrying a pot of *avgolemono* soup, prepared the night before. Sophia cradled her homemade loaf of *Christopsomo*, the slightly sweet, light, buttery bread. The car was immediately filled with the fragrance of cinnamon, cloves, and orange, the familiar smell of Christmas Day for them.

Arianna felt shell-shocked. Sophia was consoling, her own pain set aside. Faith was a rock. For this to happen at such a special family time made it all the more difficult to process.

They all agreed a turning point had been reached. Quietly, each in their own way, they attempted to insert a semblance of Christmas cheer into the day. Subdued and saddened at times, they also found moments of laughter. The grandchildren's joy and excitement at opening their presents was not to be denied. Sophia busied herself in the kitchen or snoozed in the rocking chair. Faith, Christine, and Tad persisted in recalling good times. There had been many.

Ben slept at home, sedated.

Tad and the four women tried to create a festive atmosphere as they all pitched in to prepare the traditional Christmas pork dinner. The grandchildren were welcome distractions with their unabashed excitement. But Arianna knew this time of year would never again mean what it used to.

As she had for months now, Arianna kept silently questioning how everything could change so dramatically—even though she knew nothing in life could be predicted or controlled. She'd been through it with her parents' accident. She'd seen it happen to people she knew. But somehow that still didn't stop her from questioning it.

How could she ever move on? She struggled to accept that life as she knew it was over. Her Ben was gone. Their marriage, as it once was, was gone.

Yet Ben was still physically there. Arianna was still his wife. She still loved him and felt committed to him.

"That's the conflict," she confessed to Gloria one chilly morning in January as they walked briskly through a neighborhood park. The freezing air caught their breath in puffs.

"I feel increasingly alone," Arianna continued without a hint of self-pity. "That's the reality."

Gloria slipped her arm around her friend's shoulder. "It's frightening to watch and accept. We keep wondering how we can do more."

"That's the thing. No one really can. It's not like he's an invalid and friends can come visit, chat, take him for walks, play cards, watch a movie—all those things we want to do . . ." Arianna's voice trailed off into a sorrowful sigh.

"The only—and I do mean *only*—consolation is that I'm assured by all the medical support people that at this point he is unaware of what is happening. If I thought his mind was somehow still present, that would be torture . . . for all of us."

Gloria nodded. "So sad that this is the good news."

"For better or worse. In sickness or in health," Arianna murmured.

Their eyes met. The two friends stood at the side of the path, wrapped in an embrace of support, friendship, love . . . and sadness.

In the following weeks, Ben slipped into a heavily medicated regimen to counteract his increasingly abusive and stubborn behavior.

Nursing became necessary around the clock, and everyone advised Arianna that moving him to an assisted-care facility was best for all concerned.

Tad, Christine, Faith, Sophia, and Arianna spent long hours comforting each other as they came to terms with the inevitable decision. Arianna gave thanks constantly for her strong, loving family.

Just over a year and a half had passed since the day Arianna and Ben had sat with Dr. Spencer to hear the dreadful diagnosis. Every day since then, they really had been coping with grief over the loss of Ben as they knew and loved him. Some argued that, in certain ways, this was more difficult than dealing with death.

CHAPTER FOUR

A steady lulling sensation accompanied the increased motion of the train. As the urban backdrop of Paris began to fade away, the TGV accelerated into its legendary high speed.

Arianna's face relaxed. Her eyes softened, and her lips turned up in a half smile.

France! I'm finally here.

The bittersweet feeling that accompanied these attempts at smiles for almost two years had become part of her. She wondered if that would ever change.

She had always been a confident traveler. But she had also always had her husband with her, taking charge. He'd made it so easy. The reality that she was on this journey alone was not lost on her. However, as Faith had so accurately pointed out, she essentially had been functioning on her own for many months now.

And somewhere along the way during those months, Arianna had lost herself. She'd stopped moving forward. Each day had vanished into the next. Her focus was only on Ben. She had visited him every single day for the four months since he had been admitted permanently to Lakeview Assisted Living. Not that he knew it.

There had been much arm-twisting applied by all of her family before Arianna had agreed to this trip.

Faith and Tad had sat with her and expressed their concerns. "We're losing our father. We don't want to lose our mother too. Please, Mom . . . listen to us."

I've got this. I promised the kids I would do it . . . and I will.

She settled into the comfortable seat and blew out a quiet sigh. She was glad her train connection at Charles de Gaulle Airport had been easy. Her anxious anticipation of what lay ahead during the next weeks in Provence was replaced by a calm that descended upon her like a soft blanket.

Arianna was going to participate in a two-week art workshop. The website made clear that this particular course was for seasoned artists, not beginners. Applicants had to submit photos of four completed pieces and give a detailed educational and practical history of their experience. The stated goal was to "guide you into a deeper understanding of your craft, *en plein air*, surrounded by the light, color, and atmosphere that has inspired painters for centuries."

After letting go of art in her life for so many years, she had worried her application would be futile. She'd waited with a combination of excitement and anxiety to see if she would be accepted. Now she was on her way.

The location was a bonus. Arles was where van Gogh had his most productive years, and she had been drawn to his art ever since she was young, when she tacked up posters of his sunflowers on her bedroom wall. At university, her attraction had turned to infatuation. Here she would have the opportunity to walk in his footsteps. A dream come true.

And there were no shared memories with Ben in France. This was her choice. These would be her memories to make. She wondered if she could.

The window beside her was wide and surprisingly clear, somehow missed by the graffiti artists who had spoiled many of the others, she noted. It didn't much matter, though, as the train rolled past blocks of suburban apartments that looked like any other city outskirts, with no hint of the magic of the City of Light.

She planned to have time to enjoy the treasures of Paris for a few days after her course in Arles. Faith had helped her plan a week of travel. She had arranged a rental car and would spend a few days on the Côte d'Azur before flying back to Paris, and then home. A twinge of pleasure ran through her.

Her thoughts slipped back forty years to when she had spent a month in Paris as part of her final year at university. The students had been immersed in museums, galleries, and art classes for those four weeks. Arianna had been torn the entire time between her love of all of that art and obsessive thoughts of her fiancée, Ben, back home waiting for her. That had been the last time she'd seen Paris.

She turned her attention to the window again. Soon she was thankful for her unimpeded view as the countryside surrounded the train. She felt herself being drawn into the contentment offered by the rural landscape: a blur of spring's green on the brown and yellow palette.

Young crops reached skyward in some fields. Orderly rows of vineyards stretched endlessly in others. Freshly plowed furrows offered the promise of new yields.

Arianna felt a sense of renewal as she watched the scenery unfold.

Bursts of color, as if applied by afterthought, would intermittently appear as the train sped by. Splashes of bright-red poppy fields and golden rapeseed in bloom dotted the landscape. The solid, jumbled-limestone mass of an ancient village with clay-tiled rooftops punctuated the scenery from time to time. Rivers and forests changed the perspective. The cloudless May sky layered on a shade of blue that inspired only optimism.

She took out her new art journal, bought for this trip, and worn leather pencil case. Without thinking, she briefly caressed the soft, caramel-colored lambskin with her long, graceful fingers before she opened the zipper. The pencils had been changed a few times through the years, but the case had aged along with Arianna. The fine lines in the leather represented the passing years.

Like the lines in my face, she mused as she traced along the front of the case and lost herself in thought. *Goodness knows I've added many more in the last two years.*

She had purchased the pencil case in Paris during her student days, and it had fueled many dreams. The familiarity of that touch soothed her even more now. It had been too long since she had felt that.

A brand-new little tin field kit of paints was in her travel bag, to use when she wasn't in motion. Everything she needed to get started. She felt excited to open the first page of her journal and begin recording this artistic journey.

She drew with a fine-tipped waterproof marker. Then, choosing each freshly sharpened pencil with care, she created a patchwork of colors as she saw them. Where others might write in a journal, Arianna sketched, rubbed, and blended to create the desired shades and hues that captured her eye, creating memories. Every once in a while she added a word about how she was feeling.

Excited, nervous, curious . . .

As far back as she could remember, color was as integral to her as breathing.

Her childhood dreams centered around primary colors, with secondary colors blending in as she grew. Even without understanding about mixing colors in those early years, she was soon using the complete spectrum of the color wheel in her coloring and painting. She would entertain her parents with stories about the taste of color. Sophia would chuckle, hugging her young daughter with delight. Nikos would shake his head, wishing she would talk about the taste of food.

Arianna left those thoughts behind now, contentment wrapping around her as colors filled the page. She had missed this feeling. Missed these tastes.

The truth of the matter was, she had not touched her paints, pastels, pencils, or any other art materials since Ben's diagnosis. It occurred to her several months after that day in Dr. Spencer's office that she was seeing things only in stark black and white.

Her thoughts had focused solely on how to get Ben through the day. How to get herself through the day. She had even stopped watching the news. Her family's sorrow was all she could handle. There had been no color.

Books had been her escape. Always an avid reader, she was able to lose herself in the pages of good stories and was grateful each time she sat down with her current read.

Thanks to Faith, she had an e-reader fully loaded with new books. Her daughter had been instrumental in bringing technology into her life in the last few months. Arianna had to admit it was so much easier than packing a bunch of print books, as much as she still loved to turn the pages of a book in her hands.

She flipped another page of her journal, surprised at how she much she was enjoying creating in this way again. Old feelings might come back after all.

Again, she was pleased to have the seating space to herself. Her luck was holding, she thought, as her mind wandered.

The flight from Toronto had been without incident and not full. Arianna felt it was a good omen that the middle seat in her row had been empty. She and the woman in the aisle seat had appreciated sharing that extra space. Arianna also appreciated that the woman was not particularly chatty. After a few initial pleasantries, each had settled into her own involvement with the entertainment system, reading, and catching some sleep until breakfast was announced shortly before landing in Paris.

Arianna liked that. She wasn't one to easily engage in small talk with strangers. She had always been a bit of an introvert.

Ben, like Nikos, had been the chatterbox and the über-friendly guy in the room. That was one reason why both men had been so successful at running the restaurant for so many years. It took that kind of personality. Arianna loved that about her husband, along with a lot of other things.

Ben . . .

How she missed him. She thought about the saying that you don't know what you have until it's gone. Well, not with Ben. She always knew what she had and was always so thankful luck had shone on her when he came into her life. Even when he was dating Gloria during their high school days, she'd secretly adored him.

His smile lit up a room, never mind her heart. Everyone wanted to be his friend, chat with him, share a few laughs. He always saw the good in people but was perceptive and an intuitive judge of character. No one took advantage of Ben, but plenty of people received help from him. He always made life an adventure.

Arianna knew there were many other types of men who would not have brought as much laughter or love into her life.

And he cooked. He cleaned. But most of all, he loved his family with a passion. He had so much more to give.

Tears filled her eyes and rushed down her cheeks before she could quell them. Fumbling for a tissue in her pocket, she turned her head to the window and dabbed at her face. She decided to let the tears silently continue, knowing they would anyway. She had learned these outbursts were brief. It wasn't going to be one of her loud and painful sobbing fits. She could now sense those in advance and find a private place to let go. And even those moments were diminishing . . . she was well aware of that.

How she loved him. What a solid marriage they had shared. They had weathered the ups and downs and put effort into making their commitment to each other work. Plenty of their friends had not been so successful. Arianna and Ben admitted to a certain smugness about that.

It had been excruciating to watch him be eaten alive by a terrible disease and disappear into himself.

And Sophia . . .

Bless her mother. Eighty-five years old. Ageless in her attitude. She devoted herself to helping however she could, constantly thinking how Ben's illness was so wrong. "It's just not fair. It should be me," her mother would say every day, even as she tried not to. "This would have devastated Nikos. He loved Ben so."

When they had coffee together the day before Arianna left for France, Sophia clasped Arianna's hands in hers. "My darling daughter, I've been a widow for twenty-two years. I've lived like this, carrying the loving memory of your dear *baba* with me, as I should, and as you will always keep dear Ben in your heart. But Greek women of my generation dressed in black and mostly never moved on with our life. I don't regret it. It was my role. But it is not your role. You have a lot of life to live, and I hope you live it. Ben would want you to live it."

They had cried together. Arianna had vowed to her mother that she would try.

Tadeus, Christine, and Faith, our little family . . .

She thought how her gratitude to their children knew no bounds. They had stepped up to meet this crisis in ways she would never have predicted. The two grandchildren, Nicholas and Isabella, had provided a beautiful, unconditional love since the day each was born and during recent times had often been a much-needed distraction.

Faith remained home for those last agonizing months, loving her father and helping Arianna in every way possible, until the madness was over and the sadness was left to consume them.

Faith was a classic example of the benefits of never giving up on your kids.

She had been a challenging teenager, pushing limits and causing her parents many sleepless nights. Her first tattoo had been a contentious issue.

There was a flirtation with drugs and independence, especially after she lost her grandfather, her beloved *pappouli*. She had struggled with grief. That had been another reason Arianna had not returned to her previous job at the Art Gallery. She felt that the flexibility of her presence at home, as well as in the restaurant, was important.

On the positive side, Faith had stayed committed to her education through it all, but in as unorthodox a way as she could. She took many semesters in exotic parts of the world: Africa, India, Nicaragua, Guatemala, Nunavut.

Faith studied diligently, and Arianna held close in her heart the pride she and Ben shared as they attended each graduation. With a master's degree in education and a doctorate in social work, Faith applied her skills from her heart as well as her head. She chose to live without personal comfort in order to help those she saw in need.

And then, when the chips were down, Faith had quietly assumed control when she returned home.

Watching her during Ben's illness, Arianna had a glimpse, for the first time, of how Faith had taken on the cultural and societal challenges of her troubled young students in Nunavut, Canada's northernmost territory. She saw her daughter's combination of strength, intelligence, and sensitivity and felt enormously proud of her. It was apparent Faith had developed a strong ability to hone in on what was critical. She was a straight shooter.

It was a shock when Faith told her mom she had recently established contact with second cousins in Greece. Not surprisingly, Facebook had brought them together. The Greek relatives had made the first overtures, messaging Faith. She was happy to be reconnected with her roots. Her generation carried no animosity for their elders' supposed past wrongs.

More lessons learned from the prodigal daughter.

Arianna was pleased about reconnecting with the Greek family and, surprisingly, so was Sophia. "All those years we were mad at each other. Think about what we missed. Why did I have to get old to get smart about this?" Sophia said to her daughter and granddaughter.

Faith and Tad, along with his wife, Christine, and the long list of caregivers provided by the health-care system, had offered the loving and physical support Arianna needed to keep Ben at home until it had become impossible. She would be grateful to them forever for that.

Tad and his wife were both accountants. Their knowledge and assistance had been crucial in developing a financial plan that would offer Arianna ongoing security. Arianna and Ben had been diligent about contributing to savings for their senior years. However, they had never paid much attention to the possibility that the restaurant would not continue to be a source of income.

In the beginning, Arianna and Ben had talked about the reality of selling the restaurant. At the time of his initial diagnosis, Ben was still able to understand what they were facing together. Arianna was insistent that Ben continue to run what had been his lifelong passion until he could not cope. When he reached that point, he was unaware of it, and close friends within the business stepped in to help manage things and take care of the sale of Papa's to Demetrios.

Good friends had been kind and helpful, but eventually it was too difficult and painful for them to be in Ben's presence. Finding the right words became a challenge. It was easier for people not to come. Notes, cards, flowers, and meals were dropped off, and the family appreciated all of them. Ben, by then, was oblivious to the offerings.

Arianna understood the challenge of friends visiting as Ben's condition progressed. It was embarrassing, awkward, shocking, even, to see Ben's behavior . . . for her and for the visitor. She fought with her conscience over the feelings of shame and anger that more frequently overtook love and sadness.

Gloria was the only person whose presence with Ben offered Arianna solace. Her best friend was able to move beyond whatever his behavior was that day and somehow give Arianna the right kind of support and understanding. They cried together after each of her visits, and that helped too.

At times, wine also helped. For everyone but Ben, of course.

Ben's diagnosis had been slow in coming. His effervescent personality had camouflaged many of the early symptoms. Now he lay in a vegetative state in a nursing home, where it was predicted he would remain for an indeterminate time. Palliative care was still to come. It was a ponderous torture for the family.

CHAPTER FIVE

Arianna put away her pencil case and journal, which had slipped to the floor. She closed her eyes and allowed the memories to carry her back to the early years.

An only child, Arianna had a loving relationship with both her parents. Sophia was a woman of few words but deep understanding. Arianna had known that for as long as she could remember. Their bond was quiet and strong.

And Nikos adored Arianna, with her long black hair, big brown eyes framed by lush eyelashes, and quiet ways. She was his *poulaki*, his little bird.

Indeed, it was because of their preteen daughter that they tearfully bade good-bye to their extended family on the tiny Greek island of Lesvos in 1967 and moved to Toronto. A military junta had seized power in Athens, and hard times were predicted. They wished a better life for Arianna.

The Papadopoulos family had owned a popular seaside restaurant on Lesvos dating back to the early 1800s. What began as a place where the catch of the day was casually grilled and sold to locals on the beach slowly evolved into a sprawling, unpretentious patio restaurant overhanging the glistening sea in a protected cove. Sun-kissed waves in shades of turquoise and blue washed over golden-sand beaches.

Children ran and played with carefree abandon, and parents never worried. Ancient ruins were neighborhood playgrounds.

The community, and then eventually also tourists, gravitated to the friendly atmosphere provided by lively conversation, laughter, and tempting fresh delicacies. Something as simple as a salad and grilled sardines could evolve into a feast lasting for hours, as heaping plates of everything from fish to olives to fruit appeared on the table. Dripping jugs of sangria and local wines were emptied with ease. Eating was not limited to specific mealtimes but rather was an ongoing celebration of any part of the day.

The delicious fish recipes created by Nikos's family, going back to his great-great-grandmother, were legendary throughout the islands. These treasured gems of family history came across the sea in a carefully wrapped binder.

At that time in Toronto, there was already a strong cultural vibe in the stretch along Danforth Avenue known as Greektown, from Greenwood Avenue to Broadview. The area blossomed with food, music, and culture. Word spread throughout the city's expanding suburbs.

Some of the two-story brick buildings originated from the 1910s and 1920s, adding to the character of the area. It was on the ground floor of one of these older structures that Papa's on the Danforth opened its doors. Soon devoted customers were returning and bringing friends to savor the delights of Nikos's kitchen. Sophia took charge of the cash register and bill payments. And the family settled into the rambling, slightly rundown apartment above it.

Through the years, more Greek immigrants had moved in and gravitated to living on the Danforth. By the 1970s, Greektown held one of the largest Greek populations in North America.

There was a sense of being transported to Greece while walking through the close-knit neighborhood. Fresh markets, bakeries, restaurants, and patios infused with authentic food, noise, and smells brought that sense to life.

Shopkeepers called out to one another in Greek, keeping their colorful language alive. The daily arrivals of deliverymen were events on their own, greeted with noisy enthusiasm. Regulars were treated like family members.

Neighborhood dogs trotted up and down the streets, knowing which doors to check for a waiting treat. Spunky cats marked their territories, helping keep down the rodent population. Chickens squawked through the slats of their wooden crates. Rabbits wrapped in newspaper peered out at children who begged to take them home as pets, not for dinner.

Black-clad elderly women, heads covered in black lace or drab kerchiefs and shopping baskets on their arms, took their time inspecting the stands of fresh produce. At the seafood and butcher shops, every purchase was debated and negotiated. It was expected and respected. Shopping was an art, a business, a social event, and an important part of daily life.

One could sense a community built on tradition. There was unity and an underlying passion for thriving businesses. And noise! Laughter, loud voices, singing, debating . . . the life of Greek villages was being lived on these streets, in this community, halfway around the world from their country of origin.

The Mediterranean cuisine proved in demand with diners from every ethnic group in Toronto's multicultural population. A loud chorus of *"Opa!"* could be heard late into the night at various celebrations, accompanied by the traditional smashing of plates and bouzouki *rebetika* music.

All that was missing was the sea.

Some establishments only served dinner, but what made the immigrants feel most at home were the small patios, often attached to bakeries. They were the perfect place to have a dark, strong cup of coffee or a glass or two of ouzo and watch the passing parade on a warm, sunny afternoon or summer evening.

Nikos was overjoyed when he received permission from the city to create an outside patio. He would take cigarette breaks out there, mingling with his customers as he entertained them with stories, accompanied by his outgoing personality and boisterous laugh. Breaking into song from time to time became an expectation, as he harmonized with his favorite Nana Mouskouri tapes.

In 1972, while still in high school, Ben took a part-time job in the Papadopouloses' family restaurant. In fact, he always said he fell in love with her father, Nikos, before he fell in love with Arianna. No one denied that. And the feeling was mutual.

Although he washed dishes at first, Ben's interest in cooking soon became apparent, and slowly Nikos took him under his wing in the kitchen. Arianna worked as a waitress, and Nikos made it clear to Ben that his daughter was not to be flirted with.

When Nikos saw how Ben was suited for the restaurant business, he was delighted to encourage him to assist and learn in his chapel, the kitchen. In time, he even treated Ben as a son.

Slowly Ben and Arianna got to know each other.

Arianna was shy, studious, and obsessed with art, consumed with drawing and painting. A sketch pad was her constant companion. During all her spare time she took courses at the Ontario College of Art or simply spent hours lost in the exhibits in local galleries.

Her bedroom walls were covered with van Gogh posters. When an exhibit of his work came to the Art Gallery of Ontario, she saved her money and went three times.

Nikos did not understand his daughter's fascination. He proudly displayed her art throughout the house and even, to Arianna's embarrassment, in the restaurant. But he clearly saw it as her hobby and often worried aloud that she was simply a dreamer.

"What's she gonna do with that?" he would ask Sophia, exasperated. She would reassure him that their daughter had a special talent and clear ideas about how she would use it.

"She knows what she wants to do, Nikos. Don't worry, she has plans, and she will be doing work she loves. That's what we hope for, isn't it?"

Nikos would wring his hands and worry, but he loved his wife and trusted her opinion.

Meanwhile, Ben had a girlfriend, Gloria, throughout high school, and Nikos went out of his way to invite her to hang around the restaurant. He was delighted when she and Arianna became friends, unaware that Gloria told Arianna regularly how she was sure Ben favored her.

While Arianna was waitressing during the summer after high school graduation, Ben amicably broke up with Gloria.

The girls met for lunch shortly thereafter.

"I've been telling you this for years," Gloria said to Arianna, without an ounce of regret, as they shared a chocolate sundae.

As Arianna began to protest, her friend raised her hand to stop her. "Uh-uh, nope! That's not going to fly this time. You have to believe me. Our breakup has been coming for a long time. We're just friends. You are the one Ben loves. Now give him a chance, because I think you love him too."

The friends shared a look: the kind of look that comes naturally to women who truly care about each other. There was a tenderness, a knowing, and a "don't mess with me" aspect to it, and girlfriends got it.

Then Ben chose to go to the Chef School at George Brown College to hone his craft. He would work at the restaurant every evening and weekend. It was a marriage made in heaven.

While Ben was attending college, Arianna studied for a fine arts degree at the University of Toronto.

When it was time for Ben to have a three-month placement abroad, Nikos arranged for him to go to an old friend's restaurant in Athens. Afterward, Ben spent a few weeks at the family restaurant on Lesvos and returned more Greek than most of their customers. He loved the culture and never doubted what he would do with his life.

Nikos was excited about the new ideas Ben brought into the kitchen. The restaurant continued to be known as a thriving purveyor of Greek street food: gyros, souvlaki, spanakopita, and traditional family recipes such as béchamel-smothered moussaka. But now there were new seafood dishes and ever-changing *mezedes*, the popular appetizers served with ouzo.

The secret recipe Sophia used for their baklava was renowned throughout the city. In spite of premade phyllo pastry becoming readily available, she always insisted on making her own.

Two years later, Ben asked Nikos for Arianna's hand in marriage. Nikos and Sophia gave their blessing joyfully.

Arianna went off to Paris to study art for three months to earn a credit that enhanced her degree. She loved the City of Light and immersed herself in its history and art. Strolling the narrow cobblestone streets of the older quarters was a thrill she had not imagined. Even so, she couldn't wait to get back to her Ben.

In June 1978, a big Greek wedding took place. Arianna and Ben were twenty-three years old, deeply in love, and excited about the future. Nikos and Sophia glowed with pride and happiness.

Though Arianna had let her attendance lapse once she'd begun university, Nikos and Sophia still faithfully worshipped in their neighborhood Greek Orthodox church every Sunday. Arianna and Ben met with the local priest, and the wedding was arranged for June 9, 1978. Odd numbers were lucky, Nikos reminded them.

As much as it was not in keeping with Arianna's style, she had agreed with everything her father wished for the wedding. Though she was thankful that he did not insist on many of the old-fashioned rituals, like regularly spitting three times to ward off the evil eye. Always loving and supportive, Sophia helped keep Nikos's excitement under control.

After Nikos blubbered through the traditional ceremony with candles, golden crowns attached by ribbons, and three shared sips from the common cup, the party moved to the church hall.

No expense had been spared, and the hall had been decorated with splendid flowers and linens. Nikos oversaw every detail of the menu and catering. After five courses of the finest Greek specialties, the party began.

A popular Greek band played as everyone danced the Tsamiko, the Zeibekiko, and the joyful Kalamatianos. The evening was exuberant, loud, and filled with laughter.

After much pleading from the couple, Nikos agreed to forgo the plate smashing but only once Arianna and Ben consented to participate in the money dance at the end of the night. After the couple began dancing, holding a handkerchief between them, every guest took turns dancing with them and pinned money to their clothing.

Their honeymoon was in Greece.

Growing up, Arianna had realized that Nikos felt sad that his family name would not live on through another generation. After her marriage, her father beamed when Arianna told him she would keep her maiden name along with Miller. Papadopoulos-Miller was a surname she carried proudly, in spite of the time it took to write it.

As the years went by, their family expanded with the births of a daughter, Faith, and a son, Tadeus. The family took turns taking summer trips to Greece, Nikos and Sophia one year, and then Arianna and her family the next. One very special summer, they closed the restaurant for two weeks and all went together for an unforgettable family holiday.

This continued until the summer Nikos and Sophia were in a tragic car accident. As they drove the steep, narrow roads of Mount Lepetymnos to their favorite viewpoint, where Nikos had proposed to Sophia so long ago, he suffered a fatal heart attack. The car went off the road, its descent halted by trees on the heavily forested slope. Sophia received minor cuts and bruises and a broken heart that never healed completely.

Sadly, the emotional aftermath of the accident also caused a rift in the extended family that grew into a chasm. Relatives in Greece thought Nikos's ashes should be returned to Lesvos. Sophia could not bear the thought of setting foot again on the island that had claimed her husband's life. Passion overtook understanding. Unkind words were exchanged, and bitter feelings grew.

Neither Sophia nor Arianna's family ever returned to Lesvos. Over the years, as relatives aged and passed, the family connection was lost.

In the meantime, Ben and Arianna worked hard to keep the restaurant going. Eventually, they expanded into an adjoining vacant space and hired more staff. The restaurant prospered, but long vacations became impossible as they realized they needed to be there on a daily basis or problems would arise. Talking to others in the restaurant association Ben had joined, he knew this was the norm.

Arianna's mother was stoic and undemanding. Her grieving was quiet, except for the fact that she dressed in black from head to toe for the rest of her days. Gradually, Sophia returned to some of her old ways, spending time at the restaurant, sweeping the floor, and living with her memories.

An adored *yiayia* to Tadeus and Faith, she had always been a great help by babysitting when they were young and by planning special local excursions to parks and the zoo. When the children were teenagers, they still often spent part of their weekends at her cozy house nearby. She refused to move from the space she had shared with Nikos and kept the house set up as they had loved it.

The years seemed to fly by, filled with long hours at the restaurant for both of them. Arianna missed her work at the Art Gallery and occasionally took some evening art classes. But she knew her contribution to running the restaurant made a difference to their lifestyle financially, and she gave it gladly. She was grateful daily for the love Ben had for his vocation, for food, for people. Not everyone was so fortunate, they reminded each other.

Tad and Faith were good students, and their graduations from university were occasions of great celebrations at Papa's. Yiayia proudly held court and quietly reminded them, at every opportunity, how proud of them Pappouli would have been.

And so it went. The years passed. There were always plans for the future.

Until the future vanished.

For Ben, it was futile. Arianna wondered if that was how it was for her as well. The thought of life without Ben brought her nothing but agony.

This was not the way it was supposed to be. *Who planned for this?*

CHAPTER SIX

An announcement brought Arianna's thoughts back to the present. They would reach Avignon in fifteen minutes.

For the past hour, between drifting through old memories, Arianna had been listening to her French podcasts. She hoped to summon the courage to speak the language whenever possible.

Now she slipped into the restroom at the end of the car and freshened up as best she could. Looking in the mirror, she was still surprised to see her thick black hair just grazing her shoulders. It hadn't been that short since she was in kindergarten. And bangs! At sixty-two, she had bangs for the first time in her life.

Everyone at home said she looked ten years younger. Even though she couldn't agree with that assessment, she liked the change. The stress and despondency of the past two years had taken its toll on her face. Lines of worry etched her olive complexion, and a shadow of sorrow in her once glimmering eyes told its own story.

Faith, in her direct way, suggested that her mother was looking severe and convinced her this haircut would give her a lift. "Go for it, Mom. Take a leap!"

Gloria had gone to the salon with Arianna, planning to get some highlights. When Arianna began to have doubts on the way there,

Gloria encouraged her. "We can all use a new hairstyle every once in a while, my friend. Let's do it!"

Arianna shrugged her shoulders now and gave her reflection an amused look. Sophia, old-fashioned to the core, had reassured her, "A change is as good as a rest," as she patted her daughter's hair, holding her in one last hug before Arianna left for France. This new look was the first part of a change, Arianna decided.

Tad and Christine had Arianna and Faith over for dinner the night before Arianna's departure. Isabella told her grandmother she looked "cute" with her new haircut, and everyone agreed.

As Tad walked them out to the car, he put his arm around Arianna's shoulder and gave her a hug. "I'm proud of you, Mom. I know this isn't easy, but I have a feeling you are going to be glad you went. The South of France in May sounds very good to us. Christine's got me looking at travel brochures for next year!"

At the departure gate at Pearson International Airport the next day, Faith had looked into her mother's eyes as they stepped back from their farewell embrace. "Mom, I've been reading a lot of Anaïs Nin lately. This thought made me think of you. She said there comes a day when it's more harmful to remain tight in a bud than to take the risk to blossom. Good image, isn't it?"

Arianna smiled at this daughter of hers, now such a strong, sensitive woman with a full heart and warm temperament. She tucked a stray strand of hair behind Faith's ear, as she had done so often when she was a little girl, and felt an overwhelming moment of pride and love. She kissed Faith's cheek softly. "I love you."

"Go forth and blossom, Mom. I love you too."

The train pulled into the Avignon TGV station precisely on time.

A gust of surprisingly warm air welcomed Arianna as she stepped onto the platform. Her eye immediately caught the sign, "Madame Miller," on the other side of the gate, held by a young man, fashionably but casually dressed. He had the classic look of a young Hugo Boss model with light stubble, thick brown hair finger-combed off his face, and aviator sunglasses.

When Arianna raised her hand in acknowledgment, he moved quickly to greet her with a warm smile as he took her suitcase. They walked toward the reserved parking area.

"*Bienvenue*, madame. I am Jean-Marc and I work for Madame LaChapelle. Sorry about all the security. Things have changed in France during the past year."

A spark of pleasure tingled through Arianna at the sound of his charming accent, in spite of his serious words. His face shone with the confidence of youth, and his voice conveyed a genuine welcome.

"*Bonjour*, Jean-Marc. I understand about the security. We have it in Canada too. I'm happy to meet you, and I look forward to meeting Madame LaChapelle. The Mas des Artistes looks wonderful on the website."

He nodded, smiling, as he held the back door of the car open. "*Oui*. It's very calm and serene, just like Madame Juliette, the proprietor."

Arianna sighed as she settled against the dark-blue leather seat. She tucked her hair behind her ears and put on her sunglasses.

As the car exited the busy parking lot, Jean-Marc asked, "Did you have a fine voyage, madame?"

She smiled at his lovely manners, so typically European. She recalled a bittersweet memory of Greece. "Yes, thank you. It was long but enjoyable."

"There is bottled water for you. Please help yourself. Would you like me to tell you something about the area as we drive through? It will take us a half hour to arrive at the property."

"I would like that very much," Arianna said, hoping she wouldn't fall asleep as he spoke. She calculated she had been up for twenty-seven hours at that point, with a five-hour sleep on the plane that barely counted.

"We are in a . . . how you say . . . kind of . . . very secret part of Provence, Les Alpilles. It means 'small alps.' To many of us, we say this area is the true Provence."

The passing countryside, topped by a deep cobalt-blue sky, was filled with quiet olive orchards and stately vineyards. Fruit trees had dropped their blossoms and were busy producing this season's harvests. *Cherries!* Arianna hoped.

Well-planted fields had already begun offering up their bounty. The car passed many handwritten signs advertising asparagus. Arianna noted, with pleasure, some little unattended stands with a box for honest payment.

"Soon *les fraises* . . . strawberries," Jean-Marc interjected into the quiet. "The most delicious in France . . ." He chuckled.

Arianna noticed that most houses had their own *potagers* close by— small kitchen gardens. Ben often said they provided the true origins of French cuisine.

Ben . . . There was a sharp pang of sorrow in the thought, but even more, she felt regret. He would have loved this. She had known Ben would be with her in spirit on this journey, and she had vowed to make that a positive. To do him proud.

This trip was not to be about sadness. She remembered how Faith had hugged her at the airport and whispered, "Let the sadness go, Mama. Let it go. Reach for that light in Provence."

Arianna squeezed her eyes tightly shut for a moment. Then she took a deep breath and turned her attention back to the passing scenery.

Fields exploded with the bright colors of purple-pink valerian, yellow broom, and red poppies, lending an almost festive air to the landscape. She inhaled the colors, already planning her painting. How could she not?

She was certain there was more wisteria here than she had ever seen before. Great frothy clouds of mauves and purples covered stone walls and tumbled from thick vines clinging to houses and rooftops.

They drove through picturesque medieval villages, all of them bustling with life and seemingly with an inviting *bistrot* on every main square, their terraces packed. She had read how popular a tourist area this was, and the slow traffic they encountered confirmed that.

At times, the road became hilly as the car passed between rocky ridges.

"Look up, madame. Do you see the castle ruin? You may visit there during your stay. Madame LaChapelle will choose the time carefully. It's very popular. Very crowded, some days, but better now than in July or August."

Arianna took in the magical setting. She chuckled as she recalled Tad referring to the brochures of the area as "eye candy." She would have to tell him it was more like a gourmet meal. Her eager anticipation of the next three weeks was growing now that she was in Provence and not just dreaming about it.

For the last week of this holiday, she was planning a road trip on her own to the Côte d'Azur. Just for a few days before flying from Marseille to Paris for her return home. She would decide the details later. She felt a little trepidation at the thought of going on her own, but that was part of the challenge she was setting for herself.

The road suddenly became even narrower as the medieval buildings of a village closed in around it.

"It's as if time has stood still," Arianna suggested, her voice filled with emotion. Impulsively, she asked, "Do you mind if we stop here for a moment?"

"*Pas du tout*—not at all," the young man replied as he pulled alongside a small park in the village center. He quickly exited the car and held the back door open, offering his hand to help Arianna alight. Then he discreetly leaned against the car.

"Thank you. I can't resist getting out here. The simple beauty transports me to centuries ago."

Jean-Marc's eyes crinkled with pride, and he bowed his head slightly to her before looking away.

She turned around slowly and then sat on a nearby stone bench. Shaded by the broad canopies of oak trees lining the square, Arianna allowed herself to set aside all other thoughts.

It's like stepping into a storybook . . . A rush of pleasure brought her almost to tears, and she realized she was forgetting to breathe. *Some dreams are worth waiting for.*

Her eyes took in the cobblestone lanes leading in several directions from the square. The ancient stone houses, some covered with flowering vines growing with seeming abandon, glowed in the afternoon sun. Their uneven terra-cotta-tiled roofs, sprouting seedlings here and there, begged Arianna to capture them in her art.

In spite of all the years her family had spent time in Greece, her heart responded to this harmonious landscape in an entirely different way. She had known it would. It might be purely psychological, but it was what she wanted.

It fed her need to be somewhere new, without recent memories lessening her experience. As reluctant as she had been to accept the thought, she knew she was entirely responsible for how her life would move forward. The biggest question she faced, she kept asking herself, was just how she could possibly begin that process.

She watched a stooped, elderly woman walking her dog and carrying on an animated conversation with the shaggy canine. Then her eyes followed a cyclist down an alleyway with three baguettes sticking out of a rear basket. A cluster of men gathered at the far end of the park, and she recognized the *pétanque* court. *Of course, it was that time of day.*

"Thank you—*merci*," she added shyly as she returned to the car, and Jean-Marc held the door open for her. "These villages are so inviting. I wanted to have a sense, even for a moment, of what it must be like to live here."

Jean-Marc nodded. "We like to say that everyone who chooses to live here does so because they share *l'amour de la terre*. They love this land as it has been loved for centuries. We are a small protected natural park, Le Parc naturel régional des Alpilles, with our treasured *petits villages*. Sorry—small villages."

Arianna nodded. "Every one of them makes me want to come back and explore. I'll have a bit of time to do that while I'm over here."

"Each village has its own unique character, and the gastronomy is the best in France. You will see. Yes, I did say that! Parisians will chide me!"

Arianna laughed, charmed by his unabashed pride in his region. He continued to entertain her with stories about the local culture, including his favorite markets, for another ten minutes.

The car crunched along a narrower gravel road. Turning sharply onto a dirt laneway, they drove under a leafy arch that led to a sun-filled open parking area. Jean-Marc announced, "*Et voilà!* Le Mas des Artistes!"

And suddenly, there it was. Just as it looked on the website. Just as Arianna had hoped it would be.

CHAPTER SEVEN

The late-afternoon sun washed over the sprawling limestone farmhouse, turning it into a glowing, golden mass. The dusky Provençal-blue shutters, their paint peeling slightly, were unlatched and flung wide.

Twisted, thick stems of wisteria climbed around the massive wooden front door, creating a welcoming violet-tinted canopy of cascading blooms. The vines meandered across the stone walls, delicately draping over three sets of French doors that were invitingly open.

At the far end of a long flagstone terrace, Arianna could see a few people sitting at tables under grand, cantilevered umbrellas in rich rust shades that complemented the surroundings. Large terra-cotta pots overflowed with vibrant, multicolored plantings and trailing ivy spilling down the sides. Stunning bursts of bougainvillea in deep pinks and purples dotted the property.

A sizable black-and-white cat made its way along the terrace to the driveway, purpose apparent in every stride. With its ears perked and long tail pointed straight up, tip twitching back and forth, the cat left no question of its strong personality.

An attractive woman of indeterminate age followed closely behind. Her long hair cascaded in auburn waves halfway down her back and moved in unison with the flowing, cream-colored linen dress she wore.

A wide-brimmed straw sun hat completed her outfit, offering protection for her flawless porcelain complexion.

Arianna had to stop herself from staring at this woman, possibly the most ethereal being she had ever seen. It was as if she floated rather than walked. A soft golden aura seemed to hang in the air around her.

"*Bienvenue!* Welcome, Arianna! We're so happy you're here! I'm Juliette." She greeted Arianna in a warm, cordial voice that gave the new arrival an immediate sense of inclusion. Taking Arianna's hands in hers, Juliette leaned in and lightly greeted her with a *bise*. She touched her cheeks to Arianna's, one side and then the other, making a light kissing sound, not unlike the Greek greetings so familiar to Arianna.

"I'm happy to be here, Juliette."

The cat positioned himself beside Juliette, a respectable distance from Arianna, and meowed loudly.

"Arianna, please meet Maximus. Are you a feline fan? Would you like to be friends with him?"

Arianna smiled brightly, her expression indicating her delight.

Then Juliette turned to the cat. The cat stared directly into her eyes. "Maximus, this is Madame Miller." She paused, maintaining the eye contact. "She will be happy to be your friend. Please stretch out your hand, Arianna."

Arianna bent slightly and offered her hand. Going over to Arianna, Maximus lowered his head in a manner that indicated a pat would be welcome.

Arianna chuckled and looked at Juliette, who cocked her head and said, "Maximus understands English, French, German, Italian, and, apparently, Russian. He's very friendly but also respects that some guests are not fond of cats, and he stays away from them. Since you've indicated you would enjoy being his friend, he will be good company to you during your stay."

Arianna bent down farther, patting the cat's head and adding a light scratch around his ears. The cat responded with a quick *murp*. Then he sat a short distance away, purring loudly.

In Arianna's childhood, there were village cats everywhere, and she had been fond of them. In Toronto, her children's allergies had prevented any in the house.

"As you can see," Juliette explained, her eyes crinkled with obvious affection for Maximus, "he's quite a character. You will discover he is very much a part of life at the *mas*."

Arianna smiled. "I will look forward to getting to know him better."

"Well," Juliette cautioned, "I have informed everyone that if he decides he likes you, he may be so bold as to invite himself into your room. So you might want to keep your door closed. Otherwise, he may make himself comfortable on your bed for the night. Consider yourself warned." She laughed again, as did Arianna.

"Would you like to go to your room first, or would you come to the terrace and meet the rest of the group? We're having *apéros* now, and dinner will be in a while, but just a light meal."

"I'm afraid I might be tempted to lie down if I go to my room," Arianna admitted with a chuckle. "Though I won't be staying up long no matter what. I hope that's okay."

"*Absolument!* Everyone arrived at different times today and from a variety of places. I would advise you to stay up as late as you can tonight." She offered a sympathetic look, adding, "We'll do our best to keep you upright until around ten."

Arianna noticed her luggage had been spirited away by a young man who had left as silently as he had appeared.

"That was Stefan," Juliette said. "He's very shy but most helpful. You will meet him later. *Allons*—come and get to know the others."

With Maximus leading the way, they walked along the terrace to where it wrapped around the side of the rambling house. Rosebushes bloomed profusely in clouds of palest pink and ruby red. Some climbed the side of the house to meet the purple wisteria blossoms cascading from thick, well-aged vines.

Mounds of lavender, buds still forming, bordered the terrace, preparing for their spectacular explosion of color and fragrance in another month. Beds of iris were beginning to fade.

Arianna smiled at the chirping of the cicadas, their song not quite as intense as the evening temperature began to cool.

The group on the terrace rose to greet Arianna. Warm smiles, friendly voices, and extended hands made her feel at ease.

Juliette's mellow laughter preceded her words. "Ah, handshakes . . . By the end of the evening you will all be offering each other *bises. Je vous assure!*"

A pleasant voice interrupted her. "Like this. *Bienvenue*, Arianna. I am Juliette's husband, Maurice." He leaned toward Arianna and greeted her the French way. Then he offered her a woven-wicker armchair like the ones the other guests had settled back into. Arianna smiled gratefully, murmured a soft, self-conscious *"merci,"* and sank into the plump, brightly upholstered cushion.

"Now that we're all gathered, I want to offer you an official *bienvenue* . . . welcome. We are thrilled you chose to visit with us, and it will be our pleasure to have you feel at home here," Juliette said, her mellow voice instantly putting everyone at ease. "Let's go around and introduce ourselves. You, of course, know who we are . . . Juliette and Maurice LaChapelle, and our families have lived around Arles for generations. We've been offering art courses here at the Mas des Artistes for twenty years. I studied in England for a few years, long ago, but please forgive my mistakes in your language."

Maurice popped corks and poured champagne into slender flutes.

"Let me clarify Juliette's words. She is the artist, and I am her steadfast *majordome*—majordomo. It is our distinct pleasure to share our home with all of you."

When the champagne had been passed around, a welcome toast followed before Juliette spoke about the course.

"In the morning, we will begin. This drawing and painting retreat is our favorite course, and you soon will see why. Van Gogh settled here in 1888 in search of the very special light of Arles and the surrounding region. You will draw and paint in some of the same places as Vincent. The breezes, fragrances, birdsong, cicada harmonies, and, most of all, unique light that inspired him will be part of your world here. Magic will happen!"

Her gaze rested on each of them before she continued. "Tomorrow we will immerse ourselves in our art. For tonight, we want to learn about you. We want you to learn about each other. Who would like to begin?"

Without hesitation, a man and woman stood in unison. Their gleaming smiles matched their silvery hair. He was as tall as she was short, and there was no mistaking they were a very tight couple.

"I'm John Mitchell, and this is my wife, Joanie. We met in an art class almost forty years ago." He leaned back slightly and slipped his arm around her shoulder. They both chuckled. "We retired to Florida from New York five years ago and have never looked back . . ."

Joan's eyes sparkled and a warm smile lit her face. "Yup, we love the sun, surf, and palm trees! We live in a retirement community where we're almost the youngest, and we love that too! My role models are all in their nineties!" Her strong Brooklyn accent and contagious laugh immediately created a light atmosphere.

Straightening the collar of his bright Hawaiian-print shirt, John said, "I work primarily in oils. I like to get messy . . . very messy!"

Rolling her eyes, his wife shook her head in feigned dismay. "I, on the other hand, am a dainty and dedicated watercolorist. I don't like to get messy."

With a theatrical leap in front of Joan, his arms spread wide, John said, "Except with me! He-he!" Then he waggled his eyebrows Groucho

Marx style and gave her a loud kiss on the cheek. Everyone laughed, and Joan rolled her eyes again.

They described how they had exhibited their work for many years, first in New York, and then in Florida.

"We love the fun of competition . . . stress doesn't seem to bother us," John explained.

"And the characters we meet make it all worthwhile," Joan chimed in.

It was clear that art was the focus of their retirement.

"We're a bit embarrassed to admit that this is our first trip outside the States—" John said before Joan interrupted.

"Yup, like a kinda high percentage of Americans, we didn't have passports either, until recently. And after five days in Paris and then coming here, we've been kicking ourselves! Why on earth did we wait so long? I think this is just the beginning of our new life as world travelers." Smiling widely, they looked at each other and high-fived before they sat down.

A corpulent, puffy-eyed man fumbled with his chair as he stood. He appeared to be hovering around the age of sixty. "Good evening, one and all," he began in a very proper British accent. "My name is Bertram Lloyd-Goldsmith. I am from London, England. I'm here because I've studied the work of van Gogh, Gauguin, Cézanne, and other impressionists who created art in this area."

Pausing and clearing his throat loudly, he ran one hand over his thinning hair as he straightened his back and boasted, "I consider myself rather an expert on that. I have traveled a great deal in this area and was attracted to the details of the approach of this course . . . and besides, it fit into my calendar."

He hesitated as though he had finished speaking, and he was halfway into his chair when he added, "I have a wife who has no interest in art or history and is at a spa." He lifted his glass, gesturing to the group. "Pleasure to be here with you."

Then he drained his champagne, held out his glass to Maurice, and said, "I'll have a refill, my good man."

There was an awkward silence for a moment before a petite, blond, fiftyish woman with a stunning smile literally popped out of her chair.

"Hello! My name is Marti Smythe. I'm from just outside Napa, California. I'm here with my wife, Lisa Marshall, who is the true artist in our family. I'm kind of an interloper at this course. I love to draw and am more of an illustrator . . . and I'm delighted to be here."

Equally petite and blond and of a similar age, Lisa remained seated but waved her hand and looked about shyly, even as she avoided eye contact.

Marti reached over and took Lisa's hand. "Lisa and I want you to know that she has Asperger's syndrome, or what is now referred to as an autism spectrum disorder. I share this information with her complete approval, of course. You will find she may be short on words, but she's the one who pushed me to come to this course. And she is a fine, fine artist . . . which you will see. She works primarily in acrylics because she likes to charge right onto her canvas and go wild—her words—and she's delighted to be here too."

Marti reached over and clinked glasses with Lisa before she continued.

Flashing a dazzling smile, Marti raised her glass to everyone. "When Lis and I talked about this, she wanted me to end the introduction by saying that she's an 'aspie' and proud of it."

Lisa looked down and nodded. A thin smile played on her lips as she shyly gave a thumbs-up to the group.

Arianna stood next. Her pulse thumped in her neck. Then she heard her words tumble out.

"I'm Arianna Papadopoulos-Miller from Toronto, Canada. Art has been my passion for as far back as I can remember, but after a while, life got in the way and I set it aside. I'm here to rekindle that desire to draw and paint and to see this part of France."

She stopped and took a breath, suddenly aware she had spoken with barely a pause.

"Sorry. Let me slow down. I'm very happy to be here. The last time I was in France was for a month in Paris when I was twenty-three. I love everything about the work of Vincent van Gogh."

She sat down and wondered why she had added that last sentence.

An elegant, white-haired woman stood next. "Hi, everyone. My name is Barbara McNeilly. I'm from Vancouver, British Columbia, and I like to believe I am an artist. I was a high school art teacher for forty years. During the past ten years of my husband's illness, my saving grace was painting detailed street scenes and sometimes florals. I work in all mediums, but these days I seem to be favoring acrylics."

She turned to the younger woman sitting next to her and proudly told the group, "This beautiful girl is my granddaughter, Cecilia, whom I adore. I'll let her tell you her story."

Cecilia set her champagne flute on the side table and stood up. With her long brown hair pulled into a ponytail, she had a youthful appearance that was enhanced by her dimples. Arianna thought she couldn't be much more than thirty.

"Hi, everyone, I'm Cecilia Hall, also from Vancouver, and I'm so fortunate to be traveling with my grandmother. I have a confession to make, though."

She turned and grinned at Marti. "I am the real interloper here! I'm not an artist . . . not even close. I'm a travel writer and blogger. On this wonderful trip with my grandmother, I'm taking photos to post with articles about just that and also about different aspects of the places we are visiting. So thank you for allowing me to tag along and write about this experience."

Conversation flowed easily as the group mingled. Spirits were high as everyone shared their hopes for the course and gave thanks for the opportunity to work on their art in Provence.

Along with the champagne, there was a lightly fruity nonalcoholic alternative and bottles of mineral water . . . still and sparkling. Several of the guests switched before long.

"One glass of champagne is more than enough for me," Barbara commented.

"Oh, my dear, allow me to persuade you to have another. It's very good for you," Maurice encouraged. "It's been proven to benefit spatial and short-term memory, to help your heart, *et cerise sur le gâteau* . . . it has fewer calories than wine!"

Barbara laughed and held out her glass. "That was very convincing! Half a glass will be perfect, please."

Olivewood boards with pâté, accompanied by fresh figs and fig jam, were on the tables next to baskets of thin baguette toasts. Bright pottery bowls contained three different tapenades, with more fresh baguette next to them.

Satisfied murmurs drifted around the table as every dish was sampled and enjoyed.

Bertram raised his champagne glass as he held up a slice of baguette topped with a healthy chunk of pâté. "Ahem." He cleared his throat loudly. "'To paraphrase George Bernard Shaw—a wise gentleman, if ever there was one!—there's nothing better than fine food, and I am besotted with this superb cuisine! And I'll have another *coupe, merci*!"

Maurice topped off Bertram's champagne.

There was enthusiastic agreement that everything was delicious, as the enjoyment of the *heure de l'apéritif* continued.

At six o'clock, Juliette suggested everyone might wish to unpack and freshen up but cautioned them not to lie down.

"I know it will be difficult, but our goal this evening is to keep you up until nine or ten. It's the best way to get on track with the time. *Je vous promets!* I promise you! We will see you back down here at nineteen thirty . . . seven thirty . . . for dinner. If you absolutely feel you cannot make it, of course we understand. But please try."

A middle-aged couple appeared as everyone rose to leave.

Maurice said, "Attention, everyone, please. May I have the pleasure of introducing Mirielle *et* Louis-Philippe." The couple smiled and bowed modestly. "They are the indispensable people who keep our house running as it should. You may have already noticed their son, Stefan, who whisked your luggage away. He also expertly looks after our gardens and vineyard."

There were acknowledgments all around.

Maurice continued, "You may seldom see them but, *croyez-moi*, believe me, they are the people who truly keep things running. They are part of our family and will be happy to help you with anything if you cannot find Juliette or myself."

The couple smiled demurely and began to clear the terrace of dishes as Juliette directed everyone else to the house.

"I will show you to your room, Arianna," Juliette offered. She leaned in conspiratorially and whispered, "It's particularly special. Did you know your daughter sent us an e-mail with a lovely and emotional request for you to have it?"

"No! Oh my goodness!" Arianna's cheeks flushed with embarrassment.

"She must be a special young woman," Juliette added. "She certainly was eloquent, and it was our pleasure to comply. We hope you will be happy here."

Feeling awkward, Arianna wondered just what Faith had said.

She could not stop grinning as they walked across the terra-cotta tiles of the centuries-old farmhouse. The website and literature for the workshop had not pretended to present anything more than what she was seeing. It was not the most luxurious *mas*, but instead it was a collection of charmingly restored rooms that exuded an air of welcome and comfort.

The two-foot-thick textured, irregular stone walls and hand-hewn beamed ceilings surely had centuries of stories to tell. There was a unique patina of what Arianna could only guess were generations of layered paint on the ceiling and beams. Now flaking and peeling in spots, the effect added depth and character.

As she explained a bit of the history of the property, Juliette described the extensive restoration they'd undertaken over twenty years before. "It was pretty much *une ruine, un désastre* . . . but we fell in love with it."

"I can see why!"

Arianna could feel the atmosphere all around her. Wrought-iron candle holders accented the walls. The sofas and chairs, in earthy taupe shades, were large with inviting down-filled cushions. Bright Persian carpets dotted the terra-cotta floors. Tucked in one corner was a grand piano, its dark, polished wood gleaming.

"Please make yourself comfortable," Juliette said as Maurice called out to her. "I'll be right back."

Slipping her phone out of her purse, Arianna took a few photos of the beautiful surroundings. Faith would love it . . . and be amused that her mother was putting her newfound tech skill to work.

She had never been one to take photos. That had been Ben's department. Even so, they were not a family to have stacks of photo albums around. Faith, on the other hand, loved using her phone and creating albums. She had been encouraging her mother to do the same ever since she had gotten home.

Faith, Tad, and Christine had given Arianna the latest iPhone for Christmas. Finally, she had been convinced to give up her old phone that had no camera or data storage. After a couple of intro workshops at the Apple Store, she felt reasonably comfortable with it for her trip.

She had promised to text and send photos from France. For a moment, as she snapped away, she felt a sense of accomplishment with herself and this new-to-her technology.

Morning can't come too soon. I want to sit in every room with my journal and fill page after page.

"Désolée," Juliette apologized when she returned. "Sorry to have left you. There was a small flood in the kitchen . . . always something in a house two hundred years old! Even with modern plumbing!" Her laughter sounded to Arianna like tinkling crystal wind chimes.

"I hope you don't mind. I grabbed the opportunity to take a few photos to send to my daughter. Your home is simply splendid."

Juliette's eyes shone with pride. "Oh, please do! I'm so happy you like it!"

They climbed a spiral staircase that took them to the next floor, where a number of decoratively carved wooden doors opened off a wide corridor. Wrought-iron light fixtures that resembled medieval lanterns provided an atmospheric glow.

"These are all the other bedrooms. There is still an empty one if you would rather be on this floor. You can decide."

She led Arianna up a narrow stone staircase, the steps worn to a dull sheen. It was described on the website as the former dovecote, and Faith had agreed it looked like the perfect selection when Arianna showed her the pictures online.

"It looks like an artist's studio, Mom," she had exclaimed. "You'll be inspired just sleeping in that space."

The rustic wooden door alone was enough to satisfy her, Arianna thought. The ancient iron hardware and elaborate set of keyholes almost caused her to swoon. How she loved doors like this and the secrets she imagined they held.

The entire room, wooden beams on the high-arched ceiling included, had been painted a soft grayish white. A set of three shuttered windows overlooked the back garden to neighboring orchards beyond and the pointed, rocky range of Les Alpilles in the background. Above the windows was a row of small glassed-in squares that had, in fact, been how the doves had flown in and out.

"Voilà!" Juliette sang. Her eyes sparkled. "What do you think?"

Arianna's reaction was immediate. "I love it! It's even more beautiful than the photos. Thank you!"

Juliette gave an almost imperceptible bow and began to back out of the room. "Make yourself comfortable! I will see you downstairs later."

Thanking her again, Arianna then closed the door. Just being in this room was going to make her happy—she could feel that immediately.

The accent color of dusky Provençal blue on the shutters and cushions and rich pewter-gray linens gave an airy feeling to the space.

The blue-and-white theme continued into the spacious bathroom with Chinese-porcelain accessories on the floor and counter. A deep claw-foot bathtub was placed in a position to afford a splendid view out the window. Arianna tingled with delight and took another photo to send to Faith.

Then she fell back onto the thick, soft duvet and looked around with pleasure. Yes, she would like it in this room. For a moment, she succumbed to the comfort of the bed before she quickly picked herself up and unpacked.

CHAPTER EIGHT

At the appointed time in the evening, the group reassembled in the grand salon.

"*Magnifique!* Everyone is here *à l'heure*! It's a good sign for our time together! Now let's go to the back terrace and enjoy dinner."

Passing through the French doors, Arianna commented to Joan, "It's like walking into a photo from a French version of *Better Homes and Gardens*."

Joan's eyes sparkled. "Omigosh, yes—like a dream! It's all amazing! I can't believe I've lived this much of my life without coming to Europe. We're loving every minute of it! Have you been to Europe before?"

Joan's enthusiasm generated easy conversation. The two women were laughing together within minutes. Arianna shared some of her experiences in Greece, something she had not thought about for a long time.

Maximus lounged contentedly on the nearby stone wall, overseeing the gathering and happily accepting rubs and scratches.

Pausing, John stroked the cat's back so vigorously that the loud purring was interrupted by a throaty bawl. "Whoops! I think Maximus just had a purr-gasm!" he whispered to Arianna and Joan, which resulted in more giggles.

Once everyone was assembled at the table, Juliette asked them to find their names. Then she collected the place cards when seats were taken and she had the group's attention.

"We're going to switch twice during dinner, so we all have a chance to chat with each other," she announced. The sweetness of her smile and her direct, bright gaze left no doubt this was a fine idea.

While she had their attention, Juliette shared a few words of welcome. "Maurice and I are thrilled you have chosen to spend the next little while with us. We want to welcome you to the Mas des Artistes and to one of the most special parts of France. You are about to have a most unique experience in the area of Les Alpilles, Arles, and the Camargue. We trust you will create memories that will last a lifetime. This evening we will eat, drink, and be merry and get to know each other. Tomorrow we will begin to make art."

Arianna found herself between blustery Bertram Lloyd-Goldsmith and bouncy Joan Mitchell. It didn't take long for her to sense a strain between the two. Joan kept her engaged in lively conversation, as Bertram concentrated on refilling his wineglass.

"La grande charcuterie!" Maurice announced as the young kitchen staff appeared with three large platters. Each bore a colorful display of meats.

Maurice gave the diners a guided tour of each artistically arranged platter. "We have thinly sliced prosciutto and *jambon cru* . . . local uncured ham that will melt in your mouth. Here we have our very special *saucisson d'Arles*, native to our area in particular. It's a dry sausage that used to be made a century ago from—don't gasp, please—donkey meat."

In spite of themselves, there was a slight gasp.

"It is nowadays made of beef and pork fat with some garlic and black pepper. *Magnifique!* Only certain local *charcutiers* make it—*c'est authentique!* And finally, there are grilled lamb chops, seasoned to perfection. We are famous for lamb in Provence. You will see why!"

His hand moved on to the end of the platter, and his level of enthusiasm increased even more. "*Pâté maison, la recette de mon arrière-grand-mère!* Very smooth. It's made with chicken livers, lemon, onion, and herbs de Provence. Plus"—with this, he raised his fingers to his lips, as if sharing a secret—"what makes hers special is . . . a touch of *fromage de Neufchâtel.*"

He nodded conspiratorially, the gleam in his eye never fading as he continued. "And also her even more famous *pâté en croute.* It's a coarse and rich terrine of mixed ground meats with peppercorns and pistachios. After being cooked in aspic, it is wrapped in a rich, buttery crust, coated inside with lard. *C'est vraiment extraordinaire!*"

"And ever so fattening!" Bertram interjected.

Maurice responded with humor. "Don't even think about calories or cholesterol when you eat in France. Simply enjoy! A little bit never hurt anyone! Even too much on certain days never hurt anyone. We only live once!"

"Can you tell my husband is a true 'foodie'?" Juliette interjected with a grin.

He bowed with an extravagant flourish as applause reverberated around the table. "Champagne goes very well with this meal, if you care to continue, or we have a fine Châteauneuf-du-Pape red—and, of course, always there is beer for those who prefer."

After he slipped his arm around Juliette's waist, they wished everyone in unison, "Bon appétit!"

During the meal, Maurice answered questions about the difference between a *boucher*, a butcher who sells raw meat, and a true *charcutier*, someone who prepares the foods they were eating.

"Of course," he explained, "you will discover we can thank the Ancient Romans for many of our traditions."

Large olivewood bowls, lush bicolored swirls creating patterns in the grain, were placed on the table, filled with a simply dressed green salad.

When all the food from that course had been consumed, Juliette clapped her hands lightly. "*Levez-vous, s'il vous plaît!* Time to change seats."

She scattered the place cards back on the table. Chatter and laughter filled the air as everyone helped each other find their spots.

This time Arianna was at the end of the row with Marti on her left and Maurice at the foot of the table. The conversation soon became food oriented as the women discovered they both came from family-restaurant backgrounds. Delighted, Maurice encouraged them to talk about their experiences.

Marti modestly explained she was the chef in a small Napa Valley restaurant her hippie parents had begun in the 1970s.

"They became followers of the great Alice Waters. Yup! Nothing but the finest seasonal ingredients, grown locally and sustainably," she explained. "I grew up weeding and picking and always knew what I wanted to do. My parents are still around and involved, but they turned the kitchen over to me ten years ago."

Initially, Arianna felt anxious knowing she would be talking about Ben as well as her father. However, her pride in her family history and the success of Papa's on the Danforth soon had her sharing stories and happy memories.

"And is your husband keeping the restaurant going on his own while you are here?" Maurice asked.

Arianna decided to sidestep the issue. "Actually, we sold the restaurant last year, and the new owners are doing a great job." And then she deftly changed the subject.

"How does your interest in art tie into your career as a chef, Marti?"

Her eyes crinkled with laughter. "I'm really an illustrator. I've designed all of our menus and restaurant posters since I was a kid. I'm the queen of drawing fruits and veggies. Lisa is the talented artist in our family. In fact, I fell in love with her vibrant seascapes before I fell in love with her."

Marti's enthusiasm made Arianna smile. She was about to ask another question, when a two-tiered wooden cart was rolled out with a cheese platter on each glass shelf, evoking gasps and applause.

Everyone's attention focused on Maurice as he circulated around the table. He described every selection with a brief history that made it difficult to resist sampling each one. Meanwhile, Juliette made her way around the table with a silver tray containing an assortment of fancy pastries and luscious chocolates.

"Et, bien sûr, vive le chocolat," she sang gaily. "It's my belief that every day should end with chocolate. Please indulge."

In spite of the ongoing feast, eyes were noticeably glazing over, and attempts to stifle yawns were not succeeding.

"So, it appears we've kept you up long enough," Juliette said as she circled the table with her tempting chocolate.

"This evening we commenced our adventure together. We've talked about art and what it means to us. Tomorrow we will begin to immerse ourselves in our *en plein air* workshop. We will live and breathe the life of an artist in the Provençal countryside. Drawing will be a focus. Watercolor, acrylic, oil, pastels, or pencil. All will be embraced. I know that, every day, each of you will discover something that speaks directly to your artist's heart. And now, *bonne nuit*! Sleep well!"

CHAPTER NINE

After a fitful sleep, due to the time change more than anything else, Arianna awakened with a start to her alarm.

As usual, she had given herself a fifteen-minute window to lie in bed before rising. This was a lifelong habit, a time in which she liked to think about her plan for the day and sort through any possible complications.

For a long while after the diagnosis, it had been the most painful part of her day. It was so easy to wake up in the past for a few brief seconds before the truth took hold.

Feeling relieved with the way her first evening had unfolded, Arianna felt her nervousness about mingling here diminishing. *Goodness knows I've conversed with strangers most of my life. But this is different. I never really had to talk about myself before.*

Her thoughts turned to the loneliness that had consumed her life over the past year. *It's okay to feel good about this trip. I know that. I just need to buy into this workshop and not wish Ben were here. I'm becoming quite used to being alone.*

I miss Ben, our life, real laughter. I miss my heart and want to put the pieces back together. That's my goal here.

Without thinking about it, she grasped her left hand. Bringing her hands out from under the covers, she ran her fingers over her rings.

Looking at the small diamond simply set in white and yellow gold that had belonged to Ben's grandmother and the plain gold wedding band next to it once again caused Arianna sadness.

A woman in the hospital support group had said she felt better without her rings. Arianna had tried to go without them, and that only brought her more sadness and confusion. The conflict was one she had yet to resolve, but in the meantime, she'd decided to keep wearing them.

I am still married to Ben. I know that. I feel that.

She fussed over the dilemma for a few moments and then allowed it to fade, as she had many times before. It was time to get on with her day.

Still in bed, she stretched her arms wide and then brought her hands to her knees. Bending her knees, she pulled them up to her chest, holding them there for a count of sixty, letting herself feel the pull in her lower spine. Since her back had seized up a few years before, every morning began with this stretch repeated six times. Her doctor had stressed the importance of this exercise, and the problem had seldom returned since. Arianna knew keeping her back strong was important, along with staying in decent shape.

Her friend Karyn Spencer had made a point of picking her up for Zumba class once a week, and Arianna would always be grateful for that. In spite of the number of times she'd wanted to quit, she recognized the good it was doing, especially during the most trying times . . . on a lot of different levels.

Daily walking had also been part of her regimen, and for the past months, Faith had accompanied her to the gym twice a week where they would swim for an hour.

Thank goodness for Faith. "Mom, after all those years I drove you and Dad batshit, I'm doing my best to make up for it," Faith would tease her.

"That you are, my girl. That you are." Arianna knew that the conditioning had gone a long way to keeping her sane as well as fit, although she knew she still had a few pounds to shed.

Another gift Faith had given her was an introduction to meditation.

Now, Arianna made a nest with her pillows on the bed. She settled herself cross-legged on one to raise her back to a comfortable level. Then she elongated her spine, brought her shoulders back, and placed her hands together at her chest, in a namaste pose. Tucking in her chin, she opened and closed her mouth a few times to relax her jaw.

Dropping her hands to rest palms up on her thighs, she brought her gaze loosely to a spot about three feet ahead of her on the bed. Focusing on her breath, she let herself slip into a peaceful space for about ten minutes. Her body told her when the time was up.

Thank you, Faith. Namaste.

She showered and dressed quickly, eager to see what the morning would bring.

In the front salon, she saw *"On y va"* painted on a piece of wood with an arrow pointing to the front terrace.

Everyone converged about the same time. Enthusiastic greetings were exchanged. Wicker baskets brimmed with warm croissants, *pains au chocolat*, and *pains aux raisins*, accompanied by bowls of locally produced fruit preserves.

While Maurice tended to espressos, cappuccinos, and assorted teas, Juliette spoke about the atmosphere they hoped for that morning.

"Our desire is to introduce the influences that inspired earlier masters. The unique light that changes throughout the day is key. But the history and culture, the scenery and architecture, must also be considered. Tomorrow, we are excited and honored to welcome Monsieur Jacques de Villeneuve, an artist and *gardian* of the Camargue. On Thursday, we will spend a day at the Fondation Vincent van Gogh and be treated to the expertise of several of their staff."

At the mention of van Gogh's name, Arianna's entire body tingled with excitement. She smiled inwardly, thinking how close she was to realizing a dream.

Juliette motioned to a stack of folding canvas chairs and stools leaning against a thick stone wall, which was partially covered by a lush vine with delicate leaves and soft blue blossoms that resembled morning glories. About three feet high, the wall separated the garden and olive grove from the breakfast area.

It was difficult for Arianna to take her eyes off the timeworn wall, which Juliette commented was around three hundred years old. She was startled to see color calling to her from the stones that at first glance appeared dull and achromatic. The longer she held them in her gaze, the stronger the attraction became. She locked in the memory, determined to come back to the power these stones seemed to hold for her.

"Please pick up a chair or a stool. The early artists in this area would fashion a leather strap so they could sling a chair like this over their shoulder and carry it to their chosen spot to work. They're surprisingly comfy. If you did not bring your own easel, you will also find some there."

After collecting their seats, everyone followed Juliette into the olive grove and set up in a semicircle, shaded by a large, gauzy beige canopy. Maximus led the way, his long tail waving proudly as he skirted around the plants and clumps of grasses.

Maurice had placed a flat screen on an easel under an umbrella to control any glare. He proceeded to click through a slide show of paintings, as Juliette led the group through a retrospective of work by Cézanne, van Gogh, Gauguin, Picasso, Signac, Matisse, Braque, Derain, Dufy . . . and so many other revered names.

"These artists, among many others, all spent time in Provence. They loved this land that is so generous in a multitude of ways to the artist's soul. Color, light, subject, history, and culture combine in endless variations in all of their work." Juliette paused and looked around with a luminescent smile, her deep affection for her surroundings clear.

"These masters found their inspiration in many different ways and from a variety of sources. We will investigate those factors. Of course we must always consider how emotional stability—or instability—also impacted their work. Please stop me when you want to spend time with a painting so we can discuss one aspect or another."

As she had been from the first, Arianna was captivated by Juliette's voice. Her words seemed to float into the air, sparking thoughts and ideas.

"What we hope to do with this course is not to focus on how you ply your craft or on what your subject matter is but rather to encourage you to consider why you are making the choices you are. The 'why' of your art."

The discourse became animated as thoughts were expressed, questions asked, answers debated. Arianna found herself becoming engaged as the morning went on. It had been a long time since she had immersed herself in these subjects she so loved.

She felt encouraged, excited at the possibility she might truly taste colors again.

There was a break for water, coffee, and fruit. Then Juliette posed her first challenge.

"For the rest of the day, consider subjects, color, and light on the property. Move around. Use cameras, your journals, sketch pads . . . however you prefer to plan a project. This is an expeditionary task. Go for a walk. Nap under a tree. Feel the earth, the air, the light, the vegetation. Please promise you will stay out until at least four o'clock and return with journal pages, sketches, or even a preliminary drawing you are ready to share. We will have *apéros* in the garden for a while and relax. After that, do as you wish until we gather for dinner at seven. We're taking you into Arles."

Maurice smiled at the group as he said, "For lunch, there will be freshly made baguette sandwiches on the dining table and bowls of salad and fruit. If you would like something different, just ring the bell on the sideboard, and one of the great kitchen staff will be happy to help you. Help yourself whenever you feel hungry. There will also be fruit and *petites pâtisseries* on the table all day."

Then Juliette stepped forward once more. "The other component to your task today is that you are not to talk to anyone until we meet for *apéros* . . . rosé, pastis, wine. We're going monastic for a few hours. Revel in the silence. Feel at one with your surroundings and be inspired. See you when the bell rings."

A silence settled around them. Everyone bought into the challenge quickly, after exchanging wide-eyed looks.

There was no problem finding secluded spots in the vast gardens. Arianna found herself moving from one place to another, discovering images she thought inspired her. But for the most part, her sketchbook and paper remained blank.

She had been certain the stone wall would waken her muse and was disappointed when it did not. The hint of inspiration she previously felt was gone.

Frustrated and feeling close to tears after little more than an hour, she gathered up her things. Hoping no one noticed, she slipped away to her room.

In her spacious bathroom, along with the old-fashioned claw-foot bath-tub, there was a porcelain sink. A small separate WC adjoined the space.

Arianna filled the tub to the top after adding some of her favorite bath oil that she had brought along. She opened the nearby window with its clear view across the olive grove and vineyard. Her thoughts drifted, picturing Vincent setting up his easel in a setting like this.

The relentless chirping of cicadas filled the room. A warm spring breeze carried in a perfume that seemed to float into every corner. Breathing in deeply, she let the sweet, fresh air of the countryside fill her lungs.

A long soak in the bath had always been her favorite way to relax. Never more so than since Ben's diagnosis, and often more than once a day.

Slipping under the water up to her chin, she closed her eyes as tears squeezed out between her lashes and ran down her cheeks. She felt herself fill with doubt and sorrow, like so many times before.

Purposeless. That was how she had described herself to her friend Gloria when they'd met for lunch shortly before Arianna had left for France. *Purposeless.*

Gloria, her BFF since high school. Arianna treasured their friendship. She felt lucky to be able to talk without explaining and know Gloria would understand whatever the problem was. Her support had carried Arianna through many dark hours with Ben's illness.

She had also encouraged Arianna to take this trip.

Gently swirling the water around in the tub, Arianna recalled their conversation from that day.

Over coffee after lunch, Gloria had said, "Faith told me the doctors were glad to hear you were doing something for yourself as they have been suggesting."

Arianna let out a long sigh now. The memories were vivid.

She had told Gloria, "They keep stressing I am dealing with grief. I keep saying I still have a husband, and they gently remind me 'in name only.'"

She recalled how she had twisted a tissue in her hands and confessed to Gloria how broken she felt. "I've tried to keep up a brave front for my mom and the kids, for our friends. But, honestly, I feel like I am disappearing into an empty shell. On the outside I appear almost normal, but when I look inside, I see nothing. I feel completely vacant. Hopeless. Purposeless. Intellectually, I understand I will heal. Who knows when? Emotionally, I can't imagine it."

Gloria had held her hand. She had offered Arianna comforting, supportive words. Arianna loved her and appreciated all the help she tried to give. Arianna also knew that Gloria realized at that point it was falling on deaf ears. But like the good friend she was, she would not give up.

It had been Arianna's hope that, while she was on this trip, she would be able to move away from those feelings she'd expressed to Gloria. Apparently, it was not going to be easy.

After topping off the hot water a few times, Arianna stepped out and wrapped herself in a soft, large bath towel. She then lay down on her bed and promptly fell asleep.

CHAPTER TEN

At seven p.m., the group was transported by van to a restaurant in Arles. The chatter was nonstop, as everyone compared notes about their afternoon of silence and introspection.

Concerned inquiries were made about Arianna's absence that had been noted when they had gathered for *apéros*. Most of the group assumed she had found a very private place to paint.

She explained that a migraine had caused her to retreat to her room. Then she asked a lot of questions, encouraging others to talk so she did not have to create any other falsehoods about her day. After all, she rationalized to herself, she had stuck to part of the instructions and not communicated with others.

What worried her was that she had come away from her afternoon of introspection wondering if she should really be there. She was afraid her artist's soul might truly be gone . . . lost along with all the other parts of her life she could not find.

She had spent the last year or so of her life inside the secure cocoon of her family, rarely having anything more than cursory interactions with other people, medical staff aside. She felt herself being gripped by anxiety that her social skills had disappeared. How could she interact normally with these people? Did she really even want to do so? And her art?

She had gone so far as to check with the airlines about changing her return ticket to Toronto. It was possible—with a hefty penalty, of course. She'd decided to give herself another day but felt a certain relief at knowing she could slip away if her disconnect continued.

For the moment, Arianna pulled herself together. Even if she had made a mistake in coming to the course, she could at least make the effort to enjoy a pleasant evening out.

The challenge of the afternoon seemed to have been a very powerful experiment for everyone else except Bertram. He had apparently fallen asleep after several glasses of rosé under an olive tree that hadn't provided quite enough shade. Sunburned from head to foot, he was obviously uncomfortable and embarrassed.

"We're just a ten-minute drive from the magical heart of Arles," Juliette told them. "You can actually walk there almost as quickly on a lovely hiking path from the property. Driving takes so long because of our convoluted country roads."

"We will be the first arrivals, since Gaston, the owner, is opening half an hour earlier than normal for us. We know most of you are still not ready for late nights."

Maurice acted as driver and tour guide. "Juliette gave you an excellent overview of our wonderful Arles and its romantic history. Once you spend time here, I know you will agree it's a unique town. Centuries ago it was a kingdom, and in some ways we locals still see it that way!" He paused and chuckled. "While we have you as a captive audience, we will do our best to make you a *vrai Arlésien* or *Arlésienne*. The French tend to be very loyal to the communities we call home."

The country lanes twisted and turned. Bertram interjected comments from time to time, noting the "crepuscular light" as the sun had just set. He appeared delighted when some didn't know what he was talking about and he was asked to explain.

Suddenly the van was on a paved road with the river on one side and town on the other. "*Voici* le Rhône, one of Europe's major rivers. Just south of Arles it flows through the Camargue and into the Mediterranean. So you can see why this was an important area for the Gauls, the Greeks, and the Romans . . . And they left us many reminders. That's the first thing to think about when you visit this town."

He pulled into a parking spot as heads swiveled, taking in the striking setting. Stepping into the midst of structures that had stood for centuries, people commented on the bizarre sense of going back in time.

Maurice finished his remarks. "After dinner we can split up for a short while and explore." He gestured to a stone wall in front of them. "We will meet here after dinner, but if you get separated, don't worry. These are the remains of some of the original Roman gates to the town; everyone knows where they are, if you have to ask. The restaurant is just a five-minute stroll from here."

As the group followed behind him, there was a collective gasp as the street curved slightly. At the end, up a slight incline, was a dramatic view of the Roman amphitheater. The evening lighting on the symmetrical limestone arches created an enchanting effect that seemed to bring history alive.

Although she appreciated the ancient history, what it meant to Arianna at this moment was that Vincent had been there, drawn it, painted it. She was walking the same streets he had walked—or raged—through. His angry behavior had been well documented. Her pulse quickened.

"Two thousand years of history, more or less, right in our faces," Bertram announced. "One of the largest Roman amphitheaters in the world." And he began to list the few comparable ones.

"Yes," Maurice replied, with good humor, when the Englishman finished his spiel, "Les Arènes, we call it. But it is the largest amphitheater in Arles, and that's what counts for us. We're proud of how it is still used to this day. The season began with our exciting *Feria de Pâques*, Easter, last month. That's the first of the *tauromachies*—bullfights—but not just that. It's an exciting festival filled with the music and dance of our culture."

"Bullfights!" shrieked Joan. "They have those here? I thought that was only in Spain! Yikes! No way we're going, John!"

John held up his hands in submission.

Maurice chuckled. "They're a big part of the history and culture of this area. We have two kinds of bullfights, so you could see one where the bull is not killed. There might be one of those . . . *courses camarguaises* . . . but I believe it's the weekend after our program ends. I will check."

"That might be exciting, Joanie," John cajoled his wife.

"No blood, John. No blood! Be kind to the bulls. That's the rule, okay?"

John patted Joan's knee and planted a loud smooch on her cheek.

Bertram looked at them in disgust and muttered something unintelligible.

The group arrived at the front door of a charming two-story building with blue shutters and window boxes overflowing with a colorful mix of annuals. Spring had come early to Provence this year, and the gardens, pots, and planters were already putting on shows.

A classically attired waiter in a white shirt, black pants, and long black apron greeted them in a reserved manner, as he indicated a long table by the front windows. A mouthwatering blend of garlic, butter, and other cooking aromas wafted from the open doors of the kitchen. Delighted murmurs were exchanged as the group entered.

"Oh, this is perfect! Look at the view we have of the amphitheater!" Cecilia exclaimed to the group as they were seated.

Bertram launched into a flow of information about the Roman ruins in Arles that would have been interesting had he not had such a blustery, obnoxious way of speaking.

Arianna was delighted to see she was seated across from Barbara and her granddaughter, Cecilia. They had only spoken briefly before, and she was eager to get to know them better. But then Bertram briskly pushed his way around the table to take the seat next to her, breathing heavily, and she shivered a bit.

"I'm so glad to be sitting with you!" he wheezed, a strong odor of whiskey accompanying his words. His chair scraped on the tile as he moved closer to her than she would like.

Arianna smiled weakly.

She was relieved when Cecilia jumped in and began a conversation, including everyone at their end of the table. "You've probably noticed me taking notes nonstop. I travel quite a bit for my work, but most of my trips have been in North America and Asia, since I live on the West Coast. This is my first time in the South of France. How about the rest of you?"

Bottles of the local *vin ordinaire*, red and white, were placed on the table as menus were handed out.

Bertram had a way of inserting his opinion into every topic of conversation. In spite of his often brusque, rude manner, however, he appeared to have a tremendous depth of knowledge, particularly about the history of the area. But he also drained his wineglass faster than anyone else.

He loudly explained to the table that he was a scientific researcher and historian by profession. But within minutes, he caught everyone's attention when he described his involvement in the retrieval of the two-thousand-year-old Roman boat that had been raised from the silt in the Rhône and was now on display in the Arles Archaeological Museum.

Surprisingly, he proved to be a gifted storyteller, taking them into the polluted depths of the Rhône as he described a diver finding a large section of wood sticking out of the muddy bottom in 2004.

He paused for dramatic effect, his arms spread wide, clearly enthralled with his subject matter. His face glowed with enthusiasm, and his personality seemed to soften.

Clearing his throat, he took a long sip of wine as he continued the amazing story.

There were exclamations around the table urging him to keep talking. He obliged, all the while topping off his wineglass.

He brought suspense into the details of his story as he explained the knowledge that, within minutes of being in the open air, the ancient wood of the boat might begin to disintegrate. "If indeed they could even raise the boat! And besides, there was no money to pay for such an undertaking. So there were many issues at hand."

Suddenly the waiters appeared with the first course on trays raised shoulder high. Maurice stood to announce with a grand flourish, "*Soupe de poireaux et pommes de terre!* Or in Julia Child–speak, Potage Parmentier! Traditionally served during the cooler months, it's such a classic that we wanted to present it to you tonight."

Bertram sat down. "Enjoy your soup, sir," John said. "But promise you will finish the story, please." The others all concurred as baguette was passed around to accompany the soup.

Arianna chuckled as Joan gave her a little kick in the shins. Within minutes, Bertram had inhaled his soup and was back on his feet, apparently enjoying the spotlight.

Wiping his face with his napkin, he looked around for approval and then continued with his story. Arianna wondered if his face was increasingly flushed from wine or from excitement at being in the spotlight.

"So! No funds in Arles, right? Then Julius Caesar himself—who had once personally conferred Roman citizenship on the people of Arles—old Gaius Julius saved the day! In 2007, an amazing marble bust was also discovered in the river. It was identified as the old man himself."

Indicating with his hand for John to replenish his wine, Bertram could barely contain his enthusiasm. "An exhibition built around the bust brought hordes of visitors to Arles, and, from what I've been told, that was the start of funding becoming available! The project could move forward! It was incredibly exciting . . . and unbelievably challenging!"

Maurice murmured a comment about how French bureaucracy sometimes moved at a snail's pace, before Marti stood and raised her wineglass. "I propose a toast to Julius Caesar!"

Voices and glasses were raised and cries of "To Julius!" filled their corner of the room. Other diners peered over to see what the hubbub was all about.

More bottles of wine appeared on the table. Cecilia had pulled out her ubiquitous notebook and was scribbling frantically.

"So what happened?" John asked.

"Well," the Englishman said with a distinct tone of pride as he puffed out his chest, "that's where yours truly came into the picture, playing a small role along with other scientists. There's an amazing video on YouTube about this entire undertaking. Watch it! No . . . wait . . . there's an excellent short film here at the museum where the barge is. Make sure you go and watch it! I urge you! I'll take you! It's such a fantastic story!"

Bertram's brow glistened with sweat now, and he mopped it with his napkin while he paused to catch his breath. He looked around the table to see faces glued to him.

"Let me finish by saying we were told it was an impossible task, timewise. That it simply could not be completed before the barge just disintegrated. Again the gods—or Julie, old boy—were with the team."

Arianna smiled to herself, somehow pleased to see this side of the fellow she had thought curious and rather revolting. She could see he was becoming quite inebriated, though, and dinner had not even been served.

Animated and surprisingly emotional, Bertram related the end of his story, describing how the most unpredictably mild winter weather played a vital role. "That, combined with the passionate dedication of all involved, who faced tremendous challenges, resulted in the success of this historic project."

He looked around, picked up his wineglass, and drained it. "Here endeth the story! The gods were with us!"

There was applause all around as each person thanked him sincerely for such an interesting story. The Englishman appeared overwhelmed by their admiration. He nodded to the waiter that a refill was desired. "Another glass of this *puissant* red, *s'il vous plaît*, monsieur!"

Maurice told them that a trip to that museum was also on the agenda during their course. "*Merci*, Monsieur Lloyd-Goldsmith, for those details. Arles is so proud of this barge and the amazing team that saved it. And now we can thank you personally. *Sérieusement! Bravo!*"

Glasses were raised toward Bertram. He blushed furiously and his eyes teared up. "It truly was one of my proudest moments."

Maurice looked toward the kitchen and barely motioned with his hand. Waiters appeared with the main course. Two choices had been presented to the group earlier in the day for this meal. Some had picked a classic coq au vin and the mussel lovers chose *moules-frites*. Everyone expressed their satisfaction in murmurs of delight throughout the dinner.

There was much ongoing chatter throughout the rest of the meal. Bertram was plied with questions, appearing to relish the attention even as he spoke quite modestly now. His blustery demeanor softened as the evening went on.

She had to admit the man could be interesting, his normally pompous attitude notwithstanding, until he overdid the alcohol.

Looking around the table, she could see the group already beginning to gel. Bertram appeared to have settled into a more contemplative mood as he chatted quietly with Barbara.

Juliette spent time with each of them, while Maurice paid attention to the delivery of the food. He quipped with the waiters with a familiar ease. From the laughter and bonhomie that flowed among them, it was obvious he was well known and well liked.

When the last morsel of crème brûlée had vanished from each diner's colorful pottery bowl, Barbara stood and gently tapped her knife on a glass. "Attention, please! I would like to offer our compliments to the chef and all the restaurant staff. This was a delicious meal!"

Everyone stood and applauded as the chef appeared from the kitchen and gathered the waiters around him. Their beaming faces mirrored their pleasure.

Maurice stood and looked at his watch.

"It's ten o'clock, and there's a concert beginning in the main square, Place de la République. We'll walk over together, but then everyone is free to explore as they wish. *D'accord?*"

Before they left the *mas*, Juliette had given them each a throwaway phone with Maurice's number already in it. "There's a minimal amount of time on each one, but enough to call us for assistance or directions if you don't find a local to show you the way. You will find people friendly and helpful here."

Taking Arianna's hand, Juliette tucked it under her arm as they began to walk. "Is everything all right?" she asked, her voice gentle with concern. "You vanished this afternoon."

"I'm sorry," Arianna apologized, her anxiety somewhat calmed by Juliette. "I had no idea I would sleep through the entire afternoon. I told the others I had a migraine." She paused.

Juliette gave her hand a comforting squeeze but said nothing. The evening air was still and a comfortable temperature for strolling. The streets were quiet in this part of town. There had been enough wine with dinner for Arianna to feel a little less vulnerable and more open to disclosing what she had been keeping locked inside.

She continued. "The truth of the matter is I simply don't know what to do. I didn't have a migraine. I had such hopes for this course . . . that I would find my way back to my art. So far it's not happening. Nothing is happening. I stare at my blank paper . . . I feel nothing." She let out a long sigh.

Juliette answered softly. "My sense is you are in a difficult place in your life. I hope you don't mind me getting too personal." She paused, looking for approval.

"Not at all," Arianna answered, wishing she could release the tightness in her chest. "I probably should be talking about this." She knew in her heart that she needed this. She had been denying it for too long, as Faith kept telling her.

With that, she revealed to Juliette, in brief snapshots, all that had transpired over the past two years. She was surprised at how she was able to hold her emotions in check. It was easier talking to a stranger somehow. At least to this stranger.

"And so here I am, at the behest of my children and my mother, on a quest to rediscover some of the life I seem to have lost."

They walked along in silence for a moment before Juliette spoke. "*Désolée.* I'm so, so sorry for all you and your family have been through. It's not the story I anticipated. It's heartbreaking. I understand why you are struggling. *Eh bien*, it's a strange thing. Some people throw themselves into their art when something like this happens . . . and others turn away."

Arianna continued. "I was certain that once I was here, I would slip right back into my artistic self. In fact, I was hoping to lose myself in my art as I once did. Maybe I was too excited to focus . . . Perhaps my expectations were too high."

Nodding, her voice thoughtful, Juliette slowly chose her words. "There's a Buddhist saying that guides my life. 'Peace comes from within. Do not seek it without.' I want to give you those words as a gift."

Arianna took it as a sign. Juliette was offering her the same thoughts that Faith had for so many months. It was time she began to heed them.

They stopped walking and stood looking at each other. Arianna swallowed the emotions filling her throat. She murmured, "I know I shouldn't expect this course to change me. I have to want that change and make it within myself. I know that. I'm trying."

"Precisely. Take your time this week and next, my dear Arianna. Listen to what is within you, and you will begin to find your way. Life throws things at us when we least expect them. All we can do is try our best to make good choices. Having friends and family to help is an added bonus. I hope you already feel you have friends here."

Arms linked, they began walking again. The moon was high now and cast a soft light into the narrow streets.

"Please know you are not alone," Juliette assured her.

"It's a good group here from what I've seen so far," Arianna replied. "And as for family, I'm blessed. I have a wonderful son and daughter-in-law who have given us two sweet grandchildren. I have a daughter"—her voice caught here for a moment—"a daughter who truly is a gift. And also an amazing mother—in her eighties, for heaven's sake—who has such strength and quiet wisdom! They've all been tremendous supports—to Ben, to me, and to each other."

"I'm glad to hear that. You're fortunate. I trust you'll continue to feel support here too. Be open to it . . ." She repeated softly, "Be open to it."

They walked together through cramped, cobbled streets. Surrounded by medieval history that came alive to her, Arianna reveled in the atmosphere created by the doors, windows, and weathered stone walls of the buildings. She could visualize inhabitants of the past, from the poorest villagers to wealthy aristocrats, hurrying along in the darkness. The visuals never stopped in her mind. She chose to omit the negatives of that time, like mud streets, lack of sanitation, and the abundance of poverty and disease. The romance of it all was what called to her.

Arianna did not want to sound like some silly schoolgirl, so she kept her thoughts of Vincent to herself. But she saw him. In shadows, down moonlit lanes, she saw him.

Her spirits lifted after her chat with Juliette.

Wooden doors with enormous and ornate keyholes, handcrafted lifetimes before, bore witness to the centuries of history that had crossed their portals. They fascinated Arianna, and she was surprised to feel the urge to sketch them. Perhaps something was stirring in her after all, she mused.

Voices tumbled from the ancient town's houses, shutters and windows open on this warm evening. Arianna found it difficult not to peer inside, curious about the spaces and occupants.

Soon, lively music filtered down the street. Turning into Place de la République, they saw that the square was jammed with people of all ages. Many were dancing in front of the stage, while others in the crowd swayed to the rhythm and sang along. The atmosphere was akin to that of a large, friendly party.

A full moon softly bathed the crowded square, in contrast to the glaring spotlights on the stage. Ancient buildings surrounded this heart of the old town, with the Romanesque church of St. Trophime a highlight. Juliette offered a few details about the intricately carved twelfth-century sculptures around the façade and the tympanum over the door.

"This is another UNESCO World Heritage Site," Juliette said. "Rest assured we'll spend some time here in the coming days and also in the attached cloister, which offers a meditative and prayerful atmosphere. Hard to believe with this party going on!"

The thought of exploring these mystical buildings excited Arianna. She would set aside some time to do that on her own, so she could dally as she wished and puzzle over the cryptic and esoteric symbolism created so long ago.

Maurice pointed out the obelisk and fountain in the center of the square. "We'll meet right here at eleven thirty. Is everyone okay with that? If you are not here, we will look for you at the gates where we parked. That's the backup plan."

There was a buzz of agreement as they all looked around to note their surroundings. Bertram pointed to a nearby bar and said he would be waiting there. "Time for a nightcap."

Maurice held their attention for a few moments, while the band was between songs. "Originally fabricated in the fourth century, this obelisk was abandoned and not discovered again until the fourteenth century. In the 1600s it was installed in this square. Through the ages it's become a popular meeting place. See you in a bit."

Juliette turned to Arianna. "Do you mind if I hug you?"

Arianna smiled, and before she could say anything, Juliette had her arms around her. "I have adopted the hug from my non-French friends. There are times when it is the only thing that feels right."

Her eyes teary, Arianna thanked Juliette for encouraging her to let down her barriers. Then she repeated the Buddhist quote, saying, "Thank you for the gift of those words. I will work on that."

As others meandered away, Arianna and the Mitchells strolled off together. "Join us for the best ice cream in town," John said in an attempt to entice her.

"Seriously," Joan muttered, rolling her eyes, "he has built-in radar for it."

"We just finished eating an enormous meal," Arianna protested with a laugh.

"So? Ice cream is a completely different matter. We all have separate ice cream compartments in our bodies. Don't worry! You'll see I'm right." John chuckled heartily as Joan nodded at Arianna and smirked. Arianna couldn't help but laugh too.

The streets were crowded now, with late-night diners walking off their rich meals, concertgoers heading to the Place du Forum for a nightcap or, like them, a visit to the *glacier*.

"You weren't joking," Arianna said to Joan as her husband soon had them joining a long line at a busy *glacier artisanal* on the far side of the square.

Giving her a knowing look, Joan nodded her head and pointed to the long list of ice cream and sorbet choices. "We were here Saturday afternoon. Never tasted better—"

John interrupted, a rapturous expression on his face. "In fact, we came back again that evening too. This is the work of a true master, a gold-medal winner in any competition. The classic flavors are divine, and the original creations even more sublime—*lavande, figue, rose, violette, cassis, passion* . . ." With a theatrical pause, he cleared his throat before ending in a dramatically dulcet tone, *"Et la spécialité de la maison—caramel au beurre salé!"*

Joan laughed, fanning her face with her fingers. *"Oh là là!* There's almost nothing sexier than Johnny reciting ice cream choices in French."

He grinned with exaggerated false modesty. "It's my best French. No question." He lowered his voice a few octaves and growled, his eyes blazing with melodramatic sexual desire. "Joanie, *mon amour, mon coeur.* I'm saving a few for our boudoir, to whisper in your ear."

Joan's laughter ended with a loud snort, and they all cracked up. "That might have broken the spell," she sputtered.

When they got their orders, they sat at a table trading superlatives as they savored the flavorful ice cream.

Arianna noticed the couple exchange a questioning look, and then Joan said, "I hope you don't think we're being nosy . . . but we noticed your absence this afternoon, and we were concerned. Is everything okay?"

Flushing with embarrassment, Arianna felt like a child who had misbehaved. She knew she was not ready again tonight to articulate her emotions. "I had a migraine. It came on suddenly, and I knew I had to lie down in a darkened room and take some meds. I'm fine now."

Her new friends expressed sympathy, asking if they could help. Arianna was touched by their concern. They talked briefly about migraines in general and the art course in particular, and then changed the subject to what was happening around them in the square.

The Place du Forum was still filled with activity punctuated by the squeals and laughter of children who had not fallen asleep on laps. Watching the lively commotion, they commented on the number of children still up. "It seems to be the French way, we've noticed," Joan remarked.

Out of the corner of her eye, Arianna spotted the yellow awning of Le Café La Nuit, much as van Gogh had painted it, at first glance anyway. He had spent a lot of time there, misbehaved there. She would go to the café on her own soon.

Arianna's eyes fluttered with fatigue, and she was struggling to stifle her yawns. "Aren't you starting to fade?" she asked her companions. "Jet lag is quickly overtaking me!"

"We spent five days in Paris before we came down here on Saturday. So we're pretty much over it," John told her.

Joan took Arianna's arm. "Your eyes look like they're about to slam shut. Let's go back to the fountain. It's almost time anyway."

By the time the van arrived back at the *mas*, in spite of the fact that Bertram was snoring in the backseat, Arianna was sound asleep. The Mitchells gently woke her before they each took an arm and guided her to her room.

It was all Arianna could do to strip off her clothes and pull on her nightgown before falling into bed, groggily conscious of how good it felt.

There'll be no meditation tonight . . .

As she lay half awake, her thoughts returned to the feelings of guilt that had brought her down that afternoon. She had worried that she should not have left Ben. She had berated herself for being selfish about coming on this trip. She had given in to defeat at painting again. Clouds of regret scudded through her mind. She wanted to shake off those misgivings.

Talking with Juliette had been therapeutic, no doubt about that. For the first time, she had uttered words long held inside. She was thankful that Juliette's warm sensitivity had drawn those words out.

As her eyes began to close and sleep wrapped around her, she felt an understanding begin to settle inside her. One she had refused to recognize before. *There are two realities in my life at the moment: Ben's is one. Mine is the other. Until I come to terms with seeing them separately, I cannot more forward.*

Peace comes from within. She thought about Juliette's words and promised herself that that would be her focus.

Tomorrow will be a better day was her final thought as she drifted off to sleep.

CHAPTER ELEVEN

The morning breakfast table was irresistible to Arianna. Just looking at it brought a smile to her face. Fresh *pâtisseries* and still-warm baguette, accompanied by local conserves and a large bowl of colorful fruit salad, brought back happy memories.

Looking around, she chuckled as she noticed so many of the group busy drawing in their art journals. She took hers out without worry of embarrassment. She was happy to be reminded that this is what artists did. Quickly, she drew the display on the table, including a vase of flowers that looked like they had come straight from the garden.

Ever since that month in Paris in her university days, Arianna had admired the French art of baking pastries. Once back in Toronto, she had made it a priority to locate an authentic French boulangerie not far from her home.

She smiled now, remembering how her father had felt she was being disloyal to her Greek heritage when she began bringing the sinfully rich and buttery treats home.

"What's wrong with *tiganites*?" he would ask, refusing to eat her pastries. She had liked those little pancakes as a child, especially the ones Sophia had made with yogurt, but once she had tasted French pastries, there was no going back.

Now she alternated among the choices at the *mas*, finding them all equally melt-in-her-mouth delectable.

She slipped into a chair and set her plate down at a small table with Joan and John. After fibbing about her migraine the night before, she felt she owed them an apology.

They both were understanding as she explained how she could not get her creative juices flowing, although she did not tell the whole story.

"Oh, I've had mental blocks before," John said sympathetically. "Not Joan, though! She never seems to get stuck! Right, Joanie?" He raised his hand to his wife, and they high-fived in agreement.

Then John became serious for a moment and spoke in a more philosophical way about how he thought Arianna might ease back into her art by using watercolors. Joan gave him a lighthearted punch in the arm and accused him of "waxing lyrical".

"Come on," he encouraged now with a chuckle, "watercolor is fun. It's Joan's poison. She's a master at layering! Right, Joanie?"

Joan nodded in her spirited way and patted Arianna on the knee. "I know sometimes it's difficult to get started. Trust me, I've been there *so* many times. But I've got an exercise that is incredibly helpful and then I just power through! I'll show it to you later. Honestly, I've never let the dreaded block stop me!"

Arianna grinned at them both, grateful for their encouragement and good humor.

She reached down and gave Maximus a scratch behind the ears. To her delight, he'd been searching her out.

Juliette reminded them a guest would be visiting after the morning break.

"Jacques de Villeneuve is well known internationally for his commitment to the Camargue area. In addition to being a respected artist, he is also a member of the ancient Brotherhood of the Camargue Horsemen—quite a dying breed. So you'll have the unique opportunity to not only study certain aspects of his approach to art but also have an intimate introduction to the life and philosophy of these *gardians*."

Juliette went on to explain how the Camargue was the Wild West of France and the *gardians* were the cowboys. They rode the wild horses that still roamed there, and they tended the storied black bulls.

"There are not many true *gardians* left. They are talented riders, proud of their métier, at one with the animals and the land. Monsieur de Villeneuve is truly a man for all seasons."

There was much murmuring among the group. Everyone had read about this man in the notes about the course. They all eagerly anticipated meeting him and learning from him.

After breakfast, the plan for the first part of the morning was for each person to return to the location they'd chosen the previous day.

"Take your time," Juliette instructed. "Put something to paper: a sketch, color blends, however you wish to begin. Think about texture, shape . . . what you want to communicate. Last night you all confirmed you had found your spot and the subject matter for your work, but do you have an idea of the why?"

Before she had given up on art the day before, Arianna had considered the texture and subtle shades of the stone wall. But she was also drawn to the olive trees with their gnarled and twisted trunks speaking to her of survival through centuries. The silvery blue-green colors of the slender, tapered leaves shifted in the morning's gentle breeze and challenged her to define their hues.

Even more, she felt a sense of tranquility in the midst of these aged trees. She could see the ghosts of generations of workers who had nurtured, harvested, and protected their precious bounty. Perhaps this was her "why": to capture that feeling, that history, the struggles, and the passion.

She set up her folding stool and began to sketch. Something inside her still was not quite right. And she knew it.

Arianna thought of all the encouragement she had received since she had arrived. John had enthused she should consider "the alchemy of everything that surrounds us . . . mix the brightness of the sun, the blue of the sky and the breezes that waft by with your paint and paper, and magic will happen." And so she decided to do just that. *It's a beginning . . . please . . . just let me start . . .*

As she took in her surroundings, she was reminded how working *en plein air* was all about movement . . . the sky, clouds, light, wind. *John was so right.*

She decided to begin to capture the scene she wanted to paint by dividing her paper into four quadrants. By drawing a thumbnail sketch of the scene slightly differently in each box, she could decide how her painting would begin.

Two hours later, a soft bell summoned them for coffee. Arianna welcomed the reprieve from the clash of emotions that remained with her. But she felt a hint of pride that she had finally achieved a beginning on her canvas and a detailed color wheel.

"Just leave your equipment where it is and join us in the main salon, please. We will turn you loose out there again later this afternoon." Juliette's cheerful voice drifted out to the terrace.

As Arianna made her way back, she paused at the edge of the terrace. With her eyes closed, she turned her face up to the sun. The warmth washed down over her chest and bare arms. She opened her eyes and let the blue of the sky lift her spirits. She so wanted to feel happy. How could she not in this peaceful and stunning setting?

A light poke on her arm startled her, and she let out a squeal.

"Oh, bloody hell! Sorry to scare you! I wasn't sneaking up on you. Didn't know whether to say something or simply touch your arm. You seemed quite caught up in your thoughts. I rather thought I should ensure you are well."

Arianna shook her head, slightly flustered, and assured Bertram Lloyd-Goldsmith he had not frightened her. "You just surprised me. I was taking a moment to feel that lovely warm sun."

"Well, I certainly hope you remembered to put on sunblock," he fussed, glassy-eyed, his beet-red face dripping with perspiration. Arianna could hear him hiccuping as he disappeared into the kitchen.

With her arm linked through Jacques de Villeneuve's, Juliette escorted the guest in through a door from the front terrace. Jacques promptly removed the slightly battered, soft-brimmed black hat he was wearing. It reminded Arianna of the fedora her father wore to the Greek Orthodox church in winter back in the sixties, when the men all left their hats on a shelf inside the entrance.

Juliette introduced him once everyone was sitting with coffee or tea—or rosé, if you were Bertram. Arianna wondered where he had found it at that hour.

"Please welcome our guest, Jacques de Villeneuve. He is a friend, an artist, and one of the few remaining *gardians* of the Camargue."

He was a mesmerizing figure. Tall and lean with rugged good looks, he projected an aura of quiet confidence about him even in his simple garb. Still holding his hat, he wore the standard attire of a *gardian*: gray moleskin cotton pants and a long-sleeve cotton shirt in a blue Provençal pattern.

"A *très* sexy dude," Joan whispered to Arianna with a wink and a nudge as they sat together. Arianna nudged her back and did not disagree.

In no time, de Villeneuve had drawn his listeners into the mysterious landscape of the Camargue, a vast, windy area composed of endless beaches, shifting wetlands, enormous salt deposits, a UNESCO nature reserve, and agricultural land.

"As an artist, my work is influenced by living here, and I hope I can impart some helpful reflections. I'll be interested to hear how your art has been impacted by the surroundings in your part of the world."

The group was soon captivated by his words and the slide show of photos he had brought along. It was clear they were learning about a part of France unfamiliar to them all.

"Of course, the world knows the Provence of the masters . . . and why not?" His startling blue eyes connected with them all, seeming to emphasize the power of that thought. "Arles, in particular, played a most important part in the life of Vincent van Gogh—a frenzied, frantic sixteen months when he completed over three hundred pieces of work. His memory is all around us in this town.

"Today I simply offer you other aspects of art to consider in an area where beauty is perceived in a much different way. Scrubby farmland, remnants of an ancient forest, marshy fields with towering reeds, intriguing lagoons, and vast saline flats. To some, there is little beauty in the Camargue. To me, it's endless." Bertram appeared ready to interrupt, and Barbara, sitting next to him, gently patted his arm and shook her head imperceptibly.

The *gardian*'s voice was low, inviting attention. He drew pictures with his words as he blended history with the extraordinary environment and unusual cultures that had evolved there. The group sat spellbound.

He led them through a brief history of the Rhône delta, highlighted from time to time with his stunning photography and artwork. His choice of graphite pencil for most of his art created a dramatic effect.

With a laser pointer, he outlined areas on a large map set on an easel to help illustrate his narrative. As he spoke, he switched roles before their eyes: environmentalist, artist, cowboy.

Arianna felt as though he had put everyone in the room into the basket of a hot air balloon and floated them from one part of the Camargue to the next. The timbre of his voice and his confident self-assurance kept them mesmerized.

"After World War II, the northern marshes were drained and irri-gated with fresh water. By the 1960s, Camargue rice was supplying three-quarters of the demand in France. How times are changing. I believe now it only supplies about one-quarter. The good news is that our *riz rouge* has recently been discovered by gourmands."

Marti put up her hand excitedly. "Camargue red rice! Love it! We use it at our restaurant in Napa."

De Villeneuve laughed, clearly pleased. "And do you cook it in California like we do? That's the question!"

"*Oui, oui!* Like pasta! Until it is al dente, in a huge pot of salted boiling water, with *sel de Camargue, bien sûr*! I'm a fanatic about rice."

They grinned at each other. Juliette said she would make certain she served some while they were at the *mas*.

"How about Camargue wines?" Bertram asked. "I've been told I must try them."

Jacques spoke directly to Bertram. "The vines here are unique in France. You may remember hearing about the phylloxera pandemic in the nineteenth century. It was catastrophic! Destroyed all the other vineyards in France!"

Bertram nodded. "These were the only ones spared. Rootstocks had to be reimported into France for all other vineyards. Am I correct?"

"That's correct, sir. The roots and stems here were submerged underwater. Aphids couldn't attack the roots because of the unusual texture of the sandy soil. That was our good luck."

He showed a map indicating the location of the vineyards in the Camargue. Then his voice grew more serious as he explained the threat the *vignobles* faced during World War II.

"During the occupation, tens of thousands of land mines were buried in the vineyards to deter the Allies from landing along the sand banks. They were—"

"Good God," Bertram interrupted, "the condition of this area must have been deplorable!"

"Indeed it was," Jacques agreed. "But with determined effort, the mines were cleared, and authentic, uncompromising wines are now produced. It's a unique terroir and—"

"Ah, terroir . . . Such a vital part of the French psyche . . ." Bertram interrupted again.

"You are so right!" Jacques replied, unbothered by the Englishman's rude manner. "Terroir is very important to the French; you might hear the word most often used in relation to wines. But really, it encompasses our obsession with food and where it comes from. It's simply a combination of local factors, like soil, climate, and altitude, that makes what we eat and drink unique."

He stopped to take a drink of water and then continued. "Like the chickens from Bourg-en-Bresse or butter from Normandy, melons from Cavaillon or *saucissons* from Arles. To simplify, it's something about a product that enhances community, cooking, and taste. Get the picture?"

They nodded.

It was no surprise that, once again, Bertram jumped into the conversation. From time to time, the slurring of his words was obvious. Though his thoughts were always clear and concise.

"I have long been a student of van Gogh. That's how I first learned anything about the Camargue. I read about his stagecoach voyage, in 1888, to Sainte-Maries-de-la-Mer, hoping the sea air would ease his ailments. The first work I saw of his from there was done with a reed pen. Your sketches remind me of that."

Bertram paused and asked if anyone else in the group was aware of van Gogh's works from that area. The boastful Englishman's inclusiveness of the others was a surprise.

Jacques smiled. Interest was percolating.

"You are correct, sir," Jacques said to Bertram. "Van Gogh happened upon the reed pen while he was in this region. He used a penknife to sharpen local hollow-barreled grass and obviously was very pleased with the results it gave him."

He addressed the painting to which Bertram referred. The two men engaged in a lively exchange. Finally, Bertram seemed satisfied and thanked Jacques for his expertise.

"I am always happy to discuss van Gogh's work. The paintings and drawings he made in the Camargue have their own distinct character and beauty. Between 1877 and 1890, he crafted over eleven hundred drawings. Many people are not aware of that, yet it's his drawings that have affected me the most—and have influenced my own choice of medium."

Next he played a slide show of van Gogh's drawings, many of them re-creations of paintings that the artist would send to family and friends to report what he was doing. Everyone, except Bertram, was surprised to learn that van Gogh sometimes made his drawings after he had created the oil painting.

"In his letters to his brother Theo, he said drawing helped him combat his depression. He knew, as we do, that working *en plein air*, we are able to capture light and images more quickly and from that create our interpretation."

De Villeneuve then shared a series of drawings and paintings by local artists. There were some magnificent birds. The flamingos, in particular, were depicted in ways that drew breathless comments about the graceful slender curves of their heads and necks, the textured beauty of their feathers, and the seeming fragility of their thin legs.

"The only time I think of pink flamingos is when I see them as tacky lawn ornaments," John said.

"Or as the good luck symbol for the Florida lottery ticket I buy every week," Joan added with a chuckle.

"It's rather the icon of American kitsch, isn't it?" Bertram asked rhetorically. "Who knows what a group of flamingos is called?"

Jacques had been listening to the banter with amusement. Now he watched to see if anyone could answer Bertram's question.

After suggestions of "a flock," "a gathering," "a bunch," and a few others were put forward, Bertram announced, "I believe the appropriate collective noun is a flamboyance."

Jacques clapped his hands. "Bravo!" He then turned their attention to the rest of the art he had on display. "The pink flamingo is the official emblem of the Camargue. However, the Camarguais horses and bulls are equally iconic."

His words flowed as he painted dramatic visuals of the wild horses of the Camargue, describing how the *gardians* worked with them as well as the bulls raised there. Robust white horses and sturdy black bulls, with majestically curved long horns, were captured in oils, watercolors, pastels, and graphite.

The movement and beauty of the images captured a combination of fragility and strength. The subject matter was completely different from the art of Provence they were all accustomed to.

"This is food for thought from a very different menu!" Marti exclaimed. "It never occurred to me that I would be creating works like this in the South of France. I'm definitely intrigued."

Juliette and Maurice set the art on long tables that had been arranged under a shady pergola.

De Villeneuve's enthusiasm for all the pieces and his pride in the local artists was obvious.

"I often consider Thoreau's thought that the world is a canvas to our imagination. And that has been true throughout my life. Would you say the same? I hope to hear how art is integrated in your lives."

He indicated that he was leaving a handout with the websites of all the artists whose work he was sharing. "I encourage you to take some time to explore the work and the philosophies of these artists. It will open a window into how this area inspires creative talent from all over the world. How it speaks to them in such diverse ways."

He walked over to where his work was displayed and picked up different examples as he spoke.

"I've worked with graphite pencil or charcoal almost exclusively since I began my artistic endeavors in the Camargue. It feels right. When I reduce my subject matter to black and white, it feels as though only the basic shading is left. To me, this represents truth."

The group agreed the use of black and white produced a powerful, intense piece of art.

Arianna had been sitting very still. His art had stirred thoughts deep within her.

I feel like I have been living my life in black and white since Ben's illness. I need to begin to add shading to this picture of my life. I've been numb for so long, I've closed my eyes and my heart to the beauty around me. Faith was right. I need to blossom. I need to free my imagination.

There was general astonishment that the morning had passed so quickly.

A simple but sumptuous buffet was set up for lunch, and during this time, everyone had an opportunity to speak with their guest. Questions were asked and answered. They walked around the display tables, expressing opinions, studying perspectives, and comparing techniques. Discussion ensued as to the different moods portrayed by the works of art they were viewing.

Maximus wandered up and down the tables, rubbing gently against the framed art. He purred his satisfaction at the absentminded head scratches and ear rubs he received. After a while, he wandered over to a stone wall from where he could observe all the activity.

The lunch buffet and art show lasted for two hours, accompanied by probing discussion about techniques, subject matter, and lighting. Arianna caught a glimpse of Juliette and Maurice sharing smiles of satisfaction as they observed the interactions.

There was one final aspect of Jacques's life in the Camargue that still was to be shared.

"Apart from art, which truly drives my life, I have one other passion about this area I call home." His eyes flashed, and his voice took on an intensity different from before.

"My grandfather had a dream that grew out of family stories passed along from a portrait of an ancestor on a white horse. He grew up in Arles, and when he heard stories about a man founding the *gardians*, he ran away to Saintes-Maries-de-la-Mer. I follow in his footsteps, and those of my father, as a *gardian* today."

He showed a brief video that dramatically portrayed life on a *manade*, a traditional ranch where black Camargue bulls were raised. The footage of men, the *gardians*, on the backs of wild white horses, riding through the surf and herding the bulls, evoked romantic images of a way of life that was quickly disappearing, he explained. "Let me assure you the life involves long hours and hard labor . . . not so romantic! But we all have a love for what we do.

"I will keep you sitting here for hours if I continue to talk about it. So I'm issuing an invitation instead. It would be my pleasure to have you come down to the Camargue and spend a day. We can meet at my *cabane*—my cabin on the *manade* where I work. If you like, I can arrange for a short trek on a Camargue horse."

Murmurs of interest punctuated the end of his invitation.

De Villeneuve spoke with everyone individually for the next part of the afternoon. The focus was on basic drawing skills that might be the foundation for their paintings, in whatever medium. As helpful as the group sessions were, everyone later agreed how they valued this personal attention.

Arianna felt nervous and embarrassed when it was her turn. She had managed to position herself so she was the last one. She was thankful she had at least drawn something on paper in the morning. His comments and suggestions were constructive, with tips that she could see would be useful.

His steady voice and assured manner calmed her nerves. She was surprised to find herself responding as he drew out some of the technical questions she had felt shy about voicing to that point.

As he gathered the group together to end his visit, he addressed the value of warming up before you begin drawing.

"If you are feeling stressed about something or burdened by other thoughts when you begin to work," he said, "art will be a challenge. It will not flow. The first thing you need to remember is to set aside all other thoughts. Breathe. Become present. Then you may begin your conversation with the paper." He demonstrated a few short exercises that he said helped him to "loosen his hand and his thoughts."

"Jacques," said Juliette, her rhapsodic tone the perfect complement to his throaty delivery, "thank you for taking the time to share your art, as well as the magic of the spellbinding Camargue with us. I don't know anyone who could have done this more passionately or informatively."

She was interrupted by applause from the group and a loud "Hear, hear!" from Bertram. He led the rest in a standing ovation.

Juliette smiled and nodded her agreement. "Equally as important, I believe you were able to open our eyes as observers to the endless ways of interpreting the Camargue artistically. I believe I speak for all of us when I say it was fascinating and inspiring to see the work of the various artists that you brought with you."

As Jacques wished them well, he had these parting words: "There's no doubt that art is therapeutic for the spirit. Have you examined the state of your spirit lately?"

Arianna wondered if he was giving her a message. *Had he read something in my eyes, my demeanor? Is it that obvious I'm searching for my spirit?*

"Thanks—*mille mercis*—to all of you for your interest and for the enthusiasm you showed for the Camargue. Please consider accepting my invitation to come and see it for yourselves this weekend. Juliette and Maurice have my contact information."

The atmosphere was charged with enthusiasm after his departure, and the eager artists returned to their easels.

Arianna walked slowly through the garden back to her easel and her morning's sketches. She crumpled her paper and began again, after doing the warm-up exercises de Villeneuve had demonstrated. Slowly she felt more freedom in the movements of her hand.

Her imagination was fired.

CHAPTER TWELVE

Their evening was free. Options were bandied about for dinner in town, and plans were made.

Marti suggested they walk into Arles. "We'll get some exercise and work up an appetite. Though it's not exactly far . . . Never mind! Who's with me?"

Arianna did not take long to respond. There was something about the energy Marti radiated that made Arianna want to be in her presence.

Lisa and Cecilia were enthusiastically on board. Joan and John were driving in with Maurice, who had offered to pick them all up around eleven.

Barbara was staying in and having an early night.

By the end of the cocktail hour, Bertram was in his cups. After delivering a lengthy monologue about van Gogh's history in Arles, hiccuping loudly all the while, he gave everyone a detailed description of where the famous yellow house was located before it was bombed in World War II, and later demolished. Then he demanded they promise to go there and take photos for him as proof.

"And no selfies! I abhor them!" were his last remarks as he began to stumble off to his room.

"If that's important to you, Bertie," John called after him, using the shortened name he had begun calling the Brit in an attempt to break down his reserve. "We will most definitely carry out the task for you."

Everyone was a little uncertain as to how the very proper Englishman would respond to his new nickname. So far, his only acknowledgment had been a slight twitch at the corner of his eye.

"Okay, walkers," Marti said. "We'll meet down here in half an hour?"

The path leading to town was wide and well used. The women set off at a good pace, casually dressed and wearing comfortable walking shoes. A light breeze carried with it the aromatic scents of wild sage, rosemary, and thyme.

Juliette had told them about these low scrubland plants she called garrigue as they headed out. "It's found all through the Mediterranean countryside, along with dense thickets of kermes oak and juniper that contribute to the natural aromatherapy. As you crush the plants under-foot, you'll release a fabulous bouquet. Be sure to stop and breathe deeply. The whole sensory bodhi is an ambrosial part of the hiking experience here."

Within minutes of their setting out on the path, Lisa had messaged the others: FYI—'bodhi' is a Sanskrit word meaning enlightenment. Make a note for Scrabble/Words with Friends! Thank you, Google. I had no idea.

The others laughed as they thanked her. Arianna noted how they all had their phones with them. She realized she had become one of "them."

As they walked along the path, Lisa occasionally would put her hand up, motioning the others to stop. Then she would rest her hand on her diaphragm and take an exaggerated inhalation, pointing to each of them to do the same.

"It's divine!" Marti exclaimed as she let out her breath. She reached down and grasped some of the plants along the path, crushing them between her fingers and bringing them to her nostrils before releasing them into the air like confetti.

Arianna closed her eyes and inhaled again. This worn path meandering through the idyllic landscape, combined with the lighthearted repartee of her companions, was just what she needed. She could feel even more of a release of the guilt that had plagued her the past few days.

"Truly restorative," she murmured to no one in particular.

"Could we bottle this?" Cecilia asked as she excitedly described the experience into her phone.

Winding past olive groves, beside vineyards, and through fields dotted with poppies and other wildflowers, from time to time they'd comment on the pastoral beauty. They could imagine artists through the centuries setting up easels along the way.

Arianna fantasized about Vincent painting the very scenes through which she was walking. *Was he right here? He must have breathed these same intoxicating scents!*

Lisa didn't speak but shared the occasional nod. She continued to stop and brush her hand across the landscape as her subtle expressions relayed her pleasure.

"I'm sorry I keep doing this," Cecilia apologized after speaking into her dictation app. "I don't want to miss recording how this walk touches all our senses. Listening to your comments feeds my descriptions."

Arianna felt herself grow more relaxed and cheerful in their company.

After the trail led them down a small knoll, they exited a large olive grove. Suddenly the dramatic outline of the medieval buildings of Arles rose ahead of them.

"There's no denying this is France when we see a vision like that!" Cecilia declared.

They stopped to take photos or draw in their journals, in between sighs and exclamations. It made Arianna happy to feel she was with people who were so like-minded about art. She had been away from it too long, she told herself.

Breaking the spell, Cecilia said, "And knowing we're in France also means that we can't get dinner before seven thirty."

Marti continued, "I don't know about you ladies, but we're heading straight for the nearest coffee bar. A double espresso would hit the spot. Right, Lis?"

They all laughed as Lisa held up her phone and showed them the Google map that led directly to a café.

As they sipped their espresso and *café crème* and chatted, they each formulated their own plans. In so doing, more bits of information surfaced about their respective interests and personalities.

Marti's primary interest was in supporting everything Lisa wanted to do. "As I told you all before, she truly is the finest artist. I am the dabbler."

Their affection was obvious as Lisa took Marti's hand and kissed it. Marti's always-bright eyes twinkled deeper.

Lisa texted a longer message than normal. Marti read it to them. "I want to drink it all in. To see everything. Every nook and cranny. Every ancient stone. To feel everything. Then I hope I can express that in my art."

Cecilia's youthful exuberance shone through.

"In this short time, I've already got articles and blog posts galore planned! I'm so happy Granny convinced me to come here with her.

She hasn't really shown her true personality to you yet, but she will, and you will love her even more!"

Arianna spoke last. She took a deep breath, pushed through the urge to avoid being honest, and was surprised she was so forthcoming.

"I'm on a bit of a spiritual search here, looking for something I've lost. My art, mainly. So I will probably fumble my way forward for a while, but I want to thank you for the friendship we've shared thus far. You've no idea how you are helping me. But if you don't mind, I'll wander by myself for a while when we're through here."

The others shared compassionate looks with her. She suspected they were waiting for her to reveal more. *All in good time, I hope.*

Her comments had stilled the conversation momentarily, until Marti chirped, "So how about Monsieur de Villeneuve? Is he a hottie or what?"

There was enthusiastic agreement. Lisa gave a decisive two thumbs up.

"And his presentation was awesome, wasn't it?" Marti continued. Everyone eagerly agreed.

"So are any of you going to go to the Camargue this weekend?" Cecilia asked.

Marti and Lisa nodded, already having decided. They all chatted about it some more, pondering the logistics.

Marti said, "We're kind of torn, though, because we also want to sample the cuisine and seafood of the area—don't know if there's time to do it all in one day. Arianna? Are you going?"

"I think I would like to go. I was intrigued by the art from the area and by that history of the *gardians*, the horses, and the bulls. It sounds like something different from anything I've seen."

Cecilia agreed. "I think it will be quite an adventure. I'm always up for that!"

And maybe it's time I was up for an adventure too, Arianna prodded herself.

❧

The Place de la République was just around the corner, and soon they strolled over to the fountain in the center. Already acknowledging a certain familiarity with the old town, they all agreed to meet back up there at seven thirty.

"I'm off to the Fondation Vincent van Gogh. Can't wait!" Cecilia said. "I know Juliette has organized a visit for all of us on Thursday," she explained, "but I want time there on my own. So I'll slip in now, absorb everything in the special exhibit, and do all my reporting. Imagine! Thirty originals of his work!"

Arianna nodded. "I know! That was part of what convinced me to come to this course. I can't wait to see it."

Cecilia continued, "Us too! So if I take in the exhibit now, when I go back with all of you I won't disturb everyone by mumbling into my phone through the whole tour."

Arianna politely declined an invitation to join Marti and Lisa in their explorations. She agreed to meet them back at the fountain at seven thirty and waved good-bye. She had her own plan.

CHAPTER THIRTEEN

Arianna lingered in the square, entranced by the intricate sculptures over the portal of the Romanesque twelfth-century church of St. Trophime that had attracted her their first night in town.

Seeing it in daylight for the first time, she found the rich detail overwhelming. The work had lasted through so many centuries. Sculpted stone figures of tormented souls being taken to hell in chains and others being taken to the saints. She decided the religious meaning was lost on her, but she appreciated the artistry.

Sitting on the edge of the fountain, she added a page in her journal, taking in the square from three perspectives.

Maurice had told them the recent cleaning of most of the town's antiquities had given them all new life.

She peeked through the entrance that led to the quietly elegant cloisters attached to the church. Beyond the columns, which were topped by elaborate carvings, an eerie darkness intrigued her. She felt a strong desire to return another day and explore what lay beyond the pillars that surrounded the intimate courtyard.

For a moment, she pictured crowds of pilgrims gathering there through the centuries, preparing to set out on the Via Tolosana to Santiago de Compostela.

Checking the map in her hand, she turned up the narrow Rue du Cloître leading toward the Roman coliseum. Simply strolling the cobblestones gave her a sense of connection to the history around her. She couldn't stop imagining the centuries of footsteps that had preceded hers.

On her left, a busy terrace caught her eye. Delicate vines zigzagged their way up the uneven stone walls, skirting around shuttered windows. White-shirted waitstaff, their long black aprons tied around their waists, bustled about organizing metal tables and chairs in preparation for evening diners. Crisp white tablecloths were set with round, emerald-green chargers that matched the gemlike bubble-glass goblets. The details appealed to her.

Sumptuous aromas wafted out to the street. She paused at the blackboard leaning against the gate to read the dinner choices. It was printed in the typical French style that made every chalkboard an individual piece of art. Several dishes tempted her. She made a mental note to come back another day.

Farther along, she passed under a timeworn arch and had a vision of van Gogh frantically rushing through these streets. The thought sent a shiver through her. *He really did! And I wonder where he and Gauguin had their loud arguments and fights. Maybe one night it was right here! So much to discover . . .*

Rounding a corner, she arrived at the jumble of ruins, all that is left of the antique Roman theater. Assorted large stones dotted the grounds in front of curved rows of tiered seating. They were the remains of thirty-three rows that seated an audience of nearly ten thousand. Two tall Corinthian columns kept lonely watch over the grounds. She could only imagine its original grandeur.

She had read that, after the fall of the Roman Empire, many of these historic sites had fallen into disarray. Stones and other building materials were stripped away and used to build churches and monasteries, and the theater became a quarry.

Posters advertised upcoming performances. A large movie screen indicated mixed media was used with some of the listings. She liked how theater continued to live on in the original spirit of the ruins.

The gates to the grounds were locked at the modern entrance and ticket booth. She noted the times when she should return.

Looking beyond this ruin, the two-tiered amphitheater or coliseum—Les Arènes—imposed its graceful presence just steps away. She made her way there instead.

She had been fascinated by the Roman structure when they'd passed it on the way to dinner on Monday evening. The moonlight that had shone on the two-thousand-year-old limestone arches had created a graceful, haunting visual. Vivid images of the ancient-Greek ruins of her childhood were revived from the back of her memory bank.

The ticket office was still open, but she wouldn't have much time before it closed. She paid her admission and walked through the gallery that ran under the arches. In the main arena, she climbed the stairs to the second level and sat on a stone bench. She ran her fingers lightly across the stone, sensing the ageless time preserved in its patina.

There in the fading light, surrounded by thousands of years of history, Arianna experienced an overwhelming moment of clarity.

She missed Ben . . . more than ever. She wanted him there, and at the same time she was ever more aware that he was not there. Would never be there again. She was on her own.

She had to keep all the good memories of the past alive. They had made her who she was now. That was her history. She never would let go of it. But she had to be open to new beginnings, to see if that black hole of a future could become bright again.

A haunting voice accompanied by a guitar filtered through the galleries. The deep, rich tones rose and fell with the emotions of the woman singing. They swirled up the tiers and took flight into the air. Arianna determined the words were in Spanish. Somehow it didn't matter. The passion of the song came through without any translation necessary.

The ambiance of the moment floated like a cloud around her: the history and redolent beauty of the surroundings, the setting sun painting the sky and washing the stone in shades of pink, the absence of others, and the emotional power of the song. Arianna promised herself this would be the beginning of moving forward. She closed her eyes and made a silent vow. *Peace comes from within.*

She took her journal from her bag. Drawing, and moving from one spot to another, she worked to capture the shadows cast by the setting sun. She felt like she was transferring shadows that had been clouding her thinking for too long. It was as though being in this mystical setting was pushing the darkness inside her away and allowing light to shine on the peace she was seeking.

She was sorry she had to rush now and vowed to return.

Before too long, Arianna followed the dulcet sound of the distant voice as she exited the arena. Sitting on a chair by one of the arches was a woman of indeterminate age. She was dressed in a colorful collection of mismatched clothing, and a floppy hat shaded her face, even though the sun was no longer a factor.

Her fingers danced across the strings of her guitar. Attached to each foot was a tambourine, providing a rhythmic percussion as she tapped. A small dog was curled up, asleep, on a mat tucked under her chair.

Arianna stopped at a distance. Leaning against an arch, she listened intently and felt mesmerized. The woman sang of pain, sorrow, hope, and joy. It was all there.

Although Arianna could not understand a word, she understood the emotions. There was no mistaking them. She wondered if this woman was aware of the power she possessed. A large crowd had gathered around the woman.

Suddenly, a voice spoke next to Arianna. "Are you under her spell?" Arianna found herself looking into the deep-blue eyes of Jacques de Villeneuve.

"Oh, hello again! You surprised me! And . . . yes, yes, I am totally enchanted."

"I hope you don't mind me intruding. You looked so lost in thought, but when I recognized you from the group today, I thought I would say hello."

"No, of course . . . I'm happy to see you. I'm Arianna . . ." She held out her hand instinctively.

"I remember your name," he said with a smile, reaching to shake her hand just as she began to pull it back.

"Oh!" Her cheeks flushed with embarrassment. "That was . . . um . . . awkward. Handshakes aren't very French, are they? But they're an automatic reaction for us."

He smiled. "*Pas de problème!* I've spent a lot of time on your side of the Atlantic."

Her perceived faux pas slipped away. "And thank you for today. It will take a while to process everything you shared with us. It was wonderful, enlightening . . ."

Now she felt embarrassed for gushing.

"*Merci!* I regretted I had to dash off for a meeting, and now I'm on my way to another. It's a crazy day. But this woman singing . . . I'm so glad you came upon her. She's a special character in Arles."

Arianna smiled her agreement. "Her voice is hauntingly beautiful. I don't understand a word she is saying, yet I feel the meaning of her songs so deeply. It's quite remarkable."

"*Vraiment remarkable,*" he repeated.

She saw him look at his watch. "Thank you for stopping to say hello."

He smiled as he asked, "Do you plan to come to the Camargue this weekend?"

"I'm not certain. We haven't all talked about it, but I'm sure some of us will be there."

He bowed his head slightly. "Hopefully we will meet again then. Enjoy your evening in Arles. *À la prochaine et bonne soirée.*"

Arianna's eyes followed him as he took the stairs briskly and disappeared down a narrow street. She thought there was something almost old-fashioned about him. And intriguing.

The singing stopped a few minutes later. The woman was drinking water and talking to her dog as Arianna approached her.

As she stooped to drop euros in the open guitar case, Arianna's voice was heartfelt. "Thank you. *Merci. Muchas gracias.* You are a beautiful singer." She touched her hand to her heart as she held the woman in her gaze, hoping she got her message across.

The woman smiled warmly, saying nothing as she nodded her head. Arianna could not tear her gaze away from the deep pools of emotion that glimmered in the singer's eyes. This was a face that told a story.

CHAPTER FOURTEEN

Noticing it was almost seven thirty, Arianna hurried the short distance to Place de la République. Dusk was beginning to settle across the square.

While she waited for the others, she took in the details of the fountain and the towering four-sided, tapered monolith. Maurice had told them part of the fourth-century obelisk was found buried under rubble and sand in the fourteenth century on the site of the original Roman circus, of which nothing of note remained.

Bertram had piped in during that conversation, adding, "The other part of the obelisk was discovered being used as a bench amongst the fishermen's cottages in La Roquette."

He went on to describe how it was pieced together and mounted here on a pedestal in the sixteenth century, and the fountain was installed in the nineteenth century.

Looking at it now, Arianna thought how she loved these stories that encompassed hundreds of years. It was such a big part of why travel in this part of the world was so special. She had a moment of regret that she and Ben had not taken more time to travel. *Was work really so important we couldn't have taken two weeks off?*

Then she banished the thought and focused on the fact that now she was there, making her own memories.

Sitting on the edge of the basin, Arianna dipped her fingers in the cool water and was briefly transported to childhood memories in Greece. She smiled at the pigeons nestled above the bronze masks, now aged to greenish-blue perfection, through which water spurted.

Children's laughter echoed around her as youngsters gleefully ran after the pigeons in the square. She remembered how she loved to chase birds through her own village so long ago.

As she watched Marti and Lisa walking across the square toward her, a text arrived on her phone from Cecilia saying she would be at the *glacier* in the Place du Forum at precisely nine thirty. Rest assured I will never be late for ice cream!

An agreed-upon urge for tapas and paella had Lisa googling for some dinner recommendations. They strolled the short distance to the Place du Forum, winding along meandering streets lined with closed shops. Evening commercialism had not gripped this small town. It was far more important to close the doors and shutters early and spend the evening wining and dining with family and friends.

In the growing nightfall, the bistro- and café-lined square buzzed with activity. Piquant aromas rose from an enormous pan of paella cooking streetside that would serve a crowd.

They decided a freshly made paella was more to their taste and continued their search. At the far end of the square and down a narrow alley, they discovered exactly what they wanted. They settled at a table on the stone terrace and ordered Spanish beer. A few tempting plates of tapas appeared quickly, and the waiter let them know the paella would take a half hour to cook on their wood fire.

"You can really see the Spanish influence around here, *sí?*" Marti asked rhetorically. She unfolded her napkin and passed one plate to Arianna and another to Lisa. "I could eat tapas every day."

Hearing them speak English, the waiter lingered to describe what he had brought to the table. He appeared extremely pleased to show off his mastery of the language.

"Here you have *pan a la plancha*. It's grilled bread, tomato with garlic rub, and olive oil. Next is Manchego cheese—so good to eat with that. Next is *gambas al ajillo*, sautéed shrimp, garlic, and olive oil with red pepper flakes. Nice and spicy. Last is empanadas, little pastries filled with onion, garlic, and potato."

They looked at each other and wondered why they had ordered a main course.

"Well, we walked our asses off for the last few hours. Hopefully we built up an appetite!" Marti exclaimed as Lisa flashed her thumbs-up sign to Arianna.

"I know I did," Arianna agreed. "I'm starving! Let's dig into these!"

"Did you know there's a whole system of underground galleries right below us, under this square? *Les cryptoportiques!*"

Lisa pulled up Google on her phone.

Marti continued, "We happened upon it by accident when we went into the hôtel de ville. That's where the entrance is. You really feel like you've gone back to Roman times."

"That's the thing about this town, isn't it," Arianna said, her eyes lighting up. "History lives all around you. And it's not too big, so it's such an intimate experience."

Marti and Lisa nodded enthusiastically. Marti asked, "What did you do after you left us?"

Arianna described her stroll up to the amphitheater. At first she glossed over the singer, but her voice betrayed her emotions.

"Wow, it sounds like that was truly memorable. Do you think she's there every day?" Marti wondered. "Perhaps we'll get to hear her."

"Well, if I understood correctly, she's in the same spot every single day," Arianna told them. "Guess who stopped by as I was listening?"

They gave her a quizzical look.

Without waiting for an answer, she said, "Monsieur de Villeneuve."

"Cooool," Lisa murmured in the flat, unvarying tone she normally used—when she spoke. In the time the group had been together,

Arianna hadn't heard her utter more than a dozen sentences. But even so, she had never seemed disconnected from any conversation.

As she had just demonstrated once again, there was no question she was always the first with Google answers. Marti teasingly referred to her as Quick Draw McGraw or Speedy Gonzales, which without fail caused Lisa to grin.

"So what did he say?" Marti asked.

"He said she was a well-known character and agreed her singing had a special quality. Honestly, I don't know when I've been touched so deeply by a voice."

"His?" Marti teased.

Arianna felt a blush coming on again. "No, silly! The singer's!"

"Intriguing, to say the least," Marti said. "We've got to make a point of hearing her, Lis."

The aromatic paella arrived steaming in a round, double-handled copper pan. The waiter set it on a tile in the middle of the table. The three women leaned in and inhaled the scent. Saffron added a distinct color and musky smell to the rice, which was mounded with shrimp, mussels, and squid, along with rabbit, chicken, chorizo, and assorted vegetables.

The serving was enormous and they looked at each other with a collective gulp. "We could be here for a while," Marti announced.

As they indulged in their meal, the conversation became more personal. Avoiding doing most of the talking, Arianna encouraged the Californians to tell their story.

Marti proved herself an able raconteur. She had them all laughing at anecdotes about the joys and challenges of owning a restaurant. Lisa pulled up photos on her phone to show Arianna, as Arianna plied them with questions.

The waiter was a handsome black-haired young man with an olive complexion and deep, dark, brooding eyes. After he served them the paella, Marti commented, "Now he is what I call erotic, with a capital *E! Oh là là!*"

Lisa responded with an exaggerated wink. She held up her phone, showing off a photo she had sneaked of him.

They noticed Arianna's puzzled expression.

"Are we confusing you?" Marti asked. "Make no mistake. Even though we are in love with each other, we still appreciate a great-looking guy. We both were even married to great guys at one point." They looked at each other. Marti grinned. Lisa's thumbs were up.

Arianna tried not to show her surprise.

"In fact, my ex is still one of my very best friends," Marti said. "Lisa's, not so much."

Lisa gave a thumbs-down and shook her head as she shrugged her shoulders.

"Some battles you win, and some you don't," Marti said. "It took us both a while to figure out what we wanted in life. But when we met each other, there was no question for either of us. We've been together for fifteen years, and when we were finally legally able to marry, we were among the first in line."

They leaned over and kissed lightly. Their mutual affection was obvious. Arianna liked these women.

Marti looked at Arianna. "So tell us about your family. Oh, and your Greek restaurant! I guess your husband is holding down the fort while you are here, right?"

Arianna had a moment of indecision. Hesitation showed in her eyes.

Marti reached over and patted Arianna's arm, obviously sensing something amiss.

Then her voice filled with regret as she said, "Shoot! I'm sorry. I can see you're not comfortable with my question. Is there something wrong? Um . . . but . . . that question doesn't help either, does it? You don't have to say anything. Feel free to change the subject. I tend to blurt things out. Right, Lis?"

Lisa rolled her eyes and made a face that had them laughing and eased the awkwardness.

The waiter arrived at their table to light some candles, and Arianna appreciated the delay.

When he had gone, she looked down for a moment, made a decision, and began to speak. "No, no, it's okay. I'm all right . . . really . . . well, not exactly, but I have to stop holding this in. Juliette drew it out of me the other day. I know I should get the facts out on the table."

"Only if you want to," Marti said. Lisa indicated her agreement.

And so Arianna gave them the short version of Ben's affliction and how this was her first attempt to move forward on her own. "I'm not looking for sympathy. I hope you understand. I've been struggling with finding my way back to the art that was such a part of my life . . . struggling to find lost pieces of myself, really."

She reached for her glass and finished her drink.

Marti got up and gave Arianna a hug.

"I'm sorry if I put you on the spot," Marti apologized.

"You didn't." Arianna pursed her lips for a moment and brushed her fingers through her bangs. She spoke softly now.

Her eyes searched her new friends' faces. "I have to get over this hurdle so I don't keep feeling like I'm hiding something. I'm just not sure how to do that."

There was an awkward pause.

"Well, let's start by having another beer or something," Marti said. "And some more paella, please."

Arianna agreed to both. Lisa served another portion to each of them. They all commented on how much they were eating—and enjoying every morsel.

As they ate, they deliberated about how life could be cruel at times. Marti spoke while Lisa supported her thoughts in her usual manner.

"If it's of any help, we struggled with change in our lives too. Y'know, I have a feeling we've experienced some of the same emotional journeys. It all centers around grief, loss—maybe even fear—and learning to move forward to become more authentically who you are."

Arianna looked at Marti and Lisa and could feel the strength they shared. She wanted to hear their story. "Talk to me, Marti. Tell me what you think I should hear, please."

"Well, it's not a matter of should . . . but sometimes we really are able to get stronger through another woman's experience. I know I had friends whose stories were incredibly helpful when I was struggling—and believe me, for a time I really floundered."

Lisa nodded, her eyes bright with emotion. She clearly was relating to every word.

"When I finally admitted to myself that I was gay, I was married to the greatest guy in the world. Seriously . . . he still is my best friend, along with his amazing wife. He even came with me to tell my parents. That's how great he is."

Lisa pulled up a photo of Marti, her ex, and his wife of thirty years and passed it to Arianna. Marti looked at it too and smiled. "I feel so fortunate to have them in my life. In our life. They love Lisa too."

"That's a good story, Marti," Arianna said, handing the phone back to Lisa.

"But can you imagine how frightened I was?" Marti asked. "I was afraid of hurting him, my parents, my friends . . . and it was back when society was not as open and accepting as it is now. I had to give up the dreams I thought I had about babies and family. My future became a big black hole. I'm guessing that's how you see your future."

"Oh, Marti, I can feel how frightening that must have been," Arianna murmured. "I hear what you lost . . . and yet see what you gained, as you say, your authentic life . . ."

Arianna looked at Lisa. "And you found the right life too. You both did. And you're right, I feel like I've not only lost Ben, but I've lost my future. That's why I say I feel like I'm stuck in the 'now.'"

Marti's sympathy tempered her voice as she continued. "The big difference in our stories is that your life *was* right for you. And that's a bummer. That's so not fair . . . for you or for Ben."

Arianna was nodding slowly, taking it all in. Lisa was looking down, texting wildly.

"The lives we were leading were not right for us," Marti said, "and we had to figure that out and then make the change. We had to learn to be honest in every way."

Marti picked up the water pitcher and refilled their glasses. Arianna practically gulped hers down. Her throat felt parched, partly from the spicy meal but also from the emotionally charged conversation. But she knew this was good for her to hear.

"What we all have in common is how we move forward," Marti suggested. "As I began to consider the rest of my life, it occurred to me I had to give up the pictures I had of my future. I had to create new pictures, a new way of being me. That's how I see your challenge."

Their phones dinged as Lisa messaged them. Rejection. We had a lot. We were judged, and you will be too. Believe in yourself. Believe in the choices you make. Make them fearlessly. Right, Marti, my love? That's how we got through.

"Everything you say truly speaks to me," Arianna assured them. "I know I will be judged by some. And I have to get over my fear of hurting Ben. He will never know what happens to me from here on out. Then I have to try to let myself be open to possibilities . . . to try and create some pictures for my future. I get it. I'm just not sure I can do it . . . and . . . if it's right to do it while he is still alive."

Marti's voice cracked as she said, "He's alive . . . but he's gone. He's gone. I hope you forgive me for being blunt." She reached for Arianna's hand, and their eyes remained locked.

Arianna nodded wordlessly.

Marti continued in a hushed voice. Their hands remained clasped. "You need to accept that, and I can only imagine how difficult that must be."

"I know. I know," Arianna whispered, her lips barely moving.

"Arianna, even if you can't see it yet, it sounds like you've made all the right decisions so far, as difficult as they've been," Marti said, her eyes conveying respect and sympathy. "Your family has been enormously supportive, from what you've told us. That's wonderful, and such a help."

"I'm grateful for them, no question," Arianna agreed as the two women shared a look of understanding and unclasped hands. "And I'm grateful for the compassion and straight talk you are both sharing with me."

Marti and Arianna smiled warmly at each other. Lisa looked down, nodding.

The sparkle in Marti's eyes dimmed, and she looked thoughtful. "Crisis strips us of everything we think is important."

"It narrows your focus," Arianna agreed. "I certainly learned that."

The quiet that rested among them for a few moments was almost calming. Each woman was lost in her thoughts.

The light returned to Marti's eyes. "But there's a positive outcome to crisis. Once we are stripped of everything superfluous, we're left with all we truly need in our lives."

"And I guess that's what I'm waiting to discover," Arianna agreed.

All three women nodded slowly and then raised their glasses.

"Thank you both for this. You've already helped me, and I know this conversation will resonate with me for a long time."

"Let's go have some ice cream . . . the universal panacea," Marti said, waving to get the waiter's attention. "Cecilia just texted she will be there in fifteen minutes."

They all put their thumbs up as the waiter arrived with the bill. Marti and Lisa gave him the once-over again as he walked away from their table. Arianna smiled.

As they made their way through the crowded square to the *glacier*, Marti gently slipped her arm around Arianna's shoulder. "I'm so sorry for all you've been going through. It must be torture."

Arianna turned her head and gave Marti a grateful smile. "I'm glad you encouraged me to talk about it. It helps."

She thought how it seemed easier to tell her story to complete strangers. Talking about it with friends or family was much more difficult because she was unable to avoid their pain as well as her own.

In many ways, I hurt even more for my children. They're losing their father when they still should have so much more time with him. A mother is supposed to help her children when they hurt, and I can't.

She felt her throat tighten with emotion. Her heartache was palpable. She swallowed hard as she tried to control the stinging behind her eyes.

Please don't let me lose it now.

Just because the telling was becoming a little easier did not mean the pain was gone. *Will it ever go away? Time to refocus my thoughts . . .*

The air in the square was filled with talk and laughter. The milling crowd closed in around them. Arianna pulled her shawl from her bag. Feeling a bit of an edge in the refreshing but cool evening air, she wrapped it snugly around her.

They laughed as they approached the ice cream shop and saw Joan and John, cones in hand, comfortably sitting with Cecilia. "No surprise here!" they greeted them. Before meeting Maurice, they all placed a large to-go order to share at the *mas*.

After a good long soak in the tub, Arianna was happy to crawl into bed. It had been quite an evening. Quite a day, for that matter. She was amazed when she went over all that had occurred.

She'd replayed the conversation with Marti and Lisa as she'd unwound in the bath. Gratitude was the strongest emotion that filled her right now. She could never have imagined sharing her personal life so completely with relative strangers. But Juliette had reached in and opened a small corner of the compartment where she had locked her feelings about her life. About the "now."

Marti and Lisa were so easy to be with. So honest and open in their own ways. She smiled to herself, suddenly thinking that Faith would have said, *"They have their shit together."* Arianna hoped she was getting to that point too. Each small disclosure felt like a small step forward. *Okay, an inch . . . but still forward . . .*

There was now a soft but commanding meow in the hallway. Arianna slipped out from under the covers and opened her door. She invited Maximus to join her. He looked up at her as he rubbed against her legs.

"*Bonsoir*, Monsieur Maximus. Did you sense that a comforting snuggle would be appropriate?"

She stroked his back and then climbed into bed. He sprung up lightly, barely denting the duvet, and nestled into her body.

Arianna fell asleep to his gentle purr. Her last thoughts before drifting off were content and hopeful.

CHAPTER FIFTEEN

Arianna sat bolt upright in bed. Her heart was pounding from some sudden, howling, deafening noises. It was a surprise to see it was still dark. She had taken to sleeping with the windows and shutters open, enjoying the cool night air.

Now the shutters were banging wildly back and forth. She was momentarily confused. Certain she had secured them before going to bed, the metal hooks embedded in the stone walls, she leapt out of bed.

The wind was raging. One of the shutters almost hit Arianna in the face as she reached out to grab it. She needed to approach this problem with care and timing. After a few frantic attempts, she had them all tightly closed.

Well, well, well . . . this must be the famous mistral. I've read so much about how it roars down into the Rhône valley from the Alps. I wonder how long it will last.

Maximus was nowhere in sight. When she called to him, a loud yowl replied from under the bed. Despite her pleading, he refused to budge and stared back, wide-eyed.

She felt a mix of curiosity and anxiety as she climbed back into bed, noting it was only three a.m. The clanging of metal furniture being blown about and men's voices could be heard from outside for a short while, then nothing apart from the tempestuous wind's clamor filled the air.

Pulling the pillows over her head, she finally fell back asleep.

Everyone except Bertram arrived for breakfast looking disheveled and bleary-eyed. The mistral had been effective in robbing most of sleep.

He explained he had slept through the cacophony of the night and only now realized what was happening. "I might have overserved myself last night. That full-bodied Bandol red was irresistible! I heard absolutely nothing until my alarm woke me."

The legendary mistral was the topic on everyone's lips. The Mitchells had never heard of it. "Remember, we've never traveled outside the US. We've got a lot to learn . . . and are loving every bit of our education so far," Joan said.

John interjected with a wild-eyed look, "But seriously, you didn't need to arrange this crazy cyclone for us. We could have just read about it, y'know!"

Juliette, as gracious and calm as ever, gave a brief history of the famous wind for everyone who might not know the details.

"The mistral is a fact of this area. We all simply accept it as part of the price of living here. It's the reason our farmhouses are built facing south with only a few small windows on the north side. *Mistrau,* as we call it in Provence, begins as a cold front when freezing air gathers high up in the Alps. Pressure builds and the system is pushed over the mountaintops. It has a clear path down through the Rhône valley and heads toward the coast. Saint-Tropez and Marseille often bear the brunt of it, as do we."

Bertram piped in. "That's why the trees in Provence are bent in the direction they are. But it's also the reason there are so many sunny days here."

"So true," Juliette agreed. "It does bring good things in its wake, fiercely blowing away the clouds and grime. We have a saying in Provence, '*La beauté vient après le vent*—beauty comes after the wind.'"

"Is it true it causes headaches?" Cecilia asked. "I read about that."

"Yes, for some people, because of the atmospheric pressure. And, if the wind lasts too long, you can feel like it is driving you crazy! Hopefully this won't be too bad. The *météo* calls for it to pass in three days, so we will keep our fingers crossed and hunker down."

Maurice stumbled in, his normally well-groomed hair blown wildly about. The door slammed so forcefully that everyone jumped.

"*Merde!* Oops—*excusez-moi*! It's savage out there! John, *mon courageux ami, merci beaucoup*—thanks for coming out in your pajamas to help me move that furniture during the night!"

"That was an insane experience! Never felt anything like it!" John looked around in amazement at everyone and added with a snort, "Good thing Joanie wasn't out there. We might have lost her forever!"

The program for the day had been for individual sessions outdoors with Juliette.

"We can accomplish the same goal inside. I will just have to speak a little louder to be heard above the wind," she said. "Take some time to find a space in the house where you feel comfortable working. The kitchen and dining room tables are also available. I'll come and find each of you."

The wind wailed into every nook and cranny of the house.

Maximus roamed from one room to another. His tail was puffed out like a bottle brush and his ears were flattened back. He was not a happy cat. Every once in a while, he emitted a mournful yowl, and eventually he curled up in Juliette's wicker pannier.

"Our feline friend obviously knows you won't be using your market basket today," Cecilia remarked.

Juliette said, "Max definitely does not appreciate the mistral. We won't see too much of him as long as it lasts."

During a break later in the morning, Marti ran an idea by the rest of them. "Since we're apparently housebound, why don't we all pitch in with dinner tonight? I know there's an abundance of food in the kitchen. What do you think?"

The response was unanimously in favor, and Juliette and Maurice were delighted at the suggestion.

"But let's make it even more fun and have you all create the menu," Maurice said. "I have two legs of lamb marinating for *le plat principal*, and the cheese course is already organized. You make up the rest, and I will go pick up what we need."

When they objected to him going out in the mistral, he assured them it would not be the first time.

Marti and Lisa offered to prepare a salad, California style.

Barbara, Cecilia, and—the biggest surprise of all—Bertram quickly conferred and announced they would bake a chocolate cake. Bertram's recipe, no less! Barbara's decorating skills would complete the task, with Cecilia assisting and measuring.

Joan and John were preparing the hors d'oeuvres to have with the *apéritif*. Hummus and tzatziki with crudités, using Arianna's recipe, were their choices. Maurice suggested he would pick up an assortment of olives and fresh almonds at the market to go along with that.

Arianna was making Sophia's famous *avgolemono* soup as the entrée. Juliette assured her the lemons of Provence would be the most flavorful and juiciest she had ever tasted.

"Today is market day," Maurice reminded them. "Our *marché* in Arles is one of the biggest and best in Provence, and the plan was for us all to go first thing this morning. *Laisse tomber!* With this wind, it would be no fun, and, *honnêtement, c'est dangereux!*"

Juliette nodded in agreement. "But there will be a few hard-core vendors—*probablement*, Gaston, Henri, *et* Serge . . ."

"*Oui!* They'll just be selling out of their trucks today. Those won't blow away. Hopefully we can all go on Saturday, when it is on again. *Sacré* mistral!"

They wrote down the necessary ingredients. With a hearty wave, Maurice set off with the shopping list, as they all wished him well battling the wind. He refused any assistance, knowing precisely where he wanted to go for his supplies. He also knew that each stop would require a social visit and perhaps a slurp of rosé.

Once that planning was complete, everyone went back to their art.

Juliette asked if they minded music while they worked. "We may enjoy some tunes over the roar of the mistral." She programmed a mix of Édith Piaf, Charles Aznavour, Zaz, and the Gipsy Kings. "Did you all know that the Gipsy Kings came from Arles? We're fiercely proud of them!" She went over to a bookcase and took down a framed, signed photo of the group. There was a personal message on it to "dear Maurice and sweet Juliette."

"You're kidding," Joan exclaimed. "I looooove that group."

So, it seemed, did everyone else, except Bertram, who had never heard of them. "Sorry, I've been a classical music devotee my entire life. Haven't branched out much, I'm afraid," he apologized and then added, to everyone's surprise, "except for Leonard Cohen. Do you mind if I wear my headphones and listen to my music?"

Barbara pointed to herself. "I'm in that classical music club too, but I'm going to give these tunes a go! *Pourquoi pas?* You see! I'm becoming so relaxed, I'm speaking French . . . or at least attempting to!"

Juliette continued, "Well, let me know what you think of their music. It's infectious! The father of one of the main musicians was part of a celebrated flamenco duo for years. Picasso was a fan. And Miles Davis! Anyway, after his father died, the musician, Nicolas Reyes, and his cousin Tonino Baliardo put the group together, all family members, and the rest is history . . . But lots of them still live around here."

"I thought they retired," Joan said. "They kind of disappeared. I used to see them at a casino near us, from time to time."

"They took a few years off, but they're touring again. Their latest album, *Savor Flamenco*, is in the mix here—*superbe, comme toujours*!"

Arianna said nothing. Her heart had jumped when the Gipsy Kings were mentioned. They were Ben's absolute favorite group, and for years, their passionate music had resonated through the apartment or in the car. He was fond of saying, "Their music stirs the blood, moves the soul, and assumes complete control of our bodies . . . olé!" followed by a flamenco-style foot stomp and clap of his hands. That was another of his quotes Tad and Faith knew by heart.

She steeled herself to work through the inevitable bittersweet moments she might experience listening to them again. She had always loved their music after Ben introduced her to it. She could keep loving it and remember the good memories. That's what she had to do, she told herself.

As much as she had let her life come to a halt, she knew it hadn't. Goodness knows Faith reminded her of this in her daily texts and e-mails. Arianna appreciated the way her kids were staying in touch with her during her time away.

CHAPTER SIXTEEN

The day progressed, with everyone breaking for lunch at their leisure. Arianna could tell that the private sessions with Juliette were being very positively received, and she looked forward to hers that afternoon.

The background music seemed to provide just the right atmosphere for the work they were doing. It certainly was proving an effective distraction from the mistral.

As the hours passed, some people sang or hummed along to Piaf and Aznavour. When the Gipsy Kings came on, there were moments of spontaneous hip twitching and outright dancing. A relaxed, festive air permeated the farmhouse.

Arianna was happy that all the music pleased her, even the sentimental familiarity of the Gipsy Kings.

During one of their rhapsodic acoustic songs, John slipped Bertram's massive headphones off. "Bertie, listen to this. I challenge you not to like it!"

Cringing at first, Bertram did take some time to listen, then admitted, "By Jove, it does have merit," saying he'd give the music a chance. "Later, though. I'm communing with Beethoven at the moment."

Arianna smiled to herself. Bertram was becoming a different person. She berated herself for being so judgmental about him in the beginning. Although she couldn't help notice the nearby bottle of rosé.

Barbara commented that she also always painted to classical music and was surprised to discover how much she was enjoying Juliette's mix.

Whether it was the bonding she experienced on the previous evening's stroll, the chat with Juliette, the presentation by Jacques, or her connection with the emotional singer in the amphitheater, Arianna felt a growing commitment to her art project. Her work was coming along slowly, but, like her, it was moving forward.

Juliette spent a productive half hour with her, and she beamed as Arianna indicated the breakthrough she had reached with her rough work. In their session, Juliette encouraged Arianna to identify empirically what she wanted to say with her work and then delve into her heart to create her own interpretation. Their discussion brought back memories from her days at university and art school. Arianna could feel her former excitement for the craft returning.

Juliette said, "I can tell the embers are still smoldering, Arianna. Your artist's soul is there and slowly reawakening. I'm happy for you."

"I can't tell you how promising this feels," Arianna replied. "It's what I hoped for. Thank you for the encouragement you are giving me . . . in every way."

In their meal planning, Marti had drawn up a schedule of who was to be preparing their food and when.

During the morning, while the artists were absorbed with their work, Mirielle had chopped root vegetables, filling an enormous earthenware roaster. She had been shocked when Juliette advised her that she and Louis-Philippe did not need to prepare dinner that night.

After four o'clock, art was put away and activity moved into the kitchen. Cutting boards and a selection of knives, bowls, and platters were already waiting on the rustic wood table.

As the socializing moved in and out of the kitchen, Maurice spoke a bit about the importance of terroir to French cuisine.

"As we keep telling you . . . because we can't help it. Each region in France has its own particular environment that affects the food it produces. In Provence, it is primarily the Mediterranean influences of the sun and the sea that help us create our unique cuisine." He spoke rapturously about the local olive oils and herbs.

Juliette added, with a chuckle, "You are getting to understand how we French love to talk about food. Any kind of food! We always like to know the precise origin of what we are eating. It's a habit in our blood."

Maurice laid a fire in the raised hearth in the kitchen. As the flames danced and crackled, the smell of woodsmoke wafted through the rooms accompanied by murmurs of approval.

Once the flames were well established, with strong embers, the two bone-in legs of lamb would be slow roasted. They had marinated overnight in lemon, garlic, rosemary, and cilantro, with enough vinegar to carry the flavors deep into the meat.

"Later, with dinner, especially for the lamb—we will serve a hearty Bandol red!" Maurice announced. "We have a saying here about wine drinkers. There are two kinds: the ones who love Bandol wines and the ones who don't know Bandol wines." His eyes glistened as he spoke about the excellent local vineyards situated between Marseille and Toulon. His voice almost a reverent whisper at times, he explained how many of their products never left the region because their production was so small and exclusive.

Juliette wore a smile from ear to ear as she presented white aprons and chef's hats to everyone. She explained she had a cache of them in the pantry and had never had the occasion to use so many at one time. "*C'est tellement amusant! Je suis ravie!* This is so much fun. I'm so delighted!"

They slipped on the garb with glee—even Bertram, who finally allowed Juliette to help him after some good-natured cajoling.

"Chef Bertie! Chef Bertie!" John began a chant, and the others picked it up. Juliette tied the apron around the Englishman's rotund belly, placed the hat at a cocky angle, and *bised* him on both cheeks before gently pinching them. Flushing a deep red, he cast his eyes downward and sputtered an awkward, "Goodness gracious."

Arianna had a feeling he had not often been on the receiving end of such good humor. Her curiosity grew about his story, and she wondered if it would ever come out. Alcohol definitely comprised a chapter or two.

The cake bakers were first in the kitchen. In the planning of the evening's feast, it had been determined the cake would take the longest time from start to finish.

Bertram pulled together the ingredients, enjoying his wine as he did so. Cecilia measured, all the while dictating her comments and thinking about the divine blog post this would make. Bertram mixed and sipped. They took turns whisking and beating and joked over who was going to get to lick the bowl. Meanwhile, Barbara prepared the icing and colorings she would need and began to sketch a few designs.

The aroma of cake baking in the oven elicited comments from many in the group about cooking traditions. Everyone had a favorite recipe.

"Chocolate chip cookies!"

"Banana bread!"

"Triple-chocolate fudge cake!"

The list went on.

The whole baking experience brought back sweet childhood memories.

The divine cake smells faded as the smoke of the wood fire floated through the farmhouse.

"There's something about the smell of a wood fire that makes everyone feel good," Barbara remarked to Bertram. "Ever since I was a young girl, I've been aware of that. I still have an apartment with a wood-burning fireplace."

"Jolly good! I agree with you. Sadly, my wife is allergic to smoke"—he turned his head for a moment, reaching for the wine bottle, and muttered to no one in particular—"and every bloody thing else . . ."

"Oh, what a shame," Barbara replied.

"Right! Bloomin' shame! We never have fires, in spite of the fact we have two enormous hearths in our hunting lodge in the country. In our early years together, I would sneak in a few bloody roaring infernos when my wife went off to London for a few days. Nevermore. The minute she catches the slightest hint of smoke, she goes crazy. I'm enjoying this."

After searing the roasts, Maurice flattened the flames. Then he settled the meat on a low grill over a bed of hot, glowing embers while the fire continued to smolder. "*Deux heures!* Two hours to perfection!"

Juliette smiled to herself. She knew that meant three hours, without question. Maurice was always an optimist when it came to roasts on the coals.

Maurice told them they were in for a treat, as this was Camargue lamb. "It's a delicacy because of the special flavor that comes from grazing on the salt-marsh grass."

Joan, John, and Arianna took the next shift. John chopped veggies and baked pita chips, singing along to an Eagles album he had requested from Juliette's extensive music collection.

Joan blended chickpeas, garlic, lemon, and tahini to make hummus. They had to do several taste tests to ensure she had it just right . . . or so they said. Arianna guided her on the tzatziki, a very simple recipe, also made in the blender.

From time to time, she and Joan picked up spoons to use as microphones and accompanied John as backup singers. The mood was lively, with everyone wandering in and out of the kitchen, singing along.

Arianna felt transported to a time years before when this kind of atmosphere was very much a part of her family life. It occurred to her that she had not lost it or left it behind; it was simply different now. She was having fun again.

She made the *avgolemono* soup in a broth-like style, knowing this consistency was a pleasing complement to a lamb dish. She was thrilled to add a touch of her Greek heritage to the meal.

When she asked for some salt, Maurice seized another opportunity to talk about the products of the area.

"Did you know that *fleur de sel* is harvested by hand?"

Arianna admitted she did not, even though she always used that kind of salt both at home and in their restaurant.

He continued, "In the Camargue, this salt is only produced at special times during the summer when the wind is slow and steady or, even better, stopped! This causes millions of salt crystals to form at the surface of the water. That layer is hand raked and harvested. The aroma of violets and flower-like pattern of crystals that develop as the salt dries gives it the 'fleur de sel' name."

He picked up a round container with a cork top that had a signature on it. "Each container is signed by the one who harvested that salt. The tradition continues."

"Maurice, I love that! I'm going to look at my containers when I get back home and see who has signed them. That's so cool!"

Champagne corks were popped. "It is, after all, *l'heure de l'apéro*! I hereby declare this cocktail hour!" Bertram announced with unabashed enthusiasm.

Everyone agreed they were beginning to appreciate the French love for their national drink. Foie gras on small toasts were set out, along with the newly created appetizers, and consumed with murmurs of delight. The talk was all about food.

Marti and Lisa would prepare their salad after everyone was finished in the kitchen.

"We're very familiar with the French theory of keeping the salad simple in order to cleanse the palate and aid digestion after the main course. We follow the same philosophy at our restaurant," Marti told them. "Then we serve the cheese platter, followed by dessert. It makes so much sense."

The aromas of the roasting lamb, covered with a paste of minced garlic and fresh rosemary, filled the kitchen.

"Mmmm, that is just too divine!" Arianna said as she clinked glasses with Joan.

"Normally, I can't stand the smell of lamb cooking, but this is making me salivate!" John admitted.

"Ah, these perfumes, combined with the whiffs of woodsmoke . . . My nostrils are putting me in a state of delirium!" Bertram staggered about theatrically. "More champagne, please!"

CHAPTER SEVENTEEN

It was almost midnight when Juliette stood with her finger to her lips to attempt to stop the conversation. The men were clearing the dishes from the table, leaving only a box of hand-dipped local chocolates to be passed around.

"Attention, *s'il vous plaît*! Shhhhh!" She laughed as the chatter gradually tapered off around the table. "I would say this dinner has been a great success."

The men returned to their places, and applause broke out, along with a few cheers and a loud whistle from Lisa with her fingers between her teeth. All heads turned in her direction, followed by peals of laughter.

"I want to compliment all the chefs involved!" Juliette said, looking at each one around the table, including Maurice. "This meal was *magnifique*!"

Words of praise and agreement echoed around the table.

Barbara stood up and raised her empty glass. Bertram picked up a bottle of wine to refill it, but she covered the top with her hand. "*Non, merci*, Chef Bertie! I've had more than enough! As the senior member in the room, I want to tell you this is the most fun I've had in years! I can't believe I'm still awake. *Merci, merci, merci . . . beaucoup!*"

Maurice's face reflected pride in their accomplishment. "I believe this all got started around the chopping block and mixing bowls this afternoon."

Marti grinned. "There's something about working together in a kitchen that goes a long way to develop camaraderie."

The group had become a tight unit over the course of the evening, as delectable conversation was served up with equally delicious food. Stories were told and much laughter shared.

At one point, Bertram had slipped into the empty chair beside Arianna. Joan had been sitting there and had left the room for a moment. In spite of the good company he had been in the kitchen, Arianna felt herself tense up. She didn't do well with inebriated men. Never had.

"Arianna, my dear girl," he began, slurring his words ever so slightly. "There'shomething I've been wanting to tell you since Monday. I hope you don't mind . . . and I would never have said it without the help of dear Bacchus . . ."

He swallowed a hiccup. "Damn! Please excush me! I had a sense you were struggling with your bare canvas when you first arrived, and this is what I wanted to say. It's acshually advice from dear Vincent . . . don't listen to voices saying you can't paint. Paint, my dear girl! Paint! You can do it! Then those voices will be silensh . . . shilensh . . . damn! . . . silenced! Tha's what I wanted to say . . ."

He weaved a little as he stood up. Then he patted her gently on the head. Arianna thought she would burst into tears at his thoughtfulness. She berated herself for judging him so harshly earlier in the week. She knew better than to let first impressions color her thinking.

Joan arrived back just as Bertram was vacating her chair. When she saw the look on Arianna's face, she assumed he had said something hurtful. "What the heck happened? Tell me, and I'll speak to him right now! I've got a bone to pick with him anyway!"

Arianna took Joan's hand and held her in her seat. "No! Exactly the opposite. He just stumbled over and said the sweetest thing to me . . . something very thoughtful. I think I've been misjudging him."

"Well, I'm surprised. Glad it wasn't anything bad. Seriously, I've had a score to settle with him from the day we all arrived. I won't do it while we've been drinking. But I have to agree with you. He does seem to be nicer than when he first got here."

Arianna looked down the table to where Bertram had taken his seat again. He looked back at her and gave her a crooked smile. She mouthed the words "thank you," put her hands together in front of her, and bent her head in a namaste response.

Dessert plates were set on the table. The pièce de résistance was the cake. Bertram's recipe was declared just the right melt-in-your-mouth combination of richness and simple flavor.

Now he pulled himself together in an exaggerated manner. "The recipe for thish ambrosial comestible was pashed along to me by my dear old gran, Lady Sonia Lloyd-Goldsmith. She wash the custodian of my heart throughout my formative yearsh. Not that she would ever spend a moment cooking, mind you." His oration was interrupted by a loud hiccup. "Excush me! But she maintained a treasury box of family reshipes transferred through generations and ensured they were faithfully and habitually served." He wiped his brow with a flourish.

"A gentle explosion of chocolate and butter in the land of *beaux gâteaux*!" Cecilia expressed, recording into her phone, and then shared loudly over the table. "*Merci*, Chef Bertie!"

Barbara had created a garden of sugary delights on the top, in the shapes of roses, lavender, and other colorful blooms.

Bertram refilled his wine, stood up, and raised his glass. "A toasht to everyone! To my beautiful cake-baking companions and everyone elsh at the table! Three cheersh!"

Everyone joined in the toast and then continued to compliment each other on their particular contributions to the dinner.

While the cake was being consumed, Juliette placed a clear four-inch acrylic cube filled with cards on the table. "This is a great game to connect with each other. We each take a turn and answer a question on a card. If you don't like the card you pick, pass it on to someone else. It's good fun."

How could it not be, with questions such as:

What song brings back the strongest memories for you?

Which is more important, intelligence or common sense?

If you could do something dangerous once, with no risk, what would you do?

By this time, everyone was relaxed. John had volunteered to answer the first question, and the ball was rolling.

Conversation about life, art, travel, politics, sex, and food floated around the table, ranging from deep and substantial to frivolous and lighthearted.

Maurice rolled a cart to the table. "*Voilà les digestifs*—brandy, cognac, whiskey—*qu'est-ce qui vous ferait plaisir?* What's your pleasure?"

Bertram raised his hand.

And stories were told . . . by some more than others.

CHAPTER EIGHTEEN

The mistral continued to roar for all of Thursday.

Bertram was unusually vocal as he joined some of the group for breakfast. "Jesus H. Christ! Doesn't the wind know I'm hungover? It's like a bloody banshee today! *Sacré* mistral!" He had picked up that "damn mistral" curse from Maurice.

Juliette had explained the day before that their visit to the Fondation Vincent van Gogh would be rescheduled for the following week.

With some feeling a bit foggier in the head than others on Thursday morning, the day's schedule was left to the artists. At their insistence, the music was back on. Barbara convinced Bertram to forgo his headphones for part of the day, and more than once he was caught in the act of twitching his hips to the music.

By noon, everyone was up and about. The kitchen held a wealth of leftovers to be consumed when desired. The guests favored lamb sandwiches on crusty baguette with mint from the garden. Juliette had braved the wind to pick some fresh stems, assuring everyone there was a way to deal with the mistral after you had been through it enough times.

"The biggest danger—apart from falling over—is getting hit by a flying object. Otherwise we carry on but certainly don't go out as much as normal. That's another reason some people say the mistral drives them crazy. You can be housebound for several days, depending on the strength of it. I have to admit I relish being held captive at home, but many don't."

Everyone was immersed in their work. Inspiration and motivation were the buzzwords being shared. The general consensus was that the presentation by de Villeneuve on Tuesday and then individual sessions with Juliette the day before had been huge catalysts.

"I'll be at work in the studio all day, and you know I'm available for any questions or help you may wish," Juliette reminded them. "I'm delighted several of you have already set up in there with me. There's room for all of us . . . so think about it."

Arianna liked the relaxed overall atmosphere and the fact that the course encouraged independence as well as collaboration. She had spent the morning mixing her paints to re-create the silvers, grays, and greens of the leaves on olive trees as they filled her canvas.

Occasionally, she would take a break and spend time in the pages of a coffee-table book of van Gogh's art she had borrowed from the well-stocked bookshelves in the salon.

The day passed in relative quiet indoors, background music notwithstanding.

But the roar of the wind outside continued unabated. Maurice had mentioned the mistral sometimes continued for well over a week. Arianna hoped that would not be the case this time.

Later in the afternoon, appetizing aromas began to waft through the house. Maurice had used the remainder of the lamb and roasted vegetables to put together a mouthwatering stew.

Listening to an optimistic report from *la météo*, that evening he told them it was predicted Friday would be the third and final day for this mistral. The news was greeted with cheers.

Discussing weekend plans over dinner, everyone wanted to visit the *marché* on Saturday. It would be on again, Maurice assured them, and it would be busy after the disruptive weather.

Since they had essentially missed out on two days of exploring Arles, some suggested that Saturday afternoon they take the walking tour offered by the tourist office.

"Besides, Juliette deserves a break!" John proclaimed, and there followed a chorus of accord.

In addition, they all agreed they were eager to visit the Camargue on Sunday. Maurice was amenable to driving them in his van.

Friday proved to be only slightly breezy by comparison. The mistral teased the trees and shrubs, but relief could be found.

Some spent a little time outside drawing, eager to capture the movement created by the wind. Protection could be found by stone walls or on the south terrace near the house. Others moved quietly around indoors. After the socializing of the previous few days, a hushed mood prevailed.

The artists were at work.

For a while, Barbara and Bertram set their easels back to back, apart but together. Pausing for the occasional break of tea for her and wine for him, they shared conversation in low, muffled tones.

The day passed.

Arianna spent most of it in her room with her easel in front of an open window. She liked to be alone when she painted. She'd discovered that distractions and interruptions, music notwithstanding, slowed the process for her.

If she was honest, she was also there because she still felt her work was inferior to the others'. But she was beginning to accept that, really, everyone's individual pieces were just that. Individual. She had even received some compliments about her work, for which she was grateful.

I just have to become a believer.

With much of the color and texture detail well established, she worked purposefully. Now her emotions transferred to the canvas. She looked out over the olive grove and the vineyards stretching beyond and let the natural surroundings affect her.

A long sigh escaped her lips as she took in the unfolding panorama. Her view swept across the unevenly spaced grove of olive trees with their silvery leaves to the orderly dark-green rows of vineyards. She imagined the bounteous clusters of grapes slowly flourishing on the vines.

The celebration of the olive and the vine . . . true Provence . . .

Beyond, the jagged, rocky mounds of the scrubland-covered *Alpilles* formed a dramatic backdrop. Avenues of tall cypress trees dotted the landscape, and she glimpsed, here and there, steep little roads leading to perched villages.

She thought of the proud words of Jean-Marc, her young driver from Avignon, when he spoke of his love for this region and how it embodied the "authentic" Provence. They were certainly getting a sense of the proud traditions of the area from their hosts.

Her mind frequently wandered to thoughts of van Gogh. Being in this environment made it easy to understand how he was so inspired to produce such a prolific volume of work. At the same time, the speed with which he must have worked was a cause for wonder.

She looked to the collection of vintage photos on one wall in her room that included this quotation from Frederic Mistral: "When the Good Lord begins to doubt the world, he remembers that he created Provence."

Bringing her thoughts back to her painting, she felt even more motivated. Mixing her paints, she worked with ultramarine blue and a lemon yellow to produce a dullish green. She had learned long before not to bother with green pigments but rather to mix others to create the color she wanted. Once she came close to the hue she sought, she began to experiment with a dash of violet to warm it up. Juliette had made the suggestion, and Arianna was pleased with the results.

Jacques de Villeneuve had also offered similar advice. "Sometimes you need to use your artistic license. Add different colors to express your vision, rather than simply replicating the norm."

This was not news to her. But she beat herself up a bit for having lost touch with such basics. Too much time had passed since she had been connected with her artistic side.

The hours blended into each other as Arianna was drawn into her work, oblivious to everything around her. She was excited to feel old familiar stirrings about painting. She had always loved the buttery consistency of oils—and the smell. She recalled arguing with friends about that when they disagreed and said oils didn't smell. There was some odor she found inexplicably pleasing that rose from her color palette.

She sat back and appraised what she had accomplished so far.

It's not close to being finished. But these paints are so forgiving. Because they dry slowly, I can take my time, correct mistakes, and plan my next move without rushing.

As she studied her canvas, it occurred to her that those might be good steps to follow as she moved forward with her life.

Arianna wandered downstairs at around eight that evening. Juliette had tapped on her door earlier to see if she would be down for dinner, and Arianna had replied she would find something for herself when she finally stopped painting.

All the doors were open to the terraces. The warm evening air floated through the rooms along with a hint of citronella. Maurice had explained when they had first arrived that Mirielle would set out her special concoction to ward mosquitoes off with great effectiveness.

She could hear Joan and John chatting on the terrace adjoining the kitchen, words and laughter mixing together.

"Hey!" John called out as Arianna came toward them. Then he said something that sounded like, "Hayadoin? Jeet?"

Arianna stared at him, not sure what to say.

Joan laughed, explaining, "He's talking Brooklynese! Y'know, how are you doing? Did you eat? Jeet?"

Arianna laughed. "I get it! Kinda like *The Sopranos*."

"Yeah," Joan replied, giving John a playful punch on the arm. "I think he's having a moment of homesickness."

"Beer will do it every time," John mumbled, looking psychedelic in a lime-green cotton shirt dotted with hula dancers.

"Have you seen any mosquitoes?" Arianna asked. "I noticed the scent of Mirielle's secret potion in the air. Oh . . . and nice shirt, John!"

John pirouetted around to show off his shirt. "No mosquitoes! Come and join us! We've got some ice-cold 1664 in the fridge. Want a beer?"

"That sounds good. I haven't had one since I arrived. That's a French beer . . . Kronenbourg, right? We carried it for a few customers at our restaurant." Looking around, she said, "It's quiet here tonight. Where is everyone?"

Joan explained that Juliette had excused herself to work on a canvas in her studio, since everyone was doing their own thing. "She floats in and out every so often and is apparently making good headway on her painting. You know how it is when your mind gets in gear!"

Arianna smiled.

"Maurice is out with friends. He drove Barbara and Bertie into Arles to do some walking tour they had read about, and they're having dinner in town. Cecilia took the bus to Avignon so she could write a blog post about that experience . . . said she'd be back around nine. Marti and Lisa went out for a romantic, candlelit dinner after revealing today's the anniversary of the day they met. Cool, huh?"

With a grin, Joan added, "Maurice insisted on calling a taxi for them so they could be truly on their own and not feel they had to chat to him or anyone else. He was *un vrai romantique*, Juliette teased him. Hey! How about that! I just parlayed Français!"

"Trays beans," John said. "I haven't quite mastered the language. So there you go, dear Arianna . . . all the news that's fit to print! Come join us and have one of these most-delicious-sandwiches-ever!"

Arianna was quick to agree. "For all the mouthwatering, fabulous food there is in France and the culinary delights available to us, aren't baguette sandwiches just the best? A simple, magic bread—never better anywhere else—with some ham becomes a taste sensation. Oh yes, I will definitely have one, thanks."

John went into the kitchen, and Joan got up to follow, rather quickly. "Excuse me, Arianna. Just thought of something. Be right back!"

The pale moonlight bathed the view from the terrace in a soft blue glow. Sitting by herself, Arianna felt pulled into the calm of it all. Her thoughts seemed to float out and dance among the olive trees as she considered how this course, this setting, and these moments were slowly bringing her peace.

She felt a familiar rub against her legs and reached down to give Maximus a scratch. He flopped down and rolled over for a tummy rub.

The quiet was broken as the Mitchells returned to the terrace with sandwiches and beer.

"It's a party!" John announced.

"So, Arianna Papadopoulos-Miller . . ." Joan began. "Oh, it is such fun to say your name out loud."

Arianna grinned. "My proud Greek father was so sad that the family name would disappear when I got married. I promised him I would keep it alive as best I could. He was so thrilled and touched that there's no way I could ever stop using it. And my kids have kept their last names like that even as adults."

Smiling back at her, the Mitchells asked Arianna to tell them about her childhood in Greece. "Now that we've started to travel—"

John laughed. "Yes! With our one trip so far . . ."

"But this is just the beginning, sweetie pie. You even said so!"

"I was teasing you. For sure, we'll take a trip every year, and Greece sounds like a good destination. But there are a lot of problems there now, right, Arianna?"

They talked about the economy and politics in that country right now. And, of course, about the migrant situation.

"Remember, though, I haven't been back for a very long time, so my memories are not today's realities. But, you know, talking with customers in our restaurant through the years, I still always felt it was a beautiful place to visit and that troubles could be avoided."

She told them briefly how a family rift had stopped their visits. "It's so ridiculous when I think of it now. Anyway, my daughter recently reconnected with extended family there, and I think she may visit them. I hope she does."

"Would you go back now too?" Joan asked.

"Seeing how I'm loving this trip so much, I just might. You never know. Recently I even have entertained thoughts about taking my eighty-five-year-old mother back with me. Barbara has been a good source of inspiration for that idea."

"She's amazing," John said. "And a great example of how age is just a number when you have your health. Fifty, sixty . . . eighty . . . just numbers!"

They talked about Greece some more, before the conversation segued into a focus on food. Arianna found she could talk about the restaurant and life before Ben's illness with much more ease than when she first arrived.

The Mitchells shared more of their history. They had three children, all married, and four grandchildren. They chatted about their children's various lives and professions.

"Though our older daughter and son had moved away for work, our youngest daughter and her family lived just a few blocks from us.

We were very close and saw them all the time. Those grandchildren are in college now. Amazing how time flies."

John's voice began to fill with emotion, and Joan got up and hugged him. "Here's where our story gets difficult," Joan continued, "and I'm going to skip the details. Nothing bad had ever happened to us. Even with our older daughter and son moving far away, we were happy for the lives they were building. But then, Debbie . . . our youngest daughter . . . had stage-4 ovarian cancer . . . and she passed very quickly."

"I'm so sorry," Arianna said softly.

Joan's sad smile showed her acknowledgment. "Then her husband remarried and started a new life. I mean, that's what happens, right? Married a nice lady with two younger children. But they lived in the same house as Debbie, and we just found it so difficult. That's when we started thinking about moving to Florida."

John joined in again. "At first we beat ourselves up, saying we were running away. And maybe, at first, we were."

"But we were close to retiring, and the more we thought about it, the more we convinced ourselves we were making choices for us. Not for our kids. Not for our jobs. But for us."

John said, "Yeah, it was like this big lightning bolt suddenly zapped us."

"I'm telling you, Arianna, within six months we'd moved. Retired, sold the house, got rid of tons of stuff, and . . ."

"Bada bing, bada boom!" John said. "There we were, moving to south Florida. Just like that!"

Joan chuckled. "We couldn't believe we had done it. We lived there for six months and looked around. We knew we wanted to be near Sarasota because they have such an active arts community. Then we found the perfect retirement development for us."

"You sound very happy," Arianna commented. "I love how you laugh so often. It's contagious! That's a gift."

"We lost our laughter for a while when we lost Debbie," Joan said as John gazed at the moonlit landscape. "We worked hard to get it back . . . mostly by reminding ourselves of all the good memories. We lost our Debbie and our life with her. We didn't want to lose ourselves and the rest of our life."

Arianna got up and hugged each of them. John said, "You know, the French are missing something important by not hugging. That felt good."

Joan and Arianna agreed as they settled back into their chairs.

There was a lot of talk about change and about seeing possibilities in life. "And at the same time, we're in touch with all of our kids and grandkids—thanks to the glories of the Internet. And they love to come to Florida. We couldn't be happier."

Arianna was absorbing all of this. She knew there were messages in this conversation that would stay with her.

"Yoo-hoo!" Cecilia appeared in the kitchen, followed by Maurice, Barbara, and Bertram. Juliette soon joined them, eager to hear about their adventures.

The time passed quickly, particularly after Marti and Lisa arrived home and related their splendid evening to the group.

"Never a dull moment with this crew," Arianna said as they wished each other good night. Maurice had reminded them of the early-morning departure for the Saturday market.

CHAPTER NINETEEN

On this calm, sunny morning, the sky was as impossibly blue and clear as before the clouds had assembled and the wild wind had blown through three days prior.

As the group climbed into the van, Juliette said, "I always feel it's as if the mistral was a crazed artist whose wild brushstrokes swept away the white clouds and gray haze to create this vibrant color."

Market day proved to be as Juliette and Maurice promised: big, boisterous, and beguiling. The parking lot was already full when they arrived, and people were disappearing into the depths of the market.

A forest of stalls stretched among the trees down both sides of the main thoroughfares of Boulevard des Lices and Boulevard Georges Clémenceau. Some were covered by brightly striped canopies or shaded by large multicolored umbrellas, while a few were uncovered. The atmosphere was a riot of color, smells, and sounds—and people! Even though the group arrived just after the market opened, there was already a crowd.

Before waving them off to explore, Juliette said, "Keep your cameras handy because this is a visual feast, *bien sûr*, but follow your nose. It will lead you to even more treasures! And watch your wallets. Pickpockets also love markets!"

Maurice added, "And watch for *les crottes de chien*—dog poop! That problem is getting better, but . . ." He grimaced apologetically.

Although they started out together, Arianna noticed that within minutes their group had dispersed. She had been to enough markets to know that the best approach was to go it alone. She relished this intimate experience.

Of course, there were the inevitable memories from home. Owning a restaurant had meant regular market visits in Toronto with Ben. But those vendors spoke English, and, after so many years, Arianna and Ben had known precisely which ones they needed to visit. There was little lingering, and most times they had split up, each with a list. Then they would meet at a small coffee bar on the edge of the market and watch the bustle.

Arianna realized that she was becoming more accepting about the return of memories as the days passed on this trip.

Familiar memories in unfamiliar places seem to be easier for me to work through. Just as I'm finding it easier talking to these new friends in my life. But this market is really going to make me think of Ben. How he would have loved it. I'm not going to let it be a negative.

She saw here how colorful Provençal fabrics—some already made into tablecloths, placemats, or napkins, some simply bolts of material—were stacked and hanging. Some vendors were selling goods from North Africa, including exotic spices and carvings in polished dark wood. Local soaps in all sizes and shades were exhibited in vibrant displays.

And, of course, lavender, even though it was not in season yet. The number of balms, salves, perfumes, condiments, as well as dried bunches and bottles of the pure essential oil was clear evidence of its versatile and popular use.

Arianna watched locals stopping to chat in the midst of the activity. Woven market baskets, panniers, were set down for a few moments as *bises* and greetings were exchanged. Laughter and banter floated above the busy scene, the language spoken so quickly it was impossible for her to pick out more than a few words.

She stood by the edge of an olive vendor's long counter for a few minutes, out of the way of the bodies milling around her. Staring off at nothing in particular, she was lost in contemplation and memories, reminded of words Faith had said when Arianna was packing for the trip. She couldn't recall now who her daughter was quoting . . . she chuckled thinking about all the books on positivity Faith slipped to her. But she did remember the sentiment.

"Step out of your comfort zone." "Become at ease with the unfamiliar and the unknown." I guess that's what I'm doing.

A voice interrupted her thoughts. "*Bonjour,* madame. *Vous désirez quelque-chose?* You like something? Here! *Goûtez!* Taste this, if you please!"

The grizzled face of the olive vendor smiled invitingly at her as he stretched an olivewood ladle toward her. A delectable-looking large green olive was stuck on a toothpick.

"Oh, *merci*, monsieur! Mmmm, *c'est delicieux!*"

She promptly purchased more of those olives, along with some smaller black ones sprinkled with rosemary and some green ones mixed with oil and walnuts.

The entire display was irresistible. The vendor proudly posed as she captured several photos, once again confounding herself.

I'm not a picture taker . . . or maybe I have to put that in the past tense now. It appears I am becoming one . . . .

The colorful, sizable ceramic bowls, each filled with a different selection of olives or tapenade, were too inviting to resist. Multiple shades of brown, green, golden, purple, red, and black olives sat in seasoned variations. Rustic clay jugs and glass flasks with olive oil, cider, or vinegar lined the top of the counter.

Images of still-life paintings filtered through her mind's eye. Inspiration was everywhere. Arianna could feel the artistic flame deep inside her growing stronger. She was coming alive.

Arianna was surprised as the vendor weighed each olive bag carefully, told her the price, and then added a few more olives to each bag. "*Un petit cadeau, ma beauté*—a little gift." As her visit to the market progressed, she saw that this was quite a common practice among the sellers, adding even more friendliness and camaraderie to the business at hand.

She chuckled to herself, observing as she strolled that some of the bonhomie might have been enhanced by the bottles of rosé or pastis next to a torn fresh baguette that could be seen on a table behind the main counter of many stalls. Sharing a glass or two with a neighbor or regular customer seemed to be the norm.

Dogs were also very much a part of the *marché*. There were few stalls where Arianna didn't see one sleeping under the counter or on a cushion conveniently placed to allow greetings from customers. Arianna noted some people who were obviously very familiar with offering them treats. As she had on many occasions, she wondered how French dogs were always so well behaved. Even those visiting the market with shoppers fell into that category.

And how do they get the dogs to follow so obediently without a leash?

Whiffs of organic perfume accompanied her through the market. *Juliette was so right about using our noses.*

Whether it was the sweet smell of lavender, local herbs, and freshly cut flowers or the pungent aromas of cheese, they were all irresistible in their own way. As she roamed past stall after stall, she became familiar with the particular scents of specialties of the area: Camargue salt, goat cheese, and *saucisson d'Arles*, bull-meat sausage.

Sausages of all sizes and shapes were displayed on stalls decorated with bulls' horns. The tufts of hair still attached to the horns were disconcerting initially. A few photos of those displays would be added to the file she was putting together for Faith. She could just hear Faith laughing at those.

More than once, she tucked herself safely out of the main walkway and quickly captured some drawings and notes in her journal. She thought if she never took another trip, she was taking home enough drawings and information to keep her painting forever.

But this trip is reminding me that travel must be part of my life going forward. Now I'm kicking myself for so many memories I've missed making with my family.

Arianna munched on small spring strawberries, sweeter than any she could recall eating before. Their irresistible perfume had insisted she buy them.

She needed to keep reminding herself she was there to observe, sample, and enjoy, and not to stock up. It was difficult to pass by the temptations of the rotisseries strung with golden-skinned chickens, as potatoes and onions cooked in the drippings below. The air was thick with a smell of such roasted goodness that Arianna thought it should be bottled.

And the cheese displays! For those who didn't know a good deal about cheese, it would be worthwhile to bring a guide along. It was not a simple matter of choosing a cheddar or a Brie or a goat cheese. Taste, texture, smell—goat, cow, sheep—there was so much to take into account. She considered herself a fairly sophisticated cheese connoisseur, but one look at the choices these *fromagers* presented had altered that thinking.

As she continued to wander, Arianna found herself considering just how much her thinking had been expanded in many more ways than cheese. In just short of a week, through the kindness of strangers, she was learning to open herself to life again, to laugh, and to be excited about art.

It was all much more than she had expected. Now she had to convince herself that she could take all of that back home with her and keep the momentum going. She thought about the myriad art galleries in Toronto she could spend untold days visiting. She would get involved in the Art Gallery of Ontario volunteer program again.

Maybe even rent some small studio space in one of the many art collectives I've read about . . .

As she continued her musing, she dreamily noticed a most commanding aroma floating from shallow paella pans bubbling away on gas cookers that drew long lines of patient customers. Arianna stopped to breathe in the tempting combination of herbs, then suddenly felt a hand on her elbow, and her focus snapped back to the present.

CHAPTER TWENTY

"What do you say? Should we cave and get some?" She turned to see the Mitchells. They debated the question for just a moment. "Those lines kill the idea for me," Joan said, pointing to the crowd queuing in front of the paella pans, "but we just passed the most amazing *pâtisserie* stand. Let's go get something there and have a coffee over by the carousel. Are you ready for a break, Arianna?"

Arianna readily agreed. Checking her watch, she was amazed to see she had been there for over two hours. "I've sampled so much already, I'm not sure I can eat another crumb of anything, but a coffee sounds good."

"I know, us too!" Joan agreed. "It's a fantastic market, isn't it? But I can still do with something sweet . . . No problem there!"

John put his hand on Arianna's shoulder, and his expression turned serious. "Remember my philosophy about ice cream? Well that works for sweets too. There's that separate compartment!"

Laughing, they stopped at the stall Joan had mentioned. The array of pastries, cakes, and other assorted enticements was artfully arranged. Arianna could not resist the rows of macarons in every shade of the color spectrum.

"I'm going to take some of those back to the *mas* for everyone," she announced. The vendor patiently placed her choices in a shallow box.

Then he wrapped the box as carefully as a special gift. He took time to complete his task by tying a bright ribbon into a bow.

Arianna, Joan, and John watched with delight and all three uttered their thanks at his thoughtfulness. The vendor grinned, saying a cordial, *"Pas du tout."*

Using hand signs and hilarious facial expressions, John assured him his purchase didn't need to be wrapped, as it was going to be eaten immediately. Two slices of charlotte *aux fraises* were each placed in plastic containers. Joan had extracted a promise from Arianna that she'd share with them. Heaps of fresh strawberries topped creamy vanilla custard, all supported by sweet, spongy ladyfingers, making a rich, fragile treat.

They quickly walked through an extensive seafood section, giving each other eye rolls as they held their breath. Soon they found a table that was being vacated and congratulated themselves on their good timing.

After ordering coffee, they chatted about their morning experience as the town carousel whirled gaily behind them. The music was old-fashioned and repetitive, but they found it amusing rather than annoying.

The line of children snaked all the way around the square. They giggled and jostled each other as they waited for their turns.

"At least the kids have a good, long ride once they get on," Joan observed, laughing at their antics. "They're so cute . . . and they all speak such perfect French!"

"Trust Arles to have a black bull as one of the animals to ride on." John chuckled. "It's a true Camargue carousel."

Within minutes, Bertram and Barbara spilled out of the market crowd and came to join their friends, pulling over a couple more chairs and placing a box of cherries on the table.

"I say!" Bertram exclaimed. "I've been through a lot of superb markets, but this is a real winner! What an outstanding assortment of products. And that cheese vendor by the memorial statue . . . best pastis I've tasted in years!"

"Bertie!" John said as he gave him a hearty pat on the back, "you even managed to have a snort at the market?"

Bertram chuckled and said he was sure the drink was offered because he had purchased a rather large round of Brie from the man. He put his bag on the table and lifted the hefty package out to show them.

"I thought we would enjoy it later. And Barbara bought these cherries, which will go very nicely together. No collaboration either! We just bumped into each other now. How about that?"

"Did we lose Cecilia?" Arianna asked.

"Oh, she was as happy as can be when I bumped into her a while back, taking notes, dictating, and photographing. That girl knows how to multitask!" Barbara said. "She said she would find her way home later."

John walked over to a stall and begged two more plastic forks.

As they were poised to pass the sweet pastry around, Bertram held up his hand and, with a serious expression, intoned, "Wait! Before we delve into the deliciousness of this, let us first admire its pulchritude. Is it not a work of art? Are we not here to study art? It behooves us to express some thoughts, perhaps, about the color, the texture, the contrasts . . ."

Acknowledging the wide grins around the table, John said, "Bertie, I believe it behooves us to eat this work of art immediately. Barbara, please lead the way. *Bon appétit!*"

"*Avec plaisir,* monsieur," Barbara replied as she sampled a dainty amount.

The others followed as Bertram continued to share his observations about the vibrant red and perfect shape of the strawberries, the delicate creamy sheen of the vanilla custard, and the fragile texture of the ladyfingers.

"Is that you or the pastis talking?" Joan teased him. "You better start eating before we finish it."

They all shared the charlotte, smiles and murmurs of scrumptiousness accompanying each bite.

Sitting contentedly after they'd polished off the dessert, Arianna checked to make certain no one would be offended before she took her journal from her handbag.

They all laughed. "That's one question you never need to ask this group! You should know that by now."

"I can't believe the number of photos I took this morning! It's such a new thing for me . . . and so easy with these phones! I managed to squeeze in a few pages in here too, and now I want to get this view."

She turned her attention to the carousel and the bustling market scene in the background.

"Good idea," Barbara said as she did the same. "Arianna, you seem to have broken through your artistic block. I'm happy for you."

The others offered words of agreement. Everyone had noticed.

Smiling, Arianna conceded she must be making headway. "Most importantly, I feel eager to be painting. I'm feeling the spark again." She continued to sketch.

Joan and John were looking through their photos, most followed by murmurs of approval and the occasional burst of raucous laughter.

"Joanie has the best—but occasionally extremely weird—eye!" John explained.

Contentedly, Bertram took in the scene as he sipped on another pastis. "I should go buy some more cheese. That bloke's pastis was better!"

All of a sudden, all their cell phones beeped. Maurice had texted to see where everyone was. He was waiting at the drop-off spot for those who wanted a ride now—or offered to return again later.

They looked at each other, and then Arianna said, "Bertram, would you be interested in taking us to the museum to see the Roman boat?"

Bertram looked surprised and pleased. He nodded enthusiastically as everyone else agreed it was a fine idea, then they texted the others to let them know what was up.

Maurice replied he would swing around the back street behind the carousel and collect their market goodies so they could get rid of their packages. John negotiated a beat-up empty box from one of the nearby produce vendors, and they all carefully placed their purchases in it.

"Look! The tourist office is right here," Bertram said as they waited for Maurice to pick up the box. "Unless things have changed since the last time I was here, there's a little *navette* . . . erm . . . a tourist bus that can take us to the museum. I'll pop in and check the schedule. Back in a tick!"

John scratched his head and chuckled. "In a tick? That Bertie is so darn British, isn't he?"

Money was left on the table for the coffee. Arianna commented how she liked the way the waiters left the bill every time they brought an order. "You never have to wait to pay. It works for everyone!"

The tourist bus pulled up at the stop right behind Maurice and beeped for him to get going. Free of their purchases, they quickly dashed to catch it. Marti, Lisa, and Cecilia met them at the museum.

Bertram relished his role as guide. Arianna noted how genuinely pleased he was to share his knowledge and to see their interest. His involvement in this project had been a highlight of his life, he reminded them, as he led them all in to sit and watch the impressive video.

There's more to him than I first assumed. I know better than to make assumptions.

Somehow she had lost that attitude, along with a lot of others once important to her, in the recent past.

After the movie, Bertram ushered them to the display area with a grand flourish. Everyone stood spellbound.

The wooden boat, complete with mast, oars, and some tools, was exhibited in a bright, airy space that had been specially created. The openness and the lighting were perfectly planned and offered a breathtaking sense of history. The surrounding display of artifacts—recovered amphorae, jugs of all sizes, and other objects as old as the boat or older—were considered trash by the Ancient Romans, which they had tossed into the river for centuries.

They all agreed with Marti when she said, "This is a tale about which the city of Arles and everyone who worked on the project has every right to be proud."

Bertram beamed.

"It truly takes your breath away." Arianna sighed to no one in particular as she wandered from one exhibit to another in the spacious, modern building. "The visitor is transported back in time. The entire museum is a work of art."

Bertram caught up with Arianna as she approached the other highlight of the museum.

"Here he is, Arianna. Meet Gaius Julius Caesar. Amongst other things he was a Roman general, an author of Latin prose, and a man who influenced my life. Quite a guy!"

"I'll say," Arianna agreed. "I can't get over how well preserved the features are."

"I would suggest he had the best mudpack facial ever"—he chuckled—"buried in the muddy Rhône for two thousand years or thereabouts. The best guess is that, after he was assassinated, this bust was tossed in the river. As I told you all before, when it was found, visitors flocked to view it from all over the world, and enough money was raised to make the boat project happen."

"What a great story . . . and a fantastic outcome. Hail Caesar!"

Bertram smiled broadly, and Arianna thought he might actually get teary-eyed. "Hail Caesar, indeed. I know I told you that working on this project was what I'm most proud of in my life. Most of my time has been spent in laboratories and libraries doing research. This was my first opportunity in decades to truly apply what I had studied. Caesar kind of changed my life too. I'll tell you about that some other time."

Arianna wondered at his last comment. She made a mental note to follow up.

Then they all spread out around the museum with sketch pads, notebooks, and cameras. There was work to be done.

Later they gathered in the main entrance area.

A consensus was reached to catch the *navette* back to the tourist office and go to a bar for a drink. Dinner plans might follow. But Barbara and Arianna both decided to call it a night.

"It's been a great day," said Arianna by way of explanation. "In fact, my mind is going a mile a minute, and I want to get back to painting."

Barbara smiled at her. "Do you want to walk back, Arianna? I would love to do that, and it won't take us much longer than if we wait for Maurice, right?"

CHAPTER
TWENTY-ONE

"I'm glad you chose to walk back with me," Barbara said as they wandered along one of the many cobblestone streets that led out of town. "We haven't had a chance to really chat on our own."

"I agree! This was a good idea," Arianna said. "I've enjoyed the time I've spent with Cecilia. She's so bubbly and full of life. Such a positive spirit! I love the fact that the two of you are traveling together."

Barbara's eyes twinkled with delight.

"Fortunately for both of us," she said, "her husband is completely supportive. They also have a nanny who is Mrs. Doubtfire reincarnated, so my three little great-grandchildren are well looked after. Being away for this extended period is most unusual. She's never taken so much time away before. But this trip was special, and we couldn't pass it up! We figured we might never have the chance to do it again."

"You were right to do it, because you just never know what life has in store around the corner. Sorry! I didn't mean to sound so negative . . ." Arianna's voice trailed off.

Barbara took Arianna's hand in hers for a moment. "I know what you mean, and it's not negative. It's simply life. Grab opportunities when they present themselves! I have a friend who calls that being a possibilitarian. Great word, isn't it? We should all be that!"

Sadness clouded Arianna's face suddenly. "I wish I could, Barbara. I'm working on it, and I'll take that word to heart."

Taking in their surroundings, Barbara changed the subject. She was hoping to lift Arianna up on this stroll, not drag her down. She remarked on the ancient doors of the medieval residences they were passing. "This was obviously a poorer part of town back in the day, but not anymore! These cramped *allées* stir my heart! Do they yours? Cecilia and I have walked through such history these past few weeks, but I never tire of it."

Arianna agreed, sounding enthusiastic again. "I've even been taking photos of buildings, shutters, and, yes, those doors . . . It's something I've never done before. The urge to sketch them is growing, especially those fascinating keyholes!"

"That's splendid news! I know you were searching for your muse."

The two women locked gazes, transferring an understanding of shared experience. Barbara said quietly, "I've been there, my dear, not for the same reason, but I understand the struggle."

"It has taken me most of this week to break through," Arianna admitted. "I feel so fortunate that I ended up here with our little group in these inspiring surroundings. I had done a good job of denying how tightly I was locked inside myself."

Barbara's voice was almost a whisper. "It can happen so easily . . . to any of us . . ."

They walked quietly for a moment, neither quite ready to pursue that thought. Arianna sensed Barbara had something important to share with her. Something not easily expressed . . . something that might match Arianna's own despair.

The only sign of activity on the street was a small dog briskly pattering along, focused on his path. Both women followed it with their eyes. Arianna thought it a welcome distraction just then.

"I'm always fascinated by how dogs in Europe seem to be such a part of life in small towns . . . citizens in their own right," Barbara remarked. "We had such laughs watching them in the local piazze and *campi* in Venice. I find it so pleasing somehow."

"It reminds me of growing up in Greece," Arianna said with a chuckle. "We knew all the village dogs—and cats—and you are right. They are part of everyday life. Everyone knows them."

"How long did you live there? What are your memories? Do you ever go back?"

Arianna was content to revisit those thoughts, sharing stories as they strolled. "It's interesting, though," she concluded. "I thought being in the French countryside might remind me of Greece, but it doesn't. And I'm pleased to be having a completely new experience. It's what I need."

The peacefulness of the street captured their thoughts again, and they walked without speaking for a while.

"I thrive on being surrounded by this charm and antiquity," Barbara murmured, seemingly hesitant to break the spell of their surroundings. "My only regret in life is that I didn't travel like this sooner. It's a lesson learned that I try to pass on to the younger people in my life. Just because your spouse, partner, whatever that person is called in these times, doesn't wish to travel—don't sacrifice your dreams like I did. I wish life had offered me more opportunities to paint scenes like this."

Arianna smiled at her, nodding in agreement. "Is there something specific that calls to you, when you consider what you want to capture in your art here?"

"My passion is painting detailed scenes as opposed to focusing on a single element." She stopped and gestured at the cobblestone lane. "I want to recreate the ambiance of this timeworn street, the buildings, the shutters, the rooftops—the entire milieu—and bring the viewer into it. I want them to hear the sounds, smell the scents in the air, feel the surroundings, as well as see the beauty."

Then she laughed, a bright and cheerful sound that floated in the air. "Um, do you think I'm asking a bit much here?"

Arianna returned the laughter. "That was quite a wish list."

They continued to share observations as the street led them to a narrow path through some trees. Suddenly they were on the same trail that Arianna had walked earlier in the week.

"Here we are," she said, relieved. "It's an easy stroll to the *mas* now. I was a bit nervous that I was taking you the wrong way. There are so many of these little streets, it can get confusing."

Barbara laughed. "You know, I never worry about getting lost. Ceci and I refer to it as 'having an adventure.' Somehow it's always possible to find your way, even if you have to ask and make endless U-turns."

"That's a fine attitude, Barbara. Tell me more about your travels together."

"Well, we've gone on trips together since Ceci was a tyke. At first, she would simply spend occasional weekends with my husband and me. Then, from the time she was six, we began taking small excursions together, just the two of us. She loved her grampy, but he wasn't the traveling type."

"Barbara, you just caused me to remember the many happy hours our two grandchildren spent at our restaurant. We didn't travel with them but took them on little journeys of imagination within the walls of Papa's on the Danforth, our Greek restaurant." She was thankful for those memories now and surprised that she was sharing them happily.

"There you go," Barbara replied. "We've each built special memories with our grandchildren. That's what's important."

"It sounds like they lived close by."

"My daughter and her husband live in Vancouver, not far from us. Ceci and I would drive or take the train to a nearby town like Steveston or White Rock. When she was older we would take the ferry over to Vancouver Island and visit Victoria, Nanaimo, and places along the coast. We even went to Tofino once and hiked in the rain forest. There are beaches that go on forever, begging to be explored.

"Then, as Ceci got into high school, we went farther afield. I took her to Paris when she graduated. She tells me that all those childhood trips are the reason she chose to go into travel writing as a career."

"Wow! That's very cool!"

Barbara chuckled and grinned broadly before she continued. "Once Ceci married, she and her husband moved to Calgary. Even so, once a year we would still plan a getaway. Usually a long weekend, but once in a while she took me along on a weeklong cruise or an organized trip through her work. Her husband didn't go on all of those trips with her after they had children. He's such a great dad and partner!"

Arianna smiled at the proud expression on Barbara's face. "That's a wonderful story, Barbara. You're giving me good ideas. Since we no longer have the restaurant, perhaps I can plan some little trips with our grandchildren."

"Perhaps you can . . . and, trust me, you will love it and so will those little darlings."

Arianna asked, "Did your husband go with you on any of those trips?"

"No, he didn't. He loved Cecilia dearly but didn't have the patience for our adventures." She paused before adding, "Then, in his later years, he became an alcoholic."

Arianna felt awkward. Searching for the right words, her eyes met Barbara's with compassion. She said softly, "Oh, Barbara, I'm sorry . . . I . . . I don't quite know what to say. That must have been difficult to live with."

Nothing could have prepared Arianna for Barbara's matter-of-fact response. "It had its moments. But he's been dead just over a year now . . . and I have to tell you that it's a relief, for all of us. To be honest, this trip is a celebration of that."

Arianna's face registered shock.

Barbara's expression showed no sign of embarrassment or anger, although there was a hint of chagrin in her voice. "My dear, when you get to be my age, one of the most important lessons you learn is that each of us has a story. Though, up until ten years ago, my life was fairly normal, if not exactly what I wished for."

"I've learned more than once that life can change dramatically," Arianna said, "and I'm still coping with that. I'd like to hear your story."

They had reached a small area where the trail had been cleared and a bench installed. "Just what we need!" Barbara exclaimed. "The French always seem to give thought to their elderly citizens. I'm going to assume that's why this rest spot is here."

She sat on the bench, patting the spot beside her. "Here. Join me. And I promise not to blather on. I just want you to understand why I said what I did. Some people do not."

They sat in the quiet of a narrow field bordered by stately cypress trees on one side and a thick forest on the other. The backdrop of the ancient town was no longer visible. The sweet-smelling air was filled with the daily chorus from cicadas.

Barbara let out a long sigh and reached down to rub her calves. Arianna worried that going on this walk together might not have been a good idea. Her worry was quickly allayed.

"Walking is something that has been a constant in my life, and I credit it with keeping me going. Somehow I've managed to avoid arthritis and other afflictions, and I'm thankful for that every single day! I can deal with minor cramps. It's good to have a chance to sit for a few minutes, though."

Arianna agreed and told her that she walked every day now too. "It helps to sort things out in my mind. It's not just exercise for the body but for the soul as well."

Barbara patted Arianna's hand. "Ceci told me about the difficult time you've had recently. She said you told her it was fine to share that information with me."

"Yes. It was a surprising relief for me to spill my story to Marti and Lisa the other evening. It all just came tumbling out. Ceci got the short version when she met us for ice cream later."

"It sounds like you've been carrying quite a load on your shoulders. I'm glad to hear you're feeling relieved about releasing it. I learned that lesson a long time ago."

Barbara explained how she had loved being a high school art teacher. "For all the negative comments we so frequently hear about teenagers, working with my students gave me hope for the future. I loved those kids . . . and I tried my best with the few bad apples. Kids are growing up in such a different world than my generation, and even yours." She continued, her voice now wistful. "Then I retired when I was sixty-five and was excited about what would happen next with my life."

"We were looking forward to that too," Arianna whispered.

"I can imagine you were. It was fun to have time to do whatever I wanted, and that's how I approached life. I figured my husband would have the same attitude. Not so, unfortunately! He retired three years later and immediately went into a deep depression that affected both of our lives dramatically."

"I've known a few people who have struggled with that situation," Arianna said. "Loss of identity and not knowing what the future holds . . . I've had a bit of that myself in the last two years."

"I can imagine. It's not unusual . . . and it's a perfectly natural reaction to such an enormous change in your life. But I believe it's vital to look beyond that and explore all the possibilities that are open to us. Don't be retired. Be rewired! That's my motto!"

Barbara paused, and Arianna saw an expression of frustration and sadness briefly flicker in her eyes.

"I tried to interest my husband in all sorts of projects, both for us to do together or for him to do on his own. He rejected them all. George decided he needed stiff shots of vodka to help him cope, and that grew into a problem he could not handle. Although, he did not see it that way."

They sat without a word for a moment. Arianna was briefly thankful that she and Ben had never gone through anything like that.

Barbara continued, "To be honest, the last few years of our life together almost ruined the fifty that we had shared before. George turned into someone I did not know. Someone I did not care to know. I felt like a prisoner, and yet I couldn't bring myself to leave him after all those years. I did my best to keep the problems away from our daughter and her family, but Allison twigged pretty quickly. She would encourage me to go live with them or at least move out on my own. But at the same time, she felt badly for her dad. It was a messy situation."

Arianna searched for the right words, but none came. She could only look at her friend and shake her head in sympathy.

Barbara let out a long sigh and looked off into the distance. "So I stayed. I had a busy life with girlfriends, as George increasingly refused to socialize. I had my once-a-year little adventure with Cecilia. I volunteered. I painted. I worked very hard at seeing the positives and spent as little time at home as I could manage. But almost every time I walked into our house, I walked into a well of negativity, criticism, and complaints."

"Oh, Barbara, that's awful. No one deserves that. It must have been hard to stay. I can't imagine living with that," Arianna sympathized.

"Honestly, I regret that I stayed. I missed out on a lot of dreams during the past ten years. And I experienced many painful and sad moments with George. Experiences I did not deserve—hurtful, mean words hurled at me for no reason or perceived slights. And I took it. All because I could not convince myself to let go of what used to be."

"I get that," Arianna said. "Leaving must be the most difficult of all decisions."

Barbara's eyes clouded over. "Yes, but I think it's even worse to allow yourself to be robbed of the life you desire. When you get to be my age, those ten years can be crucial in still having the energy and ability to follow dreams. My loss began long before George passed away. I lost the partner I once loved. I lost the marriage I once loved. I mourned all of that for years before there was a true death to mourn."

"What happened to George?"

"He developed health problems—mostly heart related—and, of course, he didn't exercise at all. He spent a lot of time on his computer or reading or sleeping on the couch. Then he would begin his midaft-ernoon cocktail hour and drink himself to sleep, often becoming very unpleasant in the process. Then last year he died of a massive heart attack. On the couch. With a vodka on the rocks at his fingertips."

"What a shock that must have been," Arianna said, her tone sorrowful.

"Yes. It was a shock. But do you know, I felt very little sadness. I felt more relief than anything. For him as much as for me. He had spent many years being a most unhappy man, and there had been nothing I could do to help him. Even though I was married, I really was living alone. At times I felt like a prisoner. And that's not a nice way to live. Now I have my freedom back, and I'm very happy. Does that make me sound selfish?"

"Not at all. I just never thought of getting old in terms like that. Listening to you, I am sure you are not alone in that experience."

Sad agreement registered on Barbara's face. "The truth of the matter is that I know more older women than I care to admit who are living their senior years with this kind of unhappiness. We women have to remember to take care of ourselves at every age and not feel we always have to take care of everyone else. Let's face it, many women get caught up in that at some point."

Arianna nodded thoughtfully, recognizing herself in those words.

Barbara stood up, stretched, and sat back down, obviously not fin-ished. "Let me just share this with you, Arianna. I feel I had a thorough lesson in dealing with grief. Perhaps just not in the way most people think of it. If nothing else, I believe it's important to pass that lesson on to others."

Arianna replied, "I've done a lot of reading about the different types of grief recently. I recognize I've been fighting grief for a while. It's hard. Complicated. I haven't sorted through it. I think I keep feeling it's not time yet for me to move on with my life, because Ben is still alive. I grew up thinking grief is what comes after a person dies."

"That's the misconception," Barbara said. "The most important thing I learned about grief is that none of us can even begin to comprehend it until it happens to us. And then, it hits every person differently. And—this is something I didn't grasp until later—grief doesn't just visit us when someone dies. I think you have probably been trying to cope while being in the clutches of grief all along."

Tears welled up as Arianna nodded. She swallowed, blinked, and willed them away. She was tired of crying.

Slipping her arm through Arianna's, Barbara gently held her hand. "Life can be so cruel at times. What has happened to Ben and to your family's time together is tragic. But it didn't erase the love and the life that you built and shared. The positive memories will last. It's vital to hold that close to you. We often try to push grief away from us. Sometimes we need to accept it sooner than anticipated and work through it."

Silence hung in the air. Both women contemplated the truth of that last thought.

Barbara continued, "I read somewhere that there's a juxtaposition between grief and serenity, between heartache and relief. Really, we need to embrace grief and ride it out until we see through the sadness to the laughter and beauty in life again."

"My kids even tell me I'm not being realistic at times," Arianna confessed. "I know Ben will never be home again, and yet I can't bring myself to give away his clothes. They don't even fit him now. They tell me—in the kindest way—that I'm living in a bubble. And I know I am. I simply haven't been able to move away from where my life is now."

"Yes. That's normal. But look, Arianna, you are here. In France. You've taken a step forward. A big step. Surrounded by this pastoral beauty and history and visuals that must make your heart sing—if you will let it. I hope you will."

She squeezed Arianna's hand lightly, and they both stood up. Arianna reached out to hug this wise woman who had taken the time to revisit her heartache and share what she had learned.

As they embraced, Arianna said, "I can't begin to thank you for all you've shared. I'm sorry for your loss and the hurt you had to endure . . . and I'm so happy you are here on this course. I certainly lucked out with this group!"

Her face glowed as Barbara closed her eyes and breathed in the aromatic air. "I think several of us are feeling that. Life moves in mysterious ways and brings us opportunities when we least expect it."

Bending down, Arianna grabbed a handful of the greens bordering the path. She rubbed them together and held them to her nose and then to Barbara. "Breathe this in! How good is that? We were taking in these scents the other day as we walked this trail."

As the women drew closer to the *mas*, they watched something moving purposefully toward them on the path and then laughed as they recognized Maximus. "This cat has a special wise soul of his own, don't you think?" Barbara asked.

Arianna smiled in agreement.

CHAPTER TWENTY-TWO

Arianna opened her shutters early Sunday morning to see the day had dawned in typical Provençal splendor.

She felt refreshed and primed for the adventure they had planned.

In meditation before her shower, her thoughts took her to a place she had not been for a long time.

In the stillness of her mind, she focused on letting go of the tension she knew had tethered her emotions. She pictured her heart opening and taking in warmth, love, and hope. She had lived with those feelings for most of her life. The familiarity felt good, although it was coupled with regret for its absence.

The wisdom of her new friends' words about crisis and grief were magnified in her thoughts.

Looking out the window over the view that was becoming so pleasingly familiar, Arianna fixed her gaze on the horizon.

Yes, I was stripped of everything that I thought was important to me: our family unit, the routine of our life, our restaurant, our security, our dreams—my husband! Those I will never get back. I've been grieving those parts of my life. But there are things I thought were gone that now I can see I will recover: love, laughter, different dreams, a new family dynamic, plans for the future . . . I needed to step away from where I was to catch a glimpse of this.

What she was learning from the rest of this group was an unanticipated bonus, added to the inspiring effect of living in the heart of this splendid countryside. The visuals constantly filled her heart. Walking the timeworn pathways and strolling the ancient winding streets had not ceased to thrill her. And to finally feel that all of this had stirred her creative desires again, to see the proof of that in her art and feel it in her hands, her heart, and her thoughts.

I know I only see how that applies to one day at a time at the moment. But that's something I couldn't do before I came here. My only focus was Ben. Now I am looking at my own desires each day, even though it's not without twinges of guilt. It feels good to laugh so freely and to look forward to doing what I want to do. Somehow I still don't see past my life with Ben. But I am learning that I will . . . and that's an enormous step.

She sat in the window seat and composed an e-mail to her family. Until then, she had sent only brief messages and photos about her surroundings, the food, and the people she was with.

Faith, Tad, and Christine had all responded with humor, teasing her about taking so many pictures.

Now, she was able to begin to express what had just filled her thoughts, and she knew they would be pleased.

The plans for Sunday's excursions divided them into two separate groups.

Arianna, Barbara, Cecilia, and Bertram were expected at Jacques de Villeneuve's *cabane* at ten a.m. He had sent them clear directions to the ranch where he lived and worked as a *gardian*. Per Jacques's instructions to Juliette, they were all wearing jeans or slacks. And they were eager to get going.

"In case anyone has forgotten in your obvious excitement," Juliette added with a chuckle, "you are artists first on this trip and tourists second. Don't forget your sketching materials, colors, and whatever else you need for recording."

They were taking Juliette's car, and to everyone's surprise, Bertram insisted on driving.

"I've spent my life navigating the hedgerow-lined lanes of the English countryside!" he said, looking very pleased with himself. "Nothing I've seen here so far compares to that!"

Marti, Lisa, John, Joan, and Maurice were headed to the west side of the Camargue in search of special seafood.

"I know some secret spots that you would never find otherwise," Maurice assured them. "And I never pass up an opportunity to go there. We'll head to Le Grau-du-Roi and then Sète and then simply play it by ear. If my friend Bruno is around, you may get to eat the most delicious fresh fish of your life. He doesn't have a phone, so we will have to take our chances. *Allons-y, mes amis!*"

"*Eh bien!*" Juliette laughed. "We have the nature lovers in one group and the foodies in the other! What tales you will have to share tonight when you get back! *Bon voyage!*"

With a hearty "*Au revoir!*" the foodies set off.

Before they left, Cecilia and Arianna quietly expressed some concern to Barbara about whether Bertram would drink too much during their expedition.

"Absolutely not!" Barbara said rather indignantly. "I have no fear of that. I believe he is an honorable man—and I've formed an opinion about his drinking, which I will share with you at another time. Besides, we have three other competent drivers here, if need be!"

❦

A short while after the group left Arles, the scenery changed abruptly. The road cut through agricultural flatlands where rice paddies, small vineyards, fruit orchards, and fields of wheat and rapeseed were farmed.

"There's no obvious way through this area if you get off the main road," said Cecilia, reading from her guidebook. "A maze of marshes, canals, and back roads that go who knows where."

"Thank goodness for Jacques's directions," Barbara said.

Bertram commented on the landscape as he chauffeured them, expressing how it "metamorphosed from the bucolic, rich countryside of Provence that we love to this flat, marshy environment that demands a whole different mind-set."

Roadside stands displayed local salt and *riz de Camargue*, a nutty red rice grown in neighboring paddies. They had passed a few signs for horseback riding when suddenly Bertram slowed down and turned into a parking area next to a wooden viewing platform. "By Jove! There you go, mesdames, the feral horses of the Camargue."

He had spotted a small herd of the white horses standing among tall reeds, their heads and shoulders just visible. The group noticed there were some that appeared younger, dark in color, and Cecilia told them she had read that's how they are born. "They gradually become white after three of four years."

Bright, alert eyes stared back at them from the broad, handsome faces.

"Shhh!" Bertram reminded them. "Let's not startle them." Everyone excitedly whispered about their beauty and took photos. Then they urged Bertram to get going.

"I can't wait to get close to some of those horses," Cecilia squealed, back in the car and barely concealing her excitement.

"Are we all game for a horseback ride?" Bertram asked.

With some initial reservations from Barbara and Arianna, they all finally agreed. Bertram told them how he had grown up riding and how much he was looking forward to this experience.

"These Camargue horses are a breed unto themselves, you know. They're seldom stabled and roam as freely through their surroundings as the limitations of modern changes allow. Their solid bodies and hooves are uniquely suited to the unusual conditions here, and their history goes back forever. Bones of their ancestors from the Paleolithic period, seventeen thousand years ago, have been found here."

Cecilia looked up more information about the horses and shared it as they drove.

Just over an hour from Arles, as instructed by Jacques, they turned onto a long dirt lane. There were more trees now, and great stretches of marshes disappeared into a large body of water.

"That's the biggest saltwater lagoon in the Camargue, the Étang de Vaccarès," Cecilia read. "I'm excited to see the masses of pink flamingos that are around here!"

They all concurred. Cecilia texted Jacques to let him know they were almost at the *manade*, the ranch where he lived and worked.

After one more left turn, the sandy driveway led them to a large ranch house. A wooden sign had the name, *"Manade de Saint-Dominique,"* burnt into it, and a broad set of bull horns sat atop it. A large iron sculpture stood beside the sign.

"I've noticed the symbol of that sculpture a few times now. I'm sure we will discover what it means," Arianna observed. It bore a resemblance to an anchor, with three prongs at the top followed by a heart on a center support that ended in a curve.

"Oh, look," Barbara pointed out, "there's a smaller one on the chimney of the house and another on the wall of that tractor barn. Let's remember to ask about it."

A little farther along, in a wide field bordered by towering reeds, they could see in the distance a small stucco structure with an unusual-looking roof and a rider on horseback approaching them from it.

The image startled Arianna. She had seen these dwellings in van Gogh's painting *Trois cabanes blanches aux Saintes-Maries*. It was like seeing the portrayal of this unfamiliar landscape come to life. She felt a long-forgotten twinge of excitement at what adventures might be ahead of them today.

CHAPTER
TWENTY-THREE

"*Bienvenue,*" Jacques called as his horse stopped next to the car, and he quickly dismounted.

He was again dressed in the traditional attire of a *gardian*, wearing black moleskin pants, a red paisley shirt, a black vest, and round-toed leather boots. In greeting, he put his fingers to a wide-brimmed hat just like the one he had worn to the *mas*. "Welcome! I'm so pleased you were able to come."

He had ridden bareback on a sturdy white Camargue horse, like those they had admired by the side of the road. With a low whistle and a flick of his hand, he showed he had clearly trained his steed well. The horse turned and galloped off.

"And now let me take you into my world," Jacques said. "Come and meet the madame of this *manade*." The visitors expressed excitement at being there and eagerly agreed to Jacques's suggestion.

He led the way into the ranch house, after a light rap on the massive wooden door, adorned by a majestic set of bull's horns. They would later learn this represented good luck.

The house's exterior of simple white stucco and red-tile roof did not prepare them for what was inside. They immediately felt transported as they entered a bright, spacious living area that seemed more like a Texas ranch than a home in France.

Aged, unpainted wooden posts and beams supported the ceilings, crammed bookcases of the same wood covered one wall, and a gallery-like display of photography and posters of bulls, horses, and *gardians* filled the others. Leather chairs and couches, with a mix of side tables crafted of iron, invited one to sit and absorb the ambiance. Whitewashed walls and wood plank floors added to the rustic country charm. Sunlight poured in through a series of windows that looked out over the porch at the front of the house.

A petite woman, her silvery-gray hair tied back in a long braid, greeted Jacques with an affectionate *bise*. She murmured a few words to him before he turned to the visitors and said, "It's my pleasure to introduce you to Madame LeClerc, who is eager to invite you to enjoy her family's *manade*. She asked me to apologize to you for not speaking English better. That's her opinion, though; I believe she does very well."

Her warm smile caused them to feel welcome instantly. Madame LeClerc spoke English haltingly with a charming accent. She gave a brief history of their ranch going back to the late 1700s, her pride evident.

She led them along the gallery pointing out family and important events—first in paintings and sketches, and then in photography. She indicated several pictures of her husband, explaining that he was currently out working the land, accompanied by their daughter.

"We are proud that our daughter had a passion to become a *gardian*—or *gardianne*, if you prefer. We normally don't bother with the latter in these days. *Oui*, Jacques?"

He nodded in agreement. "We are all one, madame."

Their close friendship was obvious. Arianna found it interesting that Jacques never called her anything but "madame" and always with such respect.

"In time, she and her husband will take over our farm and business. She was among the first few women to come into this male-dominated world," she stated proudly, looking to Jacques again for confirmation.

He smiled broadly as she continued. "And how lucky we are that she had the best *gardian* in the Camargue as her instructor and mentor." She put her hand on Jacques's arm, and he grinned and replied it had been his pleasure.

The collection of photographs, from the cracked and aged sepia prints to colorful recent posters, told a bold and yet intimate story about the property and the lives that had been such a part of that narrative.

Indicating one faded photo, Madame LeClerc said, "This man was our star . . . a *gardian* extraordinaire whose son followed in his footsteps. We just lost this fine gentleman two years ago at the age of ninety-nine, and we will never forget him. In fact, he is buried on our property. But I will let his son tell you more. *Oui*, Jacques?"

Jacques's face flushed with pride and emotion. "I'll be happy to tell them all about my father. I will do it as I take them around this Camargue he loved with all of his heart and soul."

Madame LeClerc's eyes glistened with devotion. "There are few times in one's life when a man as special as your father comes along. He will always remain such a part of our family, our history."

The others felt touched by the moment, unsure quite what to say.

Then Jacques broke the spell and said, "Would you like to talk about what we do here before I whisk our guests off?"

She laughed, her eyes crinkling with delight now. "*Oui!* You know I love to do that."

She walked over to a grouping of animal photos and first pointed to a few posters featuring massive black bulls. "As you may know, our bulls are semiwild and live in the marshes of the Camargue as they have for centuries. First and foremost, we raise them to perform in the bullring. Secondly, for their meat. I'll let Jacques explain bullfighting to you later, since that is an important part of our culture."

As she moved on to a collection of photos of horses, her voice filled with affection. "We love our Camargue horses. They are playful, smart, and strong. It can be very hot here but that doesn't bother them."

"They are fun-loving creatures whether at work or at play," Jacques confirmed. "Also, they have no fear of flies and mosquitoes. Those insects can be fierce here."

"I was reading out loud in the car how dreadful the mosquitoes are," Cecilia said. "Juliette sent us off with repellant she described as 'super-duper jungle-strength extra strong,' and she instructed us to slather it on! Is it really that bad?"

Jacques and Madame LeClerc looked chagrinned. "*Malheureusement, oui*. Although some days the wind makes a difference. The mistral this week will have helped."

A stunning photo of several horses thundering through water, surf spraying, with their long white manes flowing, drew Bertram's attention.

Their host laughed, her face beaming with pleasure. "They love to splash through the sea and gallop across the beaches and dunes. That's why some call them 'horses of the sea.'"

"They're carefully monitored these days because of development in the region. Most importantly, we want them to be safe. Yet still they are allowed to run wild, within boundaries," Jacques added. "It's very special, and photographers come from around the world to capture shots like this."

"And they love to show off!" Madame LeClerc expressed, her affection for them undeniable.

Everyone commented and exclaimed as they examined the posters and asked questions. There was much to discover about the way of life in the Camargue.

Bertram pointed to the same iron symbol they had noticed outside. There were many of them scattered in among the photos. "Might I ask what this represents, madame?"

"*C'est la croix de Camargue*—it's the Camargue Cross. It is the emblem of the town of Saintes-Maries-de-la-Mer, not far from here."

"Oh yes, I read about that town!" Cecilia exclaimed. "It has quite an unusual history."

Madame nodded. "*Oui!* There is a medieval legend that says the three Marys—Mary of Cleopas, Mary Magdalene, and Mary Salome, all friends of the mother of Jesus—landed near there in a boat after Christ's crucifixion. They were fleeing from persecution after finding the empty tomb. Bones were discovered in the fifteenth century that were proclaimed by the Church to be relics. Pilgrimages became popular. The bones are still treasured in the crypt of the church. Who is to say, really? There are always other interpretations."

"So this cross represents their story?" Bertram pressed, wanting more information.

Jacques interjected, "Partly. But really it's more modern than the legend. The Marquis Folco de Baroncelli commissioned the design in 1924 by the artist Hermann-Paul. I'll tell you more about the marquis later. In 1930, a large iron Camargue Cross was forged by a local man and installed near Saintes-Maries. Since then, you find smaller ones everywhere. It's a popular souvenir."

"Yes, it is. But it is very meaningful to those of us who live here. It represents culture but also the three most important Christian virtues, as well as the three Marys," Madame LeClerc added as she pointed to each part of the sculpture. "The cross represents faith, the heart stands for love or charity, depending on who you ask, and the anchor symbolizes hope. There is also the Holy Trinity at the top."

Jacques pointed to the three-pronged fork at the top. "These are also supposed to represent trident spears, traditionally used by fishermen. So that brings in the fishing customs of the area. But also, this is the long tool used by the *manadiers*—a type of *gardian*—who work with the bulls. They use it like a shepherd's crook to help keep the bulls together in the herd."

Bertram was clearly engrossed in these stories. "I say! That's a wealth of symbolism there. Will we pass by a shop to perhaps purchase one of these?"

Jacques assured him that would not be a problem. Arianna chuckled to herself. *I hadn't thought of Bertie as the souvenir type.*

Next, Madame LeClerc directed their attention to the photos of individuals as well as groups of men on horseback. "As you know from Jacques, our powerful black beasts are tended by our *gardians*—you might call them cowboys—who ride our semiwild horses. Some people like to say the *gardians* are semiwild also."

She chuckled and reached over to pat Jacques on the back. He frowned at her in mock dismay and then winked back.

"That was *une petite blague*—a little joke! We take great pride in our *gardians*. Most of them have a family history with us, and we value their loyalty as well as their tremendous talent as equestrians. *Gardians* and horses form bonds with each other. The *gardians* respect the horses for their stamina and agility, as you will see. Most importantly, these men . . . and now some women . . . understand that the horses have an innate ability to communicate with the bulls. *C'est magnifique.*"

She paused and looked at Jacques once more, her eyes glistening, her affection and respect obvious. "You know those words describe our *gardians* too."

"Madame, it is always an honor to do the work we do. And to work on this *manade* makes it even more special."

Madame LeClerc cleared her throat, and her voice cracked with emotion as she addressed her visitors once more. "I hope you fall in love with the Camargue and come again. Now I will stop my tourist talk!"

She put her hands together and bowed gracefully. All four guests offered words of thanks at the same time.

Bertram bowed low and said, "Madame LeClerc, you have been most gracious and congenial. *Merci beaucoup.*"

"*Oui, merci*, madame. We have a busy day planned," Jacques said. "Perhaps we can see you again later today."

"*Pourquoi pas?* If it fits with your schedule, why don't we dine together here?"

CHAPTER
TWENTY-FOUR

Once outside, Jacques indicated they should climb into his Range Rover. "I'm going to take you on some back trails where you would not like to take your vehicle. We're going to the conservation area to see the birds first. You're here at a good time of year! There will be babies."

They soon turned off the main road into a parking lot. There were few cars, and Jacques explained that the conservation area did not open to the public until noon. "We're being offered special access."

A strapping young man who looked about thirty years old came out of the entrance office. Arianna noticed that he and Jacques exchanged three *bises*. Juliette had explained this was common between very close friends. For others, it would be just two.

Jacques introduced him. "This is Henri. He is the chief guide here and has graciously offered to give us a tour, answer any questions, and lead you to the very best opportunities for photos. Then feel free to wander and take as many photos as you wish."

"*Bienvenue au parc ornithologique*—or bird park, to simplify things." Henri opened his arms wide as he gestured across the shallow expanses of water. Varying heights of reeds, grasses, and other native plants, as well as sporadic groves of trees, created pockets of vegetation among the bays and inlets before them.

"These wetlands and marshes are part of a large UNESCO-designated biosphere reserve. They provide a major staging point for hundreds of thousands of migrating birds, including our famous pink flamingos."

"A twitcher's paradise, I daresay!" Bertram commented.

"A what?" Cecilia asked.

"Oh, sorry, that's our British term for bird-watcher or birder," he explained.

He took a professional-looking pair of binoculars from his backpack and slipped the strap around his neck. Next he slung his camera strap over his shoulder. Arianna noticed he had put a new lens on it, the most massive she had ever seen.

She felt somewhat less than prepared as Barbara and Cecilia also took cameras out of their bags.

I guess I'll just keep using my phone . . .

Henri's enthusiastic voice brought her attention back to him.

"*Mais oui!* Bird-watchers and visitors come here from around the world. Our star attractions are the pink flamingos that live here throughout the year. In mating season, we may have forty thousand of our pink-feathered beauties nesting here. Let's go see them."

Arianna had never given much thought to flamingos or, really, birds of any sort, except for the cardinals, chickadees, and blue jays that visited the feeders in her mother's backyard. So she had been surprised at how stirred she was by the artistry of the photos and drawings Jacques had shared during his presentation at the *mas*.

Seeing the flamingos now, just a few feet away, almost close enough to touch, she found herself drawn to their seemingly fragile beauty. Graceful slender necks curved up to black-tipped pink beaks. Searching for algae or shrimp, the birds stepped slowly through the lagoon, dipping their heads underwater from time to time. Many were resting on one spindly sticklike pink leg at a time.

There was just a hint of pink in the delicate cream coloring of their feathers. A bright-pink slash could be seen on the wings, where they folded against their bodies.

Everyone gasped with surprise when one bird lifted its wing and a vibrant red-and-black contrast suddenly flashed, hidden underneath.

Barbara exclaimed they must be quite spectacular in flight and Henri assured her it was a sight to behold. "We have a beautiful poster of a large number in flight that I will show you back at the office."

"I expected their coloring to be more pink," Arianna commented.

Henri explained that the depth of color in their feathers changed according to their diet. "It comes partially from the carotene in the shellfish they eat. Some of these birds are still quite young and won't become more pink until they are three years old."

Their deep honking and squawking sounds seemed at odds with their elegant appearance and movements. A constant conversation filled the air.

"That's what I call chuntering," said Bertram to no one in particular.

"Another British term?" Cecilia asked.

Bertram chuckled. "Maybe. It means to mutter or grumble incessantly. And that's what this sounds like to me." Then he screwed his face up as if annoyed, and then offered a surprisingly accurate imitation that made them all laugh.

After Henri finished giving his tour, the four artists each found their own quiet spot, tucked under the shade of a tree or protected by a tall clump of reeds. From time to time, someone would wander elsewhere. Drawing in their sketch pads or project books, photographing from many angles, and simply observing, they found that two hours passed in a flash.

Meanwhile, Jacques moved around, taking photographs and jotting in a small notepad he carried in his back pocket. He took the time to sit with each of them, examine their ideas, and talk about style, content, and anything else they wanted to ask him. Arianna found herself observing him as much as she was the flamingos.

He appeared to be at one with his surroundings, calm and peaceful in his approach to everything. He dispelled any feelings of awkwardness she had about her art. She felt comfortable to be speaking so openly about her struggle with drawing.

"So, Arianna. Is this the kind of subject matter you're accustomed to?" he asked as he crouched next to where she sat on a large stone near the water.

"No, it certainly is not," she replied. "I'm completely mesmerized by these birds. Seeing so many—and so close—is quite remarkable." He grinned as she continued. "Your drawings you showed us at the *mas* inspired me to turn to pencil here. I'm getting a lot of enjoyment from working on these, but it is work. I'm not having an easy time of it."

Arianna noticed how deeply his eyes connected with hers, and she shifted, feeling suddenly shy. She had been aware of his eyes as she observed him talking to others, but when he turned his gaze on her, it felt more intimate than she could comfortably handle.

"I've always liked the quote that refers to drawing being the honesty of the art. That philosophy speaks to me. You can't cheat with it. I tend to see life in black and white anyway. So the clarity in drawing is real to me. If I remember correctly, you prefer oils."

"Yes, I do. But this change is good for me, and I want to improve. Particularly with these birds. I'm working on that heron as well." She pointed to a majestic blue bird perched at the water's edge.

"*Bonne idée*—a handsome bird. May I show you something?"

She handed him her pencil and watched as he added a few simple lines that brought her drawing to another level.

"Thank you for that," she said. "What a difference, with such a minor change. I will remember that."

"You're doing very well. Don't doubt yourself. I like how you've added some asymmetrical elements here. It's a good effect."

As he moved along, Arianna felt a tingle of pride at his comment. She felt like she was having a schoolgirl moment, feeling flustered holding the pencil he had just used.

When Jacques suggested it would soon be time to go, they took a few minutes to leave their work at a satisfactory stopping point. Then they said their good-byes to Henri and wished him well. To his evident delight, they all expressed a desire to return one day.

The enthusiastic chatter did not stop as they settled back into the Range Rover. They all agreed that it had been an extraordinary experience.

"Who is hungry?" Jacques asked. Everyone admitted they were ready for a light lunch. "Great! I'm going to swing around to Saintes-Maries-de-la-Mer. Does everyone like seafood?"

There were enthusiastic nods all around. He told them about his friend Yves. "His family has been fishing this area for five generations. They have the best petite *friture*—fried small fish—I've ever tasted, and *croyez-moi*, trust me, I've tasted many!"

On the quiet, two-lane road, they could see what looked like an enormous church towering over the town in the distance.

"That is the local church, Notre-Dame-de-la-Mer. It's revered here and famous for pilgrimages. It began as a fortress between the ninth and twelfth centuries. In fact, it still has a freshwater well inside that was dug for times when refuge was necessary from attackers, including pirates."

He continued to answer a barrage of questions about the history of the area as they drew closer to town.

"And I would like to add this thought," he said. "You had some time just now in the *Parc ornithologique* to simply draw. For the rest of the day, I would ask you just to take photographs and make observations. No more drawing. There's much for you to discover and, more importantly, to feel. *D'accord?*"

"*D'accord!*" they all chorused back.

CHAPTER

TWENTY-FIVE

It did not take long to reach the small seaside community. The country-side appeared more open and wild here, and they passed several *manades* along with way. Jacques explained that this was the only main road. "There are also a few side roads, many walking and bike trails, and a system of small canals crisscrossing the region. When traffic is heavy for a festival, it's a *cauchemar*—nightmare!"

Glimpses of horses and bulls along the roadside drew exclamations of delight, but Jacques assured them they were in for much better sights.

"After lunch we will return to Manade Saint-Dominique. Madame LeClerc texted to say there are horses grazing near the ranch house. Sometimes we don't see them for days, so you brought good luck with you. You did say you wanted to ride, *oui?*"

His expression drew laughter from them. They could tell it was not really a question.

As they entered the small town, they noticed several impressive sculptures of bulls.

"It's the bulls that are the rock stars here," Jacques explained, as he recounted a few local stories. "They all have names and statues are often erected to the best of them when they die. There are few villages here without them."

The women all stressed how much they liked this philosophy of bloodless contests. Bertram had a different attitude about traditional bullfighting and quietly made a comment about appreciating the deeply rooted cultural traditions that accompanied it.

"It's an ongoing debate that has become much louder with the advancement of animal rights," Jacques agreed.

Fascinated, they urged Jacques to continue his commentary.

"Each village has its own bull festival in the summer and they're something to see. The organized events include bull runs through the street and tons of other activities. But the main attractions are the contests in the arenas. Some of the bulls who aren't champions there become tasty meals thanks to a life of grazing on the rich, marshy pastures here."

"C'est la vie," Bertram murmured.

"But as Madame LeClerc mentioned, bulls are truly the heart of the Camargue. They are raised for victory in the bullring, not to be the main course at dinner."

"And are these competitions truly bloodless?" Barbara asked.

"These are. Some called *corrida* or *mise à mort* are the fight to the death. But I'm not talking about them now. A *course camarguaise* takes place every week all summer long. Some towns have one every day. The goal is for the animal to become the winner of the 'course.' The bulls are surprisingly light and fast. And intelligent. Trumpets blare. The bull runs around the arena with a ribbon or other decoration attached between his horns."

He stopped the Range Rover beside the arena, which was right on the beach. "Come and see some photos here at the bullring. It's easier to understand that way. But, all in all, it's a rather crazy part of our culture. And much loved!"

They piled out and gathered around an exhibit of black-and-white photographs. Jacques continued his explanation. "You see, these men dressed in white are the *raseteurs*. They use a claw-shaped metal tool, a *crochet*, to try to grab a knotted ribbon called the *cocarde* tied between the bull's horns and then two little *ficelles*, strings attached to the base of the horns. They get two points for the *cocarde* and four for the *ficelles*. There are bonus points if the bull slams the barrier. The points accumulate all season. Being crowned the season champion is a great honor."

He pointed to another young man in the ring. "This is a *tourneur*, and he tries to distract the bull. At the same time, the *raseteur* runs at the bull, hoping the bull will charge him. Make sense so far?"

"Better him than me," muttered Bertram.

"If the two men cross paths, it might confuse the bull. That's the best time for the *raseteur* to try to grab a ribbon or string with his hook. More often than not, the *raseteur* then tries to leap over the fence and grabs onto the arena wall or railing. He doesn't want to get trampled. Sometimes the bull tries to jump over too."

"Sounds like a wild time! I would love to see that!" Barbara said.

They began to chuckle at some photos showing the men taking flying leaps into the stands, a bull hard on their heels. "Remember what you've heard today. These bulls are the celebrities and no harm must come to them. If something happens to the bull accidentally, the contest may be stopped. If the guys who go in the ring get a little hurt, *c'est la vie!*"

"It looks rather chaotic!" Bertram observed.

Jacques nodded. "*Absolument chaotique!* There's an announcer talking quickly, usually in a very loud voice. Also, there's sometimes shrieking the entire time by enthusiastic others near the microphone. The audience cheers. The band plays the overture of *Carmen*—or sometimes there's just a scratchy record played over the speakers. It's quite a spectacle!

"The most fun for the *gardian*," Jacques continued, "is a *bandido*, when we bring the bulls to the arena, or *abrivado*, when we return them to the meadows. A street is cordoned off, and everyone lines it to cheer as the *gardians* drive the bulls from one end to the other."

He explained it all happened at a frenzied pace, with possibly ten riders galloping in close formation around the bulls.

Bertram was pointing out various photos to go with Jacques's commentary.

"There's a lot of noise and dust! We keep the bulls in the middle, but sometimes one manages to get out. *Honnêtement*, sometimes we let that happen to make it even more exciting! Then we bring the bull back into the group, and the announcer yells, *'Le taureau est enfermé.'* This means the bull has been captured and once again there is great cheering and whistling."

He paused for a moment, looking around with a crooked grin, before he ended on a serious note. "Everyone is warned to stay behind the barriers. Accidents sometimes happen, sadly."

The thought of bullfights had always made Arianna feel disgusted and even angry. But these local contests sounded like a lot of fun. She smiled at the thought that the bulls were revered for being the winners. Jacques's storytelling skills were keeping them amused with his tales of colorful local traditions.

Looking around, Cecilia commented, "You can feel that lively atmosphere on the streets here. The shops and bars are all so festively decorated!"

"It's very much a gypsy town, filled with their rich folklore and music," Jacques replied. "You're just a bit early for the main event of the year here, the Gitan Pilgrimage. Thousands of gypsies gather, mainly from France and Spain. Fields, roads and laneways are jammed with caravans. Most are modern, but even today there are some horse-drawn. The highlight is when *gardians* on horseback accompany the chosen gypsies who carry the statuette of Black Sara into the sea. Night and day, tantalizing cooking smells waft through the air. Music, some fantastic flamenco, and dancing fill the streets! It's quite the party! Did you know the Gipsy Kings got their start playing here as teenagers?"

They described to Jacques how they had been painting to the sounds of the Gipsy Kings, and that Juliette had told them all about their local history.

"I'm a convert!" Bertram announced, looking quite pleased with himself. Then he twitched his shoulders rather clumsily and sang, "Bambolooli, bambolooli . . ."

"That would be 'Bamboleo,' Bertie!" Arianna corrected him with a grin as they all laughed.

He repeated it several times, aided by Jacques, who continued the song for a few more lines in perfect Spanish.

"By George, I'll master that yet!" Bertram promised.

Soon they were perched on stools at a boardwalk stand on a long, sandy beach that seemed to stretch out to the horizon.

A short, burly man in a T-shirt, jeans, and bright-yellow rubber boots rushed over from the dock. He had been busy gathering and sorting piles of fishing nets while laughing and exchanging comments with men on nearby boats. They appeared to be cleaning up after an early-morning return from the sea.

He and Jacques greeted each other with the customary *bises* and much back slapping. Yves received his guests warmly. "*Bonjour et bien-venue!* Nothing chichi here! Just the best *friture* you've ever tasted—did *mon ami* Jacques tell you?—and fresh from the sea this morning," he assured them, as he walked around the counter into the open kitchen.

Conversation moved easily from French to English between the men, and they made a great effort to keep everyone engaged.

After scrubbing his hands, Yves fired up a gas fryer, and he tossed a mixture of small whitefish, baby octopus, and calamari in flour, seasonings, and a light batter. Once he filled the fryer and lowered it into the oil, Yves took greens that were in the fridge and dropped them into a large olivewood bowl. He tossed in some chopped onion, cucumber, and tomato, then scooped out some herbs from a container. "My secret recipe," he said with a conspiratorial wink, as he rubbed the herbs between his fingers and into the greens. Next he squeezed the juice from half a lemon and finished with a flourish, adding olive oil.

He turned and lifted the fryer onto a drainage rack, then returned to the wooden bowl and tossed the salad with great panache.

"*Et voilà!*"

Jacques grinned. "As I predicted! And now for some Camargue wine to go along with it."

Everyone agreed lunch was as delicious as promised.

After lunch, they had a quick drive around, with Jacques giving nonstop commentary.

Cecilia sat next to him, recording as they went. She had asked for his permission to do a podcast about this visit. "To have the voice of a true *gardian* describing the Camargue will be very special," she told him, her words filled with adulation.

He nodded with a slightly embarrassed expression.

Arianna liked the way his subtle sense of humor shone through his observations. She could feel his connection to the region and the way of life and realized she envied that. She felt connected to nothing these days except her family. Her horizons were being expanded in so many ways on this trip.

It's up to me to do something about that . . . and slowly that urge is growing. I've got to plan more travel. That's a given!

CHAPTER
TWENTY-SIX

Soon they headed back to the *manade*.

"*Alors!* Now you will experience the passion of our region: our horses and bulls."

Jacques parked the car by the ranch house and passed around a bottle of mosquito repellant, adding, "It's strong, so don't get it in your eyes. Hopefully, though, we won't really need it today and I know you put some on earlier. This is simply backup."

He then asked, "Are you ready to ride a horse?"

Bertram offered a crisp salute. "Absolutely! I'm looking forward to this." During conversation in the car, Jacques had inquired as to each one's riding experience. Cecilia had said she had taken riding lessons as a child and was sure she would be fine. Arianna and Barbara had looked at each other. "I will if you will," Barbara had said, her expression a mixture of amusement and concern.

"Not every visitor gets to ride a true Camargue horse," Jacques told them. "But we have a few horses here that the children rode growing up."

He spoke in a most reassuring way. "As Madame LeClerc mentioned earlier, these are very special horses. Their calm temperament gives them a great affinity for their riders. You will have absolutely nothing to worry about. Do you trust me on this?"

"Implicitly, monsieur!" Bertram said. "Ladies, don't worry. A true horseman would never mislead you."

Arianna and Barbara hung back and talked quietly about whether they were really up to this. Overhearing their concerns, Jacques asked if they would like to have one of the ranch hands stay with them, and they both agreed that might be wise.

He led them past a barnlike wooden structure, open at the front and stacked with equipment, where he introduced the group to two ranch hands, Marie and Lucille. The women said they would be happy to give Arianna and Barbara some assistance with the horses.

Barbara said, "I have a spirit of adventure, but this might be pushing things. I'll need all the help I can get."

"Ditto," Arianna agreed. She couldn't believe she was getting caught up in this Camargue adventure. Her family wouldn't believe their eyes when she sent them a photo of this. She chuckled to herself.

They walked through a field to where they could see some white horses among the tall grasses, and Jacques repeated some of their history. "We learn so much from these horses. As Madame explained, they do not fear the bulls and the bulls sense this. There's a mutual respect and it almost appears playful as the animals interact instinctively."

He answered many more questions as they walked toward a marshy area. Madame LeClerc had said working in the Camargue was "a passion." Jacques made that clear with the emotion they could all hear in his voice.

As they drew closer, several of the horses approached without any trepidation. Shorter than most horses, their compact bodies appeared strong and muscular. Deep, dark eyes with long lashes gazed at them with a calm intelligence.

Once the horses had their halters on, the ranch hands led them to the barn. Jacques said, "They will just follow along with you. *Pas de problème.* If we didn't do this, they would simply wander off again to continue grazing. I assure you, we are not putting you on wild stallions!"

Barbara and Arianna expressed their exaggerated thanks for that clarification. "I think we can handle this," Arianna said.

The grins were wide as they led the cream-colored horses along, turning to admire their broad expressive faces as they walked. Marie and Lucille walked with them, answering questions.

Jacques explained that the horses were accustomed to this, as guests were welcome on the *manade.* "It helps with expenses and also educates visitors about life here."

"I've never been this close to a horse before," Barbara said. "Can you believe that? Eighty-two years and never even petted a horse's nose or offered one a carrot. I wonder what that says about me?"

"Are you certain you don't suffer from equinophobia?" Bertram asked.

"It means it's never too late to try something new," Arianna said, surprising herself at the suggestion.

Barbara laughed. "I may need a boost getting on, though."

As they waited at the barn for the horses to be saddled, Jacques explained a bit more history.

"In Paris in 1905, the Marquis Folco de Baroncelli-Javon was inspired by 'Buffalo Bill' Cody's Wild West spectacle. France was fascinated by it all. It motivated Marquis, as he was affectionately known, to create La Nacioun Gardiano. This order is dedicated to preserving the traditions of the Camargue. He revived rituals established as far back as the 1500s that had been prohibited during the Revolution."

Then Jacques went on to describe more of the American connection. "Marquis invited Buffalo Bill and his Dakota Sioux to bring their show to his estate here. Through their legends, he helped reshape bull and horse breeding in the Camargue."

"Who would ever have guessed there'd be that kind of American connection in this little corner of France?" Cecilia asked. "This is going to make a good story."

"My *cabane* is nearby. You can see it," Jacques said, pointing across the field as he whistled for his horse. "He tends to hang around there when I am on the *manade*. Being a *gardian* is no longer a full-time job for me. I want to let younger men take over, so I am back and forth."

Jacques indicated they should mount their horses. He offered his assistance to Cecilia, who was next to him. As he held the reins, the horse stood quietly waiting. Cecilia put her left foot in the stirrup and after a few hops, she sprung lightly up onto the saddle.

"Oh to be young," Barbara murmured, with admiration.

With surprising agility and obvious familiarity with a horse, Bertram easily mounted and encouraged the others. "Trust your steed, ladies. Trust your steed."

Marie and Lucille placed wooden stools on the ground to make things easier for Arianna and Barbara, who expressed their embarrassment but also their gratitude.

The group set off at a slow walk. Barbara and Arianna both acknowledged relief at having a "minder" beside them.

"I can honestly say I'm feeling a bit nervous about this," Arianna admitted to Barbara. "I hope my horse is as docile as was promised."

Barbara gave her a supportive look. "We can do this, Arianna."

They first passed by the one-story structure where Jacques lived, similar to others they had passed on the drive earlier. "This was my father's *cabane* in the old days, and I still stay in it when I am working here. As you can see, it is rather basic."

He described how originally the walls were built of clay.

"The thatched roof is made using the reeds—*sagno*—that line the canals. There are far fewer *cabanes* now, and most newer ones are built with brick and cement. However, the thatched roof is still used today. Historically, it has held up well against the onslaught of the mistral."

Bertram spoke up. "It also retains the special charm of the *gardians*, and, with all due respect, it enhances the romantic notion of the cowboys of the Camargue."

Jacques's face became slightly flushed. He brushed the remark away with a wave of his hand and a somewhat bemused expression.

Arianna was startled at her strong attraction to his modest response. He was a handsome man who definitely had an air of romance about him as he led them through this unique environment. She had to admit she was enjoying his company.

"It looks like such a simple abode," Barbara observed, changing the subject. "Is it one big room inside?"

Jacques rode to the wide front door and pulled a rope to open it, without dismounting. "Yes, it is one room with a bed, chair, bookcase, and desk—quite bare, and with a chemical toilet, in case you are wondering. Ultrabasic, you might say. You can have a look, if you wish."

They all graciously declined.

Bertram had been scrutinizing the structure. "This is pure geometry: a polyhedron of parallelograms plus a cylinder, a cone, and a prism."

Jacques studied the Englishman for a moment before he smiled broadly and said, "Monsieur, of all the people who have visited my *cabane* with me, you are the first to make such an observation. An accurate observation, I might add."

Cecilia, Barbara, and Arianna looked at each other and rolled their eyes, but not without admiration.

"Who says things like that?" Barbara asked.

Cecilia and Arianna answered in unison, "Bertie."

Bertram chuckled and puffed up, as he did when he was immensely pleased with himself.

The horses sauntered along a comfortable, well-worn path that went briefly through an herb-scented grove of trees. After rounding a corner about fifteen minutes from their starting point, they found themselves on the sandy shore of a large body of water. There was a sudden collective gasp.

Grazing on a grassy field that bordered windswept dunes was a small herd of bulls. Some stared intently at the riders. Others ignored them. Ten intimidating, broad-shouldered, dark-black bulls with long pointed horns and smoldering eyes.

"*Mes amis*—my friends," Jacques said, admiration obvious in his eyes and voice. "*Voilà le biou*. This is our legendary bull. He's quite a specimen, *n'est-ce pas?*"

They quietly stared at the magnificent beasts.

"They are even more impressive in real life than in their photos," Arianna said.

"They exude power and are rather handsome," Bertram observed.

"Their horns are so graceful, like a lyre," Barbara said.

Cecilia was taking photos from every angle. "Don't worry," she said, "I'll take pictures for all of us. You ladies concentrate on staying upright."

Bertram's face shone with glee. "This breed is mentioned in writings dating from the Gallo-Roman era! I've hoped to see them in this setting for a very long time."

Jacques looked on proudly. "'All nature is but art unknown to thee.' Thank you, Alexander Pope."

His love and understanding of this area were apparent in the stories he told them. Arianna admired the combination of his sensitive artistic side and strong *gardian* image that included a passion for nature and, in particular, the unique environment of the Camargue.

"We won't disturb the bulls now," Jacques said. "But if you have an opportunity to return and see them herded by *gardians* on these horses, it is something to behold. It's also important to remember they are powerful and dangerous."

As the trail turned through marshy wetlands, Barbara began to swat at mosquitoes. "They aren't landing on me, though! That repellant is very effective. But they are enormous!"

Jacques laughed and agreed. "Let's head back to the house. I believe we will be feasting soon. We don't want them to!"

When they arrived back at the barn, Jacques indicated that Bertram should stay on his horse.

When the women were standing, he pointed to Madame LeClerc on the porch waving to them. "*On y va*, mesdames. Madame LeClerc is waiting for you." Turning to Bertram, he said, "And you, monsieur, would you care to take your steed for a gallop?"

Bertram looked like a young boy who had just seen Santa Claus. "With immense pleasure, I would love to. Many thanks, kind sir."

Jacques motioned for him to follow and whistled at his horse. They shot off across the field, hooves thundering, Bertram whooping with excitement at the top of his lungs.

As they washed their hands in the barn, the women exchanged thoughts about how certain muscles might be rather sore in the morning.

Barbara's eyes sparkled. "It was so worth it, wasn't it?"

Arianna and Cecilia nodded their agreement as Barbara continued, a bit breathlessly. "It was so exciting, and I must say I loved the feeling. There's a horse park not far from our home, and I might just sign up for lessons. What do you think, Ceci?"

"I think that's a fabulous idea, Gran. You should definitely look into it."

"I'll see if they have a 'sauntering for seniors' program," Barbara said with a chuckle. "I don't want to go any faster, but that walk was perfect. Those horses are so beautiful. I can't wait to try and capture their image and spirit in paintings."

Arianna agreed that the ride was pleasurable, thanks to Marie and Lucille being there. "I feel the same, Barbara. Well, not about taking riding lessons, but I want to draw those horses too. I'm sure we all have some excellent photos."

Arianna felt grateful to her kids for pushing her to get the new phone and showing her how to use the camera. She had taken thirty-seven photos so far that day. She smiled as she scrolled through a few now.

Who knew? How else would I ever remember all of the wonderful experiences I've had this week—and so many today!

After her momentary elation, Arianna suddenly felt her heart drop. It was something she'd been struggling with all week. As much as she had opened herself to loving the highs of this adventure, she was still being hit by the lows of her soul as well. She felt conflicted about the happiness, laughter, and, yes, hope she had begun to feel in this little cocoon at the *mas* with her new friends.

Barbara and Cecilia noticed Arianna's change of expression.

"Arianna, did something upsetting just happen?"

"I'm sorry," Arianna replied. "I didn't realize it was obvious. I had a little relapse into the reality of my life at home. Sometimes when I'm caught up in the amazing experiences I am having with all of you, I hit a bit of a wall. Really, I'm okay. It was just a moment."

Barbara and Cecilia both hugged her.

"Thanks," Arianna said. She wasn't really a hugger, except with her family. But she had to admit these hugs did help her feel better. "I just have to keep working through it . . . and I will. I've come a long way this week, and I have to keep believing I'm on a path to a good place."

"Well, you certainly made a breakthrough with your painting. I took that as a good sign," Barbara agreed.

Just then, they heard a loud clanging and turned to see Madame LeClerc standing on the porch with a large bell and a wide grin.

"*Venez, s'il vous plaît! Le dîner va commencer.* We are ready to begin the dinner! Please join us!"

CHAPTER TWENTY-SEVEN

Madame was eager to hear of their day and to answer the many questions they had brought back with them. After having seen the horses, bulls, and flamingos in real life, they studied the photos on the walls of the main room with renewed interest.

A short while later, a smiling Jacques and a flustered but happy Bertram came into the house. Arianna, Barbara, and Cecilia stared at them in amused surprise.

Bertram was no long wearing his long-sleeved dress shirt, always primly buttoned to the neck. It had been replaced by a bright-red paisley shirt that was obviously not his. A colored scarf sat tied around his neck at a jaunty angle.

"We stopped at the barn to wash up," Jacques explained.

"An absolute necessity," Bertram piped in, barely able to contain his elation and still breathing heavily. "I was soaked in sweat! Jacques borrowed this shirt from another *gardian* who was more or less my size. Sorry, that may be too much information, but, seriously, that was the most excitement I've had in ages!"

Bertram received congratulations on taking his first step to becoming a *gardian*. "You are wearing the outfit well, monsieur!" Madame complimented him.

The room filled with laughter and bonhomie as introductions were made. Monsieur LeClerc; their daughter, Danielle; and her husband, Michel, had joined them for dinner.

The entire family wore the traditional shirts, vests, and scarves of the *gardians*. The men wore leather pants, and Danielle and her mother wore elegant, long soft-leather skirts. "We wanted to wear these outfits for you this evening," Danielle told them. "You have no doubt gathered we have a strong commitment to preserving our traditions in the Camargue."

The long dining table was set up in an enormous room that Arianna was certain had seen its share of festivities. The walls were covered with spectacular, massive photos of horses and bulls that were obvious works of art. The effect was stunning and captured the beauty and power of this wild area.

Monsieur LeClerc explained that photographers from all over the world came to their *manade* for photo shoots. "They often express their thanks by gifting us photos. We are extremely proud of our animals, and these photos honor them."

Michel brought a tray around with small, narrow glasses. "*L'apèritif* this evening is the pastis Le Camarguaise. It's a liquor produced from anise, licorice, and forty other plants. Some people find it kind of strong, so you always add water to suit your taste. It's produced at Distillerie A. Blachère, which was founded in 1835."

Everyone added water and then raised their glass to toast. "*Santé.*"

After taking a long sip, Bertram sighed loudly. "Ahhhh, I do love pastis. This is a fine degustation indeed!"

The taste and smell reminded Arianna of the Greek ouzo that Nikos loved dearly. He used to let her have a sip when she was a child. She put more water in her drink than the others and quite enjoyed it. Memories of her *baba*, Nikos, her childhood, and black licorice filtered back. Silently she toasted all that and felt happy that she was welcoming these memories and not keeping them buried. Rather, she was mixing them with the new ones she was making.

Danielle passed a platter with toothpicks stuck into small chunks of sausage. "Our own recipe, courtesy of our bulls."

Monsieur LeClerc and Michel had been pointing to some of the bulls in the photos. "The bull is both respected and promoted here. We want to raise bulls that are winners in the Camarguais bullring, where no blood is shed."

"No blood from the bull, at least," Michel said with a laugh.

"That's right," Monsieur LeClerc continued. "The bulls are the stars of the posters advertising the *course camarguaise*. With each course, the bull becomes more shrewd. They are incredibly smart, and we can see they like to win. Not many are taken to the kitchen."

"*Eh bien,*" Madame LeClerc said, "let's go and enjoy one of our boys who did end up there."

Dinner was delicious. The meal began with an entrée of *tellines*. Jacques asked if their guests were familiar with the dish.

Bertram spoke up immediately. "They are delicious! I've eaten them on a previous visit to the area." Turning to Barbara, Cecilia, and Arianna, he said, "They are edible mollusks that resemble small clams, native to this area. Each morning they are traditionally gathered by dragging nets through the sand. In my humble opinion, they are beyond delicious."

The *tellines* were served *en persillade*, in a simple parsley and garlic sauce, and the women murmured their appreciation as they ate. Conversation flowed easily, with the LeClerc family equally interested in their guests' stories.

"It's not often we are so honored to share our table with friends from Canada and England," Madame LeClerc declared. There was friendly laughter as everyone attempted to juggle both languages.

The main course, *gardianne de taureau,* was a delicious slow-cooked stew of bull meat in rich dark gravy with carrots, onion, garlic, and green and black olives. The addition of orange peel provided a special flavor. *Riz rouge de Camargue* was also served with simple greens on the side.

Jacques explained it was a local specialty. "And Madame LeClerc's *gardianne* is known far and wide as the best in the Camargue!"

Compliments abounded as the guests all agreed the dish was delicious, with a slightly stronger taste than conventional beef.

Madame looked down modestly and said, "It's thanks to our fine *taureaux.* They are the secret ingredient."

Costières de Nîmes wine was served, a full-bodied local red. The atmosphere around the table continued to be relaxed with spirited conversation.

To his companions' surprise, Bertram had one glass and refused any more. "I have a responsibility as the designated driver. So I will imbibe nothing more alcoholic this evening."

As the others were exchanging comments about the delicious meal, Bertram leaned over to Arianna and whispered, "Besides, I've had enough of feeling crapulous. Time for a change!"

She looked at him, rolled her eyes, and whispered back, "Crapulous?"

He gave her a subtle "later" wave of his hand.

Monsieur LeClerc told stories of local winemakers, including this one to murmurs of amazement. "There is even one *vignoble* that sits in the same location as a Roman villa once did. During excavations, recipes of Roman wines were discovered. Now three Roman wine recipes are produced there in the ancient method. Wine is fermented in casks buried almost entirely in the ground and about ten thousand bottles of the Roman wines are produced annually. *Les vendanges,* the grape harvest, is a grand celebration there."

A creamy rice pudding, accompanied by Armagnac and coffee, completed the meal.

Again, Bertram passed on the liqueur. "Even though I am aware that Armagnac is the oldest brandy distilled in France and truly a treat, I fear I must once again refrain. I am the driver, and with that come certain responsibilities: one being to remain sober."

Darkness had set in as the guests thanked the LeClerc family for their gracious hospitality.

"This has been a day to remember, capped by this evening of fine dining and conversation," Bertram said, his voice thick with emotion. "Thank you for welcoming us into your home and for sharing the exceptional joys of the Camargue with us. I have no doubt we will all be treasuring memories of today's peregrinations. We are indebted and grateful. *Merci mille fois!*"

Arianna, Cecilia, and Barbara all echoed his thanks. "He speaks for us all," Barbara added, "although we don't always know exactly what he has said."

Everyone laughed and promptly agreed with her.

Jacques walked his guests to their van. "The night is rarely silent here," he said.

The chirping of frogs broke the stillness around them. He suggested they look up to see bats swooping through the moonlight, enjoying a nocturnal feast. Soft lowing of bulls could be heard from deep in the darkness.

Looking embarrassed at the thanks and praise they heaped upon him, Jacques smiled in his low-key manner and lowered his gaze for a moment. "It has been my pleasure to share the Camargue with you today . . . and there is so much more to experience. You didn't see the salt flats or other villages or take a canal ride for yet another perspective. Come back anytime. In the meantime, I wish you great success with your projects this week."

Bertram went to the passenger side of the car and held open the doors for the women.

As they waved good-bye to Jacques, Bertram said with great respect, "That is a most perspicacious gentleman."

Everyone agreed.

Conversation did not still for the entire ride. A challenge was issued by Cecilia for each to determine a particular highlight of the day. "No duplications!"

The challenge was easily met.

Arianna could not stop reflecting upon all she had experienced that day thanks to Jacques. She ordered her imagination to be still but kept coming back to the fact that he had opened a number of doors for her today, and she had, without real hesitation, stepped through. Rather than fearing what tomorrow might bring, she was eager to see for herself.

Few words were exchanged after arriving back at the *mas*. It was past eleven o'clock, and it appeared the others were already back in their rooms. Grinning, they *bised*. They praised Bertie for his fine driving, and agreed with each other that the day had been so special.

Arianna sank down into her steaming tub, filled to the brim, with soothing, rose-scented bath oil added. As she swirled the water around with her fingers, thoughts swirled in much the same way in her mind. She felt it had been a most remarkable day.

The landscape and culture of the Camargue had been educations on their own, much of it quite surprising. The opportunity to meet the LeClerc family and experience a glimpse of their life had been a bonus.

Riding a Camargue horse and seeing the bulls in their natural habitat was something she would never have imagined. It wasn't something that fell into any sort of wish list of hers, and yet it had been exciting.

Seeing all of this through the eyes and heart of Jacques de Villeneuve, in his roles of both artist and guardian, was a unique opportunity Arianna knew she would never forget.

Bertie is right. That man is exceptional. We're fortunate to have spent the day with him. It would have been so easy to miss!

The constant activity of the day caught up with her now. But as much as she felt exhausted, she felt renewed. She planned to rise early and get straight to her paints.

Another step forward—no, a giant leap forward. That's what I feel happened today.

She had messaged a couple of photos from the Camargue to Tad and Faith, as was her habit most days after she had decided to stay. Often, she would add a sentence or two, and they always replied how happy they were for the adventure she was experiencing. They had all agreed before she left that they would only mention Ben if there was some change.

It was Faith who had urged her mother, and convinced her brother, that Ben should not be the focus of their communication during Arianna's time away. "If there's a change, of course we will tell you. But, if not, we don't want to make it a regular reminder."

Tonight, for the first time, Arianna felt compelled to express to them the deeper feelings of change in her heart.

It was the biggest step yet, she felt. She thought of Marti and Lisa's words and how they worried about hurting people they loved by expressing their truth. That conversation was inspiring her now. *Not that this is on the same level, by any stretch of the imagination.*

She had to take a similar risk and hope her family would not feel she was abandoning Ben. She knew other people might judge her, but she trusted her family would understand.

Because, really, this is what they had been encouraging me to do.

So she began.

Dearest Faith, Tad, and Christine,

As you could tell from my photos today, we had quite an unusual adventure in the Camargue. It was our good fortune to be introduced to that unique area and culture by someone who has spent most of his life there.

The day was so special. A complete departure from anything I've experienced before. And today was just one part of how my time here at the Mas des Artistes is helping me contemplate a new outlook on life.

I want you to know that this trip has been the finest step I could have taken. Thank you for pushing me to apply for the course.

The people here have become very special to me. Who would have imagined that these strangers could help me work through what has been holding me back?

I have so much to tell you, but I will save most of it until I return home.

What I will say now is that I am beginning to feel positive about life again. I am falling in love with my art like so long ago, with the challenge of it, with the desire it stirs in me that I thought I had lost forever. I am beginning to allow myself to feel like a whole person again—to laugh, to care about the bigger picture of life, and to hope.

Of course, I think of your father and my heart crumbles. But I'm able to put things in perspective, bit by bit. He will live in my heart until it stops beating. That is a given.

I hope reading this makes you feel as happy as it makes me to write these words to you. Please read this to Yiayia too.

I love you, my sweet family, and will forever be grateful for this opportunity to rediscover myself. I wish I could beam you all over here right this minute!

Love,
Mom xoxoxo

She slipped under the covers and fell asleep with hope in her heart.

CHAPTER

TWENTY-EIGHT

Arianna found it challenging to keep up with the conversation at breakfast, with everyone speaking excitedly at once. It seemed the foodies had had quite an adventure with Maurice.

His fisherman friend, Bruno, had been difficult to track down, and they had spent a good deal of time driving up and down from one beach to another, checking out the fishing boats as they went.

John embellished the story as only he could. He had them all in gales of laughter as he described a Keystone Kops–style chase when Maurice thought he saw Bruno's truck going the other way. "Death-defying U-turns, brakes screeching, and Maurice apologizing all along the way. Turned out it wasn't even Bruno!"

"You may recall," Joan reminded the rest of the group, "this guy, Bruno, doesn't believe in cell phones, so it became quite a challenge to finally track down someone who knew what was going on."

John continued, "Maurice must have asked a dozen people. Some of whom sent us on wild-goose chases—only trying to help, of course! We were staaaaaarrrrrving!"

Looking abashed, Maurice apologized. "*Désolé! Désolé!* I am so sorry . . . again!"

John walked over and put his arm around him. "I'm teasing, *mon ami*. You made up for it, a thousand times over!"

The others chorused in. "Absolutely!"

Marti said, "Besides, it was fun seeing so much of the coast, watching the windsurfers and everything! I can imagine what it's like in the full thrust of summer!"

Lisa nodded and extended her arms as wide as she could. "The beaches were amazing," Marti said, backing her up.

They'd finally found out that Bruno was not in the area, having gone to Marseille to visit his ailing grandmother. So Maurice had gone on to plan B.

Joan picked up the story. "He took us to a beachside restaurant in the village of Le Grau-du-Roi. Maurice was welcomed like royalty. They couldn't do enough for us. We ate a deliciously stunning five-course seafood lunch that took three hours to consume. We also heard some stories about the history of the town and how profoundly it was affected during World War II, with German troops stationed in the village. The local resistance was heroic, in spite of the coast being on the front line of fighting."

They all commented on the tragic and heartrending stories and how so many people had been courageous during those times.

"It's something that every part of this country lives with, and yet it is really so foreign to us," Marti said softly. "I feel it's important for us to be reminded of that part of the history here. Hopefully we all learn in one way or another and carry that with us."

Murmurs of agreement and other respectful comments followed.

"It is part of understanding the full experience of our culture," Maurice added.

"And we thank you and your friends for sharing that with us," John said.

"Then, after the stories and that food, we all just wanted to take a nap," Joan said. "So we went down to a bar on the beach that had hammocks under gauzy shade nets and did just that!"

"There was a considerable amount of wine consumed," Marti added, looking sheepish.

"Before we left the town, Maurice's friend came out with a cooler full of fresh fish and *tellines* for us to bring back here for dinner. You have got to try *tellines*! They are delicious!"

"We had some last night," Barbara told them. "And you're right! They are incredibly delicious!"

"After that, we visited Aigues-Mortes," John said, "which is a very beautiful and cool, totally walled thirteenth-century town. You guys should try and get there this week, if you can."

Lisa passed her phone around, sharing photos as they chatted. "We drank copious cups of coffee there," Joan continued. "We saw a few horses in the fields on the way home, and Maurice stopped at a park so we could see flamingos. It was a great day!"

Marti concurred. "We were, as they say, tired but happy."

Then the nature lovers launched into their story of the day they'd spent with Jacques. Everyone agreed their separate Camargue adventures had been superb. They also all agreed that they would go back in a heartbeat.

They gathered in the garden after breakfast to share how their projects were moving along. All were open to hearing comments, critiques, and questions from each other.

Marti had disappeared for a few minutes, and when she returned, she was carrying a large canvas on a frame, the front hidden from view. Lisa's face had turned a bright shade of fuchsia. In a gently teasing voice,

Barbara said, "Lisa! You would blend in with that bougainvillea if you stood beside it right now."

Marti asked for a drumroll, and everyone beat their hands on their thighs. John had started them on this during their mistral evening when they were playing their game.

"Ta-daaaaaa!" Marti sang as she turned the canvas around. "Can you believe Lisa has created this beauty in a week?"

They stood around and admired a stunning landscape that took in the scene from the women's bedroom window. "There are many reasons why I refer to her as Speedy Gonzales—and this is one! She's been up until all hours working on it. She simply does not like to waste time."

They all knew better than to heap praise on Lisa. But they knew they could praise her work, instead, and she would be happy with that. She simply could not bear being the focus of attention.

The praise was unrestrained and celebratory.

"Honestly," Arianna said to the others, "I've admired Lisa's blending of shades throughout this whole course. She has such a touch, and discovers combinations I would not have imagined."

"It's not finished," Marti told them. "But I wanted you to see how awesome this is before Maurice crates it up for us. It took a little persuading for Lis to agree."

"Well, we're glad she did agree," Barbara said. Everyone applauded. Lisa looked down and grinned, giving them a thumbs-up.

"I stand in awe of her talent," Bertram said to Marti, but bowed respectfully to Lisa. "No way I could make that much progress in so few days. It often takes an inordinate amount of focus for me to get in touch with my divine afflatus."

Yet again, they all looked at Bertram as if he were speaking an unknown foreign language.

John asked, "Are you talking about farting, Bertie? Or, should I say, referring to divine flatulence?" He said the last part with an exaggerated English accent.

They all laughed, including Bertram. "Well, that too, my good man. However, I happen to like the term—it means inspiration, discovering my vision."

"You've certainly expanded our vocabulary during your stay," Juliette told him.

He blushed as he replied with a courtly bow and slight click of his heels.

CHAPTER

TWENTY-NINE

The day was calm and mild with no breeze. The sky was so perfectly blue as to be almost unnatural. The mistral had done its job.

The cool morning air meant working out in the open was very comfortable. Arianna decided to continue with an oil she had begun before the weekend. She found a quiet spot by the stone wall she was calling her own and set up her stool and easel.

She closed her eyes, took a deep breath, and let her surroundings create a visual in her mind.

It's an orchestration of the senses out here today—for the eyes, the ears, and the nose. The blue sky, the golds of the stones, the ochre of the soil, and the silvery greens of the olive leaves. The comforting song of the cicadas. The low, gentle buzz of bees in the garden. The earthy smell that combines the garrigue, the herbs, and the simple freshness of the air. I do love it here.

She was satisfied with the progress she was making. Her painting highlighted the olive grove with a portion of this stone wall where she sat. It was the same wall that had captured her attention on day one. After two hours, she was ready for a change.

She carried the painting into the house, setting it in a corner of the salon with some other works in progress. She stood back and let her eyes take in the variety of subject matter being painted by the group. The different perspectives eight people could produce made her smile.

Finally, she was having confidence in her own efforts. She appreciated the opportunity to compare her work with what others were doing, to hear their critiques and compliments, and to learn from them.

While she was in the house with strong Wi-Fi, she checked her e-mail and text messages. It wasn't like her to even think about them. But after her e-mail to her family last night, it was definitely on her mind. Then she reminded herself of the time change. The kids would still be sleeping.

Calming her thoughts, she picked up a bottle of water on her way out. The day was heating up, so now she moved her stool to the shade of the front terrace.

She flipped through her sketches. Choosing between several variations, she decided on a particularly appealing single flamingo. Balanced ankle deep near the shore on one seemingly fragile leg, at that moment this bird had defined tranquility for Arianna.

But right now, the graceful curve of its long, sinuous neck was presenting a challenge. She wanted to get it just right. So she put into use the simple methods Jacques had shown her.

Using the side of her pencil, she created some contrast in the feathers. It felt right to use her pencil now, rather than the charcoal she might have used long ago. It gave a clarity she had not found before that made sense in that entirely new setting. She could thank Jacques for helping her to see that too.

As Arianna moved her pencil across the paper, she thought about the contrast between the setting that surrounded her now and that of the Camargue.

The differences did appeal to her. She liked that it was possible to move from one environment to the other so easily.

She thought about everything that had been new to her yesterday. Not the least of which were the moments of pure enjoyment that frequently surprised her throughout the day, in spite of the few surges of guilt that pushed into her thoughts. Every once in a while, an image of Ben would slip into her consciousness. But now she was able to think of him lovingly, and then set the thought aside. She was here now. He was not.

She was beginning to feel like this drawing was reaching completion when Barbara stopped by.

"Arianna, that's looking beautiful. I've learned quite a lesson about the power of the graphite pencil on this trip. Before Jacques set up his presentation last week, I paid little attention to that medium."

"I have to agree, Barbara. It just didn't call to me either, apart from for preliminary drawings, outlines, and things like that. Now I'm intrigued, although I know I'm going to do some watercolors of flamingos too. Those colors are lurking in the back of my mind, and this course has definitely opened my mind to considering all options. More so than I ever would have before."

Barbara smiled and gave her a knowing look. "I had a student throw me a line once about art being an adventure that never ends. The more I thought about it, the more I agreed."

Arianna chuckled. "Too true. Let's go have some lunch."

A strong urge to meditate overtook Arianna after lunch. She knew she needed to listen to that voice before getting involved in anything else that afternoon.

She slipped out of her clothes and into a long silk robe.

After opening all the windows, Arianna arranged her pillows into a nest on the bed. She settled herself cross-legged on one cushion to raise her back to a comfortable level and went through the rest of her routine.

But today she felt her breathing wasn't quite under control. She wondered if she was having some guilt after feeling so free and happy. She decided to count her breaths, an ancient remedy to the problem. On her outbreath, she silently counted one, then two, then three, then four. Then returned to one on her inhale.

With her focus on her breath, Arianna gently let go of her thoughts. The silence was healing. She concentrated on allowing the outer quiet and her inner silence to meet. Her goal was to rest in the moment.

Fifteen minutes later, she began to slowly bring herself out. Her body seemed to know when it was time.

After a silent thank-you to Faith again, she stood and stretched.

For the rest of the afternoon, she worked at her drawing from the Camargue until she felt like it was close to complete. She was reminded that the precision required in working with pencil was as time consuming as creating in paint. She needed to step back from it for a day or so.

Checking her e-mail again, she wondered why she had not heard from any of her family. She hoped it had not been a mistake to write them so candidly about how she was feeling. They would just be starting their day. Maybe they hadn't opened their e-mail yet.

Then she picked up her Kindle and went to find a shady spot to sip a glass of wine and read for a while. It was that time of day.

By four p.m., she couldn't stand it any longer and went inside to check for messages again. Everyone had responded. Faith, Tad, and Christine had e-mailed her. Sophia had sent a message via Faith.

A surge of love moved through Arianna. Tad and Christine had each written to say her message had made them very happy and that the way she felt was even more than they had hoped for. Faith was exuberant. "Blossom on, Mom. Blossom on!"

Sophia, too, had expressed pleasure that her daughter was discovering happiness once again.

Arianna knew she had made the correct choice in sharing her feelings with them. And with their voiced support, she felt even more justified in wearing that new outlook comfortably.

She lay on her bed, thinking of all that the past ten days had brought into her life. The whole picture was so important: her surroundings in the *mas*, the settings in which she found herself, the history, the thrill of creating art, the food, and the people—oh yes, the people. And the stories they had shared.

Before she knew it, the dinner bell was calling her downstairs.

Maurice announced that dinner was going to be a bit of a potluck, courtesy of the Camargue. He had arranged for a *gardianne de taureau* to be delivered from a restaurant near Sainte-Maries. He wanted his foodies to have a taste of this dish, since they had not the day before.

"Well," Bertram said, "it may not be quite up to Madame LeClerc's standard, but it's more than acceptable. Now let me try that fish!"

The elusive Bruno had sent a cooler full of fresh fish as an apology for not being available the day before. Maurice baked it in a subtle but flavorful sauce of cream, garlic, olive oil, and potatoes, and Juliette cooked *riz rouge de la Camargue*. A simple green salad and fresh baguette completed the dinner.

As they enjoyed the standard cheese selection after dinner, Maurice had words of praise for everyone. "I must say, I'm impressed with the progress of this entire group when it comes to your appreciation of *le monde magnifique des fromages français*."

They all congratulated each other and agreed it had been pure pleasure to have the tutelage of an aficionado such as Maurice.

A few of the group decided to go into town after dinner to have drinks and hear some music.

⚜

Arianna and Juliette took their coffee into the grand salon. They settled into the comfortable chairs and chatted about the weekend and how all the individual experiences would impact the work they were doing.

Arianna described how she had worked on pencil sketches in the Camargue. "I think I'm going to focus on that medium for now. It feels right. My oil work is coming along, and I may even wait to finish it back home. I've become energized by the challenges of the graphite pencil. What do you think about that?"

Juliette looked amused. "Ahhh, the lure of drawing." She sighed. "Have you examined van Gogh's drawings from the Camargue and in Arles? I find them as intriguing as his paintings."

"Memories are returning from my early days as a student. I first learned how drawing was a necessary beginning to everything I worked on," Arianna recalled. "As you have shown us here, it's a process different from painting. You've helped me remember that most of it is exploratory. That part of it feels so good to me right now."

"Does it feel like you're going back to your artistic beginnings? Starting over? And, if you don't mind me asking, is this return to those beginnings helping you to better contemplate starting your life over . . . moving out of the 'now' that you so aptly described to me?"

Arianna took her time to reply. "In terms of my art . . . right now, my focus is on observation, problem solving, and composition as a means of preparation for a painting. It's all about discovery, and I think that's where I need to be right now as an artist. Oddly, when I move those thoughts into how my life might change, all of this also applies."

Juliette raised her eyebrows in a slightly quizzical expression as her gaze met Arianna's.

Arianna's face clouded briefly, and then a hint of a smile returned. "My life is also about discovery now too. I've learned that here, and I'm making progress. I know that."

Juliette murmured, "*Petit à petit.* Little by little. As Oscar Wilde said, 'Life imitates art more than art imitates life' . . ."

They sat quietly for a moment before Juliette steered the conversation to a lighter topic.

"You'll have a chance on Wednesday to see van Gogh's drawings at the Fondation . . . or you can google some tonight."

Arianna smiled. "Nope! I spent so much time, so many years ago, studying his work. I'll wait to see the real deal. I'm looking forward to it. Right now, I'm going to go to my room and read. I think I'll probably nod off pretty quickly. Yesterday was exhausting . . . but inspiring."

"That's the Camargue. People either hate it or love it. From what I gathered listening to all of you, it won everyone over yesterday!"

CHAPTER THIRTY

They were off to an early start the next morning. Juliette cautioned she had a full day's excursion planned, with several surprises. The twinkle in her eye and the way she struggled to keep her grin under control had everyone guessing just what was in store.

Cecilia waved the rest of the group off as they climbed into the van. She had opted to remain behind and write. "Deadlines loom," she moaned, "and time is slipping by!"

Once on the road, Juliette pointed out the location of the ruined Montmajour Abbey, where van Gogh had loved to draw and paint. "He often walked the hour-long stroll from town, and in late spring he drew and painted over a dozen landscapes there. It's said this was one place where he found poppies. However, there don't seem to be any there now."

Juliette shared the medieval history of the area, embellishing with colorful details about invasions, plagues, and religious wars. Maurice skillfully navigated the hills and curves. Around each bend another enigmatic hilltop village or hamlet appeared.

"Ah, look at that," Joan murmured. "I'm never going to get over the thrill I feel when I see these beautiful villages. They just seem to tumble down the hillside into the valley. How the heck did they ever get built? That's what I want to know."

"And what if you had to go from top to bottom and back again every day?" Barbara asked. "I hope they used donkeys."

As they passed through one tiny cluster of buildings, Maurice made them laugh as he informed them, "I know for a fact there are forty-five inhabitants in this village—and five hundred goats."

Soon, the tree-lined road brought them up a steep grade and into the parking area of just the type of perched village they had been admiring.

"With a castle ruin on top!" Arianna exclaimed. "The perfect finishing touch!"

They walked up a short but steep flight of stairs and found themselves in the classic heart of the village. Chestnut trees bordered the small square, with a warren of narrow lanes leading away in all directions.

"Just as on your first morning with us, we are sending you off on your own. Your task today is to find a small detail, the smallest you can find, that calls you to paint. If possible, try to discover something entirely new to your eye. We'll reconvene at the Café André, next to the boulangerie, in an hour and a half. Perfect timing for a caffeine break, *n'est-ce pas?*"

As the group dispersed through the beckoning narrow alleys, Bertram and Arianna began walking with Barbara. "I know we're supposed to be on our own, but either one of us would be happy to accompany you," Bertram said, and Arianna nodded.

"No, no, no!" Barbara shook her finger at them and chuckled. "I don't want you peeking at the treasures I'm going to find! Off you go on your own separate ways! I'll see you at the café! This will be fun."

"Promise you won't climb to the top without someone with you. Please," Arianna pleaded, hoping she did not sound overprotective.

"I promise. I may be old, but I'm not stupid!"

They all grinned and headed down different streets. Arianna wondered if anyone else was going to walk to the top of the village. That castle ruin was calling to her.

As she climbed through the maze of streets and stairs, she felt like no one else was around. She had become accustomed to exploring by herself, and somewhere along the way on this trip, she shed the feeling of loneliness. She was enjoying her own company.

Just over an hour later, Arianna was on her way back to the village square. She laughed as she made her way down the hill in so much less time than it had taken her to go up. *And without becoming breathless!*

Her journal was filled with drawings of the panoramic patchwork of orchards and vineyards that stretched across the valley, which she simply had not been able to resist. She had plenty of small details as well: from ancient rusted hinges on what was left of a door among the ruins, to random poppies poking up alongside a rocky path, to her pièce de résistance, or so she thought: an ornate sculptured detail from a small, crumbling fountain she had discovered in a hidden cul-de-sac.

The scene in the square was like something from an ad for an artists' retreat. Arianna smiled as she approached.

Marti, Lisa, and Joan were perched on the edge of the village fountain concentrating on drawing or adding color in their journals.

Bertram was busily sketching, his pad on his knee, as he sat on a bench in the shade of a chestnut tree.

John was sitting with Maurice, both sipping espresso, while John was recording the scene in his journal.

The artists were at work.

Juliette appeared from a side street with a concerned look on her face. "Has anyone seen Barbara? I've been strolling around trying to meet up with her."

The others looked around, and slowly they each indicated they hadn't.

Juliette tried Barbara's cell phone.

No answer.

Everyone got up to begin searching the village. Maurice organized them into small groups, each of which was to look in a separate quadrant so they weren't duplicating their efforts. "We should all be back here in ten minutes easily. I will go up to the ruin. Juliette will remain here at the café. Do we all have our phones on?"

As they were about to start off, a young boy of about ten came running through a small archway. He stopped at the group and began speaking in a frantic voice.

"Au secours! Au secours!" he shouted, asking for help.

Juliette calmed him, her jaw dropping as she listened, Maurice at her side.

"I think Barbara is down this way," she said to the others as Maurice began to follow the lad. "It sounds like she may be hurt, and the boy's mother has called *les pompiers.*"

They all fell in behind Maurice, who was now running.

"Pompiers?" Marti asked. "Doesn't that mean firemen?"

"Yes," Juliette answered over her shoulder as she hurried along. "They are faster than the ambulance and have a vehicle that can get down these narrow streets. They're also finely trained paramedics, and, in fact, they are our first responders in health emergencies and accidents."

Now the group moved as one, puffing and panting from keeping up with Maurice, trying to move quickly but not panic.

At the end of the street, they saw a woman bending over a mass on the ground. Barbara was lying there, absolutely still. The woman had put a pillow under her head and had covered her with a blanket.

Maurice immediately kneeled down and confirmed that Barbara was breathing, but she appeared to be unconscious. He inspected the area for blood and saw none. Taking her pulse, he announced it was very low. "I believe she has fallen and injured her head. If she had a heart attack, her pulse would be higher."

He then used his fingers to make sure her airway was clear and that she was not wearing dentures. "*Excusez-moi*, Barbara," he whispered as he checked.

The rest of the group huddled together in a worried state. They could see that Maurice had the situation well in hand. They knew from a conversation during their mistral dinner party that he was certified in both first aid and CPR.

The piercing claxon on the *pompiers'* truck could be heard drawing closer. Maurice continued to hold Barbara's hand and speak to her in a muted voice. She wasn't showing any response.

The *pompiers* were professional and efficient. After asking a few questions of Maurice and carefully checking Barbara's vital signs, they gently placed her on a stretcher. The slim red-and-yellow vehicle left for the Arles hospital, with Juliette going along inside, saying silent prayers.

The rest of the group hurried to the van. Pale and shaken, they were solemn, chatting little on the way back to the farmhouse.

Maurice called Cecilia to update her on the situation. He assured her that her grandmother was receiving the very best care and tried to calm her worry.

"I will come to the hospital as soon as I drop everyone back off at the *mas*. Stefan will take you to the hospital now. I'll call him right after I hang up with you. You may even get to the hospital before your gran. Bring her passport and any health insurance papers."

As he drove, he apologized to them for canceling the rest of the day's events.

They all assured him it was completely understandable, and that they wouldn't be able to think about anything but Barbara anyway.

Once everyone was back in the *mas*, they all settled around the long kitchen table. There was something about that space, ever since the day they had cooked and baked together, that felt comfortable and welcoming.

Bertram plopped a bottle of pastis on the table and got some ice and a pitcher of water from the fridge. "I don't know about anyone else, but I know a calming beverage would do me quite a lot of good. Anyone else? Shall I get some wine out as well?"

"I'll join you in a pastis, please," Arianna said. John and Marti also agreed that would be a good idea. Joan and Lisa opted for white wine.

"A toast to dear Barbara," Bertram said, his voice cracking. "May this be a small blip in her lovely life."

Everyone toasted, and then they speculated as to just what might have happened.

They nibbled on the baguette sandwiches and croque monsieur that Mirielle had quickly prepared after Maurice had called Stefan. Like some food fairy godmother, she had them waiting on the counter when the group had returned, though she was nowhere in sight.

After a short while, they all drifted off in various directions to paint, read, or snooze as they waited patiently for word about their friend.

Arianna found Maximus curled up on her window seat. She sat beside him, stroking his back and taking in the view she loved and knew she would miss. Barbara's accident had been a jolt in this period of such peace and serenity. It felt like a reality check that life wasn't always going to be as idyllic as her days had been here.

Another reason to wake up grateful each morning and make the most out of what is before us. "Isn't that right, *mon petit chat*?" she mumbled out loud to her furry friend. "I'm going to miss you."

Maximus kicked his purring up a notch and settled back to sleep.

After a few hours, Juliette texted them all that Barbara was in with doctors for tests and observation. She was awake and groggily alert. However, because of her age, there were concerns.

The doctors were not taking any chances and would do some additional tests before discharging her. They would definitely keep her overnight.

Cheers resounded through the *mas*. That was better news than was anticipated, and they would continue to hope for the best.

Arianna continued working on a watercolor she had begun of the view out her window. As she painted, she sent out a prayer to the universe that Barbara would be well and back with them soon.

She is such a kind soul who loves life so much right now. Please let that continue. I've learned some important lessons from her and look forward to a long friendship.

Juliette was making arrangements for Cecilia to stay with Barbara at the hospital. Then she and Maurice would come home for a quiet night.

This had been more than enough excitement and stress for everyone.

CHAPTER

THIRTY-ONE

The first announcement of the morning was a text from Cecilia to everyone. Barbara had a restless night but is feeling better this morning, except for a headache. They are considering medication now.

By the time they were gathered on the terrace for breakfast, Cecilia had phoned and given diagnosis details to Juliette.

"Cecilia reports they are releasing Barbara before noon today," Juliette told the group. "She had good test results, and the doctors are all praising her for being in such great shape. Her tests show a minor concussion, and she needs to take it easy."

"There will be no wild tango dancing for our Barbara tonight!" John decreed. Everyone chuckled and murmured their relief.

"Maurice will pick them up when he takes you into town and bring them back here. I'm sure Barbara will want to rest," Juliette said. "We will see whether Cecilia will join you."

Maurice announced that this was to be a "wingy" morning, a favorite term of his. *"On improvise!"*

Laughing at the quizzical looks Maurice was receiving, Juliette explained, "We will wing it . . . play it by ear! *Oui?*"

Some were going into Arles to do the van Gogh walking tour. Arianna was glad she had walked that route by herself. It had been so special for her to pause where he saw beauty and created lasting images through his work and also to gain a sense of where he lived his daily life.

Arianna put her plan together. There was one place to which she wanted to return.

The only requirement was for all of them to meet at the Fondation Vincent van Gogh by two p.m.

Where and when they ate lunch was up to them. How they got to the Fondation was also their choice. The van would leave from the *mas* again at one thirty with anyone who had stayed behind.

Everyone's relaxed level of comfort with their surroundings, and each other, was evident. Arianna was sure their hosts were pleased with how the course was going.

"It's beginning to feel like home," Marti had said just that morning, followed by a chorus of agreement from John and Joan, who were standing nearby. Some had eaten breakfast together, and others had wandered off with a coffee and a croissant to sit in the garden or olive grove on their stools and contemplate their next steps.

Around nine thirty, Maurice drove Arianna, Bertram, and the Mitchells to Arles. Marti and Lisa would go in later.

Arianna's first stop was to spend some time sitting quietly on a bench in the midst of the colorful garden in the courtyard of Espace van Gogh. A plaque nearby indicated that it was originally the Old Hospital of Arles and was also known as Hôtel-Dieu Saint-Esprit, built in the sixteenth and seventeenth centuries.

She found herself alone in this garden, having slipped in as soon as the gate had opened. A print mounted there caught her eye. It was of Vincent's painting of the courtyard and garden when he was a patient. It pleased her to see the town had restored the space in great detail, down to the colorful plantings.

Today she could see that the town was proud of the fact that Vincent had lived there, although only for sixteen months. He was lauded in Arles now, but it had not always been that way.

Arianna had read that with all his bad behavior, he had not endeared himself to the townspeople. She knew most had considered him a terrible nuisance. They had called him *"fou roux,"* the redheaded madman, and had basically run him out of town.

An overwhelming melancholy came over her, thinking how troubled Vincent must have been during the months he stayed at that hospital intermittently.

There was a sad irony to it all. Now everyone wanted to be in van Gogh's space.

That melancholy briefly transferred over to Arianna's own situation. She considered how she was making her dreams come true by coming to Arles. But it was about more than realizing her van Gogh fantasies. Bit by bit, she was accepting that.

She filled several pages in her journal with drawings of the gardens, doors, windows, and the arched yellow colonnade. Before hordes of tourists flooded in, she left.

As she strolled the surrounding streets, Arianna was reminded of a book of letters Vincent had written to his brother Theo. At one point he described Arles as pallid and shabby, but then conceded that after a little time one saw the charm.

She felt there was no question the old charm was everywhere. It certainly appeared that way to her.

Next, Arianna headed back to Les Arènes, the ancient amphitheater that had so captivated her on her earlier visit. She was eager to sketch there before the morning grew too hot. She was also hopeful the singer would be around again. John and Joan bumped into her and decided to go along, but were soon sidetracked by a gallery along the way. Arianna promised to text them if the singer was performing.

But it was quiet when she arrived, and she was happy to see no school tours had turned up yet. Checking with the woman in the little office that sold entrance tickets, she was disappointed to learn that the singer did not usually arrive until midafternoon.

The stones were beginning to warm in the morning sun. Just enough to feel comfortable as Arianna settled on them. She had double-checked the print of van Gogh's *Spectators in the Arena at Arles* and now positioned herself at an angle where she speculated he might have sat. Closing her eyes, she pictured him sketching as he was surrounded by a crowd watching a *feria*. She wondered if anyone paid attention to him. *They probably thought he was an oddball for not watching the excitement in the ring.*

As she worked on her own drawing, capturing the lines and angles in the empty stadium, she was sorry she would not experience the music, costumes, and noise of the crowd that must fill that space during the festivals. She had been drawn to the photos and posters around town. She could feel the energy.

Then her phone signaled a text. Surprisingly, Bertram was inviting her to join him at noon for lunch, at a *bistrot* that Juliette had recommended near the Fondation.

Had she received such a message a week earlier, Arianna knew she would have resisted accepting. However, all week he had continued to reveal a different personality than she had first assumed, and his drinking had lessened. Their day together in the Camargue had convinced her he was actually a good man. He had been thoughtful, interested, kind, and—even more unforeseen—he had been fun!

See you there, she texted back. Thanks!

The time passed quickly at the arena. When she was satisfied with her work, she still had another hour before her lunch date. So many places in town beckoned. The dark, mystical cloisters had been closed the last time she stopped by, so she decided to go there.

From the first night she was in Arles, when Maurice had brought them to the Place de la République, she had promised herself she would come back there. When she purchased her ticket, she decided to pay for a tour that was about to begin.

There was a different feel now without the eeriness of moonlight creating cryptic shadows in this once holy space. Even so, it was easy to imagine the chanting of hymns and prayers ringing through the passageways so many centuries ago.

Arianna walked through the peaceful courtyard, the quiet broken only by the cooing of pigeons. As she stepped into the surrounding cloisters, the tour began with just her and a couple from Wisconsin. She was glad to have someone explain the details of the twelfth- to fourteenth-century sculptures. It was one thing to feel the mysterious ambiance and quite another to understand some of the meaning imparted to pilgrims so long ago.

She had just enough time to sit for a few moments on a stone bench on the roof to contemplate all she had seen. Arianna felt that whenever she stood on all these ancient grounds in Arles, something touched her spirit. She was growing in many different ways on this trip.

Hopeful her photos would turn out, she noticed the time on her phone.

With a start, she realized she would have to hurry to be on time to meet Bertram. Turning down the wrong side street did not help, and she was breathless by the time she reached the restaurant.

She recognized it as one she had passed on her wanderings the previous week. The cream-toned building had pale-pink shutters and a large terrace with a vine-covered pergola stretching its entire length.

Arianna noticed bunches of grapes hanging that looked like they needed a little more time to ripen.

A blackboard leaned against the wall at the entrance with the day's specials on it. Wrought-iron tables and chairs with striped pink cushions lent a sense of dining in a secret garden.

Arianna spotted Bertram and waved. "Sorry I'm a few minutes late!"

"No worries, my dear girl!" He leapt to his feet and pulled out a chair for her. An open bottle of rosé was on the table, and Arianna was happy to have him pour her a glass.

"I'm so pleased you accepted my invitation. *Santé!* And let's toast to Barbara's health while we are at it. What a relief she is all right."

"For sure!" Arianna said. "*Santé* to Barbara and you. You rose to the occasion. I was worried."

"So were we all! How was your morning?"

"I had a very satisfying morning, thanks! I finally went inside the cloisters and am so pleased I did. It exceeded my expectations, and I pretty much had the space to myself . . . at the arena, as well. If you haven't been, Bertie, you should . . ." She caught herself in midsentence.

He stared at her, waiting for her to finish.

"Sorry, do you mind if we call you Bertie? You insisted we all do so on the night of our group dinner . . . but there'd been a certain quantity of wine involved. And I don't want to be rude. I felt a bit uncomfortable saying it without checking."

The Englishman smiled, almost shyly. "To be honest, I like it very much. No one has called me that since I was a child. Now finish telling me how you felt about the cloisters."

Arianna described her experience in detail, ending by saying, "I could go on and on about what a mystical charm it has, but I'm sure it affects everyone differently. The intricately carved capitals atop the stately columns are each a work of art—such detail! The interior is so dimly lit, the statues take on lives of their own. I could almost hear the echoes of the pilgrims gathering there all those centuries ago."

Bertram rubbed at a slight tick that had appeared at the corner of his left eye. "I spent some time in the church and the cloisters when I was in Arles working on the boat recovery years ago." He took a sip of his wine. "However, I'm ashamed to say I was so inebriated at the time, I barely recall anything about it."

Raising her eyebrow, Arianna said nothing as she looked at him. The waitress arrived in time to end the awkward moment.

They both ordered the *plat du jour* from the blackboard: *pâté en croute*, a baked whitefish topped with a hot butter meunière sauce, and a lemon tart. Mouthwatering aromas wafted out from the kitchen.

"I never eat a rich meal like this for lunch at home," Arianna confessed. "But it just seems so right here . . . along with the fact the food is all so delicious."

Bertram licked his lips lightly and dabbed them with his napkin. "There's no question we Europeans somehow eat better without making a big deal about it. I guess it comes from centuries of practice!"

They chuckled and raised their glasses in a toast.

"Fine," Bertram said. "No more circumambages. I called this meeting for a specific reason."

CHAPTER

THIRTY-TWO

Arianna looked puzzled. "Circum-what-ages?"

Bertram chuckled. "Sorry, can't help myself . . . no more beating around the bush."

A faint bead of perspiration appeared on his brow. He took a linen handkerchief from his pocket and wiped his forehead. "Excuse me, Arianna. I'm feeling rather nervous about this. It's not my usual modus operandi."

Reaching out, Arianna touched his hand as it gripped the stem of his wineglass.

"What's wrong?"

"To be precise," he began, his proper British accent causing the conversation to sound of the utmost importance, "nothing is wrong. Now. Quite the opposite, my dear girl. There are some things that are more right . . . for me . . . than they have been in eons. I want to share them with you."

He took a large sip of rosé, and then beckoned to the waitress. *"Une carafe d'eau, s'il vous plaît.*

"Do you mind tap water, Arianna? I should have asked you first . . ."

"Oh, that's perfect. I've finally learned how to order local water by saying *'une carafe.'* Before that, I kept ending up with bottles of mineral water, and I much prefer this." She chuckled, hoping to lighten the atmosphere that had suddenly become a bit tense.

"I tend to drink a lot when I'm feeling anxious—usually wine—and then, well, you've seen what happens to me. I'm a terrible drinker . . . no tolerance."

He held her gaze. Arianna blinked and nodded, feeling uncomfortable. "Um . . . yes, I have noticed." She shifted awkwardly in her chair.

Once the water was poured, Bertram immediately gulped down half a glass. Then he began to speak quickly, his sentences tumbling together, as if he wanted to make certain he said everything before something stopped him.

"Arianna, this past week has been quite an unimagined experience for me. I've never participated in a group 'thing' before, always been a bit of a loner. I have to believe it was extremely fortuitous for me to land here with all of you. After this short time together, I feel like a changed man, or perhaps I've just rediscovered the person I once was. Sounds rather phantasmagorical, perhaps?"

He paused, mopped his forehead, took another long drink of water, and continued before Arianna could respond to his question. She had no idea where this conversation was going, but she recognized there seemed to be something important he wished to say.

"Let me give you a very brief history. I came from a lovely childhood and good education. A privileged background, veritable Brahmans. Went to all the best schools and was a reckless party animal. The downside was that I married a girl I impregnated thanks to one of my regular youthful booze-ups . . . but we were never in love with each other. The good news about that was the birth of my twin daughters, Rachel and Rebecca. They are now married with children. I have grandchildren!" He stopped and beamed.

"The unfortunate news is one lives in Indonesia and the other in Australia, so I rarely see them except on Skype and FaceTime. God bless them! Back to my story. One thing I will say is that my wife was a good mother, in the early years. And, if I do say so myself, I am a good father. However, as a couple we are hopeless, and yet Miranda—that's my wife—refuses to divorce me. And I don't take the bull by the horns either . . . a somewhat appropriate analogy in this area . . ." He paused and rolled his eyes as he took a long sip of wine this time. "So we live in a horrible mess of a marriage. Why, you ask? Well, you didn't, but I'm sure you are wondering . . ."

He stopped. The waitress placed their starters on the table.

"Bon appétit, chérie!" he said to Arianna, picking up his knife and fork.

"Bon appétit, Bertie! Would you like to take a break from your story?"

Chewing a mouthful slowly, he shook his head.

"Now that I've started, do you mind if I carry on my true confessions? Quite frankly, I can't believe I'm even telling you this. But this is what this week has done to me."

"Bertie, whatever you want." She felt genuine empathy for him now. "You certainly have my attention. Oh goodness, this pâté is delicious, isn't it?"

He smiled his agreement before his eyes clouded and the tone of his voice dropped. "So, since the girls went off to live their own lives, I've buried myself in my work. Traveled a lot for business. Meanwhile, my wife lives a life of luxury, lunching with her friends, all of whom apparently have foreheads that do not move. Cosmetic surgery is her hobby, as she hasn't responded well to aging. When we are home together, she berates me constantly, and I drink, which exacerbates the berating, and it becomes a vicious circle. Oh, I should add that she is a raging alcoholic and addicted to pills. And I keep trying to help her. You've heard about the battered wife? Well, meet the battered husband."

He sat back in his chair, lifted his wineglass in a toast, and drank deeply. Arianna noticed a slight tremble in his hand as he set his glass down.

The waitress set their main courses in front of them.

Arianna stared at her lunch companion in disbelief. She was flabbergasted he would divulge such intimacies, and she was still uncertain as to his purpose. Her heart broke for him.

"Bertie, I don't know what to say. I'm so sorry you have to live like this."

"Mmhmm," he replied, tucking his napkin into the top of his shirt, under his chin. "Oops, my apologies. Does me wearing my napkin like this embarrass you?"

Arianna wondered if he had done that for comic relief, because the sight of him with his tucked napkin did make her laugh. It was so unlike his very proper British comportment.

She shook her head and said, "Whatever works for you."

"You see, Miranda would be aghast if I did this in public. She never even let me do this at home. Get the picture?"

Arianna smiled weakly and felt glad that type of criticism had never been part of her world. "I'm kind of surprised you're sharing all these details with me."

Bertram's face relaxed as he savored his fish. "Crikey! They know how to cook fish to perfection in this country, *n'est-ce pas*? No wonder there's not a seat left in here!"

"*Magnifique,*" Arianna agreed in between bites.

They ate in silence for a few minutes. Arianna worried about losing her appetite, in spite of the delicious meal. Bertie seemed to be a decent man trapped in an abusive relationship. She felt sad for him.

"Well, I'm surprised too," he said, getting back on topic. "But there's a reason I want to tell you this. Oh . . . just keep reminding me to drink water too, or I'll slurp back this entire bottle of rosé before you have a chance to finish your glass. Here, let me top yours up."

"And that's fine. Enough for me or I won't make it through the Fondation later without having a catnap somewhere."

"So," Bertram continued, "I've had three epiphanies—well, major ones—in my life. The first was when my daughters were born, and I felt that new dimension of love one feels as a parent. I already knew I had a shitty marriage, but I committed myself to being the best father I could be. The second was working on the restoration of that amazing boat. That experience gave me a renewed lease on life; it was almost a religious experience. Working with materials two thousand years old. Feeling connected to something so ancient. I vowed to try to become a happier person."

He gestured with his fork as he said, "You know, I always credited Gaius Julius Caesar with that change in me. Like I told you at the museum, he was really responsible for the recovery of the boat. So I decided he brought about my recovery too."

"Perhaps you're right, Bertie. Why not?"

He chuckled before becoming serious again. "Part of that recovery involved taking up art again after a long absence, as I slipped into semiretirement."

"Did you spend more time at home then?" Arianna asked, adding hopefully, "Did things improve with your wife?"

"In fact, the response to both of those questions is a resounding no," he replied. "And I have to say, alcohol became a crutch for me. I'm fortunate it didn't become an addiction, just a very bad habit."

Arianna's face showed her sympathy. She had grown fond of him. She reached over and took his hand. He held her fingers gently for a moment. His eyes reflected gratitude for her caring.

Pursing his lips, he squinted his eyes as he looked directly into Arianna's. "In fact, the relationship only got worse. I got tired of her hurling abuse at me and even throwing things, with amazing accuracy . . . But, still, I did not leave the marriage. You know, after so many years it can be complicated, but that's a poor excuse, and I know it.

There's the London town house and the country estate. We go for weeks without seeing each other . . . or even speaking. We just text now."

"Do your daughters know about all this?"

His eyes filled with such sadness, Arianna thought he might cry. Her heart went out to him. "They are another reason I haven't pursued divorce. The girls don't realize how catastrophic things are at home. And then there's me being a coward. But . . ." His voice tapered off.

"I can't imagine being caught in such a terrible relationship," Arianna said softly. "How heartbreaking to live your life in such despair."

"I just kept painting and drinking more and more once the girls moved away. I never really touched alcohol after the girls were born. Mainly because my wife drank enough for both of us. Believe me, I've tried to help Miranda many, many times. She refuses it all."

"Not unusual," Arianna murmured. She thought back briefly to when Faith was rebelling with drugs during her teenage years.

"I've been treading the slippery slope to becoming an alcoholic myself . . . as you may have observed. Somehow I always manage to catch it in time. But only after having made a fool of myself more times than I care to recall."

"You seem to be drinking far less this week than last," Arianna said, hoping to bring some positivity to the conversation and lift her friend's feelings a bit.

"Yes, that's true. And it is because of this group and the time we've spent together. This probably sounds hokey, but I feel this is a very special mix of personalities, and it has been my good fortune to be amongst all of you. I've spent a lot of time observing, listening, and thinking. I've also been aware of the kindness, genuine interest, and even, dare I say it, respect that everyone has shown to each other. I feel it's quite remarkable. In fact, this time together in Arles has brought about my third epiphany."

"Bertie, that's wonderful. I'm happy to hear that. Of course, I had no idea you were carrying such sadness and frustration in your heart.

You're right. I've felt the same as you about the time we have all spent at the Mas des Artistes. I've never done anything like this before either."

"I made a few mistakes in the beginning. When I first met Joan, I immediately pegged her for a brash American, and I rudely insulted her. The next few days, as I drank way too much to cover my insecurities of being in this group, as is my wont, I added a few other derogatory comments."

"Oh, Bertie . . . You must feel awful. They are the nicest couple."

"I did feel awful. She's so forgiving, she let it slide and never mentioned it to John. She told me that when I apologized to her the day of our cooking adventure during the mistral. She said she was determined to work on me and charm me until I changed my attitude and became her new best friend!"

"Good story!" Arianna said, happy to feel their conversation move forward on a good note and to see Bertram's composure return and his despair fade.

"And now forgive me if I am intruding too much into your personal situation. Please hand me a cease-and-desist order, if that is the case."

Arianna tried to hide the surprise in her expression. She had not expected this turn in the conversation.

Bertram reached across tentatively, his expression sincere, and this time he took her hand in his. "In our time here, I've seen you begin to blossom from a closed, solemn, and perhaps sad woman. I've heard you share bits of your tragic crisis concerning your husband. I've understood why you have emotional obstacles in your life. I'm so sorry for the tragedy you and your family are living."

Arianna began to comprehend that this conversation was not so much about Bertie as about her. She felt genuinely touched, but unable to speak.

"My dear girl, I wanted to tell you about my pathetic situation to express how some of us get stuck in life. Stuck, where we lose love, dignity, hope. Stuck, and for whatever reason, can't move on. I hope that somehow my sharing my story helps you discover impetus to move on with your life. I know your circumstances are completely different, but I think our solutions may be somewhat similar."

She nodded and still said nothing, swallowing hard.

"Watching you and listening to you when we were discovering the Camargue was a beautiful thing. You seemed to enjoy every moment, as did we all. I'm not certain that would have happened a week ago. Are you?"

Arianna shook her head. She took a long drink of water. Little did her friend know that he was reaffirming the realization growing in her. She was learning to let go and perhaps finally giving herself permission to move forward. To become, as he suggested, "unstuck."

"Bertie, thank you for telling me your story. I am so appreciative of you being this open and frank. It's kind of you, and your words do help me. Truly."

He touched his wineglass to hers. Their eyes met with an intensity that might have taken years to forge . . . or simply a few meaningful days of honest interaction.

Bertram said, "I'm very glad . . . and relieved. I wasn't certain it was proper of me to touch on something of such sensitivity."

Arianna's expression was calm as her lips turned up in a soft half smile. "I've come to realize there aren't any rules for honesty and caring."

Bertram told her, "You said something a few days ago that really hit home with me. You said you felt you were stuck in the 'now' of your life. That is my problem too. I've stayed in the 'now' far too long, and I'm going to get unstuck. In fact, before I went to sleep last night, I looked up airfares to Indonesia and Australia. I plan to go on an extended trip. Alone."

The lemon tart was served by the waitress, who asked if either of them would care for Chantilly.

"Whipped cream, but the most divine ever," Bertram translated, giving Arianna a look that said, "Let's do it."

They both said yes.

CHAPTER

THIRTY-THREE

Arianna and Bertram strolled to the Fondation Vincent van Gogh, just down the street from the restaurant.

She told him she had read quite a bit about it before the trip. "I was so excited when I realized this exhibit would be on while we were here. Vincent was my first major influence when I was old enough to appreciate art. I had posters of his sunflowers and fields in my bedroom as a teenager."

Within minutes, they had walked through the sliding gates, on which was painted van Gogh's characteristic signature, and into a spacious courtyard. Arianna pointed to others of their group already in the two-story, glassed-in entrance area.

"The Fondation only opened this beauty in 2014," explained Bertram as they walked toward their group. "When I was here before, there was some van Gogh information displayed next to the amphitheater. It was an old building equipped with neither the security nor the climate control proper for showing van Gogh's masterpieces."

"Imagine!" Arianna exclaimed. "But you know that's not unusual in Europe, where so much priceless art was often in attics and barns for centuries."

Bertram looked around in delight. "Now this fifteenth-century mansion has undergone an eleven-million-euro transformation! I'm excited!"

After they joined their group, Juliette offered a brief preamble before they went upstairs to the paintings. "While the Fondation showcases and promotes van Gogh's art, it also constantly is searching to discover the ongoing impact of it all. They hope to achieve this by ongoing exhibits of promising new artists. "

They could see that the space was intimate but well laid out to exhibit the thirty-one originals. The masterpieces were on loan from museums around the world.

Juliette explained they would have an hour to explore the exhibit as they chose, then they would meet in a conference room on the main floor for a presentation before a guide would take them on a private tour.

"So make a note of questions you might have about any of these pieces. We have a unique opportunity here."

Everyone wandered off on their own but frequently came together studying one piece or another. It had been a long time since Arianna had even gone to a gallery or an exhibit, and she beat herself up a bit about that. *No excuses . . . I promise this is going to become an important part of my life again.*

The remainder of the afternoon was like an intensive immersion into all things van Gogh. The presenter and guide were knowledgeable, articulate, and entertaining in bringing so much information to life.

Everyone appreciated having time to simply stand in front of original works and absorb the experience however they wished. It was all very personal.

There was shocked silence when Barbara appeared with Cecilia, who told them, "I couldn't keep her away."

"And the doctors said I could go out if I wanted. I just have to take it easy. I mean, how could I miss this? I know you are almost ready to leave, so I will be quick."

Everyone gently hugged her and expressed their concern. She thanked them all. "I'm fine. Don't worry. The care I received was excellent."

There was complete agreement that this was a rare opportunity when they thanked Juliette for arranging the visit.

Arianna felt a lifetime dream had been realized, immersed as she was in the life and art of this man whose work had always been an inspiration. She wished she could share this joy with Ben.

More and more, she was able to accept that Ben would want her to keep living. He would be happy for her. At this moment she knew.

Thank you, Vincent. And thank you, Bertie, too.

It was seven o'clock when they finally left the Fondation, debating what to do next.

"Well, here's what I'm going to do, and anyone who wants to is welcome to join me," Arianna said, surprising herself by taking charge. "I admire how Arles keeps the story of van Gogh alive every day. I know some people consider it touristy and tacky, but I like the frequent references to him . . . even the souvenirs."

There were chuckles at her last comment. "I bought some," John said, "and I'm not ashamed to admit it! Even a pair of van Gogh boxers . . . for those, he-he, special artistic occasions . . ." He ended with his now-familiar Groucho Marx eyebrow waggle at his wife.

Joan punched him in the arm. "Gawd, John! You don't have to blab everything!"

Marti added, "What's wrong with tourists learning about van Gogh and wanting to buy those souvenirs? They're showing an interest in his art and helping the town's economy. Tacky or not, I support it too!"

"And let's face it," Bertram said, "I bet every one of us had coffee or a drink on the terrace of the Le Café La Nuit in Place du Forum, right?"

All hands shot up.

"Okay, I didn't intend to start a debate about it," Arianna said with a chuckle. "What I wanted to say is that I'm truly besotted with Vincent, and I'm going to stay in town until after sunset. I want to sit by the river near where he painted *Starry Night Over the Rhône* and watch the sky. It was from this work that his more famous *The Starry Night* evolved. Call me crazy, but I just feel the need to go there."

It turned out she was not alone. Everyone said they wanted to stay with her. Juliette shook her head as she looked at them all with admiration. "You've definitely morphed into a family . . . or the Vincent van Gogh fan club. Since I don't want to miss the party, I'm going to stay with you too."

There were cheers all around. Then they all looked at Barbara with concern. "We don't want to leave you out. But we don't want you to push yourself too much. Are you sure you are feeling up to this?"

Barbara nodded resolutely. "I wouldn't miss it for the world."

Juliette continued, "Well, we will all go with you and have a bit of a rest, my dear. Why not? I'll get Maurice to meet us. A friend of ours owns a very casual bar just down the street in the La Roquette district. I'm sure he can squeeze us all in for dinner . . . and it will be our treat, since we're not going back to the *mas* to eat."

More cheers erupted now. Juliette led the way to this other distinct area of Arles.

At 8:37 p.m., as the sun set, they were all sitting on stone steps leading to the walkway along the banks of the Rhône. They weren't too far from where the little yellow house once stood, where van Gogh had famously lived with Gauguin.

Bertram was talking about Vincent's love of painting at night. "I read more than once where he expressed the sentiment that the night was more alive with color than day."

Juliette agreed. "And by painting from this vantage point, he also captured the effect of the newly installed gas lighting reflected in the river. With the growth of the town and the addition of electric lighting, we won't see anything close to the same sky he did."

"And, of course, he painted it in September," Bertram added. "But never mind, we're here as much to pay homage to him as anything else, poor tortured soul, aren't we?"

Murmurs of agreement were interrupted by beautiful music as the voice of Don McLean floated up around them, singing "Vincent (Starry Starry Night)." Lisa held out her phone, where she was streaming that emotional anthem to the painter.

Not a word was spoken until it ended. "Please play it again," several voices chimed together. So she did.

"I've never heard that," Bertram told her. "That was wonderful."

"It's on iTunes with a slide show of his paintings. You should take a look at that, Bertie," Marti said. "I think you would enjoy it. We've been playing it for years. It's Lisa's favorite song."

"This has been a remarkable day," Barbara said to no one in particular.

In more ways than one, Arianna said to herself. *And not for the first time.*

CHAPTER
THIRTY-FOUR

Arianna awoke after a relatively sleepless night.

The reality that her stay at Mas des Artistes would soon be over was suddenly causing her to feel conflicted. She didn't want to leave. She didn't want the transition that was slowly awakening within her to end.

Maximus moved up to her face and rubbed his head under her chin. His whiskers tickled her neck, and before long she felt the velvet pads of his paw gently tap her cheek. He seemed to know she could use some tenderness. Arianna was going to miss him.

Less than two weeks earlier, she had boarded the plane in Toronto with trepidation. Then she had struggled for days to find her place here, to feel like she fit in, and to feel her artist's soul come back to life.

She shook her head, recalling that she had seriously considered leaving the course.

And now . . . *Funny how things can change in such a short time . . . can I keep moving forward on my own with the same positive attitude I reached yesterday?*

She opened the shutters in time to see the landscape dimly lit in a predawn silver-gray hue. As the sun began rising behind the jagged *Alpilles*, the light rolled in like a gentle tide. For a moment, in the morning stillness, Arianna had a vision of a van Gogh painting precisely this view.

After spending so much time in the midst of his original works and hearing such personal details about his life, she felt the painter had truly come alive in her mind. The more she learned about him, the stronger her empathy for him grew.

The glowing embers of desire to draw and paint that Arianna had buried for so many years had begun to burn deep within her.

Thank you, Vincent.

The song that Lisa had played for them the previous night had haunted her. She had played it over and over after she got into bed. Then she had cried herself to sleep.

She wondered now what that had been all about.

Was I crying for Vincent? For Ben? For myself? For Barbara? For all of us? She conceded she was feeling very emotional.

Whatever it was, it had been cleansing.

Now she sensed it would be a good idea to spend time meditating before she joined the others for breakfast. She needed to calm herself.

The morning was taken up with an informative watercolor and water-based media presentation at the studio of a British artist who lived in nearby picturesque Eygalières. This was not a hands-on workshop but more a lecture where they all took notes.

The focus was how to capture light and atmosphere, starting from direct observation. Arianna was not surprised that several of van Gogh's works were used as examples. The instructor quoted the painter often and reflected van Gogh's feelings as he encouraged them to listen to the language of nature.

As soon as the workshop ended, a quick buffet was waiting for the group. It was served on the terrace behind the artist's studio, where Juliette had a surprise to greet them as soon as they stepped outside.

A field ablaze with brilliant-red poppies swaying gently in the light breeze stretched before them. It was a compelling visual.

Lunch was initially forgotten as everyone drank in the view. Cameras and journals came out to record the splendid image.

"I didn't want you to leave our course without having the pleasure of enjoying a dazzling field of *coquelicots*," Juliette said as she was showered with thanks. "We haven't had as many poppy fields in our area this year—most farmers don't like them—and this one is kind of our little secret."

Juliette was aware of the emotion on everyone's face. "So please, take some time now to let this beautiful scene soak into your soul."

Arianna walked over to the flowers and knelt down to feel the softness of the delicate petals. The rich color made her heart swell with something she couldn't quite define. But it was powerful. She felt herself deeply touched by the fragility of the thin fuzzy stems and the exquisitely silky petals.

A moment of pure emotion rushed through her as she thought of Ben and the fragility of life. Absorbing the beauty of this simple bloom, she was reminded how quickly life can change. There is a delicacy to life that cannot be predicted. These poppies carried that message to her.

She wiped a tear from her eye and stood. She knew the vision of this poppy field would forever play a part in her promise to move forward with her life. She would embrace the fragility of life and believe in the resiliency that these humble blossoms have come to represent.

Still excited about their unexpected surprise, after lunch they climbed into the van for their final road trip. A half an hour down the tree-lined road, they arrived just outside the charming town of Saint-Rémy-de-Provence.

Their destination was the asylum, or sanatorium, the monastery Saint-Paul-de-Mausole, where Vincent had voluntarily admitted himself in May 1889. The people of Arles were fed up with his behavior. Here in Saint Remy it was said he was happy and relieved to find a peaceful and understanding atmosphere among the nuns and nurses who cared for him.

Although at times his mental illness took control, there were other times when he was inspired and driven to create. He had produced 143 oil paintings and over one hundred drawings in fifty-three weeks.

Maurice dropped them off at the gates to a long pathway. It was a dramatic setting with the eleventh-century priory attached to the hospital, the latter still used to treat psychiatric patients.

They walked down the pathway toward the Romanesque two-story square steeple rising above the trees. Arianna was disappointed that the massive flower beds were between seasonal bloomings. She could imagine the color and fragrance they would add to the setting, although she felt some were modern additions to the vast property. It had been a surprise when Juliette informed them the newer building was still an active health institution.

How many patients find interest in knowing Vincent himself was a patient? I wonder if art therapy is offered here? In many ways, it's art therapy that is helping me now, the life-affirming pleasure of making art.

A tour of the premises did not take long. One room was a reproduction of Vincent's room, with a window overlooking a wheat field like the ones he had studied and painted. There was lavender in one area now, and Arianna wondered if that had been added later.

Here and there a lone scarlet poppy stood out. *Just to remind me,* Arianna was certain.

She spent quite a long time at the window, consumed by her thoughts.

Bertram came back upstairs in search of her after the others had left.

"Are you all right?" he asked, slightly out of breath. "I suddenly noticed you were missing."

"Oh, Bertie, I am so caught up with the ghost of this man. He has come alive in my mind, and I don't want to leave him. Come look out this window. Can't you just imagine Vincent leaning on a windowsill like this, contemplating . . . sometimes tormented, other times not. What thoughts did he have to create such powerful beauty in his work?"

"When I think of him and all the devils he fought, there's one thought that has stayed with me." Bertram let out a sigh and his voice was full of reverence as he uttered, "Vincent believed that art consoles those who are broken by life."

They stood quietly looking out the window for several minutes. Bertram rested his hand on Arianna's shoulder. She laid her hand on top of his.

"He certainly was broken, wasn't he?" Arianna's voice was barely over a whisper.

"Terribly," Bertram replied, his voice tender and filled with emotion. "And perhaps we all are in one way or another. Maybe that's why we are all here. Maybe that's why we want to draw and paint and create."

Arianna turned and looked into his eyes, pleased they were no longer puffy and bloodshot. He had come a long way on his own journey on this course. She felt such warmth for him now, after their rocky start almost two weeks before. She wondered if he knew how helpful he had been by sharing his personal story and encouraging her to "come unstuck."

"Maybe, maybe," she replied, "but nothing close to Vincent. And guess what? I don't want to feel broken anymore. The poppies freed me."

He leaned toward her and gently planted a kiss on her forehead.

"That's very good news. I'm pleased to hear it. Vincent would be pleased, I'm sure."

Arianna chuckled. "You're too much, Bertie. Thanks for making me laugh. Now I need to lighten up."

For the rest of the afternoon, the group spread out through the property with easels and sketchbooks.

Some of them walked up the road to see and sketch the Roman ruins of Glanum.

Barbara had confessed to Arianna that she was feeling rather tired and was going to stay and paint in the cloistered garden.

Arianna had no desire to leave the monastery, and she wanted to keep Barbara company. Cecilia was having a meeting to interview the woman who oversaw the tourism part of the property.

Being on these grounds brought Arianna to a new sense of contentment. She had turned a corner with her art and within herself.

As she and Barbara sat drawing by the tranquil courtyard garden, they shared feelings about the calm that the color palette of greens wrapped around them. The geometric patterns of clipped shrubs and boxwood hedges created symmetry and order in pathways that led to the softly cascading fountain in the center. They wondered if van Gogh had felt this too among his tortured moments here.

When Juliette stopped by to chat, Arianna happily confessed, "I'm taking enough sketches and ideas back home to keep me busy for years. I'm beginning to find my peace within, Juliette. I've begun the journey."

CHAPTER

THIRTY-FIVE

This was it. Her last day at Mas des Artistes.

Arianna awoke well before her alarm went off. She gently stroked Maximus's back and thought how she might have to get a cat when she got home.

When she got home.

That thought played over and over in her head. She had not reflected about home very much this past week. The day Bertie had confided in her over lunch—*was it really just two days ago?*—had been the last time she had spent more than a few minutes contemplating the situation with Ben. With her. Until yesterday, with the poppies.

Bertie's vow to make a change from the horrendous truth of his homelife inspired her. While acknowledging that his pain was very different from hers, she knew his point was well taken. She needed to take care of herself.

There had been general agreement the night before that the group would gather at nine a.m. to share their paintings, sketches, thoughts, or anything else. Bertram suggested he might line up wine bottles. "Just being jocular!"

Juliette wanted them all to be completely relaxed about it. "It's no competition. *C'est pas obligatoire!* It's not mandatory. If you don't want to display any work, don't worry!" she assured them.

John piped up. "Are you kidding me? With this prolific group? You might have to rent one of the galleries in Arles to accommodate us!"

Fortunately, the terrace proved more than ample for everyone to set up easels or place paintings, complete or in progress, on the long tables. The day was once again cooperating, and the warm sun, clear sky, and still air, filled with sweet morning birdsong harmonizing with cicadas, provided the perfect setting.

It was a pleasant surprise, everyone agreed, when Jacques de Villeneuve appeared with Juliette. Her melodic voice undulated across the terrace as she announced he was joining them for lunch.

Barbara, still a little frail but mostly recovered from her fall, leaned close to Arianna. "I'm going to miss the spellbinding sound of her voice. Perhaps I'll call her every once in a while to get my fix."

Arianna nodded in agreement, whispering, "The sound of a Zen goddess."

Joan nudged Arianna, as she had the first time they had seen Jacques. "As I said that first day, a *très* sexy dude! That assessment has not changed!"

Arianna nudged her back and grinned. "And I agree even more today. Now that we know so much about him."

Juliette connected with each person for more than a moment, her face glowing with emotion. "This is always the most difficult part of our course. In bidding farewell to our guests, we want to convey that we hope you will return. We want to see you again!"

Maurice nodded his agreement as Juliette continued. "You probably think I say this to each of our groups, but this course truly was very special because of who you all are and what you brought with you: your unique personalities, humor, and willingness to experience and be open to change, and your creative diversity. Each one of you is a real artist."

Arianna's gaze rested briefly on each member of the group. She felt such warmth for all of them and gratitude for their individual roles in her transition.

Be open to change. Of everything I've learned here, that's the most important. My renewed commitment to art has been secondary, even though that was my purpose in coming. Every one of these people, strangers to me almost two weeks ago, has shared a personal story that has impacted me. How could I ever have imagined I would be so fortunate as to find myself here with them?

The group mingled for a while longer, studying the paintings and sketches, along with a series of simple caricatures Marti had whipped up at the last minute. Hearty laughter hung in the air.

Arianna found herself trying not to watch Jacques as he paused at her work. Her pulse beat rapidly as he made a few comments to Juliette, who was standing beside him. She noticed Juliette smile and nod as they moved on.

"What do you think, Arianna Papadopoulos-Miller? Have we learned anything here?" John asked, sidling up to her and using her full name as he always liked to do. And always making her smile. "There's some mighty fine-looking works of art here! Wouldn't you say?'

"I couldn't agree more!" she replied. "I know I've gained so much from being here. How about you?"

His head bobbed enthusiastically.

The soft ringing of a bell drew their attention back to Juliette.

"And now for the awards ceremony," she announced, eliciting a lighthearted applause.

At the mention of prizes, Arianna briefly felt anxious. No one had said anything about that! She hoped she wouldn't be too embarrassed. When she saw some of the art others had done during the course, she felt humbled. But where she had felt nervous and inadequate at the beginning of the course, she now had a new confidence and pride in her work.

She was displaying her *Olive Grove with Stone Wall* oil. It was not quite finished, but Juliette had praised her grasp of the subtleties of shades, patterns, and textures in the leaves, wood, and stone.

She also was showing the flamingo sketch from the Camargue. "Had I known de Villeneuve was appearing today, I might not have been quite so brave," she whispered to Barbara.

The prizes—certificates made with elaborate calligraphy and graphics by Juliette—turned out to be thoughtful and funny. And they had nothing to do with art.

- *Joan: best laugh and ability to have others join in*
- *John: best connoisseur of ice cream and finest French pronunciation of flavors*
- *Barbara: best role model for proving age is just a number*
- *Cecilia: best artist in a non-painting category*
- *Marti: brightest smile and generator of positive energy*
- *Lisa: technology expert and text sender extraordinaire*
- *Bertram: most impressive vocabulary and rosé consumption*
- *Arianna: most improved and winner of Maximus's affection*

Once they had finished congratulating each other, Maurice directed everyone's attention to the field just beyond the stone wall and the olive grove where Mirielle, Louis-Philippe, and Stefan waved from a cleared space in the freshly cut grass. They obviously had been hard at work there.

Shaded by substantial umbrellas, tables were set with white linen tablecloths topped with colorful Provençal fabrics. Large ceramic vases filled with showy combinations of wildflowers punctuated the tabletops. Wicker baskets, olivewood boards, and multicolored ceramic bowls hinted at a delicious picnic feast awaiting them.

Maurice walked over to a tub filled with ice in which bottles of champagne were chilling. "We began with champagne on our first evening, and we'll begin our last afternoon together with a *coupe* or two. This is our final official meal together. Juliette and I want to toast each one of you for all of you have accomplished this week and for the memories and friendship you are leaving with us."

Many toasts were proposed before they began to eat.

Arianna found herself standing next to Jacques as she planned her attack on the buffet.

"This is quite a feast, is it not?" he asked.

"So classically French." Arianna sighed. "I'm going to miss this food."

Marti was on the other side of Arianna. She turned to both of them and said, "We've never had a meal that wasn't absolutely scrumptilli-umptious! I'm sorry I don't know how to say that in French."

They all laughed, and Jacques told her, "I don't think we can match that. Perhaps if we could figure out how to join these words together: *'délicieux,' et 'époustouflant*'!"

They all focused their attention on the dazzling choices displayed on the long table.

The centerpiece consisted of a deconstructed salade Niçoise to be put together as each diner desired: a large bowl of greens surrounded by several platters with artistically displayed small fillets of seared tuna, hard-boiled eggs, al dente green beans, boiled potatoes, thinly sliced onions, plum tomatoes, olives, capers, and anchovies. On each side of the display were small pitchers of lemon vinaigrette.

Bertram was exclaiming over the *tarte à la moutarde*, which he explained to Joan and John was actually a tomato-and-mustard pie. "Once you taste this, you will develop an instant addiction and make it at least once a month when you go back home. I guarantee it! It's a good thing there are two of them on this table."

A large, creamy quiche Lorraine; a platter of grilled lamb chops; and another of grilled sardines completed the main dishes. An enormous dish filled with colorful sliced crudités surrounding a vinaigrette dip looked like it was straight off the cover of a gourmet magazine.

At the dessert end, there was fresh fruit, chocolate, and cheese. "Ah, the cheese!" Joan exclaimed. "Will I ever go a day without it again? I think not!"

"Arianna, where do you go from here? Directly back to Toronto?" Jacques quietly continued their conversation.

"You know, I'm not entirely certain. I'm renting a car, and I have to return it to the Marseille airport a week from today. I was going to head straight to Nice and the Côte d'Azur. I'd like to experience that area in person."

"Ah, of course it must be seen. Don't miss Antibes!"

Arianna responded with a broad smile. "That's my first stop, actually! How did you know?"

He grinned back. Once again, she was struck by the intensity of his eyes. She tried to pinpoint their mesmerizing color. *Is it cerulean, cobalt, ultramarine, lapis? Such a blue blue . . .*

"However," Arianna continued as she became aware she was staring, "after hearing you describe Aigues-Mortes, and then listening to those of our group who visited there, I'm altering my route slightly. I'm going to leave early tomorrow and go there first."

"Good idea!" he exclaimed. "You won't be disappointed."

"Then I'm going to drive to Aix-en-Provence in the afternoon and spend a couple of hours there before I go on to Antibes. What do you think? Is that too much driving for one day?"

"No, not at all. May I be so bold as to invite myself to meet you in Aigues-Mortes? It would be my pleasure to show you the secrets of that town."

Arianna was surprised at the suggestion. She was also pleased to accept, knowing he would make her visit much more interesting than following a tourist brochure.

"That's so kind of you," she replied, brushing her bangs aside and suddenly feeling awkward. "I . . . I accept your offer!"

"If you tell me your phone number, we can text each other. I'll let you know where we can meet. Come early to avoid hordes of tourists . . . say, nine a.m.? How does that sound?"

Arianna smiled her thanks, giving her head a slight nod. Her voice had briefly vanished as the realization hit her: *I've just accepted an invitation to meet a gorgeous man by myself.*

She was taken aback that she'd thought the word "gorgeous." She felt guilty. *I'm a married woman, and I can admire a man anytime. He's going to show me this historic village, and maybe we will have lunch together. So what? We're two acquaintances who have already spent time together. He's a gentleman. I'm a lady. An adult. What the hell is my problem? I can do this.*

She realized she had been standing there with a blank expression on her face.

"Is everything okay?" Jacques asked. "I mean . . . if I text you. Is that okay?"

"Oh yes, yes . . . sorry . . . of course." She told him her number. "See you tomorrow. And thanks!"

She turned back to the buffet table, feeling ridiculously juvenile. Serving herself way too much salad, she was relieved when Joan came over to chat.

"Mon amie!" Arianna marveled at how Joan's smile and eyes never ceased to light up the space around her. "Can you believe we're all going to be saying au revoir tomorrow morning? In some ways it feels like we just got here, and yet, in others, it feels like we've been here a long time. It's been awesome, hasn't it?"

Arianna admired her ever-optimistic attitude. Instead of sounding sad about leaving tomorrow, Joan exuded glee about the time they had spent together and the friendships that had been formed.

They found a spot to sit and relived some of the moments that meant the most to them. It didn't take long for the entire group to join the exchange.

"It seems to me your family has expanded," Jacques teased Juliette and Maurice. "No one wants to leave!"

Maurice grinned as he looked around at everyone. "This has been a unique group."

Everyone was excitedly talking about how the course had affected them and their work. There wasn't one of them who felt it had not been a successful undertaking on many levels.

Individually, they each took a moment to offer their thanks to Juliette and Maurice. Gratitude abounded. Bertram outdid himself when he declared that their artists' retreat represented "the umami of life. Ordinary days were infused with extraordinary flavor, the memory of which shall never fade. Today was an exquisite denouement to the entire experience."

Arianna could see Juliette and Maurice were touched. Their words were grateful in return. Juliette's eyes shone as she emotionally shared a thought with each of them individually.

Jacques bid everyone *"Au revoir et bonne continuation"* and invited them to visit him in the Camargue anytime. "I leave you with this quote from Horace: 'A picture is a poem without words.' I urge you to go forth and make beautiful poetry."

"Keep enjoying yourselves here, and we will see you all back at the *mas*," Juliette urged as she and Maurice excused themselves to walk Jacques back to his car. "We still have the rest of the day together."

Some planned to go later that afternoon to Juliette and Maurice's favorite wine store in town and arrange for a couple of cases of fine wine to be delivered after their departure. It would be a gesture of thanks to which all were contributing.

Cecilia had been off to one side speaking on her cell phone. She joined the group now, looking frazzled. "Gran, the travel company changed our reservation and put us on the overnight train to Paris. They're concerned the transportation systems may strike in the morning. They are sending a car for us this evening to take us to the TGV in Avignon. It's part of our package."

Barbara frowned. "Oh, darn! That means we've got to get packed! I wasn't prepared to say good-bye just yet. Never mind, good of them to take care of us like this."

Arianna smiled to see that Barbara's boundless energy had begun to return. She had given all of them such a scare.

For the remainder of the afternoon and evening, they were all going on a special tour of several photo galleries in Arles.

First, Maurice drove them by the ultramodern tower, next to the historic center, under construction and designed by the famed architect Frank Gehry. "As I mentioned, this unique complex will contain contemporary art galleries and archives. There will also be opportunities to rent studio space and artist housing. The cost is expected to be more than a hundred and ten million euros."

"Aha!" Bertram exclaimed. "The LUMA Foundation is going to boost the fortunes of your beloved town and the arts communities long nurtured here."

"Precisely," Maurice agreed. "We're excited! This will be an interdisciplinary art center, and of course, with our history of photography here, that will be a major focus—pun intended. Come back and see in a few years!"

Juliette quietly expressed her hope that the expected influx of tourists and visitors would not change the personality of the town.

Bertram explained to them, as Maurice drove to their drop-off spot, "The world-renowned Les Rencontres d'Arles is an annual summer photography festival that was founded in 1970. It's famous for exhibiting material that's never been seen by the public before. The exhibits are set up in displays all over town, from twelfth-century chapels to twentieth-century industrial buildings. It's brilliant, simply brilliant!"

"Very, very cool," Lisa murmured, giving a thumbs-up.

Marti said, "We'd really like to come back here for that some year. But today, I'm excited to see what the galleries will display."

Their enthusiasm was palpable. As often happened when groups of people had bonded, there were talks of a reunion of sorts a year later, in July, to attend Les Rencontres and to paint.

Maurice said, "There's not much point in us planning to tour the galleries as a group. There are so many exhibits that will distract us individually, we will be holding each other up constantly. Let's plan to meet at our usual spot around seven p.m."

Joan said, "Yes, we still have to pack up our wet paint carriers, and of course we want time to say good-bye to Barbara and Ceci back at the *mas*."

"And aren't we relieved that Barbara is there so we can say good-bye!" Arianna said, and everyone murmured in agreement.

CHAPTER

THIRTY-SIX

Before she went to bed Friday night, Arianna Skyped with Faith and described the slight change in her itinerary.

"Mom, it sounds like your art course morphed into much more. I'm googling all the places you've been visiting."

As she had during any communication with her mother while she was in France, Faith assured Arianna all was fine on the home front. She reported that she spoke with Sophia every day and visited her father every second day, though he continued to be unaware of anything.

"Nothing has changed here. But something has definitely changed where you are. Mom, when you first arrived in France, your guilty feelings kept sneaking through your words. I'm not hearing that now."

"Faith, when I tell you the past two weeks have been life changing, I'm not exaggerating. We'll have a lot to talk about when I get home."

⚜

The next morning, Juliette drove Arianna to pick up a rental car. They held each other in a long gaze after exchanging an emotional *bise*, and then a spontaneous hug.

"I'm repeating myself, but thank you for everything," Arianna said, her voice filled with gratitude. "The time here was much more than I ever hoped it would be. You rekindled my love of being an artist. And—as you know—more than that, you gently encouraged me to open a door and explore parts of my heart I had locked away."

Juliette's eyes reflected her feelings. "*De rien, ma chère* Arianna. This course became a special experience for all of us. It was quite an amazing time together with a unique group of individuals."

They stood hand in hand, smiling at each other for a moment.

Juliette continued, "Please keep in touch, and know you are welcome in our home anytime. I wish you only the best."

As she left the streets of Arles behind, Arianna telegraphed a heartfelt au revoir to this enthralling town that had seduced her in so many ways, with the vestiges from ancient Roman times, through medieval rise and decline, to the spirit of van Gogh that lingered everywhere.

I will be back. I'm sure of that.

She was pleased the drive to Aigues-Mortes was straightforward. The morning was bright, clear, and warm: perfect conditions for a road trip. She had a great deal on her mind, and the less she had to concentrate on the road, the better.

Her thoughts turned now to the good-byes that had been said as the course at the Mas des Artistes came to a close.

It began with Barbara and Ceci's departure the evening before. There was relief still mixed with concern after Barbara's fall. Cecilia assured everyone that she would have Barbara see her doctor in Vancouver to follow up. They both promised to update the group.

The rest of the group left in the van with Maurice for the Marseille airport after early-morning farewells.

In both cases, everyone was dry-eyed and upbeat, filled with a warmth and with promises to stay in touch; Juliette assured them she would forward e-mail addresses. There was laughter as they all *bised* each other, and Juliette reminded them how she had predicted this would become something they would all adopt. There was no question the course was considered a great success, as much for the camaraderie as for the art lessons.

They all expressed certainty these friendships would endure.

Arianna and Bertram had found a quiet corner to say a heartfelt farewell and promised to Skype each other. *I will miss dear Bertie in particular,* Arianna thought as she waved good-bye.

Arianna was not a crier, at least not in public. She had certainly added many tears to the bathwater over the past two years. But today she felt strengthened by everything that had happened since she had stepped off the plane in Paris, and particularly since she arrived at the Mas des Artistes.

It continued to be a wonder to her that this group of strangers had bonded so strongly.

They had collectively decided that the mistral had something to do with it. Those two days of being housebound certainly had resulted in some "close encounters of the third kind," as John had described it.

Arianna's good-bye with Maximus had been tender. She would miss the charismatic cat that had offered her so many moments of comfort and affection.

The fortifications of the town appeared in the distance like a Disney set.

Arianna pulled to the side of the road and parked for a moment, taking it all in. The entirely walled, mid-thirteenth-century village of

Aigues-Mortes was a study in contrasts. It sat before her like a mystical time-travel mirage, the walls surrounded by seven centuries of urban expansion. Instead of Crusader ships, powerboats and sailboats lined the canal that ran along the west side of the ramparts. A rail line paralleled a wall. Yet there the village remained in its ancient, simple splendor.

Is this where the arriving Crusaders gathered? she wondered as she drove into an almost-vacant parking lot. Her imagination filled with images and sounds of crowds of men on foot or on horseback from all over Europe, the air filling with foreign languages and smells. She was excited to go in.

As planned, she texted Jacques to let him know she was there.

He answered immediately, saying he would meet her at the main entrance with the two towers and arched passageway.

Today he did not look like a *gardian*. Wearing black jeans and a T-shirt that matched the blue of his eyes—*cerulean,* Arianna had decided—he waved as he saw Arianna and quickly walked toward her.

The *bise* followed naturally. Arianna felt very French . . . and comfortable, like meeting an old friend.

"Perfect timing," he said. "I arrived just a few minutes ago. What would you like to do first?"

"I'm in your hands, *Monsieur le guide touristique*! Tour guide, did I say that correctly?"

He laughed, replying with a bow. "*Magnifique.* I like being in charge when it comes to introducing people to my neighborhood. Let's walk through to the main square and have an espresso under the gaze of King Louis. I'm so glad you agreed to come early. No one is here . . . but that won't last long."

The charm seen from outside of the ramparts only intensified as Arianna stepped through the gates of the old town. The narrow streets, full of character, appeared to be in a perfect geometrical grid. "Like most medieval towns," Jacques explained. "Only here, because the walls were never destroyed, the maze of meandering streets that accompanied the growth of other towns never happened."

As they strolled, Jacques gave her the history in short sound bites. "King Louis IX was one of the most revered of French royalty. He is described as wise, fair, and a model of good government. He is also the only French king to be given sainthood. He reigned from the age of twelve in 1226 to his death in 1270."

"Is that the same Louis who oversaw the building of that gem in Paris, the Sainte-Chapelle? I have to admit I never could keep all the kings straight."

"One and the same, *oui*! He was quite a guy. The story goes that he fell deathly ill and made a promise to God that, if he recovered, he would lead an army to reconquer the Holy Land. To make good on that vow, he had to build a port from which the French Crusaders could set sail. Back in the day, this town was on the sea."

Jacques pointed out small details as they strolled. Arianna chuckled as he was interrupted frequently by cordial greetings from shopkeepers and other people he obviously knew.

"I've spent a lot of time in this part of the country," he explained with a grin. For the first time she noticed dimples deepen near the corners of his mouth.

It wasn't long before they reached Place Saint-Louis, an open square bordered by leafy plane trees. Shaded terraces belonging to a varied selection of cafés lined three sides. Jacques led her to a corner table on one of the smaller patios and returned the jovial wave of a woman behind the bar. A waiter arrived promptly to take their order for two espressos.

In the middle of the square, a four-sided marble fountain was gracefully topped by an impressive bronze sculpture of King Louis. Arianna could see it was positioned perfectly so every visitor arriving through the main entrance gates would be aware of it. Overflowing flower baskets hung from lampposts that dotted the square. Broad benches offered opportunities to rest and absorb the beauty of the surroundings, and people were already sitting down.

"This looks like it would be a happening place once the crowds pour in," Arianna observed as they drank their espressos.

"When you can see through the mass of visitors," Jacques added. "You're lucky to get a seat by midday during the summer. It's the best place to people-watch if you don't mind crowds. And I do! As much as I think everyone should visit this town, I much prefer the open space of the *manade*—or even better, the sea."

Arianna was surprised to hear him mention the sea. It had really never come up in conversation with him before. "Are you a fisherman or a sailor . . . or a windsurfer?" she asked, recalling seeing many windsurfers and parasailers on the previous Sunday.

"All of the above," he replied. "Although my windsurfing ventures in recent years might be considered rather lame by the younger set. I'm happy just to cruise along with simply enough wind to keep me upright. No more riding the wild waves, I'm afraid. There are a few things in life to which we have to adjust as the years creep up on us."

Arianna nodded. "I'll say."

He shared more history as they relaxed in the leafy shade. "People tend to focus on Louis and the building of the fortification and the Crusades. But there's a rich history of the Greeks and Romans too."

Their coffee finished, he suggested a walk around the ramparts. "Let's do it now before it gets too warm. It will take us about an hour, but these are views you cannot find elsewhere. It's magical, trust me."

Just as she had felt during his presentation at the *mas* and again on Sunday, Arianna liked his candid enthusiasm. He bought a bottle of water for each of them, saying they would need it.

"It's often wondered why Louis chose the mudflats of these mosquito-infested marshlands for his port. But in those days, the sea came very close to the fortifications."

"Hard to believe today!" Arianna exclaimed.

"Louis traded some other lands with the local Benedictine monks who owned this area. He rebuilt the village and created a road to it through the delta and added some canals."

Arianna plied him with questions that he was more than happy to answer. History was obviously something he enjoyed, and laughter punctuated the conversation. Arianna kept remembering how she used to love to laugh. Ben had always been so good at making her laugh.

Laughter had been such a part of the past two weeks, once she'd opened herself to it. And now it continued.

As they walked along the ramparts, on one side they had a clear view over the terra-cotta rooftops of the ancient houses. Arianna felt a sense of invading privacy as she peered down into the narrow streets and secret gardens, and yet she didn't want to stop.

Jacques pointed out several fine restaurants scattered down the narrow streets. He described the town's atmosphere as a combination of medieval splendor and a laid-back attitude. On the other side, they overlooked a canal that led up from the sea. Jacques pointed to a particular sailboat. "That's my boat. My home, really."

Arianna looked at him in surprise. "I thought you lived in that *cabane* on the *manade*."

"Only when I have to. You did notice it was sparse." He went on to explain that for a good part of the year, he called the boat home. "I usually keep it at a small marina in Port-Saint-Louis, which is less than an hour from the *manade*. It's easy to go back and forth. I sailed over here last evening."

They stopped and leaned against the stone wall as they talked about the boat for a few minutes. Arianna was surprised to hear him describe two bedrooms and two bathrooms, like a compact condo. Then they continued to stroll.

Jacques directed Arianna's attention to an elegant building he described as a fifteenth-century mansion. "Now it's a popular luxury hotel. I'm happy to say the owners have remained true to the original style and decor."

"Hmm, a swimming pool and electrical wires break the medieval mood somehow," Arianna said.

"Well, wait until we get to the end of the rampart here," Jacques said, pointing ahead. "I think you will be amazed."

CHAPTER

THIRTY-SEVEN

"You're right! The colors are breathtaking!" Arianna confirmed as she looked over the wall toward the sea. Across ponds that were shades of azure and, surprisingly, bright pink, a small mountain of sea salt shimmered in the sun. "Where does that color come from?"

Jacques explained it was from algae that produced beta-carotene as protection from the sun. "It's also how the flamingos get their color when they eat that algae."

"I've never seen anything like it!" Arianna declared, taking a series of photos. "It's such a kaleidoscope of color."

"The sun is the determining factor with those colors," Jacques said. "Those ponds alternate between blue, pink, and purple, depending on the angles and strength of rays."

Arianna stared at the scene before her, taking it all in.

"There's a train that can take you on an hour-long tour of the salt flats. I highly recommend it, because I'm willing to bet you will be fascinated at how the *fleur de sel* is harvested, as it has been since antiquity. And another thing, the sunsets here are very special."

Arianna looked at her watch. "If I do that, I'm going to have to set speed records to get to Aix and then Antibes by tonight."

Jacques asked if there was a specific reason she needed to do that.

"No, it was just my plan."

"Well, plans can be broken," he suggested, his voice subtly persuasive.

Arianna hesitated. "Yes, they can. You're right. It's a shame to be here and not see everything I should."

"*Une idée,*" Jacques said, "why don't you check into a hotel and spend the day here in a relaxed fashion. You can leave tomorrow. Why rush?"

It wasn't like Arianna to make such a spur-of-the-moment decision. The thought of acting impulsively sent a frisson of excitement through her now. His suggestions were hard to resist. After a moment's hesitation, she was surprised to hear herself agree.

"*Magnifique!* Why don't we have lunch to celebrate after we see if there is a room for you at the hotel I just pointed out. I know the owner and may be able to help. It's an experience you shouldn't miss."

In no time, they had walked to the mansion and everything had been arranged. Looking around the lobby, Arianna felt pleased with her decision to stay for a night. The hotel had an available room with a lovely view. Jacques walked to Arianna's car with her to get her things.

"You have everything you needed for two weeks in here? I'm impressed!" Jacques said when he took her suitcase out of the car.

"Yes. My daughter took charge of packing, and she knows just what to do. Also, I shipped my art supplies directly to the Mas des Artistes, and Juliette is shipping the box back for me. Most of us did that, just to be safe. You can't always trust airport security these days. I only have my sketchbook and travel paints and pencils in this bag."

After dropping off the suitcase at the hotel, they sat outside a busy bistro to eat a light lunch. Jacques made a reservation elsewhere for dinner.

As Arianna studied the menu, she asked for suggestions. "Well, the area is famous for its shellfish, so I recommend the oysters or mussels. They're exceptional."

"I'm not a fan of oysters, but I love mussels."

"Excellent choice! Let's eat light now and feast this evening. Sound good?" Jacques ordered the *tielle de Sète*, or octopus pie, which he explained was a typical local dish.

Arianna made a bit of a face. "It sounds more palatable in French than English. I've never been a fan of octopus."

"Well, you should taste this when it comes. I think you might change your mind."

Arianna's eyes gleamed. This was fun. She gave herself permission to admit she was having a very good time.

Sitting near the open kitchen, they watched the chef preparing bouillabaisse as they ate. Jacques said the chef was noted in the area for his rich, garlicky recipe.

"Of course, Marseille is the place for *la vraie* bouillabaisse—the real deal. In spite of the variations by chefs around the world, the truth is that it is a very specific dish with a specific history. It must contain five requisite fish and the addition of shellfish is optional . . . and frowned upon by many. Purists say that a real bouillabaisse can be made only in the direct vicinity of the Mediterranean."

Arianna smiled. "That is such a French thing to say when it comes to food."

Jacques smiled back and nodded his agreement. "We are very snobby about our food. But there's no alternative. If you don't have the right fish, you cannot make bouillabaisse. It is as simple as that."

They chuckled as they raised their wineglasses. "Here's to having the right fish!" Arianna toasted.

Conversation flowed as they lingered over their meal, followed by double espressos. Arianna felt content and at ease. She enjoyed Jacques's warm smile and light banter. She appreciated the easy way he had of making her laugh.

After lunch, with additional gentle persuasion, Arianna agreed to take the train tour. She insisted that Jacques not go with her, guessing he could probably repeat the tour from memory. He laughed and conceded she was not far off in that assessment.

"I'll slip down to the boat and do a few things. Why don't I meet you at your hotel for an *apéro* before we go to dinner. Say seven o'clock? We can walk out beyond the walls and see the sunset before we eat."

Arianna purchased her ticket for the one-thirty train and joined the lineup by the sign that said, *"Embarquez à bord du Petit Train."* In just a few minutes, the miniature blue-and-white train stopped at Les Salins du Midi welcome center. It soon set off into the seemingly endless area. Here, she read, the sun, sea, and wind combined to make very special salts, from La Baleine table salt, whose whale logo was immediately recognizable in France, to the prized *fleur de sel* de Camargue.

Who knew there was so much to learn and appreciate about salt? Arianna thought as she read along with an English brochure, since the tour was conducted only in French.

She learned that the area of this *salin*, or salt marsh, was bigger than the city of Paris. Every year the ponds were filled with seawater that was then allowed to gradually evaporate; then, over the summer, a salty crust "cake" several inches thick formed on top. In September, the salt cake was harvested.

Arianna understood enough French to learn that *fleur de sel* was the very fine top layer of salt, which accounted for its high cost. That top layer was painstakingly skimmed by hand by men known as *paludiers* or *sauniers* before it sank to the bottom. The work had been done in the same manner since antiquity, using a process that took several months.

The ride was bumpy as the train lurched along. It was impossible to take any photos of the spectacular pink waters until the train stopped at one of the *camelles*, or giant salt hills. The climb was not difficult, but a bit slippery, and she wished she had worn better shoes. Though there was no question it was worth a few slips for the views over the marsh.

Graceful flocks of flamingos waded in some of the ponds, feeding on algae. Passengers only got glimpses of them as the train passed by. Arianna was thankful for the time she had spent up close to the birds the past weekend.

In spite of the beauty of the salt marsh, it was also a vast semi-industrial landscape. Steel conveyor belts towered over the *camelles* and irrigation channels. Arianna had a sense of slow motion as she watched trucks crawl along dusty gravel tracks. She took some photos of those views as well and lost herself in thought in the middle of the unusual landscape. *To remind me there are usually two sides to everything. Somehow I need to stay open-minded today. I seem to be making unexpected decisions.*

By the time the little train arrived back at the welcome center, Arianna had learned more about salt than she ever thought possible. She had a feeling she was learning something about herself too.

Time for a break at that gorgeous little hotel. I'm kind of excited about that!

Although she'd been shaded by the canopy of the train, the sun had been extremely hot in the exposed salt marsh. A shower was definitely in order.

After a swim in the hotel pool, which she was delighted to discover she had all to herself, Arianna walked up two flights of stairs. She took some time to admire the seventeenth-century furnishings that added to the allure of the establishment. They were documented in a book about the hotel placed on a desk.

Staying here—in this magical town and this charming hotel—is like a mini history lesson in itself, another experience I might have missed.

She showered and then, moving aside the luxurious bedspread, stretched out on top of the fine cotton sheets. The rhythmic rotations of an overhead fan lulled her into a relaxed state of drowsiness.

She was glad things had worked out the way they had. It felt good to have a bit of time here and not have to rush off to more towns to do more sightseeing. Even though she had enjoyed private times at the *mas*, now she had time to reflect about the whole experience.

Closing her eyes, she considered the new friends who had become part of her life in such a short time, and the stories they had revealed that had begun to shape a change in her thinking. She had set off on the trip to France to awaken her dormant artistic side and was coming away at the end of it with so much more of her spirit revived. She entertained fleeting thoughts of her growing friendship with Jacques.

Content, she drifted off to sleep.

CHAPTER THIRTY-EIGHT

The ringing of her cell phone startled her.

For a moment, Arianna was disconnected from where she was. She heard the husky voice of a man say her name in a way she had not heard for a long time. She hesitated, not so much from drowsiness as from a twinge of indecision as to how she was allowed to feel.

"Arianna?" the voice repeated. "*C'est toi?* Is that you?"

"Oh yes . . . yes . . . Jacques . . . excuse me. I drifted off to sleep for a little while."

"Oh no, *désolé.* I'm sorry I woke you up."

Arianna laughed softly. "No, it's fine. No problem."

"I wondered if you might like to have an *apéro* a little earlier than I suggested. In fact, I thought perhaps we could have a drink on my boat. Then we can take a short walk on the boardwalk to watch the sunset before dinner."

"That sounds lovely. I would just need a half hour. Is that fine?"

"*C'est parfait!* I'll be in the lobby in thirty minutes, with a good book. Take as long as you want."

Arianna examined her reflection in the mirror. There was a look in her eyes she recognized from what seemed like a long time ago.

As she massaged in a face cream, she felt an almost-forgotten desire to make herself attractive for someone else, for a man. She enjoyed the feeling as she continued to put on her mascara, eyeliner, and lipstick. She had been wearing makeup throughout the trip, but now she paid more attention to how she looked.

Tipping her head from side to side, Arianna brushed her hair, and then ran her fingers through it for a casual effect. She was pleased with her new haircut. There was never any fussing with it, and the layers all simply fell into place. That had been a good change.

Thank you, Faith. Thank you, Mom.

She slipped into a sleeveless red dress she had bought specially for the trip, because it was a good color for her, lightweight, and made out of a silky fabric that traveled well. And, if she was totally honest with herself, because Faith told her it was slimming.

I need all the help I can get these days. I think I'll go to Weight Watchers when I get home—all the baguettes and croissants of the past two weeks won't have helped.

She had worn this dress the day of her lunch with Bertram and the tour of the Fondation. Bertram had told her the color suited her. That memory gave her a little boost now. *Dear, dear Bertie . . .*

Warm thoughts flooded her memories about the Englishman and how her feelings toward him had changed so dramatically in that short time.

Black strappy sandals and a small black shoulder bag completed the outfit. With one final look in the full-length mirror, she smiled at what she saw. She wondered if her attire was fitting for having a drink on the boat.

I can always pop up and change if Jacques thinks I should.

With a tingle of excitement, she picked up the large key that fit the ornate lock on her door.

This key is so cool! It reminds me of all those doors I loved in Arles. Thank goodness I hand it in at the desk and don't have to lug it around.

She saw Jacques sitting in the lobby. He appeared absorbed with something on his phone. She hesitated, not wanting to interrupt his concentration, and he looked up just as she began to approach his chair.

They smiled at each other, and he stood and *bised* her as if it were just the most natural thing to do. "You look lovely, Arianna, and perfectly dressed. It's become quite muggy out there. Have you been standing there a while?"

Arianna felt like a schoolgirl and hoped she wasn't blushing. "You looked involved, and I didn't want to interrupt you."

"I was reading," Jacques explained. "I have my library on my phone. It's become a bit of a habit, I'm afraid."

Bemused, Arianna asked, "You read novels on your phone? Isn't the screen too small?"

"Look," he said, showing her the page he had been reading. "I carry all my books with me wherever I go. What's better than that?"

Arianna stared intently at the text on the phone. "Hmm, that looks very readable. I'm surprised! You'll have to show me how to do it."

"*Avec plaisir*, madame! *C'est facile*—it's easy!"

Arianna amused him by describing how her children had forced her into the world of the new phone technology. "I really have been behind the times when it comes to that."

Jacques chuckled at her remarks as they left the hotel, and Arianna felt comfortably at ease.

The town had come alive while Arianna had been at her hotel. Side streets were crammed with tourists, and lengthy lineups were forming at the bistros with patios. Laughter and lively conversation surrounded them wherever they went.

As they headed toward the main gate in the ramparts, Jacques pointed to a small patio with a portcullis covered by a lush grapevine.

Clusters of green grapes hung from it. Classic wrought-iron tables and chairs sat on the gravel in between large terra-cotta pots overflowing with colorful geraniums and trailing ivy.

"This place is famous for its crêpes, in case you would like some tomorrow before you leave," he said, rubbing his stomach and rolling his eyes. "You should not miss that delicious experience."

Arianna couldn't help but notice his fit physique. She composed herself quickly.

"I'll probably head out very early," Arianna said. "Since I'm a day behind in my planned road trip."

Jacques smiled and said, "*Ah oui*, but look at what you would have missed. How did you enjoy *le petit train des Salin*? I was worried that you might be cursing me for suggesting it!"

Arianna chuckled as she said she probably knew more about salt now than she ever needed to. "All kidding aside, it was very interesting and unusually beautiful. I also learned I've been making a big mistake for years . . ."

"Because?"

"I've been putting *fleur de sel* in dishes when I'm cooking. Now I know it should only be used as a finishing touch on a completed dish or a salad to enhance the flavor."

"*Quelle horreur!*" Jacques reacted in mock indignation. "We will just keep that our little secret. Do you like to cook?"

As Arianna began to answer, they reached the main gates and walked out to the busy street that ran between the walls and the canal.

Jacques took her arm in a manner that was familiar and relaxed and guided her through the traffic to the marina entrance. He gestured to a guard in the gatehouse and led her along the concrete walk to a wooden dock.

They stopped at his sailboat, and he waved his arm with a modest flourish. The craft appeared old and loved. That was obvious in the gleaming brass and well-polished wood trim. The name *"Mon Esprit"* was painted across the stern in clean, artistic lettering.

"What a beautiful boat. It has such character, and I love the name," Arianna said. Jacques smiled his thanks and took her hand to help her walk up the short gangplank and onto the seating area in the stern.

"Would you like a tour? It doesn't take long." He chuckled.

CHAPTER
THIRTY-NINE

They stepped belowdecks into the salon with a U-shaped dinette and a small couch. Arianna was surprised at the light the small windows provided, creating the illusion of spaciousness.

Everything was upholstered in earthy tones with a clean, masculine feel. The orderly stainless-steel galley had a well-used, lightly tarnished finish.

"One aft cabin with a head and shower," Jacques said as he opened one door and then pointed to the door at the other end. "And a V-berth with access to another head through that door. This next room is for storage. It's rather messy in there right now. It's where I toss all my 'stuff'—easel, paints, pencils, paper—you know what I mean? I'm not the most fastidious artist."

"Do you paint and sketch while you're on the boat?"

He nodded amiably and rolled his eyes. "Unless I'm on horseback, it never ends. Art is my obsession. Do you know the feeling?"

Arianna sighed. "Once upon a time I knew it well."

Jacques's expression registered a look that seemed both knowing and sympathetic before he lifted the mood. "Let's go up top and have a glass of wine . . . and talk of other things."

The upper deck had U-shaped bench seating in the stern and an awning-covered cockpit area with a removable plastic front and sides. A screen could be rolled down to enclose the cockpit.

"*Bienvenue au gouvernail!* Welcome to the helm! We'll sit in here behind the screen, so we don't have to worry about a mosquito bombardment," he suggested.

"What a beautiful steering wheel!" Arianna commented, hoping she was using the proper term as she ran her hand over the ship's wheel. Eight richly varnished cylindrical wooden spokes were joined at a central hub. They attached to an outer rim, creating a series of handles.

She had a flashback to her childhood and the strong hands of her father and uncles steering out to sea to fish. She hadn't been on a boat since those days in Greece, and yet it all felt strangely familiar. Those boats were rustic and rusty, often with peeling paint, and piled high with fishing nets and lines. Still, the feeling of being on the boat was reminiscent of those days long ago.

"Thanks! It's quite an old wheel that I found at a *brocante* years ago, if you can believe that! One never knows what will turn up at those flea markets. The sale was in Marseille, and there was a lot of equipment from boats. It was in terrible shape, but after countless hours of loving care, it turned out to be quite a beauty!"

"It did indeed."

Jacques opened a small refrigerated cabinet. "Would you like a glass of rosé, chardonnay, or champagne? Or would you care to join me in a pastis?"

"It seems I've turned into a pastis fan on this trip. Not only do I like the taste, but it's revived some happy childhood memories. Thank you."

Jacques asked about those memories as he poured the anise-flavored Pernod into tall, thin glasses. Next he picked up an ice-filled water jug.

"Tell me when to stop," he said as he slowly added water, and the amber liquid turned to milky white.

After doing the same to his drink, he placed a long-handled spoon in the jug. "Purists argue not to add ice to pastis, as you have no doubt learned—more of our obsessive French nature with food and drink! But when it's this hot out, I like to make sure my pastis stays cool. So it's your choice if you care to add some later."

He raised his glass to her as their eyes met. *"Santé!"* Arianna did the same, giving herself an internal pinch at her surprise to be where she was.

They sat on benches on either side of a narrow table and looked out across the canal. Arianna was captivated by the atmosphere of the other boats moored around them and the sun-kissed stone walls of the medieval town that filled her view. It seemed almost surreal.

Jacques broke the silence. "All of our conversations have been about art and life in the Camargue. Why don't you tell me something about your life now?"

Arianna hesitated, thinking the next part would be awkward.

Jacques spoke again before she could. His tone was soft and kind. "At the picnic yesterday Juliette mentioned to me that you had come to the Mas des Artistes to reconnect with your artist's soul."

Arianna stared into her glass for a moment, biting her lower lip. Then she nodded her head slowly as she raised her eyes to his. "Juliette described that well. Perhaps I should start at the beginning."

She recounted some of her childhood in Greece and how her father had brought them to live in Toronto. This led into her early days studying art and her excitement and love of working immersed in the surroundings of a major art center.

"I married a wonderful man, who supported my career while he and my father ran our family restaurant. But fate intervened. My father was killed in a car accident twenty years ago, and life changed. I set aside my career and eventually lost the time for art. But I had a very happy, busy life as my husband and I managed the business and raised our family while also caring for my mother."

Jacques listened quietly. His expression and slight head movements indicated his interest and encouraged Arianna to continue telling her story.

Arianna kept the details to a minimum without losing the impact of her words. As she described the current state of Ben's existence, she ended by saying, "And once again, years later, fate has knocked on my door."

She picked up her glass and took a long sip. Jacques reached for her hand, which was resting on the narrow table between them. He laid his hand gently on hers. "Such sadness is difficult to overcome. But overcome we must."

"This trip is my first move in that direction," Arianna said, her voice strong and eyes clear.

Jacques cocked his head. "Do you know the words of André Malraux? He said, 'Art is a revolt against fate.' Let's toast to that."

They raised their glasses.

Arianna smiled ruefully. "I don't know much about Malraux . . . but I like the quote! I've never considered myself someone who revolts against anything, although I've been reminded lately that it might be time to begin."

For a few seconds, she studied the shadows beginning to fall on the walls of Aigues-Mortes. Her fingers tapped lightly against her glass.

Then she turned back to Jacques and smiled. "Now it's your turn. Where did you spend your childhood? How is it you speak English so well, with barely any accent, and yet you seem so very French?"

The corners of his eyes wrinkled as he laughed. The deep blue of his eyes intensified. Arianna was charmed by his easy manner and good humor—and, she admitted to herself, those eyes. It was refreshing to feel something like an attraction after so long, although she accepted it only as a momentary aberration.

"Well, I must admit I'm only half French . . . in heritage. In my heart I am a hundred percent a Frenchman. So you are right."

He raised his glass to her in a relaxed manner. "Are you ready for a long story?"

Arianna chuckled. "I have a feeling this is going to be a good one."

Jacques spoke easily, with a sense of comfort and confidence as he related his past. "My mother was American, and I spent much of the first twelve years of my life on a ranch in Colorado. My father was a true *gardian*, and, in fact, a bit of a gypsy. One summer, he made a pilgrimage to the States to trace the connections that had so determined the life of Marquis Folco de Baroncelli-Javon. Do you recall me speaking about him?'

"Of course," Arianna said, recalling that strange connection between the *gardians* and the American West.

"My father saw him as a hero but found his story heartbreaking, because he did not finish the last years of his life in the best condition. If I'm honest, my father was rather obsessive about it. He was fascinated by Baroncelli's connection with 'Buffalo Bill' Cody that influenced the founding of La Nacioun Gardiano in 1909. It's all kind of crazy, really . . ."

"That story was bizarrely curious. I remember you talking about Baroncelli, and I even looked it up on the Internet after our afternoon with you. Please keep going."

"I'll keep it short—and, of course, this is my father's story as he told it to me. So at the age of twenty-two, my father took a trip to Kansas and Wyoming trying to trace Cody's life there. Can you imagine stranger places for a French cowboy to go?" He interrupted himself to say, "Oh, and did you know that Buffalo Bill even lived in Toronto for a while as a child? How about that! My father did not go there, though . . ."

They shared a laugh.

"I did not know that," she said. Arianna was enjoying the company of this intriguing man who was so full of surprises. For a moment she considered this completely unexpected experience that had come her way and was glad she had not shied away from the opportunity.

"He went on a whim, hardly spoke any English. Eventually he ended up at Cody's grave in Golden, Colorado. He fell in love with Colorado and also with a young artist, my mother, Rosemary Curtis. He met her shortly after he arrived when he was looking for work as a ranch hand or wrangler. She lived and worked on her family's ranch and was establishing a name for herself as an abstract artist, exhibiting wherever she could and winning prizes. When I was older, my father described her as wild, beautiful, and free and like no one he had ever known. They got married after she became pregnant, and my father was accepted by her family and welcomed on the ranch. However, it had never been his intention to stay permanently in the States, and he missed France passionately. They agreed to stay married and live separately, as my mother had no desire to live in France . . . or even visit. Can you believe she never came here?"

"I feel like you're recounting a novel for me," Arianna said. "And, no. I find that so hard to understand."

Jacques chuckled. "As they say, fact is often stranger than fiction. *N'est-ce pas?*" He added some ice to their glasses.

"So how did things play out?" she asked, curious about his story.

"I would come to my father during the summer holidays, and he came to see me a few times during the winters. In spite of the fact my parents eventually were not in love with each other anymore, they both put a lot of effort into ensuring I had a good relationship with them both. They both loved me, and I knew that."

"Good for them, and lucky you. You don't always find that." Arianna had a moment of gratitude flicker through her for the loving family she had always been part of.

"So true," Jacques said. "When I was twelve, I told my mother I wanted to live with Papa in France. It was inexplicable, but I always felt I was home when I came to stay with him. So I lived here in the Camargue, and we rode horses and corralled bulls together. He taught me all he knew. I competed in the *courses camarguaises* and finished school. It was a life I loved, and my bond with Papa was extraordinary."

"And your mother never came to visit?"

"No. Never. The situation kind of reversed, and I would go to see her in Colorado during Christmas break from school, mainly so I could ski those fabulous slopes. Winter there was something special, and I loved that, but I didn't want to miss a minute of the rest of the seasons in the Camargue. Mom became an increasingly eccentric hippie artist. We grew apart."

He stopped speaking for a moment and became contemplative. His voice was more subdued when he continued. "This region spoke in a powerful way to my soul. The older I got, the stronger the connection became. And then I began to draw. I eventually accepted that my mother did give me something special, after all."

Jacques freshened their drinks. The conversation segued into comparisons of how their childhoods had affected their artistic leanings.

Arianna felt transported away from the worries and concerns that had occupied her all these months. Away from the conflicting emotional loads she had wrestled with over the past two weeks that had allowed her to reach this moment.

With boat activity moving slowly up and down the canal, *Mon Esprit* rocked gently at its mooring.

"What a peaceful motion this is," Arianna murmured. Leaning back and turning her face to the warm rays of the sun, she closed her eyes and enjoyed the calming atmosphere.

Jacques stretched his arms up and clasped his hands behind his head, as he also leaned back in the sunshine. "It's a biological fact that we all have salt in our blood, in our sweat, in our tears. We are tied to the ocean—physically and emotionally, don't you think?"

"My father was constantly quoting Zorba the Greek, and most of those quotations involved wine, food, and the sea," Arianna said, laughing. "The sounds and smells of the sea were what he missed most about Greece."

Jacques chuckled. "He sounds like he was quite a character."

Briefly melancholy, Arianna agreed.

Jacques pointed out that the sun was now sitting much lower in the sky. "The sun will begin its performance in about an hour. We should have a stroll on the boardwalk before we go back up on the wall, so you can experience the sun setting over the salt marsh: a glorious spectacle courtesy of *la belle dame nature.*"

CHAPTER FORTY

By the time they had arrived back up on the upper walkway of the rampart, quite a crowd had gathered along the southern edge. Jacques apologized for not getting there earlier, as they squeezed into a spot where Arianna could just see over the stone wall.

Arianna shushed him. "This is just fine! You've managed to make so much happen today already."

She could feel his closeness. There was a lingering scent of pastis on his breath that made her smile. She allowed herself the pleasure of breathing a man in. It was a pleasure long lost in her memory.

Looking over the salt marshes, Arianna gasped as she had before at the colorful beauty of the waters. "That pink is so vivid and deep one moment, and then shimmers into something light and delicate the next," she said.

"It's called 'water rose,'" Jacques told her.

The strikingly iridescent colors offered tremendous photo variations, as they continually changed hue. In spite of being jostled from time to time, Arianna could not stop taking pictures.

"Look at the cloud formations," Jacques said, directing her eyes to the sky. "The effect today will be even more glorious once the sun is below the horizon."

Arianna tried not to sigh out loud as the slowly fading golden globe melted into the Mediterranean. The rosy-pink backdrop diffused into shades of azure as it vanished beneath the waves. It was a delicious moment that elicited buzzes and hums of delight from the crowd.

As Jacques predicted, the show became even more spectacular after the sun dropped from sight. Pinks and blues swirled in the sky in a fiery blend.

"It's so interesting how many people walk away thinking a sunset is over, just because the sun has gone down," Arianna agreed.

He grinned. "That's just the foreplay."

Arianna felt herself blush and turned her head slightly, hoping Jacques wouldn't notice.

For a moment, she basked in the warm glow that illuminated the evening sky. A sense of tranquility settled over her. She wondered if it came solely from the sunset or also from her proximity to Jacques and his husky, appealing voice. She had to admit she was enjoying his company in a most unexpected way.

Maybe I've had too much pastis. I'll have to watch my alcohol intake at dinner.

As they stepped back into the heart of the town, Jacques suddenly steered Arianna onto a quiet side street, as the crowd continued to surge by. Within minutes they were in a peaceful courtyard decorated with ornate iron furniture and flower-filled urns.

Arianna was shocked to see it was nine thirty when they sat down to eat. She had adjusted well to the late dinner hours. It felt right.

Dinner was delicious and, surprisingly, already planned.

"I hope you don't mind me taking the initiative to organize this," Jacques said, almost apologetically. "I wanted the dinner to be special."

"I love surprises," Arianna replied, smiling and feeling a surge of delight at his thoughtfulness.

The courses were small and luscious, each one a singular taste sensation. It turned out that he and Marcel, the chef, were old friends.

As they sat tucked into a quiet corner of the terrace, their conversation was intimate. With the assistance of good wine, their exchanges had become increasingly personal.

The waitress, Anne-Marie, who was also Marcel's wife, had just brought them a delicate lime sorbet. "To cleanse our palate after the fish course and before our main course," Jacques explained.

"I've gotten to know a great deal about you in the times we've spent together," Arianna said, feeling both comfortable and slightly emboldened. "I've told you all about my family, but, apart from your parents, you've never mentioned whether you have any family of your own."

Jacques set his wineglass down after taking a long sip. Arianna noticed his jaw tighten before he spoke.

"We've had so much to talk about, I just never got around to it. I am on my own now, but I had a partner for over thirty years. We never married, but that is, as you probably know, very common in France. Her name was Giselle Landry. We met at Aix-Marseille University while she was studying medicine. I was taking random courses to fill an arts degree, in between working on the *manade* and hanging out in the gritty streets of seventies Marseille, trying to be accepted as an artist."

Arianna listened intently as he continued. "Giselle became a doctor and worked at clinics in the poor, rundown areas in the heart of Marseille. She did not want to have children but rather made the needs of those disadvantaged kids her needs. We both spent a lot of time doing that together. And we rode horses, sailed boats, and hiked. I built up a clientele for my art, and she practiced medicine. After a while, she also joined Médecins Sans Pays—Doctors Without Countries."

Arianna nodded. "Yes, of course I know of organizations like that. Good for her."

"She was exceptional. A beautiful woman inside and out. Part of each year she was away with MSF. Each time she returned with a broken heart. She would heal here before going away again. It was a mission that consumed her. She had such respect for her colleagues and was so inspired by them."

His eyes moistened. Emotion quieted his voice to just above a whisper. "Four years ago, she was at a hospital in Afghanistan that was bombed. She died there."

Arianna felt a sting of tears at the back of her eyes. She gulped them away and reached to cover his hand that was holding his wineglass. "I'm so sorry. How terrible."

"Yes, terrible . . . and terrible is part of life. The same word in French and English. The same pain in any language. Some people are more fortunate than others in avoiding terrible—you know that too. So we go on . . . in time . . . we go on."

Arianna dipped her head in affirmation before meeting his gaze. Her eyes signaled her understanding, her acceptance of his meaning, her knowledge of that pain.

Now he held her hand in both of his. She added her hand and they clasped them together. "Arianna," he said softly, "when people reach our stage in life—I am sixty-seven—most of us have much history behind us. Much of it good, wonderful even . . . but some of it not. Some of it terrible. We cannot spend this much time living without things happening. But whatever happens must not stop our living."

They looked at each other slightly differently after this. There was an unspoken bond built of pain, of sadness, of shared "terrible" . . .

Arianna could feel that Jacques had been stuck in his own "now."

Anne-Marie had been discreetly peeking out from the kitchen, respecting that a serious conversation was taking place. She stepped out with two plates.

"*Très chaud, faites attention, s'il vous plaît.* Very 'ot!"

Her words helped change the focus at the table.

A small, perhaps four-bite piece of rare meat in a rich sauce sat on a compact bed of Camargue rice. A modest stem of baby bok choy added green to the plate.

"Marcel's specialty! Braised bull cheek. So very tender. Marinated in Sable-de-Camargue merlot and slow-cooked to perfection. Every bite will melt in your mouth," Jacques praised, his face alight with pleasure.

Anne-Marie beamed at Arianna and Jacques. *"Bon appétit!"*

The timing was right for an interruption of their conversation. It was impossible to eat each mouthful without expressing murmurs of delight and appreciation.

A traditional salad of simple greens with vinaigrette came next, served in small, unusually shaped olivewood bowls.

"The servings are almost Lilliputian." Arianna chuckled. "And yet, absolutely just right. There's such a rhythm and blend to this meal. It's a small concert in itself."

Jacques grinned at her words. "Every meal with Chef Marcel is an experience. He makes eating an adventure."

A cheese board followed with only six choices. Jacques commented, "He knows precisely which cheese should accompany each specific meal."

The food lifted their spirits, and their conversation also moved back to lighter topics. Each asked questions of the other about interests and opinions. Arianna was increasingly aware of how attracted she was to him in so many ways. She was happy to know it was possible to have those feelings again.

For dessert, they decided to order one *café gourmand* to share with two espressos. They had discovered that neither one of them was affected adversely by caffeine.

"With any luck this caffeine will keep my eyes open until I get into bed!" Arianna admitted.

"I think that last glass of wine did me in."

The *café gourmand* arrived with six little dessert samples.

"They're called *mignardises*," Jacques explained. "*Petit*, bite-size tastes of sweetness." They then fell into a fit of laughing as he attempted to help Arianna pronounce the word.

"Every once in a while, a French word comes along that I simply cannot get my mouth to function properly around. This is one of those!" she sputtered.

By this time, Chef Marcel had joined them, the top two buttons undone on his white double-breasted chef's jacket. Jacques said this was his indication that he was through in the kitchen for the night. Marcel spoke very little English, but his French was clear, and Arianna was pleased that she could understand much of it.

Anne-Marie soon joined them as the last of the customers left the patio.

Jacques explained to them that this was Arianna's first visit to Aigues-Mortes. They had a long chat about all the areas in the Camargue and around Arles that she had discovered. They were curious to hear her observations about the region they so clearly loved.

Anne-Marie suggested to Jacques that Arianna needed to visit the Côte Bleue and the *calanques*. She spoke with such passion, with Marcel backing her up, that Arianna insisted that Jacques explain exactly what they were talking about.

Jacques began to tease her. "If you promise to stay another day and spend it on *Mon Esprit* with me, I will show you *la Côte Bleue*. We'll sail from one *calanque* to another."

Marcel joined in the good-natured kidding, explaining to Arianna she would be seeing a very special part of France that is kept secret from many tourists.

"Everyone knows the Côte d'Azur," Jacques translated as Marcel spoke, "but not everyone knows the Côte Bleue."

Arianna joined in the good-natured fun. "If I give you an answer now, it would be the wine talking. Let me sleep on this and tell you my answer in the morning."

"*D'accord!* I will meet you in the lobby at eight a.m., and *Mon Esprit* will be ready to set sail."

After heartfelt thanks to Marcel and Anne-Marie, with *bises* all around, Jacques and Arianna strolled the few blocks back to the hotel. The evening air had taken on a slight chill, and Arianna shivered inadvertently. Jacques removed the sweater he had slung over his shoulders and draped it across Arianna's back.

"*C'est mieux?* Does that help?"

"It does. *Oui! Merci beaucoup!*" Arianna giggled. Jacques slipped his arm around her shoulder and gave her a gentle squeeze.

It was a small gesture that meant a great deal to her. Yet another thing she hadn't realized she missed until that moment.

At the hotel, Arianna returned the sweater to Jacques. They exchanged *bises*. As they stepped back from each other, their eyes connected in a lingering gaze.

"Thank you for a most memorable day, Jacques."

"I enjoyed it very much," he replied.

Arianna promised to be in the lobby at eight a.m. to either go on the boat or leave on her planned road trip.

While she removed her mascara and washed her face, she examined her reflection. There was a long-absent gleam in her dark eyes. With her finger on the mirror, she traced some of the lines the years had added. This was clearly not the face of a young woman, but at this moment there was a distinct glow of happiness.

Positive thoughts spoke to her as she kept her eyes on her reflection. *Age doesn't have to preclude this happiness you see on your face tonight. You don't have to give up on it. You can always welcome it into your life, if you will just be open to it. Choose life, Arianna. Choose happiness.*

Heading to bed, she could hardly keep her eyes open.

Her thoughts replayed the highlights of the day as she slipped between the cool, crisp sheets. Drifting into sleep, she had a flicker of what it felt like to simply be happy.

CHAPTER FORTY-ONE

The moment Arianna woke up to her phone alarm, she knew what she was going to do.

She dressed in jeans, a soft cotton shirt over a camisole, and running shoes.

Jacques broke into a wide smile when he saw her. "Is that your road-trip outfit or your boating ensemble? It looks like it's for boating to me."

"So far, your ideas have turned out well. I think I should give this one a go too!"

"You are going to love this. I promise. It's a perfect day to go for a sail. However, to discover and explore *la Côte Bleue* would take us a few days. Let's just go out and see what we can see."

"I can't think of any reason not to. You'll have to show me how I can help on the boat. Are these shoes acceptable?" she asked, lifting a foot coquettishly, aware of the flutter of anticipation she felt.

Jacques checked the bottoms of her shoes. "They're rubber soles—even better than bare feet. You'll be fine. Do you have a bathing suit with you?" he asked.

When she said yes, he suggested she bring her bag on the boat rather than stashing it in her car. "Depending upon how hot the day gets, you may want to swim in the sea."

The thought flashed through her mind that it would have to be extremely hot indeed before she would want him to see her in a bathing suit. Then she let that go.

Jacques took charge of Arianna's bag as they headed to the boat.

When they passed the *boulangerie*, he popped in and purchased two baguettes. Breaking off the heel of the still-warm bread, he offered it to Arianna. Then he broke off the other for himself. "It's tradition," he said with a grin.

When they arrived at the dock, he held out his hand to help her up the gangplank. She smiled and tipped her fingers to her forehead in a light salute. "Aye, aye, Captain."

They exchanged grins as Jacques returned her salute and took charge of their departure. "Come over here, please. You can undo the fenders while I start the engine."

Arianna felt like the morning was made to order: the bluest of sky, bright sunshine, a warm breeze softly caressing her face as they slowly set off. As she looked back at the walled town, her mind filled with visions of Crusaders and sailing ships. *On how many mornings like this did the Crusaders set sail for the Holy Land under the sanction of God?*

Returning her thoughts to the present, she wondered aloud if there would be any wind to allow them to sail today.

Jacques chuckled. "That's rarely a problem here. You'll see. In the meantime, you might want to keep your phone handy. There are going to be a great many photo ops, I promise!"

They motored down the canal, past the white *camelles*, prismatic saline pools, and pink flamingos. As Jacques had predicted, Arianna could not stop taking photos.

After they crossed the Étang du Médard, the canal brought them to the seaside resort town of Le Grau-du-Roi. Arianna had Jacques laughing once again as she practiced pronouncing the town's name. "Those French *R*'s get me every time," she lamented.

"Hemingway was here in 1927 and again in 1948," Jacques told her as they passed shops, restaurants, and hotels lining the main street. "He set a scene here in his novel *The Garden of Eden*—just one of the town's claims to fame."

It pleased her to picture the writer living his life out loud in that evocative setting.

In a short while, they passed between the lighthouses that marked the entrance to the azure waves of the Mediterranean. Jacques set about raising the sails and giving Arianna instructions whenever her help was needed. As he steered their course, he described the beaches of the Côte Bleue.

"And what are these *calanques* I keep hearing about?"

"A *calanque* is a narrow inlet on the sea, mostly with steep rocky walls. The most famous Massif des Calanques run southeast from Marseille to Cassis, but we have our own here, just smaller. If we had time, I would show you all of them. They are simply beautiful."

"Will we reach one today?"

"At the speed we're going, I doubt it. Perhaps I will put the motor back on."

"No worries, Jacques. If we go nowhere, it doesn't matter. This is so peaceful, it's like a dream."

Arianna was surprised by the expansive stretches of grassy dunes and empty golden beaches. "With sand like sugar," Jacques assured her.

"I remember we saw some of these beaches the day you toured us around the Camargue. I never realized there were so many miles of them."

Occasionally, she would see a group of Camargue horseback riders galloping across the flats, sending sprays of the shallow water into the air. Phone in hand, she began to capture some of the images and felt eager anticipation of the work that would follow.

As the sails caught the breeze, from time to time, Arianna would turn her face to the sun and feel the caress of the wind and spray from the splash of water against the bow. *This is my reality today. My moments of happiness. By choice.*

Often minutes would go by without a word being said.

At other times, Jacques would offer detailed descriptions and histories of the areas they were passing. He hugged the shoreline whenever it was safe. Around Saintes-Maries-de-la-Mer, they shared the water with windsurfers and parasailers, admiring their athleticism and joie de vivre.

They talked and laughed as if they had known each other for a long time. Conversation bounced from one topic to another, as they discovered common interests and values.

After a couple of hours, back in quieter water, Jacques dropped the sails and put the boat on autopilot. "We can continue motoring while we eat. Our route is straightforward for a while now."

He brought a cooler out of the galley. "Anne-Marie came by early this morning and left this for us. She had a feeling I would be sharing it with you."

Arianna was embarrassed to feel a blush coming on. She turned her head slightly so her hair blew across her face for a moment. Brushing it back behind her ears when she had gained control of her emotions, she asked how she could help.

Together they set out a simple and delicious-looking lunch of highly seasoned, cold boiled shrimp; a potato salad; and thick, firm tomato slices full of rich flavor in a light vinaigrette dressing. All this was accompanied by a fresh baguette and a chilled bottle of Sable-de-Camargue rosé.

Arianna could not stop commenting on the thoughtful generosity of Anne-Marie and Marcel.

"They've been fine friends of mine through my entire life," Jacques said. "Marcel was always in the kitchen making meals for us since he was ten years old. Food was forever his fascination."

When they'd cleared away lunch, they both stretched out on the bench seating in the shade of the awning and before long were snoozing.

After an hour's nap, Arianna slipped down to use the head. When she returned, Jacques was standing and stretching.

"That was something I haven't done in ages," he said. "It felt so good!"

"I feel like we've run away someplace calmer and more tranquil than I've been for a very long time. Thank you for convincing me to do this. I honestly wish it would not end so soon."

"It doesn't have to" was his reply.

CHAPTER
FORTY-TWO

Arianna looked at Jacques wordlessly for quite a while. He held her gaze, speaking before she did, his tone low and engaging. "This is the first time in years that I've spent so much time alone with another woman, a friend. Arianna, I feel comfortable with you. Content. I would like to spend more time together. No strings attached. We're adults. There's no need for concern. Your company is all I ask."

"Are you suggesting we continue sailing?" she asked, wide-eyed. A slight shiver of temptation stirred inside her. She was intrigued by the possibility of something so unexpected.

He nodded. "We could take a few days to sail to Marseille. I could even take you past there to the truly stunning *calanques*. Then I could deliver you to the airport in time for your flight."

Arianna looked off across the waves. "Hmm . . . I have my rental car sitting in the parking lot at Aigues-Mortes. I need to return it at the airport; how am I going to deal with that?" She was giving this serious consideration.

They sat with large glasses of ice water and contemplated options. Anne-Marie had also included a substantial fruit platter in the cooler, and they nibbled at it, exchanging ideas. Arianna had Jacques laughing at her growing excitement.

Why not? she asked herself. *Nothing is carved in stone. Should I do what I really want to do? Am I feeling guilty about this pleasure?* "Really," she said out loud, "what's stopping me? Other than that darn car . . ."

"I think we can handle the car," Jacques said. "Give me the key, and I'll zip over to get it after I take you to the airport. I know the car rental people in Arles, and I'll just take the car back to them. I have a satellite phone here on the boat and can call them tomorrow when the office opens. We'll work it out."

"Will we be close to Wi-Fi at some point today? My data doesn't seem to be working out here," Arianna asked, feeling like she needed to let her family know what she was doing. She didn't think she would include the detail about being alone with a man. *I'll just say I'm sailing with friends.*

"We'll be at a village in about two hours and can get Wi-Fi there. It's a fishing port, and we can pick up some supplies as well. Do you think you have everything you need?"

Arianna nodded, her eyes bright with excitement. "I feel like an impulsive child! I've got this sense of waiting for someone to tell me I can't do this!"

Jacques chuckled. "It's kind of crazy, I guess. But why not? It sounds like something that will do us both good! You can take over the aft cabin, and I will take the V-berth at the back. I've slept there many times."

"That's sweet of you," Arianna told him.

Almost two hours later, Jacques steered *Mon Esprit* into a space at the end of a line of small, colorful wooden fishing boats. The weighted nets were piled high, ready for a midnight departure.

"These are *pointus*," Jacques explained. "They are traditional fishing boats of the Marseille area, and they're easily recognizable for being tapered at both ends. They're always painted two colors—white and another color—and now only a few fishermen use them. They're becoming trendy boats for local exploring."

"They're the boats Vincent drew and painted here. And of course, now all I want to do is draw and paint them too. They are irresistible!"

"I hear you. When we get to Martigues, you will see a lot of them. Let's pick up some food supplies, and then you can choose your perfect spot to work on some sketches."

A friendly greengrocer was only too happy to hand over fresh bunches of herbs, greens, and vegetables as he and Jacques bantered back and forth. Some plump tomatoes that smelled divine and juicy lemons the shopkeeper said had just come from his own tree completed the purchases. Arianna took charge of the wicker pannier, carefully arranging everything as it was handed to her.

Jacques and Arianna bantered comfortably, planning the dinner menu.

They decided to make a simple green salad with sliced tomatoes and *saucisson* on the side. Jacques had a selection of cheeses in his fridge. There was still one baguette left and the rest of the fruit from lunch.

"How's this for a plan? Tonight we will anchor in a small bay a little farther away. Tomorrow morning we'll rise at daybreak, unless you object, and we can watch the fishing boats come in. Then we'll buy fresh fish at the port after they set them up on ice on their stands. That's an experience in itself," Jacques promised her.

Arianna could not stop grinning. "I like it!" Inside, she realized she liked even more that someone was making plans that revolved around her.

"How about dinner at sunset? Does that appeal?" Jacques asked. "That gives you some time to sketch here. You're welcome to root through all my art supplies and use what you like. Then we will motor down to drop anchor in the next bay. I want to see your face tomorrow morning when you come on deck there."

Arianna felt spoiled by the way Jacques was planning surprises for her.

As she organized the food in the galley, Jacques disappeared into his storage room. He reappeared with a folded stool like the ones she had used at the Mas des Artistes and a large sketch pad. "Voilà! Here you go! Find your spot and sketch away while the light is good. Is an hour enough time? Just say the word if you want more."

Arianna impulsively hugged him, then stepped back quickly, feeling embarrassed. "An hour will be just fine!"

She settled on a raised spot at the end of the dock, facing out to the open waters of the Mediterranean. Her challenge was deciding just what her focus should be. The setting was splendidly nautical.

The protected cove shimmered in the late-afternoon sun as the distinctive wooden boats rocked gently on their moorings. Nets, rods, ropes, pails, and endless lines wrapped around wooden spools were organized in the boats for the nightly foray, each offering its own point of interest.

Arianna lost herself in her sketchbook, content and oblivious to past concerns.

They motored back out to sea just as dusk began to fall. After sailing for a while longer, Jacques trimmed the sails, and they hove to in one spot.

As the sun began to sink lower in the sky, Arianna and Jacques worked together in the galley. There was comfort in the intimacy of that narrow space. Their hands occasionally brushed, and more than once they laughed as they narrowly avoided full-on collisions with each other.

Dinner was a simple matter. Arianna prepared the vinaigrette for the salad using the recipe her family loved. She hoped Jacques would like it too and tried not to feel stressed about making a French dressing for a French man.

They brought the plates up to the table where they had eaten lunch. Jacques asked Arianna to turn on some music, and she chose a light jazz mix to play in the background.

They sat side by side, sipping wine, watching the symphony in the sky, and talking quietly, revealing thoughts and feelings about the past and present.

It was the first time that Jacques shared with her some of his struggles after Giselle was killed. Arianna recognized many of the same emotional challenges she had felt with Ben's illness.

From time to time, they reached for each other's hands to offer comfort. To give support.

The sunset they saw the evening before had been the best Arianna had ever experienced. Until this night.

As they sat outside, surrounded by gently moving waves, the shore a distant outline, the drama of the sun slipping below the horizon was magnified exponentially. Arianna watched raptly as day changed to twilight, and then dusk. Once the sun melted into the sea, the sky was awash in a rainbow of color.

Suddenly she felt her face wet with tears. Jacques became aware of her brushing them away and put his arm around her shoulder.

"Arianna, I'm hoping those aren't tears of sadness."

She leaned lightly into him.

"Not sadness, exactly . . . but it feels like some sort of letting go. I'm not certain why these tears are here. I don't think I'm crying. The tears are just happening, and I can't stop them. But they are a mix of happiness, sadness, relief, hope . . ." She wiped her eyes with the backs of her hands. "Maybe it's a letting go of what's been holding me back. I felt them coming and knew I had to let it happen. This sunset was intoxicating. The beauty, the color, the movement . . . It was so emotional . . ."

As brilliantly as the sunset ended the day, the stars began to illuminate the sky. Suddenly the entire sky was flooded with tiny sparkling lights. "And now this celestial display is continuing to remind me of nature's beauty and power."

"I never take it for granted," Jacques said, kissing her hand lightly. Arianna was surprised by the simple, affectionate gesture that seemed so natural.

"It's a different sky than van Gogh's, isn't it? I went and sat by the Rhône one evening to try and experience what he had painted."

"And what did you feel? Did you see the same starry night on the Rhône as he did?"

"I felt incredibly emotional . . . and sad for his madness. I really bought into the spirit of Vincent in Arles. Does it make any sense to say that I wanted to?"

Jacques nodded. "Totally. How can you ignore it? And why should you?"

Arianna turned to face him. "I have something to confess. Something I have not admitted to you."

His expression froze in a worried frown.

"I hope you will understand," she continued. "It's a little embarrassing, but I'm a possessed fan of Vincent. If he were alive, I'd be a groupie. I've been like this since I was very young, and spending time in Arles has brought my feelings for his work to the surface again. I couldn't get enough of his ghost while I was there. It consumed me."

Jacques threw his head back and laughed a full belly laugh. "A van Gogh groupie! I love it! You had me worried for a moment. I had no idea what you were about to confess."

For the next while, they spoke passionately about the artist and their feelings concerning his life and their many favorites of his paintings and drawings. It was a completely unexpected, spontaneous conversation that filled Arianna with elation as she appreciated the deep connection between them about art.

Eventually, Jacques started the motor and headed for the next cove. Within an hour, they had joined a few other boats anchored in the same area.

"Jacques, thanks for another amazing day. I think I'll fall into bed now. All of this fresh air is more than I can handle."

"*Bonne nuit.* It's been fun. I'm glad you decided to come on the boat. Let me know if you need anything."

They *bised.* The simple French gesture was so familiar, and yet now felt quite intimate. As Arianna went down to her room, she felt something like a flutter deep inside her. *Was that my heart or was it my spirit feeling the freedom to soar?*

She was surprised that the bed on the boat was so comfortable. It wasn't a luxury boutique hotel, but it was more than acceptable. The pillows were plump and downy, the mattress firm, and there was a soft, warm blanket to keep away the nighttime chill.

The soft lapping of water on the hull and the rhythmic clanking of halyards on the mast were relaxing. Content, she looked forward to speaking with Faith and Sophia the next day. But she felt no urgency.

It was important, of course, that they know she was fine and enjoying her last few days in France. She wanted to hear that Ben continued in good care too. But she knew he was. And she was grateful for that.

CHAPTER
FORTY-THREE

Jacques tapped lightly on her door.

Arianna stretched sleepily and took in her surroundings. A smile slowly began in her eyes, then moved down to her mouth.

"I'm awake," she called out. "Be up in a few minutes."

"The sun will soon be rising. I'd ask it to wait for you, but it has a mind of its own. Just wrap a blanket around you; it's not a formal occasion."

She grinned as she quickly slipped into the compact head of the boat and splashed water on her face and brushed her teeth. She gave her hair a quick rake with her fingers before she grabbed the blanket from the bed and went into the galley. The smell of fresh coffee filled the cabin.

"Mmmm, perfect!" she murmured as he handed her a mug. "Thank you."

"*Bonjour!* How did you sleep?" He leaned in and they *bised* as if they had been doing this each morning for a long time.

He took her hand and led her above deck. The morning air had a touch of crisp coolness to it, and she pulled the blanket more tightly around her. Jacques slipped his arm around her shoulder, holding the blanket in place as they stood together. Arianna realized she liked how natural it felt.

"*Regarde.* Watch," he whispered.

To the east, a long band of pinkish blue was layered above a brilliant band of gold across the horizon. The silvery grayness of dawn hung above them. Slowly, golden rays broke up the colors, spreading them into the sky as a fiery ball of brilliant light began to rise. The dark-blue night water of the Mediterranean turned into lighter shades of azure as the sunlight unfurled.

"It's a reverse sunset," Arianna said softly.

Jacques gave her shoulder a light squeeze and pulled her gently closer to him. "I thought you would like it."

Arianna stayed in that comfortable position and looked around.

With the increasing light, she suddenly became aware of the setting in which they were anchored. They were just inside the mouth of a small turquoise bay, and all around it, craggy limestone cliffs tumbled down to the water. A few scraggly pine trees clung stubbornly to the cliffsides. Fishing boats were docked nearby, and Arianna could see men in rubber overalls unloading their catches to the market stands on shore.

"This is a paradise."

"Ah, this is just the beginning," he said. "But we'll get some fish here and fresh croissants and baguette hot from the woodstove. It's too shallow to take the boat in, so I blew up the dinghy."

"You blew up the dinghy? When? How?"

He laughed. "Like everything else in my life these days, very easily. I stow it in the storage area until I need to put it in the water. An electric pump fills it with air on the deck in minutes. I did it before I woke you up."

Arianna nodded. "Should we go now?"

"Let's savor our coffee before we do," Jacques suggested.

They sat where the sunshine had begun to reach the boat, coffee in hand. As they chatted, Arianna could not stop admiring every detail of his rugged features whenever he looked away. What pleased her even more was the sensitive, thoughtful side of him she was getting to know. Their eyes met, and then they both laughed.

"We're like two kids playing hooky," Arianna said.

"Well, today is your day of decision. We can turn around and go back to Port-Saint-Louis and then I can drive you to your car. Or we can take our time and continue on to Marseille in time for your flight on Saturday; we could sail around for four more days and then dock in Marseille Friday night."

Arianna was silent and peered out across the water. As much as her heart was leaping, it was also aching. She felt this was a pivotal moment that was hers and hers alone. Her decision would be bittersweet one way or the other.

Jacques remained quiet until she turned her eyes back to him. Then he said, "I need to be back at the *manade* on Sunday and will be busy all that week as we have a big *feria* in Arles the next weekend. You should stay and see it . . . not that I'm trying to tempt you."

Raising her eyebrows, she smiled at him. "You've been very successful at tempting me so far! I'll just have to come back another year."

This time he said nothing. Minutes passed in silence.

Arianna closed her eyes and blew out a long breath before she spoke softly but firmly.

"Okay, I've decided. I'm going to stay with you this week. Being on the boat is a wonderful experience. It's so peaceful, calm, beautiful. And it's a complete change from my life at home. I think I need this."

The look on Jacques's face registered his happiness. "I think I need this too. I have work I need to tend to in Marseille, but it can wait. So we are helping each other. It's too early for you to call Canada, but you can use the satellite phone later today. I checked to make certain it's working."

❧

The dingy, popular Bar du Port was already open and bustling with boisterous fishermen throwing back a morning pastis or sharing a bottle of rosé. It appeared this was a regular stop on their way home after a night out on the sea.

The exposed wood beams and rough stone walls, combined with the worn, dark oak of the long bar, chairs, and tables, made Arianna feel like this room had not changed for centuries. There were ghosts in this room, and she described to Jacques the fantasies it conjured up for her. He agreed.

"That's one of the things I missed when I was a kid in the States. I'd come over here for the summer with my father, and we would go to all sorts of places just like this. There was always history, intrigue, atmosphere here. I never found that over there."

Friendly voices bantered back and forth, mixed with loud laughter. Arianna and Jacques lingered over their espressos. They bought two whitefish that were wrapped in a bag packed with ice and had been expertly filleted by the man selling them. Jacques explained they would be fine for an hour or so until they were back on the boat.

Jacques reported on his call about her car. "So I spoke with Monsieur Flaubert, who owns the car rental office in Arles. They have keys for all the cars, and he will get one of his staff to drive the car back to Arles. They will refund you the balance of the week that you paid for, with just one day's penalty for helping you out."

"Fantastic," Arianna said. "That worked out well. Thank you for doing that."

"And now we can focus on us," Jacques said. "Two friends who both need to get unstuck from what was the 'now' in our lives."

CHAPTER FORTY-FOUR

By midafternoon, the sun was beating down on the boat, and the wind was subsiding. Jacques was determined to reach a certain cove and pumped his fist as their destination came into view.

While he focused on sailing the boat, Arianna read a few chapters of her book, in between chatting with him about the history of the area. She was intrigued by his stories of pirates and smugglers.

She was increasingly aware of how easily they laughed together. Or were quiet together. It all felt right.

He asked if she was ready to call home and showed her how to use the satellite phone. Then he went on deck to give her privacy.

She came up from the cabin with a wide grin. "I spoke briefly with Faith, who thinks it is very cool that I'm sailing for a week with some friends—emphasis on 'friends,' plural. Isn't that ridiculous? The mom fibbing to the daughter! I feel I can't be honest about it."

"Arianna, it's perfectly understandable given the circumstances. I hope you won't give it another thought for the rest of the week. Just go with the flow, as you North Americans like to say."

She gave a little laugh that ended with a snort. "Oops, excuse me. At my age, I really should be able to go with the flow!" Then she added, "I also called my mother. Oh my goodness, I do sound like a child . . ." She shook her head and rolled her eyes. "It's morning in Toronto, and this is my eighty-five-year-old mother's time with her bridge group. She plays every weekday. Isn't that great? Anyway, she didn't pick up, so I left her a message to call Faith. Then I also left a voice mail for my daughter-in-law. So everyone is taken care of."

An audible sigh of relief escaped Arianna's lips, and they both laughed.

"Now I can truly relax," she said.

The location they reached was similar to where they had spent the previous night, but the bay was deeper, and sailboats could anchor well into the protected waters.

The cliffs were higher, and the water even more turquoise. Arianna could not stop exclaiming over the beauty.

"The water will be inviting here too," Jacques said. "Well, let me clarify that. It's all relative. The water will still be cool because it is early in the season, but it will be refreshing. Because it's so protected here, it will be warmer than the water you felt this morning when we were in the dinghy. I'm going for a swim. Want to join me?"

Arianna's stomach knotted. She felt her cheeks flushing and ran her fingers nervously through her hair. "Being seen in public in a bathing suit is not my favorite thing to do," she told him. "It's part of that aging thing. But, please, you go ahead."

Jacques stared at her firmly and took her chin in his hand, gazing deeply into her eyes. "Arianna, you are a most attractive woman. Don't think I haven't noticed your figure. You have nothing to hide."

Blushing, she looked away for a moment. "You are too sweet. Really. But this is a female thing, and you have to let me come to terms with it. That's all there is to it."

"*D'accord!* I hear you, and I understand. You just sit here and let the sun beat down on you for a while. Once you see me floating around in that cool, clear sea, you will be jumping in to join me in no time. That's my prediction."

She laughed and told him he might be right.

"There's a ladder here in the stern, in case you want to ease into the sea that way. I recommend a quick entry, though." He gave her a sly look. They shared a laugh as their eyes met and registered the possible double entendre.

Arianna thought, *We are adults after all.*

Jacques went belowdecks to change, and Arianna wondered if he would appear in a tiny Speedo-type bathing suit, like so many Frenchmen wore. For a moment, she considered putting on her bathing suit but couldn't quite get past her hang-up.

When Jacques reappeared, Arianna felt a certain relief that he was wearing a typical North American–style bathing suit.

He gave her a teasing look. "Ha-ha! You thought I would be wearing one of those skimpy French bathing suits, didn't you?"

She chuckled and nodded, looking a little abashed.

"As a matter of fact, I have a couple of them. But I thought you might feel uncomfortable about it . . . many North Americans do. Do you know why we wear those in France?"

She shook her head.

"It's the law in pools. Only small, tight trunks can be used for swimming in pools. The reasoning is that bigger swimming shorts can be worn elsewhere all day, so could bring in sand, dust, or other matter, disturbing the water quality. That's the way it's been ever since pools were first opened in France. So we're used to that here and scoff at tourists in their baggy suits."

"Hmm, I just thought French men liked them," Arianna confessed.

"Well, we do . . . or nothing! That's very much the French way too. We are *naturistes* at heart."

Arianna saw the teasing gleam in his eyes and couldn't help laughing.

He nodded as he continued. "Really, though, that's changing at the beaches these days, and more men are wearing looser suits. I might show you the latest style another time. It's more of a James Bond look." He winked.

Arianna laughed again, happy that they could talk so candidly.

In a moment, Jacques's taut, tanned body performed a more-than-adequate dive off the side of the boat. He surfaced after a long underwater glide and beckoned to her to join him. *"C'est magnifique! Rafraîchissant! Vraiment!"*

Arianna waved back. "Enjoy it!"

He turned and swam away with strong, clean strokes. She watched him swim toward shore and reprimanded herself for being so self-conscious. She had a lovely new bathing suit, chosen with Faith's help for her trip. She never truly thought she would have the occasion to wear it, since the *mas* did not have a pool. But she had packed it just in case she wanted it on her planned road trip to the French Riviera, which now wasn't happening,

Jacques continued to swim toward the shore. Arianna could see that the beach was pebbly, like the ones she had read about in Nice and other parts of the Riviera. She had memories of beaches of soft golden sand in Greece and was curious about the French ones like these.

She had to admit she was getting very hot and sweaty. After ten minutes, she went and changed into her bathing suit. It was a deep-blue, strapless, bandeau style with ruching across the midriff. Advertising assured her she would look fifteen pounds lighter immediately, not that she believed it.

She brought a matching sheer cover-up outside with her and laid it on the bench. Then she began to descend the ladder.

She shivered involuntarily as the water reached the top of her legs and again as her midriff slipped below. Now she let go and swam on her back away from the boat. Turning, she looked toward shore but could not see Jacques. Then she heard a loud whistle and saw him standing on the beach waving to her.

She waved back and continued floating where she was. The sea felt revitalizing and not so cold once you got in. The sun warmed her face. *Ahhhhhh—Jacques was right.* Rafraîchissant!

After ten minutes or so, she swam back to the boat and climbed the ladder. After lying in the sun for a few minutes, she was dry. She watched Jacques cutting through the water toward *Mon Esprit.* She felt herself tremble with anticipation at his return and slipped her cover-up over her shoulders.

Jacques floated and swam around the boat for a few minutes, and they chatted back and forth about the water. He smiled when Arianna praised him for his assessment of how much she would enjoy it. "You were absolutely right. It felt incredibly refreshing!"

"Your bathing suit is very nice," he said with a roguish expression, calling up to her as he floated on his back. "You look gorgeous."

Arianna glanced away and grinned self-consciously. "Stop it. Thank you."

As he began to climb up the ladder, Arianna picked up a towel to hand to him. He stepped into the stern and reached for the towel. Holding on to Arianna's hand, he let the towel slip from her grasp and gently pulled her to him.

His cool, wet, hard body felt exciting against hers. His lips brushed hers gently at first, and hers eagerly responded. Then their mouths met in a kiss that was fervidly urgent. His lips tasted subtly of salt. He smelled of fresh sea air.

His hands tenderly caressed her as Arianna wrapped her arms around his neck. She felt herself melting into the irresistible chemistry between them and arched her body into his. Her cover-up fell to the deck.

Jacques pulled his head back, his fingers now passionately entangled in her hair as their eyes met. Arianna felt an intimacy between them that only began with this kiss. She closed her eyes as he kissed her cheeks, her forehead, and the tip of her nose before his lips found hers again. Her lips parted slightly beneath this kiss, and, with the tentative dance of their tongues, Arianna breathed a low moan.

Now she stepped back, her eyes locked on to his. She took his hand and led him belowdecks to her cabin.

Jacques made her laugh as he dropped his bathing suit to his ankles. "Another good thing about loose swimsuits."

Without waiting, he helped her slip out of hers. "I knew you would look irresistible in your bathing suit. I told you so. And out of it, even more."

Arianna pulled him onto the bed with her.

CHAPTER
FORTY-FIVE

Over the next four days, Arianna and Jacques cruised from one idyllic cove to the next. In the evenings, they watched sunsets and danced under the moonlight. They decided to take their time . . . with both their lovemaking and their sailing. They would get where they wanted in due course.

In between, they sketched and painted. Arianna could not believe the stock of art supplies Jacques kept in his storage cabin. "One-stop shopping, madame."

Arianna had felt intimidated about working on her art next to such an experienced talent. But as time passed, and with all the positive conversations they shared about technique and subject matter, she soon got over her anxieties.

As they talked or walked or sailed or painted or made love, Jacques would make occasional suggestions to her about the future.

"Nothing is carved in stone, as they say," they both repeated.

Arianna was aware she felt no guilt about her decisions. It was as if, once her spirit was awakened at the Mas des Artistes, she had given herself permission to move forward with her life and her emotions.

Their evening ritual was to sit up on the bow, arms around each other, legs entwined. They would sip on wine as they watched one magnificent sunset after another. Arianna loved resting her body against him, breathing him in, knowing that his love was offered to her and hers to him.

They would not speak about the future during sunsets. They would focus only on the moment.

As the stars appeared, Jacques would quote Vincent to Arianna, and she would kiss him lightly on his face, his shoulders, his back. The gentle sway of the sea would lightly rock the boat as the calm blanket of night settled over them.

During the day, there were times for more serious conversation about possibilities. About the fact that every day was a gift and nothing was promised . . . but, even so, that making plans was something they wanted to do.

On their last scheduled day together, they settled into a mooring at a dock in another fjordlike inlet carved into the jagged limestone cliffs.

"Let's pack a lunch and hike up. You should see this," Jacques said.

The climb was steep. The mistral had made the trail even more unstable, as the ground was dry and crumbly. Jacques explained how the inland trails were all closed through the summer because of forest-fire danger. "This is the best time to walk this area. On the other side of Marseille, there are even more breathtaking trails and scenes you would love to paint."

They stopped several times to drink water and catch their breath. Arianna was not surprised at his fitness. "I've got some work to do to keep up with you, if you take me on any more of these hikes," she said.

Once they reached the top, the natural grandeur of the vista was spectacular. They shaded their eyes from the strong sun reflected in the sea. The brilliant gemlike hues of the clear, crystalline water ranged from turquoise to deep blue, stretching off into the distance. Steep silvery limestone cliffs tumbled into the waves.

"A scene waiting to be painted," Arianna murmured.

"And this is nothing compared to the *calanques* east of Marseille. If you stay longer, I will show you those."

Jacques took Arianna into his arms.

As she had the entire week, she felt secure in his embrace in a way she had almost forgotten. The stirrings deep within her were not the excited butterflies of younger years. Instead, she was overcome by an irresistible swell of tranquility mixed with desire.

"There's so much more for us to explore together," Jacques whispered, his voice catching with emotion. "Don't go. Stay with me."

Arianna listened to the beat of her heart. Her peace was within.

"You know I have to leave tomorrow," she said.

"And why is that?" he asked.

"Because that's the plan. I have a ticket."

"Plans can always be changed."

"I've heard that from you before." She laughed with a lightness in her spirit she thought had been lost forever.

EPILOGUE

In the end, Jacques did persuade Arianna to change her plans.

As they cruised toward the city, he told her about his apartment in the old port area of Marseille. He and Giselle had owned it as a rental property.

He explained to Arianna that, for years, he had alternated between the *manade*, his boat, and their larger apartment. "She worked crazy shifts at the hospital and then was away with MSP. We lived our own lives in many ways . . . a lot like gypsies, I must admit. And I became even more that way after Giselle was gone."

After Giselle was killed, he sold their large condo where she had lived most of the time. "I moved into the smaller apartment and continued to live my nomadic ways. It's time for a change."

As he held Arianna's hand and stroked her face, he asked, "Why leave when we have only just discovered each other? I know you have things to take care of . . . and much thinking to do. I respect that. But why not stay just a little longer so we can see where this is going?"

And so more phone calls were made, and Arianna planned to stay with Jacques in Marseille for another month.

Jacques returned to the *manade* for the week. Arianna remained in his apartment in Marseille, finding pleasing surprises as she explored the ancient city. Next to the warrens of the old town, exciting things were happening around the newly remodeled Vieux-Port. There was much to discover.

She went to be with Jacques in Arles on the weekend. It was exciting to be caught up in the festive atmosphere created by the *gardians* and horses working with the bulls, the *courses camarguaises*, costumes, music, and dance. He surprised her by inviting Juliette and Maurice to go to the *feria* with her. As they warmly welcomed Arianna back to Arles, Maurice said, "Juliette told me when she watched you two talking at our picnic she knew it was *le coup de foudre*—love at first sight."

After that weekend, Jacques went back and forth to the *manade* when his services were needed. Often, he was able to stay days at a time in the apartment in Marseilles with Arianna and gradually introduced her to the city he knew so well. They spent time exploring on the boat and hiking the *sentiers* between the *calanques*, which were as magnificent as he had promised.

Slowly, they settled into a rhythm together in the apartment. Arianna appreciated the freedom she felt to pursue her interests. One spacious sunlit room of the apartment was his studio. He made room for her to work there too. Her first piece was a vibrant, sun-washed poppy field.

She quickly became aware, in spite of his modesty, that Jacques was a well-established artist, represented by galleries in Paris, Marseille, and New York.

Arianna investigated art programs at the Aix-Marseille University and other studios in the city. She was committed to immersing herself in her life as an artist again. Jacques had many suggestions and plans to offer.

Marseille intrigued her. Jacques's intimate knowledge of the ancient city brought it to life for her. She discovered the lively old port neighborhood to be an artist's dream.

She returned to Toronto at the end of that month. Her visits with Ben were brief and painful. He lay or sat silently with no awareness of anyone or anything around him, staring ahead blankly.

Ben reacted violently to being touched, so she could not even hug him. All she could do was stand or sit and stare at him through tears she could not control. Heartbreaking sorrow wrapped around Arianna each time she was with him.

Gradually she accepted the urging of the staff and her family that it was better for her to be away.

There were many long, tearful family conversations. There was no question, they agreed, that what was best was not always easy. They were unanimous, though, about the reality that Ben would live in all their hearts forever.

Sophia, Faith, Tad, and Christine listened with surprise and compassion as Arianna described her newfound love of life, art, and, in time, Jacques. They understood her desire for another chance at happiness.

Gloria held Arianna in her arms as they stood together at Ben's bedside. "You must live your life. Ben would want you to do that. Don't feel guilty. Feel hopeful. It's the only way to move forward."

Arianna cried as she placed her wedding band and engagement ring in the family safe-deposit box at the bank. She vowed she would never marry again. She was simply Arianna. And she would always take care of Ben.

The new owners of Papa's on the Danforth purchased her apartment. Her furniture and boxes of possessions were put in storage.

Faith left to go to Lesvos to reconnect with family. Arianna made plans to take Sophia there for a visit once Faith was settled.

After a month at home, Arianna returned to an emotional reunion with Jacques in Marseille. They knew they had both found what they hadn't known they were looking for. Taking their time, they began to figure out their life together.

❧

One year and three months later, after several visits to Toronto, Arianna received the call in Marseille.

Within hours, she was on a flight to Toronto and went straight to Ben's bedside upon arrival. She held Ben's hand and kissed his forehead as he took his last breaths. As death was claiming him, she could touch him once again. She had never stopped loving him, in spite of the decisions she had made in the past year. Tad and Christine sat with her, recalling happier times and the strong memories they had of so many good years.

The plan had been made much earlier. One month later, the entire family met with Faith on Lesvos, bringing the ashes of Ben and Nikos with them.

Sophia was elated to be back in her homeland, past hurts forgiven. Bringing the ashes of Nikos back here with his beloved son-in-law felt right to everyone. They had been such kindred spirits, loving Greece in so many ways.

There was almost a celebratory air among the family. Peace had been made with the relatives, who joined them now on a family fishing boat that took them all out to sea.

As the ashes were gently released into the shimmering sea, there was a sense of relief that suffering was over and healing now could truly occur.

Both Ben and Nikos had left a legacy of love that would last forever. Tears mixed with laughter as words of remembrance recounted the joy these men had brought to others. The years they had lived were celebrated.

Arianna looked over at Jacques, who was standing at the helm with her cousin. Her eyes glistened with tears of gratitude for the life she had shared with Ben and with hope for what was to come.

AUTHOR'S NOTE

Writing this novel was a challenging experience at times as I ventured into new subject matter of illness and art. I hope you enjoyed the story as much as I loved writing it, even as my heart broke at times with Arianna and her family. It was my pleasure to bring you along to Arles and the Camargue, with the unique beauty, culture, and history of the area. Spending weeks researching in that part of France was a singular delight.

Please read the acknowledgments, where I have thanked many people for their invaluable assistance.

Thank you to everyone who has written to me through the years or messaged me on social media. I love hearing from readers! I'm also grateful to the many reviewers and bloggers who take the time to read my novels and write about them. I value your thoughts and opinions, so please continue to share them with me at patriciasandsauthor@gmail.com.

Have you signed up for my newsletter? It goes out once a month with all sorts of contests and information about what's coming next. Just click on "subscribe" at my website at patriciasandsauthor.com.

Anytime you take a moment to write a review, please know your efforts are appreciated. Comments from readers are helpful and inspiring to me. You are the reason I write, and your words encourage others to read my books. *Merci mille fois!* Thanks a million!

And now . . . on to the next book. See you there!

ACKNOWLEDGMENTS

It takes a village, as the saying goes. In order for a manuscript to reach that exciting point where it is finally ready to publish, a great deal of support and assistance is essential. I'm grateful to everyone who contributed in his or her own personal way to bringing *Drawing Lessons* to readers.

I cannot state deeply enough my gratitude to my gracious friends in Toronto who shared their experience with dementia-related illness in their families. In particular, I want to thank (with her permission) Lynda Douglas for so generously and candidly guiding me through her ongoing journey with her husband, Ron. She feels strongly that these painful stories need to be told. Thank you also to the health professionals I spoke with for their advice and knowledge. I offer my deepest respect to anyone whose life is touched by such challenges.

Friends and family are my rocks. My husband's patient support, encouragement, and eager first look at my words mean everything to me. And this time, I'm also grateful to him for coming up with the book title! Yes, he did . . . and now is demanding royalties!

Thanks to dear friends (you know who you are) who happily shared personality traits and experiences that added color to this story. You prove in so many ways that everyone's story should be heard.

I feel so fortunate to have advance readers who offer honest, helpful comments and read all my rewrites without losing their sense of humor. In particular, I owe big bouquets of gratitude to these honest, critical, and reliable advance readers: Terry Murphy, Gail Johnston, Martha Paley Francescato, Marie J. Maher, Pat MacDonald, May Anis, Yasmin McNeilly, and Des Chabot, to name just a few. I so appreciate the time you took to read my work and offer your valued comments. If I've forgotten someone, please accept my apology and know I value the help everyone offers.

Special thanks to artists Jo-Ann Sanborn (Marco Island, Florida), Patricia Reason (Toronto/Mexico), and Tessa Baker (Paint Provence with Tess) for their insight and sharing of appropriate details, and also for taking me inside the psyche of an artist to help me better understand that world. A special note to Irish artist Patrick McCarthy. Our chance meeting at the home of mutual friends on their stunning property with its panoramic view over the Côte d'Azur was serendipitous. When you unexpectedly sat on a stool, took out your tin of paints and art journal, and in a few strokes with your pen sketched your interpretation of that view, you opened my eyes to the world I needed to enter for part of this story. I referred often to the photos you allowed me to take of you as you worked. Many, many thanks.

Ida Young-Bondi, my friend and eFrenchCafé instructor from Nice, applies her expertise where needed and knows how much it is appreciated. *Merci mille fois*, Ida!

Thank you to Christian, from Arles, dedicated photographer, who drove me around and shared his knowledge of the Camargue.

It's serendipitous how things happen at times. It was my good fortune to connect a year ago with Heather Robinson, a woman with a special soul and a true artist in every way. She graciously shares her intimate knowledge of Arles through her Lost In Arles website and she offered particular details in response to my questions.

Thank you to Amazon's Lake Union Publishing for being the best home for an author. The support, experience, and enthusiasm offered by my developmental editor, Amara Holstein; editors Danielle Marshall and Miriam Juskowicz; and the entire Lake Union team headed by (the always available) Gabriella Dumpit are priceless. The work of my copy editor, Michelle Hope Anderson, and proofreaders, Ginger Everhart and Nick Allison, was stellar.

Thanks once again to my PA, Amy Cooper, and to Barb Drozdowich (my tech angel), for their dedication, wise advice, and active involvement in all I do.

Thank you to my agent, Pamela Harty, of the Knight Agency for her knowledge, guidance, and warm friendship.

My deepest gratitude to the amazing community of authors and readers, bloggers and reviewers, who make me proud, happy, and inspired to keep writing.

ABOUT THE AUTHOR

Photo © 2015 Carmen Blike

Patricia Sands lives in Toronto, but her heart's other home is the South of France. An avid traveler, she spends part of each year on the Côte d'Azur and occasionally leads groups of women on tours of the Riviera and Provence. Her award-winning 2010 debut novel, *The Bridge Club*, is a book-group favorite, and *The Promise of Provence*, which launched her three-part Love in Provence series (followed by *Promises to Keep* and *I Promise You This*), was a finalist for a 2013 USA Best Book Award and a 2014 National Indie Excellence Award, was an Amazon Hot New Release in April 2013, and was a 2015 nominee for a #RBRT Golden Rose award in the category of romance. Sands also contributes to such Francophile websites as The Good Life France and Perfectly Provence, and she appears as a public speaker for women's groups. Visit her online at www.patriciasandsauthor.com.